W9-BZU-407

RUFFIANS

A NOVEL

RUFFIANS
A NOVEL

TIM GREEN

Turner Publishing, Inc.

ATLANTA

PUBLISHED BY TURNER PUBLISHING, INC.
A SUBSIDIARY OF TURNER BROADCASTING SYSTEM, INC.
1050 TECHWOOD DRIVE, N.W.
ATLANTA, GEORGIA 30318

FIRST EDITION 10 9 8 7 6 5 4 3 2 1
ISBN 1-878685-78-3
LIBRARY OF CONGRESS CATALOG CARD NUMBER: 93-60820

DISTRIBUTED BY ANDREWS AND MCMEEL
A UNIVERSAL PRESS SYNDICATE COMPANY
4900 MAIN STREET
KANSAS CITY, MISSOURI 64112

This book is a work of fiction. The names, characters, places, and incidents are either products of the author's imagination or used fictitiously. Any resemblance to actual locales or events or persons, living or dead, is entirely coincidental.

DEDICATION

With love for my wife, Illyssa, who makes all things possible.

PROLOGUE

THE CROWD ROARED in Clay's ears like a storm. He was so close to Gilly that he could feel his steel mask clanging against his teammate's helmet.

"Whad ya say?" Gilly screamed.

Clay could barely hear him.

"I said, 'You stay inside . . . the X stunt is off!' " Clay yelled. Gilly responded with a puzzled look, and Clay knew that he had been heard. The Penn State offense broke their huddle and bounded toward the line of scrimmage.

"O.K.?" Clay bellowed.

Gilly glanced nervously from Clay to Coach Leary, who stood on the sideline looking intently at the field. Gilly was only a redshirt freshman. He was lucky to be on the field. Leary could change that, and would if he screwed up something like this. Gilly knew better than to ignore a play Leary had signaled in from the sideline, especially at this point in the game. But Clay Blackwell was the team's captain. He was their star, and it was his last game in a Northern uniform.

The Penn State linemen were hunkering down in their stances. Across from Clay was Keith Zard, Penn State's three-hundred-pound All-American. Clay looked intently at Gilly. His expression asked the question again.

"O.K!" Gilly said, nodding so that Clay would know.

Clay grinned, slapped Gilly on the shoulder pad, and lined up. Clay knew Leary would have a fit. They were only up by nine and with three minutes left. Penn State could win it with a field goal if they scored now. With their own quarterback out for the game, Clay knew Northern's offense would put the ball right back in Penn State's hands. Keeping them out of the end zone was critical. Northern was 5–5. They weren't going to a bowl game despite high pre-season expectations. A win against the nation's second ranked club would make up for a lot of the disappointments.

It was fourth and goal from the seven yard line. Leary had called the X stunt because he thought crossing the rush lanes of the end and the tackle would put quick heat on the quarterback. Clay knew he could beat Zard without Leary's stunt. This game was the last he would ever play at home in front of the Northern fans. Clay knew he could win it almost single-handedly with a quarterback sack.

Clay was deaf to the noise of the crowd. His concentration was so great he heard nothing. He saw only the thick, bloody fingers that protruded from Zard's black leather gloves. When those fingers left the turf as the ball was snapped, Clay lunged.

He raced three steps up the field, then threw his head and shoulders to the inside, jabbing with his right foot at the same time. Clay sensed the mayhem of the interior line. Arms and legs and helmets flashed violently. Zard went for the fake as Clay knew he would. Just before the big man's hands struck Clay in the chest, he darted back to the outside. The field was clear except for the quarterback. It was like sifting through Cracker Jacks, and suddenly there was the prize.

Clay could see himself smashing into the quarterback and rising from the turf to accept the hysterical cheers of the crowd. He couldn't see Zard spin and roll, whipping his rear leg backward at the same time. It was an old and dirty trick, an illegal trick, but Zard was a team captain too. He was thinking of a national championship.

Clay felt a sharp pain in his shin. He felt himself falling to the turf in slow motion. He reached out and grabbed for the quarterback, who stepped just out of reach and sprinted outside the pocket. Clay's glorious moment was gone forever. He tucked his shoulder, rolled, and came up quickly off the artificial turf. He was in time to see the unhindered quarterback cross into the end zone.

The roar of the crowd ended abruptly. A stunned silence overtook the stadium. Clay lined up for the extra point.

"Clay," Gilly said in a frightened voice, "what happened? Did you lose contain?"

"Fuck" was all Clay could say, slapping his helmet at the same time.

After the kick, Clay jogged back to the sideline, cursing himself. He wanted to throw his helmet, but he knew better. He avoided Leary and went to the water. He rinsed his mouth and tried to spit the sickness from his gut. The optimistic home crowd surged back to life. They wanted to see a long kickoff return. They at least wanted the Northern offense to get the ball out of Penn State's field goal range.

Clay looked at the scoreboard. Northern was still up by two. Even if the offense couldn't run out the clock, Penn State still had to score. But Clay had played enough football to know that the play he'd just called off had put his team on a slippery slope.

He went to the D-line bench. His teammates sat there, sweat dripping from their hair, heads hung low to ward off the incredible abuse that spewed from Coach Leary.

"Fuck Gillmore! Fuck you, you goddamned freshman son of a bitch! You had contain on that! You could've just cost us this game. This is the last time some of these guys will ever play a goddamn game of football! You, Gillmore! You're gone! Snead? You take this man's job. I know you'll run the play that's called."

Leary's Irish face was purple. Gillmore didn't look up until Clay spoke.

"Coach," Clay said. Leary spun on him. His teammates all looked to see what Clay could possibly say. Everyone knew better than to talk to Leary when he was raving.

"It was my fault," Clay said.

"Nice try, but Gillmore's got contain on an X," Leary said angrily.

"There was no X," Clay said. "I called it off."

Leary stared in disbelief. Clay could see his twisted, coffee-stained teeth. He blinked in anticipation of the yelling that was sure to come.

"Damn it, Clay . . ." Leary was drowned out by booing louder than any Clay had ever heard. It was almost as loud as the cheering. The Northern back-up quarterback had fumbled the first play from scrimmage. Penn State now had the ball on the thirty-two yard line going in. The Northern defense jumped to their feet, snapping chin straps in place and stuffing mouth guards into their faces. Leary turned to Clay as his teammates began spilling out onto the field.

"Get 'em up, Clay," he said with desperate ferocity, pulling Clay's face close by tugging on his mask. "Forget about the X. We can still win this. Just get those sons-a-bitches up!"

Leary hammered Clay's shoulder pads, and he dashed out onto the field. He stumbled and almost fell as he ran to catch up with the other players.

Clay pushed the earlier mistake from his mind. He had to. In the Northern defensive huddle he slapped his teammates' shoulders and helmets, exhorting them to give one final effort.

"It's our game to lose! Let's kick their ass! Come on . . . the whole season comes down to these last two minutes . . . come on!"

Penn State broke their huddle. Clay got to his position and quickly put himself in Joe Paterno's shoes. Joe needed a field goal to win. Five or six yards would put his kicker within range. Clay knew Joe would run the ball and try to get the yardage. On film, Clay had watched Penn State time and time again run behind Zard in critical situations. They wouldn't do that now. Clay controlled the ground game today.

With this in mind, Clay decided to slide a step inside of Zard. It was a bad position for a pass, and a bad position for a run to his side, but if Penn State ran the ball like Clay thought, away from him, then Zard wouldn't stand a chance of cutting him off. Clay would get to the other side in time to back up his teammates to keep the gain to a minimum.

Penn State's line set on the ball. Clay lined up over Zard. The quarterback began his cadence, and Clay slid inside, just a step. It was all he needed. The ball was snapped. Zard fired out toward Clay's inside shoulder to cut him off. Clay felt that good feeling that filled him whenever he was right about what was going to happen. He struck Zard in the chest and rammed his helmet under Zard's chin. He pushed, then shucked Zard back to the outside, freeing himself to pursue the runner. It was a sweep away. The runner broke past the outside force and headed down the far sideline.

Clay refused to let up. He watched a linebacker dive and miss the runner, then the free safety. Clay adjusted his angle and surged ahead, on line to meet the ball carrier just before he crossed into the end zone. Clay passed smaller teammates, moving incredibly fast and catlike for a big lineman. The Penn State runner thought he was clear. He'd outrun the defensive secondary and there would normally be no one who could catch him. He held the ball out and up to insult the hostile crowd with one final in-your-face gesture. Clay dived. The runner never saw him. Clay hit him in the side of his head with his own helmet, slashing viciously at the runner's arm at the same moment. The ball sprung free. Clay crashed down on top of the runner, knocking him ten feet past the sideline. Gilly dived on top of the ball in the end zone. Clay hopped up and turned to see what had happened. The noise hit him like a nuclear blast, flashing through his bones and shaking him. The crowd was on its feet. The official signaled touchback, a Northern first down.

Clay ran into the end zone and embraced Gilly as he rose to his feet with the ball held high for everyone to see. The rest of the team was close behind. They swarmed Gilly and Clay, burying them under a pile of bodies. It was almost a miracle.

The crowd continued to roar. The Northern defense dispersed. Out came the offense with renewed hope. Losing now was beyond them. They would have their part in the sensational victory too. They knew they could run out the clock. The momentum was theirs, and so was the game.

For twenty minutes after the final gun the Northern crowd remained standing and cheering. Much of the student section had spilled past the security and onto the field to knock down the goal posts. For twenty minutes the players, especially the seniors, milled about the field, hugging each other, luxuriating in the victory they would remember for the rest of their lives. Clay searched the crowd behind the bench, where Katie sat. She was at the railing, clapping with everyone else. Clay got two cops to help him bring her over the wall and down onto the field. People in the stands reached over the rail to touch Clay. Two kids who were standing next to Katie begged him for his hand pads. Clay embraced Katie, drenching her with his sweat. Then he pulled off his hand pads and tossed them to the kids. The mob around them screamed.

". . . Clay, Clay . . ."

"We love you, Clay . . ."

"Clay! We'll miss you!!"

Clay waved to them all and grinned. Then he led Katie by the hand, out onto the field amid the tumult.

"Hey, this is a first. You've never brought me on the field before. It's fantastic," she said, loud enough so he could hear.

"I wanted you to feel it, what it's like out here . . . I always talk about this." Clay raised his hands in the air, indicating the cheering crowd. "I wanted you to know what it feels like."

Her smile showed her appreciation.

"You were great," she told him. He smiled too and kissed her, then led her by the hand off the field amid the cheers of fifty thousand people calling out his name.

CHAPTER ONE

THE CONCRETE WAS COLD and made Clay's bare feet clammy. Stripped to his underwear, he stood in a line of about thirty other half-naked young men that extended around the room and out the door. The vaultlike room was cramped. Its high ceiling was a maze of corroding pipe and mold-stained ductwork. One of the players behind Clay laughed abruptly in a nervous and muffled way. Everyone turned. A fidgety silence settled among them once more. They were the rookie class of the National Football League. Every year, like cattle to the auction, the League harvested the finest football players from universities across the nation. Before the merchandise was bought and paid for, the buyers were given generous opportunity to inspect the meat.

Over three hundred college players had been flown into New Orleans from universities as far away as Hawaii and Boston College and as close as LSU and Auburn. Many, like Clay, were subdued even before they got inside. The big, dirty city offered little in the way of a warm welcome. Damp, fetid air from the distant Gulf of Mexico was tainted with smoke belched from factories and power plants. The New Orleans Superdome stood out like an enormous white spaceship, an anomaly in a town whose main attraction was the old French Quarter.

"DL7," called out the pale, spectacled man in a white lab coat.

It was Clay's turn to step onto the scales. The number had been given to him when he arrived at the NFL combines. It was printed in large letters on his T-shirt, and had been printed on the back of his hand in indelible ink as well. For as long as he was at the combines, he was DL7 and not Clay Blackwell.

"Two hundred seventy-three pounds . . ."

The lab technician paused as he jammed the metal arm hard down on the top of Clay's head.

Large and mostly overweight middle-aged men in ill-fitting clothes sat crammed into desk chairs that filled the center of the room. There were five or six rows of about ten chairs. The men were NFL scouts, and they wrote everything the lab man said like enthusiastic schoolboys, looking up only to eyeball the next slab of human flesh on the block.

The lab man said, ". . . six feet, four point one inches. Next."

Clay stepped off the scale and was pointed in the direction of a steel door at the back of the room. Not knowing what was scheduled next, he wordlessly followed a redheaded guy ahead of him who had DL6 printed on the back of his T-shirt, and stepped through the steel door into another cold concrete room.

"Walk to the yellow X and then back again," shouted a shape from behind a set of bright lights.

Clay did as he was told.

He had to squint to see that there were several lab men in this room and only a few scouts. Two cameras filmed Clay as he headed to the yellow marker on the opposite side of the room. Many coaches and scouts around the league believed a lot could be learned about an athlete's balance and speed just by the way he walked across the room.

Clay was dismissed and told to go dress himself, then report to Room C.

Strength testing was conducted in Room C. This room too was crowded with NFL scouts and coaches. They were packed in a circle around a single bench press like men in a barn about to watch a cockfight. The weight bar held two hundred twenty-five pounds and the object was to press the bar as many times as possible. The last of the offensive line group, OL43, had set the standard at forty-four repetitions. As Clay's turn approached, his armpits dampened with nervous energy. He wanted to be the best at everything he did, but he knew he couldn't match forty-four. Still, the six DLs that proceeded him had all got somewhere in the teens, so Clay adjusted his goal to be the best of the defensive linemen and not worry about the entire group.

The call came, "DL7."

Clay got down on the bench, and with a slight tremor in his hands he lifted the bar off the rack and began to press. With the first few reps his arms felt weak, not as strong as they should have been. But he figured nervous energy was sapping his mind, not his body, and he finally established a comfortable rhythm. Nineteen . . . twenty . . . twenty-one . . . twenty . . . two—his arms shook with real fatigue—twentyyy . . . three . . . twentyyyy . . .

"Aghhh!" Clay grunted as his arms gave out and the heavy bar sped toward his chest.

Two lab coats, one on either side, mechanically caught the bar and returned it to its rack.

"DL7, twenty-three reps," said one of the lab coats blandly.

Clay looked around for a sign of approval, but the only ones who weren't scribbling were other players who were not especially interested in seeing him succeed.

Clay left Room C following large arrow-shaped cardboard signs marked THIS WAY, and found himself walking through a maze of damp locker rooms in the bowels of the Superdome. Turning a corner, he was abruptly confronted with the huge expanse of the unnaturally green turf field. Artificial lights buzzed from above like monster insects, and the shouts of players, striving to run faster agility drills, echoed off the distant stands and roof.

While Clay waited for the rest of the DLs to arrive, he watched the last remnants of the OL group run through a series of drills and sprints. Clay's muscles began to twitch as he watched. He grinned to himself. This field was where he would set himself apart. For a man who was six foot four and weighed two hundred and seventy-three pounds, Clay's agility and speed was remarkable. He knew that, and he knew that after he finished these drills, everyone else in the place would know it too.

When the group of DLs was finally complete, Clay was assigned to a subgroup that consisted of DL1 through DL8. A lab technician led them to the vertical jump area. Clay watched his competition. His turn came. A lab coat marked his fingertips with chalk. Clay crouched beside the wall where he was to jump. He bounced several times, as if he was going to jump, but returned to his crouch. He got himself into a rhythm. Muscles in his legs and shoulders rippled with tension. Then, when his weight felt right, he sprang. The red marks he left on the wall were a good six inches beyond anyone else.

"Thirty-seven and a half," said the lab coat who stood above them all on some scaffolding.

Clay couldn't help noticing the incredulous looks he was drawing from the other DLs.

"Hell of a jump," DL8 said, shaking his head as he passed Clay to take his place against the wall.

The jump was only the beginning. With each passing test, more and more scouts and coaches gathered around Clay's group to watch him perform. By the time Clay got to his last test, the forty-yard dash, almost half of the people in the dome were clustered around him to see how well he would run. This was the benchmark for football players. From the time they are ten years old, football players talk about their speed in terms of the forty. Clay had worked for weeks on improving his start, and he now carefully placed his hands and feet in their proper places. He lifted his hindquarters, began breathing deeply, and then exploded off the line. Once up, his motions were smooth and fast, almost liquid, but violent, like a tethered stallion cut free. His strides took up enormous sections of the turf. If it were colder, steam would have burst from his nostrils as he churned across the finish line. The time: 4.63, the best any DL would run.

A coach who wore a Dallas Cowboys sweat top leaned over to the scout standing next to him and whispered, "That's a thoroughbred."

Clay had to wait until all the DLs were done in the dome before the group would be taken by bus to the hospital for physicals. A lab coat announced there would be no lunch and that the bus would not be leaving for at least another hour. Clay shrugged, pulled on his Northern sweatsuit, and sat patiently in a remote corner of the Dome reading a ragged paperback copy of Hemingway's *For Whom the Bell Tolls* that he had kept hidden in his bag.

At the hospital, the DLs were seated in chairs that lined both sides of a long corridor. At the end of the hall was a door that every three or four minutes would expel one player while the one seated closest would get up and enter. Each time this happened, the entire forty-odd remaining players would each get up and advance one seat closer to the door. For fifteen minutes Clay silently refused to participate. But after five empty chairs separated him from DL20, the glares from his frustrated counterparts became so malicious that he found himself distracted and unable to concentrate, rereading the same sentence in his book several times. To restore order, and his own peace of mind, Clay decided to play by the unwritten rules of the game and moved closer to the door.

As he sat, a man made his way down the hall. He wasn't a lab coat, but he carried a clipboard, a caliper, and a tape measure. He bent and fiddled briefly over each player before scribbling on his board. It wasn't until he was three seats away that Clay was able to figure out what he was doing.

"Fist," said the man when he reached Clay.

Having watched DL20, who in turn had watched DL3, Clay knew to hold out his fist at arm's length while the man measured the circumference of Clay's fist and the distance from his big knuckle to his elbow. The man then said, "Head" and fixed the caliper to his skull, measuring its diameter from front to back and side to side.

When the man had moved on, DL20 leaned over and murmured quietly, "That's the Seattle guy. I heard the Seahawks have some chart that tells how good you'll be in the league just by those measurements."

Clay gave him a knowing look.

"I'm Donny Drew," DL20 said. "You're Clay Blackwell, huh?"

It was the first time that day Clay had heard mention of his name. He nodded his head to the oversized Nebraska farm boy.

"Yeah," he said. "I don't remember when we met . . ."

"Oh, I never met you," Donny said, "but shit, everyone knows you. Northern U. superstar. Grew up somewhere around there in New York, didn't you?"

"Yeah," Clay said, "kind of born and raised, I guess you'd say."

"You're one of the top guys in the draft this year."

"Well, you never know . . ."

"Oh, my agent knows. You're a first-round pick, a one for sure. I know about all the DLs, you know, D-linemen coming out in the draft.

"I'm a three to five," Donny added rather proudly.

Finally inside the door, Clay was given a folder with eleven empty boxes on its cover.

"DL7 . . . Clay Blackwell?" asked a woman looking up at him from the desk.

Clay nodded.

"Fill each box with a circle. There are eleven stations in this room. You get one circle at each station. Don't come back until every box is filled."

Seeing that no further explanation was forthcoming, Clay turned to assess his situation. The room was cavernous, and seemed to be a cafeteria whose tables and chairs had been cleared away. There were large booths separated by heavy blue curtains. Each booth had a number over its entrance. Players milled about between booths and queued outside others. Clay headed for Booth 11, which had no line.

He entered this "station" to find two lab coats and a dentist. Clay sat on a stool while the dentist pulled back his lips. One of the lab coats took a picture of Clay's teeth. The dentist fished around Clay's mouth with a mirror, making comments into a Dictaphone. When he was finished, the dentist turned his back abruptly on Clay, and the second lab coat stepped forward to give him a round blue sticker with the number 11 on it, which he stuck on the appropriate box of his folder.

"This is a cinch," he thought.

Clay entered Booth 4 after waiting in a short line. Along with a booth for teeth and eyes and knee ligaments and body symmetry, there were seven additional booths. These housed a few lab coats and four or five physicians, one from every team represented and a corresponding trainer. Booth 4 was one of these. Someone grabbed his folder from his hand.

"DL7," that someone called out.

One of the physicians checked his hand to see that indeed he was DL7.

"Take off your shirt," someone said.

Clay did it.

"Bend down and touch your toes."

Clay saw by the stethoscope that it was one of the physicians who was speaking. The same one ran two fingers down the length of Clay's spine. Clay jumped.

"That hurt?" asked the doctor gruffly.

"Tickled," Clay said with a sheepish smile that was not returned.

"Any injuries?" asked another doctor.

Clay didn't quite know how to answer. He had no current injuries, but over his lifetime he had had his share. He couldn't think of anything worth mentioning though. He had never missed a college game because of an injury. If it wasn't serious enough to miss a game, then it certainly wasn't worth mentioning to this group.

"No," Clay said.

"No injuries, none?"

"I never missed a game," Clay answered.

It was quiet in the booth except for a lab coat who pounded furiously on the keyboard of a computer. Suddenly he looked up from the screen menacingly. "What about your elbow, fall of 1989?"

Clay thought. "Yes," he said, "I ruptured a bursar sack in my elbow, but I didn't even miss a practice."

"On the table, please," said a doctor who stepped up and grabbed Clay's arm at the forearm and the biceps. The doctor bent and twisted Clay's elbow in such a way that would have hurt any healthy elbow.

"That hurt?"

"No," Clay said.

Another doctor stepped up to the table to do more of the same. As he held Clay's arm, he noticed a scar on his knuckle. He held Clay's hand up to the light.

"What's this?" he asked.

"Oh, that was from a fight when I was in high school," Clay said.

The doctor looked up and said to no one in particular, "Make a note of that."

"What about your left knee?" said the lab coat at the computer. "Didn't you sprain your left medial collateral in spring of 1990?"

"Yeah, well, it was spring ball. I only missed a couple of days of practice, and I played in the spring game."

Every doctor was interested in this, and now each one, as well as each trainer, had a shot at not only his left knee but his right. That done, there was more general poking and prodding which had no apparent pattern. It was the guy at the computer who finally gave Clay back his folder with a green 4 fixed in its box, but not before he flashed one final look of hostility.

By the time Clay had all his boxes filled, his joints ached from twisting and turning and poking and prodding. He gave his folder to the woman at the desk. Without looking up, she told him to report to the fourth floor, Room 459 for EKG, X-rays, blood and urine, and his internal. Clay's eyes narrowed at the word internal.

"After you've completed that," she said, "you can wait for your group in the main lobby. Someone will take you back to the hotel."

On the fourth floor, a doctor who Clay had never seen before ushered him into a small examination room and asked him to drop his shorts and hop onto the table in the middle of the room. The doctor began talking about the lobster bisque at a French Quarter restaurant called Arnaud's. Clay would have been somewhat interested had he not been on all fours atop the examination table with the doctor's latex-covered finger shoved up his ass. Clay's Adam's apple bobbed as he gulped the bile that filled his throat. The doctor handed him a box of tissue and left the room. Clay got down from the table and wiped the lubricant from between his cheeks with handfuls of Kleenex.

He was just pulling up his shorts when the doctor returned. He held out his hand for Clay to shake and said, "Well, that does it for you. It was nice having met you."

Clay excused himself with a nod and a wave. "See you," he said as he shut the door. Clay could only frown and shake his head when the three other DLs outside the door looked up at his face for a clue.

In the backwoods of a small Alabama town, an enormous estate was set on acres and acres of rolling lawns and gardens, completely enclosed by a high stone wall. There were pools and fountains beyond counting. Antique sculptures adorned the grounds, and priceless artwork, period furniture, and Oriental rugs graced the rooms of the main residence, a replica of the White House. It was like a jewel in the desert, and required more than two dozen servants to staff it, catering to the whims of its occupants. It was the Lyles estate, and Beatrice Lyles was its sovereign. Her son, Humphry, had told her she could live anywhere in the world, but nowhere except here, outside the town where she and her son had spent their earlier, more impoverished and pathetic lives, could she gloat and bully with proper authority.

Humphry Lyles had risen from rags by cunning, unscrupulousness, and a certain amount of luck, and had made his fortune in the insurance industry, beginning by simply selling insurance policies and pocketing an occasional premium, taking his own risk that the owners would not make a claim. When he had amassed enough money, he opened a small office of his own, focusing his sales on the poor blacks most other insurance agencies never solicited. In a short time Humphry was successful enough to underwrite his own policies. From there, easily corrupted politicians and his own ruthlessness allowed him to expand his personal influence and business empire beyond the limits of even his own childhood dreams.

In the early seventies, he sold his interests in insurance and formed a conglomerate, borrowing and leveraging and buying up whatever struck his fancy, from textile mills in New England to breweries in Australia. His most recent and notable purchase was the NFL's newest expansion franchise which he himself named: the Birmingham Ruffians. The only problem with his new business was that unlike his other holdings, the success of this venture was not measured strictly by profit, but by victories on Sunday afternoons. His team was almost the worst in the league, and in the great football state of Alabama, winning is everything. The Ruffians were an embarrassment, and Humphry was getting barraged with criticism from every side.

That was why he was here now. Only his mother could bolster his spirits and motivate him to succeed. It had been this way ever since he had been a child. And even though Beatrice was sometimes more of an annoyance than an inspiration for a middle-aged man of tremendous wealth, it was his habit to seek her out in times of trouble.

"Well, boy, it's about time you paid your mama a visit," said Beatrice Lyles. She was somewhere in her sixties, but her rotund face and a jet black wig made her look more like Humphry's sister than his mother. It was an unusually warm day for February, and she was sprawled out on a large wicker divan beside a pool. A canopy protected her from the breeze, and she picked fresh-cut fruit from a silver tray as she spoke.

"I've been busy, Mama," Humphry replied, "with the team."

He sat down next to her in a wicker high-back. They had sat together like this countless times. In the predominant image of his youth, Humphry and his mother sat together in the barber chairs of the shop over which they lived. Humphry had few friends as a child. His appearance did little to help that. He was small and chubby and pale, and his mouth, set into a homely face, had a girlish look to it. His ugliness made growing up hard, and instead of playing with friends, he would sit for hours with his mother, talking or watching TV shows on a small black-

and-white set perched atop the barber's counter.

He regarded those meager times as the ones that had spurred him to success. Every evening after supper, he and his mother would hurry down the back stairs in time for Jeopardy.

"You see these people, Humphry?" his mother had been fond of saying. "They think they're so smart, knowing things like who built St. Peter's Cathedral. We'll just sit back and laugh. All that stuff they know, and maybe they'll win a few hundred dollars. One day that will be small change to us."

And now that was all true.

Beatrice Lyles loved her boy with a passion that only an abandoned women can give a son, but her love had become twisted into an obsession that her boy be wealthy above all else. She herself had been the painful recipient of a lesson in the power of money. As a high school girl in a small Mississippi town, she had become involved with a boy who was from one of the town's wealthy families. Her own father was a dirt farmer and a drunk. When she discovered she was pregnant, she had assumed that she would be taken in and cared for by the boy and his family. They had other ideas, however. Her father was given a modest sum of money, and she was taken to a remote cabin in the backwoods where her pregnancy was terminated. She almost died, and when she finally recovered, she ran away.

When she arrived, filthy and starved, in Baton Rouge she began to sell herself as a means of survival. She earned enough money to learn a trade as a beautician and then moved to the town of Meridian, where she now lived. She had not, however, escaped her street-walking days before she became pregnant with Humphry. So she had concocted a story about a dead husband that was believable enough for her to get a job and a place to live. And although she was now more comfortable than she had ever been, she had never forgotten that she and her son had lived in squalor.

She also never forgot what had been done to her by those who had money and power, and it was a burning, gnawing thing in her now swollen gut that never gave her peace. She was determined to instill in her son the yearning for material possessions, and power, and the cunning to acquire them. She knew the rich and how they thought. Humphry would learn the rules early in life and play to win.

He hadn't understood all she said to him as a small boy, but looking back now, he understood the significance of his training. His mother had pounded into his head the idea that it was money, and nothing else, that mattered. She tutored him in craftiness and guile, and always stressed that the end justified the means.

"I read in the paper that they want you to sell the team. I won't remind you that I told you never to buy it," his mother said, dropping a ripe strawberry into her puckered-up mouth. "They say you don't have a clue about the game, say you've got a little big man complex."

Here she snickered. "That team has been more than you bargained for, hasn't it, Humphry?

"Yes, it has," she continued, not giving him a chance to respond. "It's been a regular nightmare. Do you know what it is that you've done? You've allowed people to ridicule us. I told you long ago that money was the only important thing. This game, this . . . team is a weakness. You put yourself in a position where even my household staff can have a laugh on you. By God, after all I've taught you, after all we've done.

"I'm disgusted," she said finally.

Humphry stared silently into the pool, thinking about his dilemma. He didn't feel the need to reply to his mama's badgering. She had always talked to him in a strict, condescending manner.

"Humphry, why don't you say something?"

"Huh, oh, you're right, Mama. I'll have to straighten it out. Mama, I'll be staying a few days if that's all right."

"Of course, boy, you know you're always welcome here. This is your home, we built this together."

A black cat wandered out of the shrubbery and hunted quietly along the edge of the pool.

"Mama, there's a cat."

"Oh, that's Lidia's cat," his mother said, suppressing a yawn.

"I told her I didn't want that cat here," Humphry said, rising and grabbing the cat by the scruff of its neck. He rolled up his shirtsleeve with his free hand, knelt down, and plunked the cat and his arm into the water up to his elbow. There was only a slight rippling and bubbling on the surface of the water as the life was suffocated from the animal. Humphry stared out across the lawn and held the cat down until it was still.

"I'm allergic to cats," he said, throwing the soggy black cat into the bushes before he sat back down.

"God in heaven, Humphry! What would you like me to tell Lidia?

That cat's the only thing she has in this world."

"Tell her to do as I say," Humphry said simply.

They sat silently for a while.

Finally, Mrs. Lyles said, "You won't let Lidia's cat take three breaths in your presence, but you let those newspaper people crap all over you . . . God in heaven."

It was Clay's college roommate, Ralph Levette, or Lever, who picked him up from the Syracuse airport late Saturday morning when he arrived home from New Orleans. Lever was an enormous man. He weighed over three hundred pounds although he was not quite as tall as Clay. His arms and legs were stout, and his belly was rather prodigious. Lever was the starting right offensive guard for Northern. Like Clay, he was the physical stereotype of his position. Next year at this time, Lever too would go to the combines. He would be OL-something.

"How was it?" Lever asked before Clay had shut the rusty door of the big green Impala. Lever's car was typical for a college student, riddled with dents and corrosion, four unmatched snow tires, no hubcaps.

"It went well, but it was bad," Clay said. "Hey, Lev, can you swing by my folks' house? I gotta get my wash."

"Sure. What's that mean . . . it was bad."

"Well, I did real good in all the tests."

"Hell, I know that. Tell me why it was so bad."

Clay told him about being filmed and measured with nothing on but his underwear, and about the doctors who pulled him like taffy, and finally about the internal exam.

"That's some sick shit, man," Lever said, hawking and spitting out his window. "I don't know if I can go for that shit."

"You'll go for it . . . if you want to get drafted. No one gets drafted in the top rounds without going to the combines."

"Yeah, well, I can't see letting some guy stick his finger up my ass, even if he is a doctor. I just can't see it."

"You gonna be like Seldon?" Clay said. "Big shot. All-American. Gonna be a second-rounder. No need for a big shot like him to go to the combines. He didn't get a finger up his ass. But it cost him . . . let's see, the difference between the second and the ninth round . . . about a million. Yeah, you're right, Lev, it's not worth it."

"You know as well as I do that the guy could stick his whole head up my ass for a million dollars," Lever said with mock severity.

They both laughed.

Lever guided the old wreck through the suburban streets that were as familiar to Clay as his own backyard. Three- and four-bedroom homes sat shoulder to shoulder looking very much alike except for their color. Small lawns were bordered by dirty snowbanks and cars parked in the street. Power lines hung like attic webs, thick and black and everywhere. Chain-link fences held back family dogs and kids. Clay's own home, gray and drab, would have been a gloomy sight had it not been so familiar. His father's rusted yellow Cadillac sat by itself in the driveway, alerting Clay that his mother was out.

Clay and Lever entered to find Clay's father, Ward Blackwell, lying on the couch with the paper and a beer.

"Hi, Dad," Clay said, not looking directly into the older man's eyes.

"Clayboy!" said his father, rising to shake hands. His frame was as massive as Clay's and, taking his large gut into account, he probably outweighed his son. "How did it go? Did you kick ass? Lever, how the hell are you? Go get you and Clay a cold one in the fridge, and you might as well hit me again too. I know it's only eleven-thirty, but you girls are legal."

Lever eagerly complied.

"Well," Ward Blackwell said with a rough slap on his son's shoulder, "sit down and give me the low-down."

"I did good, Dad. I had the fastest time in the shuttle run, and my forty was four-six-three."

"Son of a bitch. Lever, pop those caps. A toast . . . to a four-six-three forty and to the million-dollar contract."

Clay's face flushed, but he took a slug of his beer and said nothing.

Clay's mother opened the door. Her arms were filled with two bags of groceries and her purse. Clay leapt up to help her. When he had set the bags down on the kitchen table, he gave her a hug, affectionately wrapping his huge frame around her petite figure. Without the tired lines in her face she would have looked like a young woman. Still, she was handsome, and to Clay she was life itself.

"Christ, Geneane," his father rumbled from the other room, "do you think you could let the kid have a little celebration here with us? We're having a beer. Either have him bring the damn bags in later, or do it yourself. Come on, Clay."

His mother smiled weakly, "Sit down, honey, I've only got one more bag, then I'll make you some lunch." She gave his hand a squeeze.

"I'll go if you'll leave the bag till later so I can get it," he said.

She smiled and shrugged, so he went into the living room and sat down. Sitting while his mother worked alone in the kitchen distracted him, and while his father and Lever talked about the NFL teams that had called their campus apartment, Clay's eyes wandered about the living room.

The furniture, like the rug, was worn, but clean and comfortable. Above the mantel was a wood imitation coat of arms of the house of Blackwell. Clay's father had gotten the curio through a mail-order catalogue. Although Clay knew almost nothing about his ancestors, he had heard his father hint to his friends on more than one occasion about a mysterious noble past. On one side of the mantel was an enlarged black-and-white photo of Clay's father in a football uniform. On the other was a smaller picture of his parents on their wedding day.

Clay's father noticed that his son was distracted. "You see that picture, Lever?" he asked loudly.

Lever nodded his head.

"Does my boy, or does he not, look like my exact replica in the pads?"

Lever nodded again. Clay shifted uncomfortably and sipped his beer, knowing where his father was headed. He had heard this story before.

"Well, the reason the picture on the right is one of me in a high school uniform and not a pro uniform is the picture on the left."

Mr. Blackwell slugged the rest of his beer. "Why don't you get us all another one, son?" he said.

Clay got up and went into the kitchen. He fished noisily through the fridge so his mother wouldn't hear what was being said in the other room, but knew his father was waiting for him to return with more beer and didn't stay long in the kitchen.

"You see," his father explained between sips, "I could have done what Clay's going to do, but I had to marry Geneane, so I went to work at the Ford plant. There wasn't really any birth control back then, if you know what I mean. Ha, ha."

Lever forced a chuckle. Clay returned to the living room, his face frozen.

"I don't have any regrets, though," his father continued to Lever, finishing his beer. "Our boy here will be rich in a couple of months, and a father can't ask for more than that."

"I've got some sandwiches for you boys in here" came the cheery voice of Clay's mother from the kitchen.

After lunch, Clay got a call from his agent, Bill Clancy.

"Well," Clancy said, "how did it go?"

"I ran a four-six-three."

"You didn't."

"I did."

There was a low whistle from Clancy's end of the line.

"You just made us a lot of money, Clay. A lot of money. You locked yourself into the first round of the draft. I don't normally say that, but you could go in the top ten. You'll go in the first for sure with a time like that."

Clay felt a rush of adrenaline. He had heard speculation that he was a first-rounder. He had even suspected it himself. But to have Bill Clancy confirm it was something entirely different. Clancy was big time. He was known for making big deals, and he was known for his accuracy in predicting the draft. When Clay first met Bill, he had been suspicious. He was an upstate kid; Bill was a New York City lawyer. But they'd hit it off. Bill was easy to talk to, and Clay talked with him almost every evening on the phone. Now, for the first time, Clay felt a twinge of what he knew his father took for granted: that he would be rich.

"Great lunch, Mom," Clay said after hanging up the phone. "Lev, let me get my wash and some things, and I'll be ready to go."

Before his father could question him more closely about what Clancy had to say, Clay bounded up the stairs and into his bedroom. His boyhood trophies lined shelves on the wall. He had to smile at the idea of all the dreams those trophies had spawned and all the work he had done finally paying off big. He picked up the bag of neatly folded laundry his mother had put on the foot of his bed. She had also left two books discreetly on his chair under his desk. His mother read constantly and gave to Clay only the best of what she found to read. It was she who had suggested Hemingway. He had told her that he liked *For Whom the Bell Tolls*, so he smiled when he saw that one of the books in the stack was *Islands in the Stream*. He shoved the books down into the clothes—he preferred his father not see them.

Clay's mother had always been an avid reader, and had been first in her high school class. She was a shy, kind woman, and her luminous eyes sparkled with intelligence. Because of her marriage, and Clay, she had never had the chance to go to college either. But she had continued her education on her own at home while she raised Clay. She didn't read romances or spy novels, concentrating instead on books with literary value. Clay had grown up listening to the stories of Charles Dickens, one of his mother's favorites. When Clay was a child, his mother would sit and read for long stretches before he would fade off to sleep.

In college, Clay learned that there was much more to the "children's stories" than he had ever suspected. Originally planning to be a business major, Clay had taken a course on Dickens as a filler that he thought would get him an easy A during football season. But the class had opened a new world of ideas for him, and he often wondered why his mother had never led him deeper into literature. He enjoyed reading, but had never been encouraged to devote much time to books. All his father's encouragement was directed toward excelling on the football field.

The spring of his freshman year, in the midst of spring football and a full schedule that included two English classes, Clay decided to become an English major. He took some kidding about it from his teammates, but the intellectual curiosity he seemed to inherit from his mother, and his respect for books, helped him deflect any needling from his friends. The most difficult part of changing his major had been his father's reaction.

"What the hell is that all about?" he had exclaimed. "What if you don't play pro ball? You don't know if you'll play pro ball yet, you're still a damn freshman. What will you do then, become a teacher? I make more on the line than a damned English teacher! A fucking waste, that's what it is. I tell you to stay with the business courses. Then if you don't make the pros, you can still make it big in life."

But Clay's mind was made up. He was feeling free in college. The full scholarship he was on took care of everything. He had earned this education, and he would do what he wanted with it. It was one of the few times he crossed his father. Ward Blackwell stayed angry through the entire spring and into the following summer. The only thing that brought him around to talking to Clay again was the upcoming football season. Then he became good old dad again, as easily and suddenly as he had become irritated. Clay felt more sorry for his mother than himself. He didn't have to face the man until he came home for summer vacation, and even then Clay could escape the house with work and training. His mother, though, took the brunt of his father's anger. He blamed her for ruining the boy and constantly reminded her of it. Clay figured out why his mother had never pushed him toward literature, and was careful to avoid the subject of books around his father.

Nevertheless, at school he spent many hours with the great works of literature and tried to live by the principles of the men he came to admire. From Homer he learned the importance of honor and tradition as well as the powerful effect love could have on a man. From Milton he learned piety and grace, and of the lures of evil. And Thoreau taught him that the simple things were sometimes the most meaningful and the most pleasurable. Clay began to understand some of his mother's behavior that he had until now thought of as rather peculiar.

Clay thought of one afternoon in particular. It was during the late summer, and his high school football practice had been cancelled because of a lightning storm bearing down on the town. Clay drove his mother's station wagon home from the school while streaks of electric bolts lit the near horizon. As he pulled into the driveway, he saw his mother standing among the clotheslines in the backyard. He parked in the driveway and hurried around the house to help her bring in the wash before the rain began. Large drops pelted him. The wind whipped the clothes and the rope line that held them bowed and swayed, but his mother was not working frantically as one would expect. She stared at the dark, angry sky as the wind tugged at her long black hair.

Clay began to pull the wash from the line. "Mom," he said, "the rain."

His mother looked at him then as if she just noticed he was there. "Look, Clay, it's beautiful. Look at the sky. Look at the clouds, the lightning."

His mother had to raise her voice above the howling gusts to be heard, and Clay almost didn't recognize it as hers. He couldn't remember the last time he'd heard her speak so loud or so clearly. He couldn't remember hearing her yell. The rain was beginning to fall hard now, but Clay looked up too. A bolt of lightning hit close, exploding in the air.

"Mom, it's raining," he said once more.

"Clay," she said, wrapping her arms around him and his wet laundry and hugging him, "doesn't it make you feel alive? Don't you just want it to sweep you up? That's what life is supposed to do, Clay, it should shake you, sweep you up, let you know you're alive."

She kissed his cheek and pressed her head against his chest, and he stood there while she held him for what seemed like a very long time. Then his mother seemed to return to herself. She let him go, and together they stripped the rest of the line and hurried into the house.

It wasn't until he was in college that he finally understood what his mother had meant.

The difference had been the books. One day, when he was finished with his football career, Clay dreamed that he might become a teacher; maybe he could even learn to write. He'd be free from materialism and greed. He dreamed of living a simple life someday. He could go into some easygoing business or teach, and spend his summers in some remote lake house in the mountains. Yet his father's training and his internal drive to succeed ran deep, and there were other things he would have to do before he could ever rest.

For now, out of habit, he hid the books, hefted the bag, and went back downstairs.

"Thanks, Lev," said Clay. He hopped out of Lever's Impala and climbed into a rust bucket of his own.

Clay had been offered a new truck by an alum who gave him a summer job, but he didn't take it. He wanted to, but he had come as far as he had because he did things the right way. His coaches had specifically warned the entire team to avoid such scandals. And now it wouldn't be long before he could buy anything he wanted. He could buy a car and a truck, for that matter.

Clay watched Lever go into their apartment while the Bronco's engine turned over and over. Finally it caught, and he maneuvered the ancient truck out of the lot faster than was safe. He was going to see Katie. Even though he had only been gone two days, he was in a hurry. He wanted to let her in on Bill Clancy's prediction.

Clay had met Katie when she was only a freshman. He had been eyeing her lean figure and long dark hair from across a smoky bar all night. When a drunken upper classman began to harass her, Clay had intervened. The scene ended with Clay popping the other guy in the nose and gallantly walking Katie and her shaken friends back to their dorm on a snowy winter night.

"Hi, honey!" she said at the door with a kiss and a hug. "How did it go?"

"Awesome," Clay said, flopping down on her couch.

"I knew it would. How couldn't it after all that work?"

"The best part is what Bill just told me."

"You spoke to him?"

"This morning, at home. I would like to introduce you to America's next young millionaire," he said with a mock bow.

Katie giggled and slapped his shoulder. "What did he say?"

"After I told him my forty time, which by the way was a meager four-six-three, he said I was a first-rounder for sure."

Katie's face was serious when she said, "Clay, I'm really happy. You really deserve it." She moved closer to kiss him softly. She kissed him again.

"Thanks, honey," he said quietly between kisses.

"Miss me?" she asked in a low, throaty voice.

Clay gently untucked her shirt and slid his warm hands up her back to undo her bra. "Always," he murmured, "I always miss you, Kate. I miss everything about you . . ."

He moved his hands to her breasts. Together their breathing grew heavy. Katie stood, bringing Clay to his feet so as not to break their kiss as she undid her jeans and wriggled out of them. When Clay too was wearing only his shirt, Katie lay back on the coach, arching her body as she gently pulled him down on top of her.

Humphry Lyles and his mother had a formal dinner together in the large and elegant dining room. Humphry spoke very little during the meal. His thoughts were on just what he had gone through to acquire the Ruffians.

When the NFL had announced its expansion to thirty-two teams in 1990, it included a franchise in Birmingham, Humphry's base of operations. He promptly went to work. The franchise was not to be had for money alone, but would be awarded to the man who could exert the most political pressure on the governor of Alabama. The NFL commissioner would accept the governor's recommendation on just which outstanding citizen of the state would be allowed to purchase the hundred-million-dollar franchise.

Humphry Lyles set out to put the governor in his pocket. He hired three private detectives, all retired FBI agents, and had them not only tail the good governor around the clock, but make penetrating inquiries into his past. Humphry knew when to spend money, and his men were the best money could buy. It took them only three weeks to get what Humphry needed. He then made an appointment with the governor.

"Jack," said Humphry, sitting across from the man, staring almost complacently out onto the lawn surrounding the governor's mansion, "I've come to tell you that I will gladly accept your recommendation to the National Football League as the franchise owner in Birmingham."

The governor looked in amazement and disgust at Humphry. "Mr. Lyles," he said, grinning with condescension and malice, "I'm glad that you're here. As a man who obviously never played the game of football, and knows absolutely nothing about it, you will be glad to know that tomorrow I am putting the first professional team in the history of this great state in the hands of someone infinitely more qualified than yourself."

Humphry smiled pleasantly at the slight and caressed the envelope in his lap.

"Of course, you don't know him personally," continued the governor, "but you have heard of Bennington Winthrop, of the Mobile Winthrops? Yes, well, Benjy and I were both Theta Chi's during our stint at Auburn . . . and with the Winthrop name, and with the fact that Benjy was himself a varsity letterman, I'm sure you understand that I really had no need to consider any other candidates for this honorable recommendation."

"Yes, when all the facts are considered, there really is only one person you could recommend," Humphry said, and tossed the envelope onto the governor's desk.

"Do consider these facts . . . Jack."

"Mr. Lyles," the governor said as he stood, now red in the face and motioning toward the door, "I will not be insulted with bribes by a man who is not even a gentleman. Good day, sir!"

"Jack, there's a hundred thousand dollars in cash in that envelope to ease the pain," Humphry said with simple innocence.

"I am appalled, sir! Now do leave!"

"Of course, please make my recommendation tomorrow, Jack, and do make sure you dispose of the documents and photographs in with that money. Of course, I'll keep my copies safe, but I'd hate to see someone get a hold of your set. Really, Jack, you gentlemen do disgust me. That child in New Orleans could not have been thirteen. And that harbor contract for your friend Brandon Wilde? My, my. Well, I guess you really needed that horse farm, though. After all, where else could you send your family while you play in New Orleans?"

The governor's face blanched, and Humphry chuckled as he left the office. The next day, he was named as that most outstanding citizen who would be recommended as the owner for the NFL's Birmingham franchise.

Owning a football team seemed to be what Humphry had always needed in his life. He loved the constant publicity. Would he build a new stadium? What would he name the team? Who would be the coach? Which players would he pick in the upcoming draft? These were the questions that filled headlines on not only the sports pages in Birmingham, but on the front page as well. A day did not go by when the Lyles name wasn't mentioned in the Birmingham paper, and not a week when it wasn't mentioned in *USA Today*. Humphry put his financial machine on autopilot. The Birmingham Ruffians became his life.

His sense of power was unprecedented. This was a southern town, and football was king.

"I want to keep the team, Mama," Humphry said quietly after the coffee was served. "I like it. It's what I want to do."

"If you want my advice," Beatrice Lyles responded after a heavy sigh, "not that you do, if you did, you wouldn't have bought this team, but if you want it, I'll tell you what I've always told you. What have I always told you?"

"Oh, Mama, you've told me a lot of things."

"Well, what have I always said about getting to the top?"

Humphry counted off on his fingers as he spoke, "Means justify ends, victors write the history, nothing more powerful than money, nice guys finish last . . ."

"No, no, no. Not that. What have I always told you about the people who work for you? What do they have to be?"

"The best."

"And . . . what else?"

"And . . . they have to be just as ruthless and just as hungry as you are, otherwise they're dead weight."

Beatrice Lyles smacked her hands together, "That's what I wanted to hear. That's your problem with your team. The people who run it are dead weight. You don't know anything about football."

"I know some things."

"Well, you know what I mean. But what do you know about computer chips? Nothing there either, but that Micro Future company paid for the house in St. Barths. Same thing here. Get the best. You've got the money, get the best."

"So you don't think I should sell it?"

"I think that you should have never bought it, but you did. Now I think you should show people why you are who you are. Isn't that why we're sitting here instead of doing the dishes?"

After dinner, Humphry took a long walk around the grounds of the estate. He agreed with his mother. The staff he had was dead weight. He didn't know football, but he knew what productivity should look like. As he passed a gurgling Italian fountain, Humphry thought about a message he'd seen go across his desk the previous week. It was from a man named Vance White. The name hadn't meant a thing to Humphry, until two days ago when he read the man's name in the paper. White had been a successful college coach at Texas State. In five short years he had taken a struggling program to four straight bowl appearances and two years ago to a national championship. But it seemed an NCAA investigation had uncovered some recruiting violations that left Texas State on probation and Vance White without a job.

Humphry's mouth erupted into a grin. White might be just the answer. He was obviously a man who knew how to win, and he was a man who knew how to bend a few rules to get there quickly. Humphry would call White tomorrow. There would be no more laughing at Humphry Lyles. There would be no more ridicule. His team would win. He would find a way, and he would succeed. He didn't need to walk any longer, so he returned to his own room.

Vance White slapped dust off his pants with the brim of his hat before placing it back over his iron-gray crew cut. He gazed across the flat desert at the distant hills. Only an occasional tree broke the monotony of the immediate landscape, but to him it was beautiful. He had made enough money from his success as a football coach to buy this small ranch near the Mexican border. South Texas was where he had grown up and South Texas was where he swore he'd always return. Since it was certainly possible that he had been permanently retired from coaching, this was the only natural place for him to come. He spat out a wad of chewed tobacco, turned his horse, and headed for the distant homestead. The morning sun was now bright, and he knew his wife would have breakfast waiting for him.

He led his horse into the barn and growled, "Chico. You rub her down good or I'll skin your ass with my teeth."

The young Mexican looked deferentially to the ground and took the horse from White. As he strode across the dirt to his house, he spotted a large black beetle. He walked over to the insect and crushed it under the heel of his boot. As he was trying to scrape his heel clean on a stone, his wife came out on the porch. Dusty wind whipped her hair.

"Vance," she said in a heavy southern drawl, "there's a Humphry Lyles on the phone for you, saying somethin' about an interview in Birmingham."

White looked up from his boot. A smile broke out across his craggy weatherbeaten face.

Humphry Lyles wasn't a man to wait. He had one of his private jets pick Vance White up the very next morning at a remote airstrip near White's ranch. By four o'clock in the afternoon, a limousine had delivered the coach to the front entrance of the Lyles estate. A butler led White to the library. The walls were adorned with exquisite oil paintings and rare books. Lyles sat at a desk at the far end of the room. A blaze burned in the ornate fireplace behind him. White was impressed, but he had something of his own to impress Lyles with. He set a fresh copy of *Sports Illustrated* down on the leather blotter in front of Humphry before he shook the owner's outstretched hand. The cover was an intensely stern picture of White's face. The caption read: WHAT NEXT FOR VANCE WHITE?

The two men shook hands. Humphry looked down at the magazine. He felt a wave of excitement. This was something that he could relate to. This was tangible even to a man who knew little of sports.

"I'm impressed, Vance," Lyles said.

"Maybe next week's issue will have a picture of you and I together with the answer," he added.

White looked impassive, but his scalp twitched slightly. The NFL would be his only chance to continue coaching. No college would hire him after the NCAA scandal at Texas State. NFL jobs were few and far between, especially for college coaches with no NFL experience.

"I've read quite a bit about you in the past few days," Lyles said, "everything, in fact, and if you're half of what they say you are, then you're the man for my team."

White nodded, still containing what he felt inside.

"Let me tell you what I want," Lyles said, "and then I want to hear from you if you've got what I need. . . . I want to win, and I want to win now. I don't want promises of success down the road and building for the future. I want results and I want them this coming season."

Still White was impassive.

"I also want you to know," Lyles continued, "that I wouldn't ask for fast results if I wasn't willing to back you up in every way possible. I mean with money, and resources, and connections. In short, I'll provide whatever you think you need in order to win immediately, and I'm not bothered by stretching the rules either. You should know Vance, that I look at your little problems at Texas State as a positive reflection on you. I want a man who is focused enough to do whatever it takes."

The two men talked for over two hours before they emerged from the library. By that time Humphry Lyles had hired Vance White and come to a verbal agreement about his terms of employment.

"I hope you'll stay with us for some dinner before heading back to Texas?" said Lyles, who was intoxicated with the progress he had made toward his goal.

"I'd like that, Mr. Lyles," White replied.

Humphry led White through the spacious mansion and up a wide set of stairs to the second floor dining room. Beatrice Lyles was already at her place when the two men entered. Her eyes widened questioningly at the sight of White.

"Mama," Humphry said, presenting his coach, "I want to introduce you to Vance White, the Ruffians' new head coach."

At the same time he gently placed the *Sports Illustrated* magazine down in front of his mother. When her typically pursed lips parted ever so slightly, Humphry knew that he had impressed her. Daintily she extended her limp and corpulent hand.

"Mr. White," she said, "this is a pleasure."

Clay knew that to be a great football player you had to run. He was in training, so he was up early in the morning. He loved to run in his old neighborhood and would drive home all the way from the Northern campus for that reason alone. He had a favorite course that never varied. He had never been able to finish the 2.2 mile course in under thirteen minutes, but today he promised himself he would. He started out fast from his parents' driveway and ran past the Murphys' front yard, where he used to play ball. He cruised downhill past streets named Ibis and Finch, picking up speed. The cold morning air began to burn his lungs and throat. By the time he could see the back of the shopping center, the sun lit the sky, an orange sliver in the east. Clay pumped his arms and legs, now heavy, almost numb from the effort of the run. It seemed like hours since he started. He looked at the stop watch he held clutched in his left hand. He was halfway at six thirty-five.

He needed a little more. He thought about the NFL. He thought about winning. Winning was everything. "Be a champion. Be the best," he told himself.

Finally, there was the stop sign. In the wintertime as a kid, that was where he and his friends would sneak up on cars, grab onto their bumpers when they stopped, and get pulled down the snowy street. He looked at his watch: twelve thirty-eight.

He had two blocks to go. He felt a rush, like an electric jolt, and a deep desire to beat his record. Now the pain was great. It filled his body. His mind was swimming and his body told him to stop. He wouldn't. Sweat flew from his face and hands. His body shook with each stride. Harder and harder, but it all seemed to be in slow motion. He could see the street sign for Kiwi Path that marked his finish line. His foot hit the imaginary line. He stopped the watch and geared down with a steady flap flap flap from his sneakers.

He fought with dizziness and staggered to remain upright, trying to hold up his head to get more oxygen into his lungs. The watch read twelve fifty-eight. He was in the best shape of his life.

CHAPTER TWO

HUMPHRY LYLES LEFT NO ONE GUESSING as to his wealth. He wore Armani suits with two-hundred-dollar ties and twelve-hundred-dollar shoes. On his wrist, he wore a Cartier panther, and his nails were carefully manicured. Likewise, his office exuded affluence. It was spacious. One sixteen-foot wall was lined from floor to ceiling with leather-bound books. The furniture was all dark wood and leather. It was all Century. Another wall was almost entirely windows and looked out over a practice field. Two French doors in the center of the room opened onto a brick terrace that afforded an unobstructed view of the action below.

Opposite Humphry's large desk was a marble fireplace. Above it hung an impressionistic painting of a storefront in a small southern railroad town. The painting had been commissioned by Humphry. In the center of the darkening shops, back lit by the orange glow of dusk, was a tiny barber shop. Shadowy figures made their way down the sidewalk toward home, and a dull yellow light shone in the window above the shop. It was a beautiful painting and it seemed to hold the viewer's eye against his will. None found it more distracting than Humphry himself, and there were times when he considered having it replaced.

It was this same painting that was holding his attention when Vance White entered. White looked strangely out of place in his black sweatsuit and gray baseball cap, but he seemed at ease. He sauntered in and sat himself comfortably in an overstuffed chair that faced Humphry's desk.

"Morning, Mr. Lyles," said White.

"Good morning, Vance. Coffee?"

White shook his head.

"I didn't want to have this talk with you until you've had plenty of time to get used to the facilities," said Lyles. "Like I said to you before, I have been successful because I know who to hire and I know how to let them do their job."

"Well, it'll take me a few more weeks to finish getting my staff together. Let's see . . . I want some more free weights in the weight room, and I think we should start putting off-season incentive packages into the contracts of all our players. Besides those things, everything else is fine, just fine."

"Those things aren't a problem. Well," said Humphry, rising to signal an end to their meeting, "I just wanted to make sure, like I said, that you have everything you need."

White seemed to hesitate as he rose.

"Yes, I think everything is fine . . ."

"Well, that's great," said Humphry. "I want a winning football team. I've got more money than I could ever spend, so don't hesitate if there's anything at all."

"Mr. Lyles," White said, "I have something that I think you could help me with . . ."

"Sit down, Vance, sit down. I didn't mean to rush you out. Go right ahead," said Humphry, holding out his hands and sitting down himself.

"Well, Mr. Lyles, I guess I should ask you something first . . . Let's say you've got a Thoroughbred to run in the derby and it comes up lame . . ."

Humphry nodded for him to continue.

"O.K., let's say you know that horse can win, but you might have to give him a little help . . . like a shot of Novocain and a little hit of Adrenalin . . . and let's say, just for the hell of it, that you could rig it so no one would know . . . would you do it?"

Humphry laughed quietly before he said, "Vance, do you really think I could get to where I am today if I had any qualms about sacrificing everything for success? I have a saying that ethics is for law professors who don't have to live in the real world, and it's a good thing for them that they don't."

White leaned forward, tilting back his hat and resting his forearms on his knees. "Mr. Lyles, I expected that's just what you'd say, but I wanted to be sure. You see, there are some things that can be had out there that can get players ready to play faster and better than everyone else. Well, probably the less said the better . . . but the fact is that if I could have access to some cash, well, it would make the whole thing one hell of a lot easier."

Humphry held up his hand. "You're absolutely right. I don't really know what it is specifically that you're talking about, but I don't want to know about it, Vance. What I said I meant. Now, how much of this cash will you be needing?"

White cleared his throat, "Uh-uh-hum, well, Mr. Lyles, initially it could require as much as fifty thousand dollars, then some more down the line if everything goes well . . ."

Humphry picked up the phone on his desk. "Wendy," he said to his personal secretary, "get me Miles Lofton of First South on the line."

Humphry hung up and sat silently. Ten seconds later, the phone rang.

"Miles? Yes, how are you? Yes, I need a safe-deposit box. I need fifty thousand dollars in cash put in there, and I want you to make arrangements for my head coach, Vance White, to have access. I don't need to tell you that this is a very private matter, Miles. . . . Thank you, Miles, you too."

Humphry hung up the phone and smiled at White.

After a moment White said, "That's it?"

"That's it, Vance. You just see Miles Lofton at First South's main offices downtown. If you need more than that, let me know."

Vance White stood and smiled ever so slightly. It was the first smile Humphry had seen on his coach's face.

"Mr. Lyles, this is going to work out very well."

The Ruffians organization was run out of a large two-level brick-and-glass building in the town of Oak Point, well outside Birmingham city limits. The top floor held the management and coaches' offices, and the bottom level was devoted to locker rooms, meeting rooms, training facilities, and a weight room. In the center of the upstairs offices was a large paneled boardroom. Much of the paneling was covered by charts and bulletin boards. Different-colored three-by-five index cards were pinned to the boards. On each card was a brief profile of a football player. The higher on the board a card was pinned, the more valuable the player.

A new coaching staff like the Ruffians had two important tasks at hand. First, they had to determine just which offensive and defensive schemes they would be using. Next, they had to fit their existing players into those schemes and figure out where they would draft or trade in order to fill the holes left by inadequate personnel. Both these tasks resulted in long, drawn-out meetings that went on day after day.

This night, like most, the coaches sat around the long table in the center of the boardroom. The air was filled with cigar and cigarette smoke, and the men's eyes were all bloodshot. It was one-thirty in the morning, and they had been in this personnel meeting since eight in the morning the day before. Vance White dropped his burning cigarette into his coffee cup with a hiss.

"Anything else?" he said, knowing everyone wanted to go home.

"I have something I want to add."

The voice was not familiar. Most of the men in the room had worked together in the past, and they were used to each other's tired, rough tones. This voice was young, almost fresh. It was as though its speaker had not undergone the grueling effects of the seventeen-and-a-half-hour meeting.

Every eye turned toward Gavin Collins. He was the new guy on the block, the coach with the least experience. He was thirty-five and neat and handsome, and he looked more like a player than a coach. He was also the defensive coordinator. The others might have wondered at someone so junior holding such a position, except for the obvious fact that Collins was black.

White's eyes narrowed at Collins, who sat rigid and calm with his hands folded neatly on the table in front of him.

"Go ahead, Gavin," said White.

"Last week we came to the decision that we would run a shifting front on defense. I have looked carefully at the existing personnel and the plan-B players available, and the one thing that we don't have is a defensive lineman that has the size to match up physically with a strong-side offensive tackle. We need someone with the athletic ability to slide out and play over the tight end when in certain blitzes he might actually have man-to-man coverage."

The room was silent.

Mark Stepinowski, the linebacker coach and the oldest among them, leaned forward, pushing his enormous gut into the edge of the table. Stepinowski had coached with White for fifteen years and was the only one on the staff who seemed to have no fear whatsoever of his boss. Like White, Stepinowski's hair was gray and closely trimmed. He rubbed his face with both hands as if to waken himself. His heavy jowls shook as he said, "You know, Vance, Gavin's absolutely right. If you've still got your heart set on not making substitutions that would give away the defense, we've got to get a guy that can slide from one position to the other, and to be honest, there aren't too many players in this league that could do it."

"How about Clay Blackwell?" said Collins.

"Have to use our number one to get a fish that big," drawled Cody Wheat, the defensive backfield coach. Wheat was a tall, lanky man who looked like he would know more about basketball than football.

"I saw him at the combines," Wheat added, "impressive."

"He was the guy reading a book in the Dome," said Jim Nelan, the offensive line coach, a burly man with sausage fingers and a deep, powerful voice. "I can't see a guy like that working in our system. Besides, both Vargass from Notre Dame and Simms from Alabama are rated higher than Blackwell."

"Those guys are tackles, though," Stepinowski said, "we need more of an end."

"That's right. I'm sorry, Jim," said Collins in the least offensive way he knew how, "but if I'm going to run this defense, I've got to be the one to make that call."

"Let me tell you something you damned . . . damned . . . you son of a bitch," the big man stammered, pointing his thick finger. "I've been in this system with Vance for three years, and it's three more than you, so if I say he won't fit in, I know what—"

"Wait a damned minute!" said White. "Just hold it. Hold it, Jimmy. Gavin, let me set you straight on one thing first of all. I run this team. I run the offense, and I run the defense. I don't care what your title is, you work for me. Second, and I don't want to drag this out into some shit-eating contest about who's right and who's wrong, so just listen. The thing Jimmy's referring to is this kid's character. I don't want you, or any of you, to forget our program. I won't have any panty-waists who fit the bill physically but don't have what it takes to win. I'm not drafting one damn player out of college that won't train under our program."

"Why don't I go up and give him a personality test?" Collins suggested. "They're supposed to tell us if the players have got what we want."

"Step?" White said, looking at Stepinowski quizzically.

"I think it's a good idea, Vance," said Step.

"O.K., Gavin," White said, "Box gets back from L.A. on Thursday. Take him with you. We'll see what the test shows before we even talk any more about this."

Later that same morning, Max Dresden, who lived in a luxury apartment building located not far from downtown Birmingham, reached out from under his covers to stop the clock from buzzing. The radio alone couldn't wake Max, he needed the buzzer. It was ten-thirty, and he had to hurry. Without looking, he felt with his foot for another warm body under his covers. She was still there, all right. Quietly Max slid out of the bed and stood over the covered form of what he remembered as a very satisfying young woman. Abruptly Max stooped and heaved his side of the bed up in the air. The girl rolled off the bed and hit the floor with a thud. A muffled shriek came from within the wrap of covers.

Max laughed until tears were streaming down his face. When she finally freed herself from the covers, the young woman gave him a dirty look that made him laugh harder.

"It's not funny, you bastard!" said the girl, pulling on her panties. "I'm leaving."

Max howled. He only wished someone else was there to share this fun with.

"That's the idea, you dumb bitch."

Instead of getting right into the shower, Max watched the angry girl dress to make sure she didn't steal anything. His wallet was in the bathroom, so there wasn't much to take. But on the wall Max had hung his football jerseys from college, the Canadian league, the USFL, and the Ruffians, and he couldn't replace them. Last night the girl had remarked about how impressive the collection was, and Max now worried that she might take them just to fuck with him.

When she was safely outside his door, she shouted, "You son of a bitch! I—"
Max cut her off with the slam of his door. He stepped into the shower and whistled contentedly as he cleaned himself thoroughly. Max was a middle linebacker who had always been obsessed with playing professional football. His first year out of a small state college in Ohio, he was cut from the Saskatchewan Rough Riders. He returned to Cleveland, his hometown, and worked nights as a bouncer so he could train during the day at a downtown gym. He had little money and lived in a condemned building. He spent what little money he had on food because it was imperative to his training.

His bed was a mattress set up on cinder blocks. The place had no heat or electricity, but it still had running water. To stave off the winter cold, Max slept in his street clothes: jeans, a wool sweater, Timberline boots, a black ski mask, and a green army jacket. This environment toughened Max to the hard realities of life. He knew that he would get no breaks that he didn't make for himself.

When the owner of the gym approached Max about using steroids, he listened, thinking that he may finally have hit on the key that would get him in the professional football door. He trained for six months under the tutelage of the gym owner, and gained thirty-five pounds of muscle. He became strong as a bull, fast as a cat. When Max returned to Saskatchewan the following season, he began his career as a professional player. The night he received his first paycheck, Max bought himself a bottle of Yukon Jack to celebrate, and then a whore.

He played for a year in Canada, then a year with the USFL's Arizona Wranglers. When the league folded, he returned to Canada, where a scout from the Seattle Seahawks happened to be at a Saskatchewan game and noticed him. He was given a tryout the following season and made the team. After three years in Seattle, he was picked up by the Ruffians in a supplemental draft. This allowed the expansion team to pick various "unprotected" players from other existing teams.

Most players detested having to leave their original team for a lowly expansion club, but Max had been strictly a backup player and what he wanted most was to be a starter in the NFL. An expansion team, he figured, was just the right place to get that opportunity.

His first season with the Ruffians was spent on injured reserve. He blew out his knee in the first pre-season game on the first kickoff of the game. Because of this, he knew that the odds were against his making the team the following year. Coaches had an innate dislike for players who spent an entire season on injured reserve. They were bad luck. When Humphry Lyles fired the original coaching staff, Max bought another bottle of Yukon. He knew that the new staff would have no preconceptions, and would judge him entirely on his efforts and performance.

When he first arrived at the Ruffians camp, Max was given an address outside downtown Birmingham and told to report to the office of a Dr. Borne. The midrise office building was newly built, and Borne's spacious office was on the top floor and had a great view of the city. As Max sat in the waiting room, he examined a plastic model of the bone structure of the foot. He looked up from the foot to see a young nurse staring at him, and he winked at her before she could look away. Max made a mental note to get her number before he left. He had always had a special fondness for nurses in bed. They had good knowledge of the human body, and he liked that. This one looked cheap with her bleached blond hair and her long red nails and matching lipstick, but he liked that too. Besides, she was tall, and her breasts were large.

Max didn't expend much effort chasing after women. In a rugged way, he was very handsome, and although he had been with women that fit into the "take home to mother" category, he was more apt to wake up next to a cheap-looking girl. Not ugly. Max was very selective and he felt that pretty girls were less likely to have any venereal diseases, so he only went with real lookers. But he did almost all of his socializing in nightclubs, and most of the lookers were the cheap ones with the tight, skimpy clothes and the high-heeled pumps. He liked it that way too because it was easier to treat them with ambivalence, taking them home after a night of sex and never even bothering to ask for their phone number. When he treated a nice girl that way, he always felt wrong.

Max suspected it was no coincidence that the young nurse was the one to lead him to an exam room and take his blood pressure. He gave her a wolfish smile and asked for her number, promising her dinner and a night on the town. She was writing it down when the doctor came into the room and she blushed. After quickly giving Max the scrap of paper, she hurried out of the room.

"Well, congratulations," the doctor said. "Boy, I know a lot of people have asked, but you're the first one I've seen get that phone number."

The doctor was in his mid-forties but dressed in the fashionable clothes of a twenty-year-old. His polo shirt was open and he wore a gold chain that sat in a bush of chest hair. He was tanned but going bald, and his comical appearance annoyed Max. Doctors were supposed to wear hush puppies and corduroys. But Max wasn't one to complain. The exclusive office and the obviously successful doctor were a far cry from Max's experiences in Cleveland, before his days as a pro. When he had gotten a steroid prescription then, the doctor's office had been seedy and the doctor himself had smelled of Wild Turkey. So who was he to complain just because Dr. Borne was a little too trendy?

But now, as a pro, he was accustomed to seeing doctors who played a lot of golf and drove European cars as a matter of course. Most of them, however, weren't jock sniffers. This one was, though. Max could spot a jock sniffer a mile away, and he also knew how to deal with them.

"I hope that's not the private stock," Max said, knowing the complimentary joke would make the guy feel like they were old and dear friends.

The doctor laughed. "No, I don't mess with the help. My wife would catch on too easily. I'm too sly for that."

I bet you are, Max thought, and stuffed the phone number into his jeans.

"Max, I'm Kyle Borne. Call me Kyle."

"Sure thing, Kyle," Max said, dropping the doctor stuff with no problem.

"Great. Boy, I'm sure glad to be helping you guys out. Not that you need it. I mean, it's tough to get started being an expansion team and all that. Boy, let me tell you, I know what it is to play on a lousy team. 'Course, I didn't really play much after high school, but we had some rough seasons and I know how it is."

Max gave the doctor an interested and serious look while he thought about what a fool the guy was. He let him run his course because he knew that he must have his nose up someone's ass or else he wouldn't be a part of something like this. If it was Vance White whom the doctor knew, it was better to have Borne tell White about what a swell guy Max was, rather than have Max treat him as he would any other sniffer.

After a few nifty stories of his successes on the field, Borne finally got down to business. He gave Max a once-over kind of physical and took his weight. He then made some calculations on a prescription pad.

"Ever used something like this?" he asked Max, taking a box from one of his cupboards.

"Yeah. A while ago I used some Debol," Max said.

"Any problems?"

"No. Nothing unusual. A little acne on my back, my balls shrunk a little, nothing noticeable. It didn't thin my hair—that I was pretty damn happy about."

The doctor looked up. "No, it didn't, did it? Any rectal bleeding, blood in your urine, unusual lower abdominal pains?"

"No, nothing like that."

"Good. Now, like I said, I'm glad to help you guys out, but I want you to remember something for me, O.K.?"

Max nodded. "Sure."

"O.K. I want you to think of me as your friend. Really, no bullshit, and if you have any problems at all with this prescription, you let me know. You can call me any time. Now, I don't mean to worry you. I spoke with a representative from the company that makes this drug, and he's assured me that it's as safe as any simple steroid. They've done plenty of tests and had no problems, but if you experience anything unusual, you just let me know."

"No problem, Kyle," Max said.

"Great." Kyle smiled, his teeth were perfect. "When you used Debol, did you take it orally?"

"Nope, used the old hypo . . . the needle."

"Good, this Thyall-D is only injectable, stomach lining can't take it. Since you're familiar, I won't bore you with the details. You'll take one three-cc injection every week. You can shoot it in your buttock, or if you want an instant effect, it can go right into a vein in your arm."

"No veins for me," Max said, "I'd feel like a junkie."

Borne nodded, not knowing whether or not Max was being serious, then continued. "Now remember, this drug has three agents: the steroid, a masking agent so you don't have to worry about it showing up on any test, and an amphetamine. It's got a kick to it, I'll say that. So use it before you go into a heavy weight workout. That will give the drug a good opportunity to run itself down a little bit. I wouldn't do it before I was going someplace where I didn't want to be irritable and hyper and . . . well, violent. During the season, you'll use it on game day. There's five one-hundred-milliliter bottles in this box and fifty syringes. Just make sure you stay sterilized and dispose of your needles properly."

"Sure."

"Here, here's a bottle of alcohol and some cotton," the doctor said, handing it over. "Well, look, Max, it was a pleasure meeting you. Listen, why don't you give me a call some time? We could go out for a few drinks."

"Sure, Kyle, sounds great," Max said.

The doctor gave Max a card on which he had written his home number. Max left the office without trying to get another look at the nurse— he had plenty of time for that later. At that moment he only wanted to get out of the office and into his car. He wanted to put some fast miles between him and his new pal Kyle. Just cruise. He just felt kind of cramped and uneasy. The steroid business had bothered him less in Cleveland, where the whole scene had kind of fit. But it didn't fit here. This was a legitimate doctor, no seedy quack. Yet the whole thing had gone off like it was perfectly O.K. I'm your friend, the guy said, call me any time, maybe we'll hit the links at my club, bang my nurse if you like.

And it is O.K., Max, you pussy, he told himself. You're getting soft. Eight years ago you'd have been impressed as hell with this setup, and happy to have some real professional guidance with this steroid routine. Lighten your load, friend, you wanted the big time, and here it is.

Max stepped into an express elevator that looked like it would take him down fast.

He continued thinking to himself. The Ruffians wouldn't let their players use something that hadn't been tested and found safe. That's what the doc said, it was perfectly O.K. An NFL franchise certainly knows how to protect its investments.

It was these thoughts that comforted Max as he rocketed downward, suspiciously eyeing the package in his hand.

He was glad to emerge into the sunlight of a bright spring day. The sun made him feel good to be alive. He now lived well, drove a Porsche 928, and stayed in an exclusive apartment building. He spent the money he made on nice clothes and exotic vacations, and women. He gave little thought to the future, and didn't intend to until he was out of the league. The new opportunity in front of him now was all he was going to think about. It was all he had to think about. He had money to spend and the job he had always dreamed of. He whistled a tune as he unlocked the car door, slid into the black Porsche, and sped off.

CHAPTER THREE

THE NORTHERN UNIVERSITY FOOTBALL FACILITY was a recent addition to the university. It was built with money that the athletic department had piled up from the three years of bowl-game money and with contributions from various jock hounds and earnest alums. The Northern players called the facility the Taj Mahal. They had everything there that college players could dream of, from a plush locker room and playing fields to hot tubs, TV lounges, and racquetball courts. The coaches' offices were also there, and that was where Clay met Gavin Collins and a scout that Gavin called simply Box.

Collins was impressed with Clay from the moment he saw him. He liked his size and the way Clay's body swayed from side to side as he walked into the room where they had been watching game films. Gavin felt he could tell if a player was quick just by the way he walked. Gavin also knew he was quick because he had just seen him run down a wide receiver on the film. He also noticed Clay's alert eyes and the slight tension in his face.

"Clay, I'm Gavin Collins from the Birmingham Ruffians, and this is Box, our head scout."

Clay thought it was an unusual nickname, but then so was Lever. In Box's case, the name fit. The man was squarely built—even his head and hands were block-like. His features were twisted and damaged, probably from years of play in the NFL. Most scouts were former players who had performed well and loyally for a team. When their bodies were worn down to the point where they were no longer of any value and they had no other place to go, they were sometimes made into scouts. A scout was the lowest man on the totem pole in an NFL organization. They didn't make much money, and what they thought of a player often mattered very little to the coaches, who have ideas of their own.

Box only nodded as Clay shook both men's hands and said, "Nice to meet you."

Clay didn't bother trying to remember the names of the men. He saw men like them almost every day. Since the combines, scouts and coaches from every team haunted his days with workouts. Bill Clancy said that it was important to give everyone a good impression, so Clay was amiable and performed with a smile on his face. He had Bill Clancy's advice in mind as he sat down to take the test.

Clay's only goal was to be drafted as high as he possibly could. Birmingham had the third pick, so if they chose him instead of, say, San Francisco, who picked twenty-fifth, the difference in salary and signing bonus would likely be over two million dollars. And for two million dollars Clay felt he could give them the answers they wanted.

He knew what football coaches liked in their players. He had been putting his knowledge into effect for the past month. They all came to test him in one way or another, and it didn't matter to Clay what the test was. All he knew was that he was going to do whatever it took to be the best. They liked a guy who was no-nonsense and who would do anything to win. Intelligence was good, but it could be considered dangerous if not coupled with a hearty dose of unquestioning obedience.

He sat down across the table from Box and Collins, and looked into their eyes, mentally converting himself into the kind of guy he knew they wanted him to be. The men both wore their hair close-cropped to their heads. Although he was heavy with excess weight, Box's posture was ramrod straight. Collins too sat with a stiff back. They both had southern accents. Collins had intense dark brown eyes, almost black, and a military bearing that made Clay think of General Colin Powell. Collins told him to take his time, there was no limit, but to be sure he answered the questions honestly. Clay would have to be careful, though. He knew from Psych 307 that these kind of tests were cross-referenced to pick up inconsistencies. He would have to watch for any questions designed to trip him up.

"There are no right or wrong answers," said Collins, "just put down the first thing that comes to mind."

The first question was: Where would you rather be on a Saturday afternoon in a strange city? (A) an art museum (B) a bowling alley (C) at home watching TV (D) in a shopping mall.

Clay thought an art museum would be his choice, but he knew that was wrong. TV was out, that was too sedentary. Bowling was a sport, so that's what you'd think immediately was what they wanted. But mall shoppers tend to be aggressive people who weren't afraid of crowds. Clay gazed at the faces of Collins and Box for a hint. Box looked like a guy who had his own bowling ball with his initials engraved on it. Clay chose B.

"I'm gonna be fuckin' rich," Clay shouted in Lever's ear so he could be heard above the din. They were perched on stools at Nelson's, and the place was crowded and hot. Clay knew it was the kind of night that would leave him smelling of sweat and smoke and beer, and that his throat would hurt from the yelling. He would certainly have a hangover, but he was very happy.

His test with the Ruffians had gone well. He was sure of that. He had given the kind of answers they wanted, and he felt he had been consistent enough to avoid those designed to keep players from lying.

He didn't even want to begin to think what he would do with all that money. He just wanted to sit back and get drunk with his friend, and enjoy one of the last few Friday nights he would have at school.

"Clay," said a very drunk Lever, "you and me forever, huh? Chug."

Lever tipped his beer to Clay's, and they both up-ended their bottles.

"Over the fuckin' top!" shouted Lever, slamming the empty bottle on the bar.

"You know, Lev, I was just thinkin', we gotta enjoy this. All this," said Clay, waving his hand in a broad sweep. "Things are gonna change."

"Nothin' changes," brayed Lever as he draped his large arm over Clay's shoulder, "only the color of the uniform changes, and if ya go to

Denver, that won't even change."

Clay's eye caught two familiar faces entering the bar, Tom Seldon and Cooper O'Brien. Seldon was a large, lean tight end for New England, and O'Brien was a beefy fullback for Philadelphia. They had both played at Northern when Clay and Lever had been sophomores. Then they got drafted. Now they looked much different. They were polished. Seldon wore gold-rimmed spectacles that gave him the appearance of an attorney. Both wore heavy black leather jackets, ostrich skin boots, and Rolex watches.

Clay looked down past his tattered jeans at his grimy turf shoes. Lever had a Timex, and Clay wore no watch at all.

Clay watched the crowds of students turn to stare at the pair of NFL players as they made their way across the floor to the bar. Lever and Clay made room between their stools so they could order drinks. Clay smelled expensive cologne.

"Hey, Tom, hey, Coop," said Lever amiably.

"Hey, guys," said Clay.

"What's up?" said Seldon.

"Hey," O'Brien said to Lever. Then, "Hey, Clay, getting ready for the big time?"

"Bet your ass," Clay said.

"What are you guys doing here?" asked Lever.

"You know," O'Brien said, "just visiting my little sister. She's a freshman here this year, and I told her I'd come. I dragged Tommy with me."

"I don't know what the fuck we're doing here," said Seldon blandly, "but I can't wait to get my ass out of this cold and get to Hawaii."

He then turned away. Clay watched him push through the crowd and stop in front of a very nice-looking girl with a spectacular body.

"You guys going to fuckin' Hawaii?" said Lever. "That's tits."

"Yeah, a bunch of Tommy's buddies from the Patriots are going out there, so we figured we'd go," said Cooper.

"Nothin' better to do," he added.

Seldon reappeared with the girl in close tow. "I'm outa here, Coop," Seldon said with a grin.

"She got a friend?" asked Cooper.

Seldon turned to the girl and said something, then he nodded.

"How about her?" Seldon said, pointing to another girl who wasn't half bad and who was now standing with Seldon's girl and looking at them out of the corner of her eye.

"Good enough," Cooper said. "Later, guys."

Clay watched them leave, keeping his eye on the nice tight ass of the girl with Seldon. "What's up?" he asked. "Why you looking at me like that?"

"Nothing," said Lever, "I was just thinking I could get a mold of that chick's ass and you could take it home."

"What's the fuckin' deal? I can't look at some nice chick's ass? I can't wait till it's that easy. Just boom, how you doin', let's get outa here. Wham-bam."

"Ahhh, those girls weren't shit," said Lever, "not next to Katie."

"They weren't Katie," Clay said, "but I'd still fuck them both."

"You're drunk."

"You're drunk too."

"Yeah, but that's crazy. You wouldn't do those girls. You wouldn't do that to Katie," Lever said.

"What are you? A knight? Sir fucking Galahad or something?"

"Aww, don't get pissed. You're talking crazy."

"What the hell is so crazy about fucking who I want? Did you see those guys? It was like clockwork."

Lever shook his head and huffed.

"What's that supposed to mean?"

"What?"

"You know what."

"Hey, it's no big deal, but sometimes I gotta wonder if you know what you got."

"What?"

"In a girl like Katie," Lever said. "You don't find a girl like her. She's pretty . . . she's nice . . ."

"You sound like a fuckin' minister or something," said Clay, taking a chug on his beer. He was so drunk now that his teeth were numb. "She's not goin' anywhere. What, you think I should tie a knot in my dick for the next two years? Hey, Lev, it's no big deal, I'll have a little fun, then Katie'll finish school. We'll get married."

Lever shook his head. "She'll never go for that!"

"You think she's gonna know, ya fuckin' dummy?"

"You're full of shit. I know you love her."

"Of course I love her. What's that got to do with it? Did you get hit in

RUFFIANS
5 5

the head?"

"Let's talk about something else," Lever said. "You're drunk. Let's talk about football."

"Let's talk about beer. Chug, you pussy."

While they were waiting for the bartender to bring them two fresh beers, Clay spotted a nice-looking blonde. It was a good opportunity to show Lever what he was talking about.

"Lev, be right back," Clay said, getting up from his seat.

Lever grabbed him by the arm. "What ya doin'?"

Clay nodded in the blonde's direction. Although the gesture was vague, Lever knew exactly what he meant. The blonde stood out in the crowd.

"Aww, that's bullshit. We're supposed to be drinking," Lever said.

"I'm not doin' nothing, I'm just gonna talk to her for a minute. I'll be right back." Clay shrugged his arm free and pushed his way through the crowd of students toward the girl.

Katie looked at the clock. It was late. She closed her textbook and rubbed her eyes. She would have preferred to be with Clay, but he and Lever were getting drunk tonight and she had a big exam on Monday. When the two of them set out to get drunk, she was better off staying home. In a funny way, she liked waiting at his apartment for him. It was kind of domestic. She liked waking up in the wee hours of the morning to feel him climbing into bed beside her.

She used Clay's toothbrush, then pulled on a T-shirt that smelled like him and got into bed. She'd get to sleep so she could get up relatively early. This way she'd have time to get some doughnuts and a paper before she made breakfast. It was something she liked to do when Clay and Lever went out drinking the night before.

Before she shut out the light, she opened the top drawer of the night table and took out a tattered paperback she had left in his apartment. After reading for half an hour the covers were warm and she hated to get out of bed. She did anyway. She had forgotten to put out a glass of water and three Tylenols for Clay on the bathroom sink. If she didn't do it, odds were that he'd be too drunk to think of it. This way he wouldn't feel so bad in the morning. When she was done, she hurried back across the cold floor and got into bed. She turned off the light, and thinking of how nice it would feel when Clay was next to her, she fell asleep.

She awoke to the sound of Clay falling into the dresser. Katie looked at the clock. It read: 3:47. Clay righted himself and clumsily began to pull off his clothes. His shirt got stuck coming over his head. He staggered and fell over again, crashing into the closet door.

"Shit."

"Clay?" Katie said sleepily.

"Hi, honey, damn fuckin' shirt," Clay said in a drunken slur, finally getting free from the shirt and crawling into the bed.

"Clay, it's almost four," Katie said.

"Yeah, me an' Lev had a long one. Closed the place, then got some chow." Clay yawned, he was almost asleep.

Katie snuggled up next to him and rested her head on his chest.

"I'm glad you had fun," she said.

Together they fell asleep.

CHAPTER FOUR

I T WAS LATE AT NIGHT and the dimly lit room was filled with cigar smoke. Gavin Collins's eyes were bloodshot from the smoke and the late hours they'd kept in the past week preparing for the draft. Clay Blackwell had been the subject of hot debate since Gavin's return to Birmingham almost a month ago. Gavin had reported his findings, and White and Stepinowski confirmed his high opinion of Blackwell after watching some game films that Gavin had brought back. There was no doubt among the staff that Blackwell had the potential to be a dominant defensive end and that he also had the speed and athleticism to occasionally drop into pass coverage. This is exactly the type of player the Ruffians needed if they wanted to change their defensive scheme from play to play without showing their hand to the opposition.

The debate, however, was about Blackwell's willingness to participate in their "program."

Two weeks earlier, Gavin had argued, "Vance, Blackwell is a perfect candidate for the program. He's bright, but he's respectful. Every coach I talked to up there said the same thing: Blackwell responds well to discipline. And let's face it, this kid is so damned impressive physically, so what if he doesn't do the program?"

"So what! So what?" White bellowed. "Gavin, don't forget this," he continued when he had calmed himself, "we are not here to have a good team, a winning team, or even a playoff team. We are here to win the Super Bowl, to be the world champions. And we are here to do it soon. Not in ten years, or two years. Next year, Collins, next year. Do you understand that?"

Collins nodded. He was embarrassed. They were sitting in the staff meeting room, and White was lecturing him in front of the rest of the coaches, the scouts, and Mr. Lyles himself as if he were a bad little boy. Well, fuck him.

"Good. Now, so we're all on the same page . . . does anyone have any second thoughts about this job?" White peered about like a hawk.

Humphry Lyles gave White an approving look. He liked a tough manager.

"Fine, then this will be the last time I will have to go over the importance of this program. Mr. Lyles has given me the goal of producing a championship team for him next year. He has put unlimited funds at my disposal to accomplish this goal. I've got the best coaching staff that money can buy." White smiled grimly. "And I made sure each and every one of you not only approved of my program, but that you were enthusiastic about it."

Gavin tried to get a word in. "Aw, come on, Vance, that's not what I—"

White silenced him with a cold stare. "I'm saying this for everyone's benefit. Because after this, I don't want our program questioned in any way. If anyone has any reservations, let me know now."

There was silence and White said, "Good. We all know that having the best staff in the game isn't enough. We know that we also need the finest players, and in this league that is not entirely for sale. We're limited by the draft. So we have to choose carefully and make the best of what we have. I have been successful in the past not by making two or three players great, but by making an entire team great.

"In my last job, and many of you were there, but for those who were not," he said, looking directly at Collins, "let me assure you that I do things as a team. What is done by one is done by all. Every team member must make the same sacrifices, must be equally dedicated to the team goals. You all know that the way to win football games is with defense and a strong running game. We will have all linemen, linebackers, tight ends, and blocking backs in this program.

"Here the goal is the Super Bowl, and one of the dedications is for each player to be the very best he can be. Not good"—White was beginning to shout—"not great, but . . . the very best they can be!"

With each word, White struck his palm.

"So, any consideration of Blackwell, or any other draft pick, will also include their willingness to participate in this program. Gavin, this is the way we will win, with an entire team effort. This program will give us the winning edge."

There was silence for some time before Collins spoke. He first cleared his throat. "Well, I think that Blackwell is the type of player that would fit into this program."

"This is something we have to discuss," said White. "Box has some concerns as to the boy's cooperation."

Each man in the room turned to look at Box. The scout looked blandly at them and said, "The test didn't give us the answer. The results are erratic. Blackwell didn't fall clearly into the positive category, although he did show some aggressive tendencies. I sent the results back out to Berkeley, and even the doctor who created the test was confused. He said in his opinion, Blackwell was a twenty-five-percent risk. Since I don't believe in taking risks, I wouldn't take the kid."

The kid, Collins fumed to himself. That "kid" was ten times the player Box had ever been. The test was bullshit and so was Box.

But Box and White went back all the way to college, when they played together at Alabama. Back then it was White who had looked up to Box. And now Box had his nose so far up White's ass that if White stopped short, Box could taste his food.

"We both know what it takes to win, Vance," said Box, "and all I can say is that this guy wouldn't have lasted at 'Bama when we were there. He doesn't have it, Vance, I can see it in his eyes."

"That's bullshit," Collins said.

The rest of the staff clamored until Stepinowski spoke up:

"I think the way to solve this problem is simple."

Everyone was silent.

"Vance, no one's saying anything against our program. Gavin's just saying that the kid is so good, that he's better than the guys we've got who are already training on the program. And he is that good, let's face it. We've all seen him on film. He's a head-stomper. He's got fire in his ass. Look at these numbers."

Step held up the file on Blackwell.

"The kid runs like a linebacker, but he's as powerful as any lineman in the league. He's also got enough brains to learn this position, which is really going to be two positions. He's perfect in every respect, so what you want to do is go up there yourself. You know what you want better than anyone. Don't listen to the test, or to Box, or to Gavin. Go up there. Sit down with the kid. Pick his brain."

The next day Vance flew from Birmingham to Syracuse and arranged to meet Clay at Northern. When Clay arrived, White was in Leary's office discussing him. Both men stopped talking and stood up when Clay walked in.

"Clay, I'm Vance White," said White, extending his hand.

"Hi, Coach, nice to meet you," Clay said standing as upright as he possibly could.

Coach Leary greeted Clay warmly, then led them to a conference room. He shut the door on his way out. Clay sat down and White sat on the other side of the table. They talked for a few minutes about Leary and what a good coach he was. Then White leaned across the table toward Clay.

"Clay," he said, looking seriously into the boy's eyes, "do you realize how much money we would be investing if we decide to use our first-round pick on you?"

Clay nodded.

"Clay, how important a goal is being a great NFL player to you?" White asked.

"Well, Coach White, it's the most important goal in my life."

"Very good," White said, smiling. "And would you do anything to accomplish that goal?"

Clay looked White in the eye and said, "Coach White, I came from a very average family with very average means. Because I worked my ass off, I'm sitting here talking with you today about maybe making millions of dollars. I got here by doing what it takes, by sacrifice, and by going one step beyond what everybody else was willing to do. So when you ask if I would do anything to be a great player, I have to tell you that I always have and I always will."

White was delighted.

Vance White entered Humphry's office to find the owner sitting at his desk intently examining a football. Lyles stopped poking the seams and waved him toward the couch. White eased himself into the soft leather chair and exhaled, deeply tired from the long trip to New York and back.

"Can I offer you a drink?" asked Humphry.

"Scotch, thanks," said White.

"No ice, right?" said Lyles.

Lyles poured two drinks, handed one to White, and sat down across from him in the other overstuffed chair. Lyles was becoming fond of White.

"I'll be honest with you, Vance, I really don't have many friends. My life is working, and I've always had kind of a policy not to mix work and friendship. To be honest, I find it hard to relate to people anyway. But I think you and I are a lot alike. We're both hardworking, and we're both successful. And after what we're going to do with this team, I don't see how we won't be friends.

"You see," Humphry continued, "I was never an athlete, but I always kind of liked the idea."

He was living out a dream. To be sitting in his lavish office, drinking expensive scotch with a tough, physical man like White gave Humphry a fraternal feeling that he had always longed for. Just two guys with a football team that they were going to take to a Super Bowl. Two guys who controlled the fates of world-class athletes as if they were commodities on the exchange. And now he would become one of the guys himself. One of the guys like Vance White. They would be like the Al Davis/John Madden team of the seventies.

"You know, Vance, I like the way you're operating this team already."

White nodded. "Thank you, Mr. Lyles."

Humphry considered telling White to call him by his first name, but then decided against it. He sipped his scotch instead.

"Winning really is a simple business concept, isn't it, Vance? Get the most out of your employees. Push them to their limits, make them produce."

White nodded again, but said nothing. Instead he stared thoughtfully at his drink. How could a man like this own a football team? But Lyles was the boss. There was always a big fish that had to be kept happy. There was always an owner, or a university president, or some powerful alumnus to kiss up to. He had to make them feel like they were a part of team's successes, like the team was really theirs.

But the only man a team belonged to was the head coach. That was why he was sitting in this office calling that chubby little puke "Mr." Lyles, because he was a coach and there was no other feeling equal to winning. He'd never talk to a weakling like Lyles otherwise.

Miffed by White's silence, Humphry said, "I said, make them produce, right, Vance?"

"Mr. Lyles, this team will kick ass all around the league."

Humphry smiled. This was the kind of talk he liked, kicking ass.

"You probably want to hear about Blackwell," White said.

"Is he our man?"

"Mr. Lyles," said White, raising his glass, "I think we have our first-round draft pick."

"Excellent," said Humphry, also raising his glass. "Tell me about him."

"Well, I must admit, I had my doubts. What with the little discrepancy on the personality test, and the fact that I felt Gavin Collins might be selling the kid just to get a big lineman to work with . . . but I gotta say after meeting him, this Blackwell is a coach's dream. He's bright but not sassy. He's certainly a physical specimen."

"Is he?" said Humphry.

"Yes, and I asked him flat-out if he would do anything to be a great football player. There's not much room for misunderstanding in that, is there? I tell you, Mr. Lyles, I really liked this kid's attitude."

"Are you sure he'll still be there by the time we pick?" asked Lyles.

"Oh yeah, we already know that Tampa has started negotiating with Roland Downs, that tailback from USC, and Memphis needs a receiver, so they'll take the DeVine kid from Miami. That leaves us. My predecessors did one good thing. Being one of the worst teams in the league last year left me with an early draft pick."

White smiled at his own humor, but Lyles didn't.

"So," said Lyles, "he's the one."

"Well," returned White, "that is, if you don't have any objections. After all, you'll have to spend a pot of money to get this kid signed. His agent is that Clancy guy out of New York City, and I want to get this kid in here to start training on our program. Clancy won't make that easy. This kid won't come cheap."

"Vance," said Lyles, "I appreciate your concern about the money, but believe me, this is the first time in my life that money is not the issue. If you think this Blackwell kid is what we need, and if he will fit into your program the way you like and help bring this team to the top, then it's as good as done."

White smiled and said, "Mr. Lyles, with your money and my coaching, this team will be on top in no time."

"This calls for a celebration," Humphry said. "How about dinner? Just you and I, the builders of a football dynasty."

White hesitated. He was tired and preferred even his wife's company to the owner's, but he knew that Humphry Lyles was a man who seldom made social engagements. To refuse would be a mistake. Maybe it wouldn't hurt to have Lyles consider him a friend. You do what you have to.

"That sounds like a fine idea, Mr. Lyles," White said, "just the two of us, like a couple of good old boys."

Lyles smiled at that idea. White knew he would.

CHAPTER FIVE

"I THINK THIS IS THE MOST EXCITING THING I've ever seen," Katie said.

Clay, nervous as a virgin on her wedding night, smiled wanly at her. She felt foolish after she spoke, but it was the only thing she could say, and she had to say something. Clay and his parents were just sitting there, staring anxiously at the set. She was wedged between Clay and his mother on the couch. The tension was thick.

On the screen, Paul Tagliabue, the league commissioner, stood next to a large black player named Roland Downs. Even Katie had heard of him, the great running back out of USC. He was wearing black leather, gold jewelry, and dark sunglasses. He and the commissioner held up a Tampa Bay Buccaneers jersey and smiled for an explosion of camera flashes.

"Son of a bitch will sign for about twelve million," grumbled Mr. Blackwell. He crumpled his beer can and opened another one despite the fact that it was only eight o'clock in the morning.

Clay said, "These first few picks don't really matter. I know I'm not going to go this early."

"When did Clancy say was the soonest?" asked the father.

"Well, Vargass and Simms will probably go before me," said Clay. "Bill thinks my first real shot is with the Jets. They pick eleventh."

"Eleventh is still big, big money," said the older Blackwell, "but what about Birmingham? You said you got a good feeling from White."

"I didn't say I got a good feeling from him. Dad. The guy gave me the creeps. I just said that they seemed to really like me. I sure gave them the sell."

"You did sell 'em, didn't you, Clayboy?" the father said. "Just like I told you." The older man turned his excited gaze toward Katie. "I told Clay," he said. "I said, 'Sell yourself to these guys, Clay. Give 'em what they want. This is business, and business is selling.' Isn't that what I said to you, Clay?"

"Yeah, Dad."

Clay didn't disagree. Everyone in the room knew that his father was just repeating the words of Bill Clancy. It was embarrassing.

"So, maybe it'll be Birmingham. Maybe. You sure sold 'em," said the father, as if he had been there when Clay gave Vance White his speech on sacrifice.

"It is possible," said Clay, but not just to shut his father up. Bill Clancy had told Clay a few days ago that the Birmingham pick was a mystery to everyone, so it really was possible.

Clay thought he had done well on the personality test he knew they were giving to everyone, and Clancy had told him that White's visit was a good sign, though not conclusive.

Clay hadn't told anyone of his conversation with Clancy. He didn't want to raise anyone's expectations that high. The third pick of the draft would bring him more money than he had really dreamed of, probably more than twice what he would get if he were to be picked only eight spots later by the Jets.

On the TV, the commentators were busy predicting that the Memphis Gamblers would pick Cory LeVine, a wide receiver which the commentators said the team could really use.

"And Clay Blackwell is another possibility," said Mel Kiper, ESPN's expert on the college draft. "They could use real help on their defensive line too, and I think that even though most people have Vargass and Simms rated higher, Clay Blackwell may be the first defensive lineman to go today."

"Oh, Clay, they're talking about you!" his mother said.

The phone rang.

"Hello," said Clay. He had purchased a twenty-five-foot cord for the phone, and had brought it into the living room from the kitchen so that he could answer the call when it came. His stomach was in knots.

"Hey, you bastard! What the hell's up? Did you get picked yet?"

It was Lever, and from the sounds of it, he was still drunk from the night before. Clay had left him at a fraternity party to spend the night at his parents' home, in his own bed.

"You crazy shit," said Clay, "they might be trying to call me right now."

Lever belched into the phone.

"Lever, if you call again on this phone, I'll kick your ass."

"Lever, you son of a bitch, come drink with me!" Mr. Blackwell yelled from his chair.

"Now see the shit you started," Clay said to Lever, looking sadly at his father.

"O.K., O.K., I was just calling to wish you luck. Don't get pissed."

"I'm not, just nervous as hell."

"O.K., see you later, huh?"

Clay hung up the phone. Memphis picked the wide receiver from Miami, and the commissioner said into the microphone, "Next up, the Birmingham Ruffians. They will have fifteen minutes."

They sat silently. Five minutes went by.

"Maybe we should let the TV people in," his father said, referring to the local camera crews Clay had asked to wait outside until he was picked. "This could be it."

"Come on, Dad," Clay said with an imploring look.

Clay's father shrugged and started another beer. The can hissed as he opened it.

The commentators speculated about the pick. One felt they would take a quarterback from Purdue. Another said the running back from Clemson would be a smart pick. Mel Kipper didn't mention Clay. They concluded that this was the toughest pick to call, Birmingham had been quiet since the hiring of college football's black sheep, Vance White. The commentators talked for a few minutes about White, and then seemed to run out of things to say. The picture shifted to the desk where the

Birmingham representatives sat among the other thirty-two teams. One of them was writing furiously, the other talked into a phone, presumably to the home office, where the coaches and staff sat in some meeting room making the decisions.

Clay's phone rang.

"Clay Blackwell, please."

"This is Clay."

"Clay, this is Gavin Collins with the Birmingham Ruffians."

"Hi, Coach, how are you?"

"Fine, fine. How would you like to be with us down here in Birmingham?"

Clay's insides went numb. Birmingham, the third pick of the draft.

"It's Birmingham," he said to his father, and stood up with the phone to pace the floor.

"I'm . . . yes, Coach, this is great."

"Well, we're going to pick you, and I just wanted to call to make sure that you're ready to join our team. Hang on, Clay . . ."

There was confusion on the other end of the phone, and Clay heard himself being put on hold. On TV, the camera followed one of the men from the Ruffians table as he left the desk and approached the commissioner's podium. He handed him a card.

Tagliabue read the card and said, "Birmingham picks . . . Clay Blackwell, defensive end from Northern University."

The room exploded with cheers, his own included. His mother, his father, Katie, they were all screaming. Through it he heard a voice on the line.

"Clay?"

"Yes?"

"Congratulations, Clay." It was Collins. "We're happy to have you."

"Yes, yes," said Clay. Katie kissed him. His father was hugging his mother, and Clay could see that they were both crying.

"Clay, we're going to want you to come down here for a press conference."

"Yes, O.K."

"How soon can you get to the airport?" Collins asked.

"Now? You mean now, today?"

"Yes, yes, the press wants to meet you, and Mr. Lyles, the owner, he wants to meet you."

"Oh, of course," Clay said, and then whispered to Katie, "They want me to come, today."

Katie nodded, smiling. His father opened the door, and a rush of reporters streamed into the house. The white light from three different TV cameras bounced off Clay's face. He smiled, not looking at the circle of people around him, but knowing they were there, dark shapes behind the light. He held onto Katie and the phone.

"Yes, well, when can I be back, Coach? We're going to have a party."

Collins said, "We'll get you back, don't worry. There're flights running through Atlanta all day. Clay, let me have our secretary arrange your flight. She'll call you back. I'm going to get you some teammates now to help you play that forty front. See you soon, congratulations."

Clay touched the receiver down, smiling at the cameras, the phone rang again instantly. It was Clancy.

"Hello, Bill!"

"Clay, congratulations. This is very big. We're going to make you a very wealthy man."

"Thanks, Bill. Hey, they want me to go down there . . . today, right now, but we're having a party here. Everyone's coming."

"Sure, you're the third pick of the draft. They'll want to see you, meet the press. You're big news down there in Birmingham. Clay, this is really very good. You were the one they wanted all along, I guess. It really is great. You go down there, the party will be there when you get back. Go ahead, call me when you're down there."

Clay hung up the phone. It rang again. It was the secretary from the Ruffians, and she gave Clay his flight information. When he was through, he unplugged the phone. The reporters began to fire questions at him. He moved back to the couch to sit. The circle of reporters followed, and he began answering their questions. He was distracted. He murmured his responses and asked them to repeat many of the questions. He was over-joyed but in a daze, and he couldn't stop thinking about himself as if he were another person. It was all real now. Nothing could change what he was this day. He felt as though he had climbed and climbed and climbed his whole life. The going had been difficult, but he was there now, at the top. Despite all the speculation, the reality of it was somehow mystical, unexpected. The thrill of the height was breathtaking. He was Clay Blackwell, football player, defensive end, and now, millionaire. It was all real. But in the back of his mind, Clay felt a lonely chill, the kind only felt at a summit. The feeling that somehow you might fall.

An hour and a half later Clay's plane lifted gently from the Syracuse runway and into the air. Clay watched for his house, which he knew he would see as the plane made its ascent. He was sitting in first class, something he felt he could easily get used to. The young stewardess recognized him and flirted without inhibition. He would probably have to get used to that too, he thought. He would soon be in Birmingham. No one would really know about him and Katie there. She would be at school, and he would be out and about with no girl, except for when she came to visit. But when she was away, he would be known as an NFL player who was not married.

He sipped his beer and turned his thoughts to the money. What would he do with it all? First thing was to buy a car, a nice car. He had never had anything but the used heap he'd bought with the meager earnings from his summer job. As a local kid who stayed home to play football at Northern instead of going somewhere like Notre Dame, he had gotten the best kind of summer jobs. They were always easy desk jobs that he got, and he was admittedly overpaid, enough so that he could afford a used car and still save enough money every summer to keep him in drinking money and gas the entire year. He still had his rusty '78 Bronco. It met his needs during school, but now he would drive in style, maybe a Porsche or a BMW. Bill Clancy had offered to lend him the money to buy himself a new car while he was still in school, but Clay refused. He wanted to wait until he was drafted, and the money was only a technicality. He never agreed with the notion of spending what he didn't have.

Clay changed planes in Atlanta and arrived in Birmingham at one o'clock. He was greeted by a driver, who led him out into the hot sunlight and then to a long black limousine. The driver opened the rear door for Clay, and he got in. He liked the elegance of the car, and smiled to himself as it pulled away from the curb. A young couple with two children and a mountain of luggage paused to try to see through the car's dark windows. Clay toyed with the air conditioning control. The driver played some annoying rap music at a volume that Clay knew he wouldn't if the car's owner were present. Clay wanted to shut the glass partition, but he felt that would be rude.

When he arrived at the Ruffians complex, the TV cameras were waiting for the car at the front door. Clay got out of the car before the driver could get around to the door. After getting away with the loud music,

CHAPTER FIVE
7 2

the driver wasn't in a hurry to help him. The cameras converged on Clay, but no questions were asked. The reporters were waiting inside, where the Ruffians public relations staff had set up a press conference. But the cameramen were outside to film his arrival in the long black car. There were seven of them from different network affiliates across the state of Alabama. Clay knew that TV cameramen were like geese—probably only one of them had the idea to shoot him getting out of the car. But when one of them starts after something, the rest always follow, afraid they might miss something.

A man in a business suit broke through them and held out his hand. "Clay, I'm Art Walton, the public relations director for the Ruffians."

Clay shook the man's hand and followed him into the building. It was a simple brick building that looked like any other structure that served as a place for white-collar business. The difference was the backdrop. They had ridden to the outskirts of Birmingham, and the building was alone in what was otherwise a rural area. Clay had seen a field of cows as they turned off the main highway. Behind the offices stretched a huge grass area with three separate football fields marked off on it. The grass fields were bordered by trees that seemed to extend indefinitely into the distance. The landscaping suggested taste and elegance, and Clay had the feeling that the whole complex belonged in a suburban business park rather than plopped down in the midst of woods and farmland.

"Clay," Walton said, "I want to welcome you to the Ruffians and thank you for coming down. This is something all the teams do with their first-round picks. The press wants to meet you because you'll be the big news item for the next few days, and probably for much of the season. Anyway, I'll take you to our press room, Mr. Lyles will greet you, and you and he will answer questions for the press. I told them they could have you for about forty minutes if that's all right?"

Walton gave Clay an inquisitive look, and Clay smiled and nodded.

"Sure." Clay couldn't get over how much his life had changed already. It was only twelve hours ago when he crawled into his parents' house, a drunken college student.

"Good. Then when you're done, the coaching staff wants to meet you, and of course, Mr. Lyles himself will want to have a chance to talk with you without the press," Walton said.

"That sounds fine," Clay said.

He entered the press room, and the TV cameramen that had been behind him scurried past to set up their cameras on tripods. The room was filled with people that Clay knew he would soon come to recognize. They were all members of the media from across the state of Alabama. At the front of the room, a man stood behind a podium that was sprouting microphones. He reminded Clay of a chemistry teacher from high school. Although he wore a suit, Clay could see that the man had never had anything to do with the game of football himself. He had a pudgy softness about him. Although his eyes looked cold, the man smiled warmly at Clay, and Art Walton motioned him forward. Clay shook a small hand that fit snugly in the palm of his grip. Clay realized then that Humphry stood on a platform in back of the podium. The platform made him almost as tall as Clay, and Clay chuckled to himself, thinking of Pat Sajak.

Lights from the TV cameras filled the room with harsh white light.

"Gentlemen," Humphry Lyles announced with a note of arrogance and pomp in his voice as he slapped Clay on the back, "I present to you, the Ruffians' newest edition and number one draft pick . . . Clay Blackwell."

The room broke into applause, then the questions began.

"Clay, how do you feel about coming to Birmingham?"

"Birmingham's great. I think you have a great city down here." Clay was doing his thing with the press. He had no notion of Birmingham, but he knew that the people would want to hear about a first-round pick that was glad to come to their town. "I'm looking forward to getting to know it better, and I'm really looking forward to being part of a winning team and building a winning tradition."

Newspaper reporters made furious notes as he spoke.

"That's right," Humphry Lyles interjected, "Clay is going to be a part of a winning tradition. I intend to give the people of this city and this state a winner that will take us into the twenty-first century. The Birmingham Ruffians are the NFL's team of the future."

Who had asked him anything? They had come to see and talk to Clay. But the reporters seemed to take it in stride, and Clay wasn't surprised. After all, Mr. Lyles was the owner, and rich enough so that he was probably used to getting whatever he wanted. As the owner, whatever he had to say would have to be heard. Still, it was annoying.

"Clay, how do you feel about playing for Vance White?"

Clay knew of White's clouded past, but that wasn't something he'd talk about. Who cared?

"I only met Coach White once, but to me he seemed like a nice guy, and his coaching record is very impressive. You probably know better than me, but I think he's taken his college teams to bowl games for the last four years as well as a national championship. Any time as a player you get to play for a winner, you have to look at it as a positive experience."

"Clay, what about the Birmingham Ruffians, are you disappointed that you were chosen by an expansion team?"

"I'm glad to be here. A lot of guys hope to get picked by a playoff team, that's only natural. But to me, there's something very challenging about being part of a team that's on the rise. I hope to contribute to what I'm sure, as Mr. Lyles said, will be a team of the future."

"Historically, Clay," said the same reporter, "expansion teams struggle for at least ten years before they experience any success whatsoever. What makes you think Birmingham will be any different?"

Here Clay glanced at the owner, who was staring at him intently. "Well, I think when you get a coach like Vance White, in a great football state like Alabama, you can't help but be successful."

The reporters all knew, as Clay did, that he was bullshitting now, but that didn't keep them from smiling and liking what he said. This was part of the game with the media, and Clay was well versed in it. No player or coach or anyone in the game of football ever told the media the real truth or their real feelings. It was all planned, and each sentence was carefully edited before spoken, omitting words that would look bad if printed, stating the positive in order not to step on anyone's toes. Although there were occasional players who spoke openly, they were considered renegades, and Clay knew that things he said to the media could always come back to haunt him.

When Clay finally finished answering questions about himself and the Birmingham Ruffians (the latter of which he knew virtually nothing about), Art Walton thanked him and led him to the staff office. Humphry Lyles had left Clay to himself after about ten minutes of questions from the media. Clay couldn't get over the feeling that the owner had left almost in a pout, miffed over the attention that was being paid to what he considered one of many employees. But it was a crazy thought, so Clay forgot about it.

Gavin Collins had met Clay and Art on their way down the hall. He wore a broad smile on his face.

"Clay, Gavin Collins, damned glad to see you again."

"Coach Collins, it's good to see you too."

"In here, in here, everyone wants to see you," Collins said, and showed Clay into a large wood-paneled office where about a dozen men sat around a large conference table. They each had notepads and papers spread out in front of them, and the room was smoky. The men all turned their heads, and Collins introduced Clay to them one at a time. Clay recognized Box and wondered at the man's indifferent attitude.

"Clay, these guys still have a full day to put in, so let me and Art take you to see Vance and Mr. Lyles."

The owner's office was a grand room, and it reminded Clay of a library. There was a large leather sofa and some other chairs that were arranged around a fireplace, but Lyles and White sat on the other end of the room. The owner behind his desk and White in a burgundy leather overstuffed chair opposite the desk. The scene had a dignity about it that didn't seem to fit with the owner's personality. Clay suspected a man like Collins would look much more natural behind the big desk rather than the short, chubby Mr. Lyles. Also, the room exuded money and power, something inherent with the NFL, but foreign to the grass-and-sod world of the gridiron.

Collins and Art Walton had remained outside, and Clay stood alone for a long minute while the two men sat silently, as if thinking, before the owner offered Clay a seat.

"Clay," Lyles said, opening his arms as if to present to Clay the entirely new world of the NFL, "welcome to the Birmingham Ruffians."

White leaned over and shook Clay's hand, "Welcome to the club, son. We're all glad to have you on board."

"Clay," Lyles said, "as you probably realize, we have to get back to the draft room and finish picking our other boys, but I did want you and Vance and myself to sit down and have a little talk to break the ice."

"Thank you, Mr. Lyles. It's a pleasure to meet you, and I'm sure I can do some good things for the team."

"Oh, I have no doubt that you will do tremendous things for my team," Lyles said with a forced smile. "And Vance and I wanted to just use this opportunity to let you know what page we're on so that we're all working toward the same goals."

Clay nodded his head.

"Clay," said White, "we have what we consider advanced training methods here in Birmingham. Methods that are integral in taking this team to the Super Bowl. So naturally, we want you here in Birmingham, working with our staff and using our training methods in order to best prepare yourself for the upcoming season. I'm sure you experienced the same kind of thing in college, but here it will be even more intense. The players on this team will not view their job as only lasting during the season. Winning is a full-time job, and we will be going at it around here three hundred and sixty-five days a year."

"What Vance is saying, Clay, is that we want you here soon . . . to get ready. Now we know that your agent—"

"Bill Clancy," Clay interjected.

"Yes, Bill Clancy. We know that he will be advising you, and that obviously you have a certain amount of trust in him. But we want you to know that we are perfectly willing to give you a very lucrative offer right up front because we want to get you into our program right away. Does this make sense to you, Clay?" Lyles said.

"Yes, I know what you mean, and I want to get down here and get into things as soon as I can. But if you and Bill don't reach an agreement right away, Mr. Lyles, I assure you that I'll be training as hard as anyone. I always have. That's why I'm here now."

"This is a team game, Blackwell, and you better get used to that right now!" White snapped, glaring at Clay.

Lyles chuckled. "Now, Vance, this is business, just business. This is the NFL. Agents are part of it, and when Clay gets his contract signed, he'll be here. All we're saying, Clay, is that sometimes agents complicate things for the sake of justifying their existence, and we want you to know that we're anxious to get you here and begin working with you."

"We've got a formula for success here, Blackwell," White said, "and if you're interested in it, then you won't mess around with your agent all summer. We picked you because you seemed like a football player, not a businessman. You tell your agent to get his job done quick so we can get going. Don't forget that you have to work for the money we'll be paying you. We're not paying you because you were a good college player. We're paying you to help take the Ruffians to the Super Bowl."

Clay sat on his hands to keep from fidgeting. He'd never really seen anyone behave so abruptly and so inconsistently before. One minute White was greeting him like an old friend, the next he was practically screaming like a lunatic. This was only the second time he had met

White. This was draft day, a day for celebration. They were supposed to be welcoming him to the team and making him feel good. It was bad manners to act like a drill sergeant at this point in the game. White's behavior was insane.

He was still staring at Clay as if daring a contradiction. Definitely off the deep end, Clay thought. But deep end or not, he also knew that he'd be working for White. Maybe this was just his way of establishing some macho bullshit between him and his players.

That must be it, Clay thought. It was just White's method of letting him know from the start that he was all business, a real hard ass. If this was the NFL, then this was the NFL. It was nothing like college, when a player was recruited and could let some hard-ass coach go screw himself if he had an attitude like White's. In that situation he could just go to another school. In the NFL, it was becoming obvious that you had no choice. You get drafted by a team and you go.

Clay said nothing, and then White said, "Well, of course Mr. Lyles is right. This is business, and I should get back to football business. Clay, let's get you here soon so we can go to work."

White held out his hand—it was gnarled like an old tree root. When Clay stood to shake it, the coach gave his hand a squeeze that was beyond any normal handshake. White's face gave away no extra effort, but he had Clay's hand in a vise. Caught in the unexpected grip, Clay could think of nothing to do but stare impassively into White's gaze. Clay had to admit to himself that he was surprised at the man's strength. Abruptly White let go, turned, and left the room.

"Coach White is very fond of you, Clay," Lyles said with a chuckle after the door had closed.

"I could see that, sir."

"Clay," Lyles said, motioning him to sit down again, "men like Vance White don't have much in the way of social graces. But he can do what I hired him to do, that's why he's here. And that's why you're here, Clay, because you can do a job that I need done. I know about one thing, and that's winning. I know I must be sounding like a broken record on the subject, but this team has a lot to prove."

Clay doubted that the owner knew a shoulder pad from a jockstrap. "Well, winning is certainly what it's all about," he said.

"And to win," said Lyles, his eyes gleaming as if he had a secret to tell, "you need a winning edge. That's why we want you here soon, Clay.

I aim to win this year. Our plan is to get all our boys here and get everyone into a special program that I have had devised by experts, the very best people that money could buy."

The owner took a bill out of his wallet, gave it a snap, then turned it over and over with his fingers. It was a hundred-dollar bill. "Oh, I know what the press says about expansion teams never winning for years after their formation. But I also know myself, and I know that I won't go through another year like last season. I won't have it. I won't have people saying Humphry Lyles isn't a winner. You see, I believe in money and the things it can do."

They sat silently except for an occasional snap of the bill. It was hypnotic, almost intimate.

"Well!" said Lyles abruptly, "I have to get back to the draft room.

"Clay," he added as he stood and stretched out his little hand, "I'm looking forward to it. I'm going to make the Ruffians into a team that few have seen the likes of. You can be damned proud that you're going to be a big part of it. Remember, let's get you here soon."

When Lyles had gone, Gavin Collins led Clay on a little tour through the building. It was an impressive sports facility. Everything, right down to the upholstery on the weight room equipment, was done in the team colors, black and gray. Everything was new. In the locker room were spacious areas for each player, and a central lounge with leather sofas, overstuffed chairs, and a television. Off to the side was a free snack bar with racks of munchies and soft drink machines. On the other end of the locker room was an enormous hot tub, large enough for a dozen big men, and a dry sauna the size of Clay's bedroom at home. Out the back door were the practice fields. Clay and Collins walked out onto them. Even in the hot sun the grass was like a soft, cool mat.

"Water 'em three times a day and cut 'em once every day," Collins said. "Looks like a golf course, doesn't it?"

"This whole place is like a damn country club on the right side of town," Clay said.

"Oh, yeah," replied Collins, "you have arrived. The only thing missing around here is a winning record, and once we have that, this will be a player's paradise . . . and a coach's."

"Well, I really hope I can help make it happen, though you'd have to wonder what I was doing here if you talked to Coach White."

Collins laughed. "Bite you a little when you were in there, did he?

Vance is just like that. Don't worry about him, it's not you. I wish you could have heard him talking about you before the draft. He really thinks you're just what this team needs, and so do I."

"Thanks, Coach." Clay was now sorry he'd brought it up. He didn't want to sound like he was begging for compliments.

"Clay, I'll take you back up to the car now and let you get back home to your friends. I have to get back with the rest of the coaches. The offensive guys are getting most of the other picks in the draft—the defensive staff had to concede that much after taking you with our first pick—but I should be up there anyway."

Before Clay pulled away in the limousine, he put down the window and shook Collins's hand once more. Clay knew he could play for this man. He was just one of those people in life who Clay knew was on his side.

CHAPTER SIX

A DROP OF AMBER LIQUID beaded on the cold blue point of the needle. All the air had been cleared from the syringe, and Max liked that. He knew that a little air was no problem just as long as it wasn't injected directly into a vein, but he could never get over the childish fear of air in his needle. When he was a boy, he had seen a TV show called "Barretta" in which an undercover cop was killed by a drug dealer who injected air into his arm. It was for that reason too that Max always shot himself in the ass. But because he was in a bathroom stall, it was hard for him to twist around and jab the needle into the soft flesh above his right buttock. He managed, though, steadying himself with his free hand on the toilet-paper dispenser. He slowly forced the drug out of the needle and into his flesh. It burned.

He knew the skin would become red and puffy in the violated area, but he also knew that for the next six hours the sore spot would be the last thing on his mind. He knew what he was going to feel like, and although he didn't particularly enjoy the feeling, he knew it would distract him from any minor bodily discomforts. Max wrapped the needle in a wad of toilet paper, tucked away the bottle of Thyall-D, and picked his gym bag up off the bathroom floor. When he left the stall, he tossed the wrapped needle into the garbage can, not even noticing that he missed. He then made his way back to his locker and sat there on his stool, waiting for the drug to kick in.

It wouldn't happen all at once, and Max liked to have a good surge going before he hit the weight room, so he would wait. He looked around the locker room.

Down a few lockers from him were two burly offensive linemen, Dan Pike and Pete Makozych—everyone called them Pike and Sick. They were always together, and Max decided to have some fun while he was waiting.

"Hey!" he bellowed.

Pike and Sick both looked up from their towels.

"What's up with you guys? You guys do everything together, don't you?" Max said.

"What's it to ya?" Sick said.

"You guys fags or something?" Max asked with his most serious look.

"Motherfucker!" Pike said, throwing down his towel and coming toward Max.

"Hey! Put your damn clothes on, Pike!" Max yelled. "I ain't no fag. If you want to wrestle or some shit like that, at least put some damn clothes on."

All the players in Max's row, even Sick, laughed at the way Pike stopped in his tracks, looked down at his naked body, and turned beet red. Subdued by the laughter, Pike just cursed and returned to his locker to dry off.

The locker room was half full with players either drying off from their showers or getting dressed to work out. Besides the few remaining draft picks who had yet to sign a contract, and the even fewer veteran players whose contracts had expired and were yet unsigned, almost the entire team would pass through the locker room at least four times a week. Some, like Max, were there up to six times a week, lifting weights, running, stretching, and doing various agility drills that would prepare them for the season. Most teams around the league had summer workouts that took place prior to training camp, but they had to be voluntary as a matter of league policy. Vance White, however, had written each of his players a letter that basically told them if they planned on having a job next season, they would be volunteers.

Max remembered the response of some of his teammates. The three of them had been sitting on stools in front of their lockers, toweling off after a running workout.

"You doin' it?" Paul Dugan had said. Doogie was a burly veteran defensive tackle whose nose was smashed across his face.

"What?" said Max.

"You know, this workout program. You gonna stay here the whole fuckin' summer?"

"Damn right," said Max.

"I was gonna go up to Alaska for a bear hunt," said Sky, a hare-lipped six-foot-eight country boy from Kentucky who played defensive end. "Not now."

"I can't believe this voluntary-mandatory bullshit. They can't do that. They're only supposed to be able to make us come to one three-day mini-camp," said Doogy.

"You don't have to stay," Max said blandly. "But for me, I think the more guys here, the better we'll be next year."

Doogie rolled his eyes. "Holy shit," he said, "you bought the fuckin' farm."

Max shrugged. "You guys want to get a beer?"

"Nah," Doogie said, "I gotta get home to my old lady. She's already bitchin' about me bein' here all day."

"Me too," murmured Sky.

Then, to himself Sky shook his head and mumbled, "Sure did want to get me a grizzly."

"O.K., see ya," Max said, and he'd gone without the two dummies.

As an incentive to comply, the players could rest assured that Vance White would make random appearances in the weight room, or on the owner's terrace overlooking the playing fields, to monitor the work habits of his men. As a reward for their efforts White would walk among his team as they trained and bestow a silent nod of approval to those players who exhibited extraordinary effort. Among themselves, the players called themselves the chain gang. They despised the rigid atmosphere and would secretly mimic White by pulling their shorts up to their armpits in honor of the unusual way in which he wore his own pants. But even the most mildly deviant behavior stopped after White walked into the locker room one day and overheard Marcus Gash, a defensive back, complaining about the rigorous work and his preference for being back home during the summer chasing skirts.

White hadn't said a word to Gash. He just stared until the whole locker room fell silent and the player, tipped off by the silence, turned to meet his icy stare. Then White turned and walked out. Max had never seen Marcus after that day, although he heard from one of Marcus's closer friends that he was later called into the owner's office, where White and Lyles had told him that if he was seen anywhere near the facility or any of their players, they would have him arrested for trespassing. Max doubted that such drastic action would have been taken against one of the better players. Marcus had only been a backup. The general consensus was that White had strategically made an example of an expendable player, but no one Max knew was up for finding out.

Max knew that many of his teammates were using the same drug he was. It wasn't hard to see who was making outrageous strength gains and who was unusually short-tempered, but he didn't talk about it with anyone, even the guys he was one hundred percent sure were on Thyall. White had encouraged him, and he assumed everyone else too, to keep the business of the drug to himself and just work hard to get the job done. Max's "job" was the workout he was assigned each day before he could leave the complex. He and the rest of the players were paid four hundred dollars a week to complete all their workouts, but any incomplete day resulted in a loss of pay for the entire week. Max wouldn't have missed a workout regardless of the money, but he knew it was a necessary incentive for many of his teammates.

In some ways, Max felt superior to his teammates. Not because he was a better player, because in fact, he was far from being the most talented, but because he knew he worked harder than the rest. Even with the drug, and Max felt sure he knew just who was using it and when they had injected it, Max out worked them all. If he himself wasn't on Thyall, there were some who could have surpassed him. But since he too was using it, no one could come close to his enthusiasm for training in the weight room. Not that there weren't some big lineman who couldn't lift more than he—there were a few—but certainly no one was as intense or improved as much.

Max smiled to himself at the thought of his superiority as he sat on the stool in front of his locker, rocking back and forth with an ever-increasing intensity. The drug was setting in hard. It was like a surge of low-volt electricity, like the kind from a cow fence, only slower and not painful. It wasn't a good feeling, though, it was uncomfortable and made him feel tight and angry, as if his clothes were too small and his skin itchy. But it also made him feel powerful and strong. He could feel it: It was time. Now he would go into the weight room and do the weights hard. He would make his workout and then some, pumping out every repetition of every exercise with an ireful purpose.

Since he'd started using the drug, the effects and the improvements were obvious. His biceps were beginning to bulge, and stretch marks were sprouting from his armpits up toward his expanding shoulders and pectorals. He was rapidly gaining strength as well as body weight. But there were admittedly some adverse effects of the drug. The veins in his legs and arms were protruding, his testicles were shrinking, acne had burst out on his upper back, and his hair was thinning on the back of his scalp. But those were small annoyances next to the gains he was making.

"Ahhgh!" Max growled to himself and drew up from his seat, kicking it with a loud crash into the back of his locker. He relished the day when he would do this before he took the field. He would be a killer. The Thyall put him in a good football mood. It made him angry and aggressive, and he knew that he would attack an opponent on the gridiron as if it were a blood battle.

Two of Max's smaller teammates, wide receivers named Spencer Clayton and Tim Tyrone, not strength players, were at the end of the locker room joking quietly between themselves. Max roughly pushed his way between the two of them.

"Pencil necks," he said, shoving open the door and disappearing down the hall that led to the clanging weights.

"Motherfucker," Clayton said when Max was out of earshot.

"Chill, man," said Tyrone, "the dude on that shit."

"That crackhead don't need no shit," Clayton replied. "He mean enough as is."

"You won't be bitchin' when that dude start killin' motherfuckers this fall an' gettin' the ball back so you can shake it in the end zone. You be on that Thyall yourself then," Tyrone said.

Clayton snorted, "You been smokin some shit to talk stupid like that. That shit for those dumb-ass animal motherfuckers. I don't need no shit, man. In case you ain't noticed, I'm smooth as silk on that field, I don't need to be nasty, just smooth and sweet. No good gonna come from that shit, man, no good."

"Chill, dude," said Tyrone. "We'll talk, not here, though. I don't need no walkin' papers."

On his way to the weight room, Max passed Gavin Collins. "Coach" was all Max said, with the nod of his head.

Collins saw the maniacal grin on Max Dresden's face, and noticed a vein protruding from his sweaty forehead. He shook his head. The damn guy looked like he was on something.

"Probably is," Collins reminded himself, "and it's probably not too much coffee."

He went into the locker room to take a piss. He spat in the urinal in disgust, thinking of the drug that he knew most of his players were now using. White was a sick bastard, but what could he do? Certainly of all the coaches he was the least able to do anything about it. He was lucky to be here, and the best thing he could do would be to not make problems. It wasn't often a black man was able to break into this buddy-buddy system of coaching, so if he ever wanted to be a head coach, he'd have to just get along for a few years until he'd built a reputation.

Something crunched under his foot on his way to the sink. He looked down and saw a used syringe sticking out of a wad of toilet paper. "Jesus Christ," he said to himself, "I'm glad I'm not mixed up in this shit."

Vance White finally noticed the flashing lights that spun in the darkness behind him. "Shit," he said, "fuckin' cops."

White got out of the car and weaved a little. The officer approached him cautiously, talking into his radio.

"Look," White said drunkenly, "I'm the head coach of the Ruffians, so this ain't gonna work."

The Birmingham police took pride in making no exceptions when it came to DWIs, and the more White talked, the worse the situation got. When he started to bully the cop, reinforcements arrived. White ended up in cuffs, but not before he had broken one officer's nose and cracked another's ribs.

Now, as he stared drunkenly out of his cell, he wondered who he could call. Drunk as he was, he knew that if something wasn't done, his coaching career was over. No NFL team could afford to have the kind of publicity that ensued from such an incident. If he lost his opportunity at Birmingham, no other team would have him. Going back to college ball was out of the question. The only person he could even hope to help him was Humphry Lyles.

White shook the cell door and shouted, "I want my phone call!"

Another drunk who was slumped near White's feet yelled, "Quiet!" in a slurred outburst. White gave him a boot in the stomach, and the bum moaned and rolled over.

Even through his drunken stupor, White could see the respect in the eyes of the cops when Lyles appeared to bail him out. The small, pudgy owner swaggered into the jail with a pompous air that befitted a monarch. They obviously knew him. Equally apparent was that he had some enigmatic authority over them.

The police speedily processed White's release.

"Make sure you misplace those arrest records," Lyles said to the desk sergeant.

"Mr. Lyles," said the sergeant, "this guy can't drive himself. Would you like me to have someone take him home?"

"No, I'll do that," said Lyles.

Inside his comfortable Mercedes sedan, he chuckled and said, "I guess they got more than they bargained for with you, Vance, huh? Did you really bust one of 'em's nose? Was there really six of them?"

White answered these questions with silence.

"I've always hated the cops," Lyles said, ignoring the silence. "That's something I wish I'd done myself, punch one of those smart-mouthed bastards."

"Maybe so," White replied, "but I won't wish it when I go before the judge."

Humphry smiled and glanced at White as he pulled his Mercedes onto the interstate. "Vance, there isn't going to be any judge, or any newspapers for that matter. This little incident never happened."

White simply stared at Lyles, waiting for an explanation. But Humphry only smiled. He wasn't saying anything until he was asked. White finally did ask.

"Those men need to put food on the table, don't they?" said Humphry.

White, still drunk, nodded.

"Well, they can't do it without a job, especially a nice city job with a nice pension when they retire. You see, I put the mayor in office . . . and the police chief . . . and enough of the district court judges so that those men don't want to displease me. I'm not about to let something like this take away my head coach. But I am glad you called me right away. The one thing I don't own are the newspapers, and if those maggots had gotten a hold of this thing, it could have gotten out of hand."

At first White was angry. He felt as though Lyles was listing off his cast of puppets, and meaning to include him in the group. "You don't own me, Mr. Lyles," White snarled. "I can hunt to put food on my table."

"Vance, you're drunk. This is no quid pro quo. What I did, I did for a friend."

White nodded and thought to himself that being Humphry Lyles's friend wasn't such a bad thing.

At the same time they were driving up the interstate, Max Dresden was pulling into a Waffle House. He looked at his watch and yawned. It was unusual for him to be without a girl this late on a Thursday night. But he'd seen nothing that really impressed him, so he'd just sat at the bar all night drinking. Now, though, he was wishing he'd taken the bartender home. She wasn't pretty, but she wasn't ugly either. Maybe she was a little heavy, but she did have big tits. Max should have grabbed her. She hadn't hidden the fact that she wanted to get fucked.

Max ordered a cheese egg special and a sausage sandwich. The food was greasy, but putting something in his stomach tonight would help to lessen his hangover in the morning. There was no other place open this late, so grease it was. While he ate, he watched a bum at the counter drinking coffee and talking to himself. Max got a kick out of the way the waitress, who was a hag herself, avoided the guy like a leper. Max imagined the bum doing something outrageous, like pulling out a knife. He imagined himself pummeling the bum and being kind of a hero.

When he'd finished eating and paid the check, he thought once more of the bartender. "What the fuck," he said to himself as he climbed into his car.

He drove back to the bar and went in. The lights were out except behind the bar, where some guy was washing glasses.

"Is the girl who was bartending here?" Max asked.

The man eyed him suspiciously, "You mean Shelly?"

"Yeah," Max said, "Shelly."

"Nope, she left about ten minutes ago. Want me to tell her you came by?"

"Nah," said Max, and he turned and went out into the night.

CHAPTER SEVEN

CLAY HUNG UP THE PHONE and stared out the window at the cold, deep Adirondack lake which was still and peaceful at the base of the worn green mountains. He needed to relax. He was uptight about contract negotiations with the Ruffians. Clancy was insistent on holding out for more money, even though the team's offer was generous. Clancy also argued there was no rush to get him to Birmingham since he was already in great shape. Graduation had come and gone, and with it the last days of college life. Clay and Lever had rarely been sober from the time of the draft party until the day after graduation. With the celebration behind him Clay began a serious training routine. He even trained on the weekends, most of which he spent with Katie at her family's summer home. The two of them would leave Fridays as soon as Clay had finished his training. They would take the Thruway from Syracuse to Route 12 in Utica, head north, then take Route 28 inside the Adirondack Park to Raquette Lake. Once there, they'd park their car at the marina and boat across the lake to the house. All the homes on Katie's side of the lake were accessible only by boat. So when Clay did his running he had to cross the lake to get back to the road. Every Saturday and Sunday after lunch, he would do just that so he could run the lonely roads that weaved through the mountains.

Katie's house was an old Adirondack camp originally built by early twentieth-century railroad magnate Pierpont Morgan. Morgan had the place built to serve as a retreat from his main Adirondack estate across the lake. He used it to get away from his estate when he needed a break from the twenties social swirl and the influx of New York City society who graced the mountains during high season. When Katie's father bought it for just twenty thousand dollars in the early seventies, the house had no electricity and no phone line. The camp had been abandoned for years and was rundown, but the immense log structure was sound and dry. It had been built on a gently sloping hill that ran down to the lake. A big, wide porch wrapped around the front of the house, and sturdy Adirondack rockers that had survived for fifty years still sat there. Katie's father had electricity and a phone line brought in, and with steady work over the years, her family had revitalized the old place until it evinced its former glory.

Clay had fallen in love with the mountains his first weekend there with Katie two summers ago. He loved the house too, and on the long drive home after his first visit he began to dream of having a place somewhere in the Adirondacks to call his own. With his sudden good fortune it was a dream that could become reality. He would easily be able to afford to buy his own place. He had never owned anything other than that old truck, and to have a house in the mountains that was his to go to whenever he wanted with whomever he wanted and do whatever he wanted . . . well, the thought gave him a chill. He would have a refrigerator just for beer, and a big porch overlooking the lake where he and his buddies would sit and drink and smoke cigars late into the night. He would buy a boat, big and fast, that would pull him out of the water on skis with no problem. But best of all, he would arrive on a weekend as a property owner, and pull up to a place that was his.

Then, of course, he would buy a nice home somewhere in Birmingham. After that, maybe a beach house somewhere on a Caribbean island, like Hemingway. Then he'd have a place to go in the winter, a place to live during the fall for work, and a place to go in the summertime. Property. Clay loved the idea of it more than the thought of nice cars and nice clothes. Property was something he could depend on. He could go there to stay, and it was his forever. It never wore out. A house like Katie's was like family to the people who owned it. It was also the best place to put his money. It was safe. It almost always appreciated, especially if it was waterfront property. He made a mental note to call a real estate broker tomorrow. He could at least see what was available. He could fly to Birmingham tomorrow if he wanted and sign a deal for six million dollars. That was what was on the table. The money was in the bag now, and he might as well start enjoying it.

Six million! It was unbelievable.

Clay thought about what it would be like to have six million dollars, or even more if Bill got his way. The signing bonus alone was two million! Not only could he buy whatever the hell he wanted, if he was even just a little careful with his money, he'd never have to work another day in his life after football.

Even after all the percentages that went to Uncle Sam and Bill Clancy, Clay would be a wealthy man. He preferred the term wealthy to rich. Wealth was a word that connoted urbanity; rich made Clay think of yellow Cadillacs and diamond pinkie rings. If he was going to have money, he would be dignified about it. He would live the good life, but never forget that most happiness came from little things like sitting on a porch in a rocking chair with a cold beer and talking, which was exactly what he was about to do.

Clay stepped out onto the porch and sat down in the empty rocker next to Katie's father. Mr. Becker said nothing, but opened a cooler, took out a beer, and handed it to Clay. The two of them sat for some time before the father spoke.

"Lot on your mind, Clay?" he said.

The stars were beginning to show, and a warm, gentle wind rippled the placid surface of the water. A bat flicked across the evening sky, and Clay rocked for a minute or two, sipping his beer before speaking. In the two summers he had spent time with Andrew Becker on that porch, he had never told Clay what to do, or judged what he had done. Instead he listened, and spoke in general terms that only suggested solutions, which was a welcome relief from Clay's own father, who felt he knew the right way to do everything.

"Sometimes the right thing is vague," Andrew had once said to Clay as they sat drinking on the porch in their identical rockers. "That's one of the first things I learned as a lawyer. Whether it's a divorce or a disputed estate, even a crime, there are always gray areas. It's not uncommon for two different judges to rule differently on the same set of facts. Why? Not because they are incompetent or dishonest men, although some are both, but because what's right isn't always clear."

It was ironic that Andrew was exactly the kind of man Clay's father had taught him to scoff. Although he stood just over six feet tall, he was a frail man. His hands and face were soft and kind, and he wore thick spectacles that tended to slide down his nose whenever it was hot. He wore dark old-fashioned suits with a bow tie at all times except when he was at the lake. It was then that he looked the silliest to those who didn't know him. Then he wore an old fishing hat with a few faded lures hooked above the brim, khaki pants with large plaid shirts from which his arms hung like two pale sticks. Clay's father had only met Andrew once. It was after a football game, and he had referred to Andrew ever since as Ichabod Crane. The irony was that Clay deeply admired the man, regardless of the fact that his own father had taught him from a young age that physical frailty was an intolerable weakness.

Andrew Becker, without knowing it or trying, had taught Clay the opposite. Initially, Clay was polite to him because he was Katie's father. But over time Clay was able to see the virtues of intelligence and kindness firsthand. The weaker-looking man had a family that was peaceful and content. And Andrew seemed to rule it with strength and compassion. Clay's own father paled by comparison. Growing up in the Blackwell house, Clay and his mother had known only an interminable undercurrent of stress and the rumblings of his father's anger which hung in the air like an impending storm on a summer night. There had never been quite enough money, his mother had never cooked dinner quite right, and as well as Clay did in school or on the playing fields, things never seemed quite up to the level that Clay's father expected.

"Lot on my mind," Clay said finally. "Talked to Bill Clancy on the phone." He paused for a moment letting that piece of information set in. "Andrew," he continued, "I'm about to have more money than I ever dreamed of all because I can play a game."

"Don't sell yourself so short, Clay," Andrew said. "We both know that you've worked hard, harder than most men work in a lifetime. And you've done it to be great at what you do, and it's certainly no more a game than what I do."

There was silence for a moment before he added, "And don't worry about the money. If God can put a camel through the eye of a needle, then he can certainly let a man as good as you into heaven, even if you will be wealthy."

Clay smiled to himself. Both men sipped their beer.

"Kate's great-grandfather, my mother's dad, used to have a saying: 'Money is the root of all evil,' he would say. 'Evil, shoot me the root.' "

Andrew chuckled at his grandfather's old quip, and Clay laughed with him.

"I thought your grandfather was a minister or something," Clay said.

"Oh yes, he was. But ministers need money to put food on the table and buy new dresses for their wives, same as everyone else."

The door swung open and Katie burst out onto the porch. "Dinner in ten minutes, gentleman, and I hope you two haven't had too much to drink. Mom and I have worked all afternoon to prepare this meal."

Katie wore one of Clay's faded flannel shirts rolled up to her elbows and tucked in to a pair of old Levis. Her feet were bare and her long dark hair was pulled back. She looked beautiful without trying.

"Dinnertime?" Andrew said. "Clay and I were just about to take the boat and head across the lake to Monte's Diner. And if it were much later we'd have been ordering breakfast."

"Funny, Dad. Now I know Clay let you drink too much."

Andrew got up and went inside. Clay stood up from his seat and kissed Katie. His movements were slow and jerky because of his three-mile run that afternoon.

"Oh, you look sore," she said.

"It's that hot pavement and these two hundred and seventy-five pounds my legs had to carry across three miles of it," Clay replied. "But nothing a late-night massage won't take care of."

"Uh-huh, I've heard that before. You love me for my body, don't you?"

"That's what you're famous for, isn't it?"

"Clay, you're a typical football player, and now I know why my father told me to stay away from football players."

"That was until he met me," Clay said.

Kate couldn't help returning Clay's impish smile because he was right. When she had first brought Clay home after they met, her father was beside himself. He had an innate dislike for Neanderthals, as he portended all football players to be. But he had given Clay a chance as she knew he would, and Clay had won him over instantly, which she also knew he would. She put her arms lovingly around Clay's large frame and hugged him, pressing her cheek into his chest. They stood silently for a few moments, then she said, "We better go in . . ."

"Katie," Clay said, holding her tight and rocking gently back and forth as he peered out across the now blackened water at the stars which painted the night sky, "this is what it's about, isn't it? Just holding each other and being here without a care in the world."

Katie looked up into his eyes as he continued to stare, mesmerized by the brilliant constellations. For some reason she felt sad. His voice was distant, as if he was reminiscing about times gone past, or saying good-bye without really saying it.

"We can always do this, Clay," she said hopefully. "We can stay happy with each other, and come here to get away."

"Things won't change between us," he said, as if to convince himself. "I mean, even though we'll be apart a little bit these next couple of years, it's not like I'm not coming back."

"Clay, snap out of it. I'll be here for you. You know that. No matter what, I'll be here. Plane ticket away, remember that's what you told me?"

"I'm not going to change, do you think, Kate?" he said after a pause, thinking of all the money.

"I'm counting on you not changing, Clay," she said pushing her nose between the buttons of his shirt until she felt his warm skin. "Let's go eat," she said. "We can take a boat ride after dinner. Maybe we'll run out of gas."

"After dinner? How about now?" he whispered, sticking his hand down the back of her pants. "Come on."

"Clay!" she whispered as he led her quickly, quietly by the hand into the house and up to the guest bedroom.

When they got to his room, Clay discreetly locked the door while Katie slipped off her pants. He started to unbutton her shirt.

"We don't have time," she whispered, and pulled him gently down onto the bed.

Clay fumbled to pull off his pants. She grabbed him gently but firmly and guided him inside her. His hands went up under her shirt and found her soft breasts. He pushed and thrust rhythmically. Katie moaned and moved her hips faster. He braced himself with one hand so he could watch her, and see the joining of their bodies. Then he collapsed on top of her and buried his face in the pillow to muffle his cry.

"Shhh," she whispered.

CHAPTER EIGHT

"MR. LYLES," VANCE WHITE SAID, "We're in full gear."

"That's excellent, Vance," Lyles said from behind his desk. Both men were sipping scotch. It was late in the evening, and the sky outside the vast windows was quickly turning charcoal.

"It is except one thing," White said. "I want Blackwell in here. I've got a guy who's going to be a rookie and starting on a team of mostly hard-assed veterans. A lot of winning football is chemistry, and if Blackwell isn't in here doing what everyone else is doing, those guys won't respect him. And if they don't respect him, they won't work well with him. So . . ."

"I know, I know, Vance. I told you I'd have him here and I will. I can't believe they haven't taken what we've offered. I've already had the Steelers and the Vikings call me to bitch about jacking up the pay structure for the whole round." He waved his hand in the air. "I don't give a damn about them, don't get me wrong. But damn it, this Clancy is just being downright unreasonable."

Humphry hit the desktop with his fist.

"Well . . . I don't know what to tell you, Mr. Lyles, but I need him in here. I don't know about money deals, I only know about winning."

"Damn," Humphry said as if to himself. "He'll be here, Vance. I'm going to do what I should have done in the first place. It's just that I thought Clancy would be reasonable. But . . . that doesn't matter now. I know how to get him and I will."

"Bill Clancy."

"Clancy, why haven't you returned my calls? Or taken them, for that matter?" Humphry Lyles asked in an angry voice.

"Mr. Lyles, the last time we spoke, I believe you threatened me, and as a former district attorney in New York City, I took offense at that. This isn't backwoods Alabama."

"Clancy, since you obviously don't want this to be pleasant, I'm not about to banter words with a cheap parasite like you, I'll just get down to business," Lyles said.

"I don't know if I'm interested in doing business with you right now, Mr. Lyles."

"Oh, yes, you are, Clancy. Do you know why? Because you're a rat, and I know how to deal with rats, whether they're country rats or city rats. I didn't get to where I am without knowing how to deal with rats. Rats like cheese, Clancy, and that's what I'm going to give you because I want Clay Blackwell and I want you out of my life. I'm talking about a good deal for Blackwell to cover your ass, and then a little cheese for you."

"I don't operate that way, Mr. Lyles. I'm not interested."

Humphry let the phone remain silent for almost a minute. Just as he thought, Clancy was very interested, otherwise the line would be dead.

"Six point five for Blackwell. That's a half-million-dollar increase that makes you look like a genius," Humphry said.

The phone was silent.

"Two fifty for you, in cash," Humphry said, and then he too fell silent.

"A million," said Clancy.

"Five hundred thousand," said Humphry.

"Done. I'll have Clay there within a week."

"Tomorrow, Clancy," Humphry said.

"Tomorrow's Friday, Mr. Lyles. Give him the weekend to get ready, I'll have him there Monday morning. I'll expect to get a package from

Federal Express on Saturday."

"You'll get half Saturday and the rest on Monday when I see Blackwell."

"Mr. Lyles, I never thought I'd hear myself saying this, but it's been a pleasure doing business with you. I don't know why it is that you're so big on getting Clay down there for some rah-rah summer training program, but with a deal like this, I really don't care."

"Like I said, Clancy, you're a rat," Humphry said.

"I'll see you Monday, Mr. Lyles," Bill Clancy said and hung up the phone.

"Clay, phone, honey," Mrs. Blackwell said as she wiped her brow. It was a hot day, and even though the windows were open, the breeze did nothing to cut the thick heat.

"Who is it, Ma?" Clay yelled from the upstairs bathroom. He had just gotten home from a workout and had taken a cold shower.

"It's Bill, honey," Mrs. Blackwell yelled back.

Clay came crashing down the stairs two at a time. Even when he was a boy, his mother had winced at the sound, always expecting the next step to bring her son through the floorboards and straight into the basement. Now, with Clay's immense size, her worry was doubled. To think of her son being hurt now, right before he signed his contract, after so many years of injury-free sports, was almost too much for her to bear. She knew her fear was justified. The house had been cheaply built on the inside to stay within their budget and still be the biggest house on the block. Her husband had insisted.

Clay didn't go through the stairs. He appeared in the kitchen doorway with a white towel wrapped around his waist, dripping wet. His mother admired her boy's handsome face and tried to remember when he was only a baby. She couldn't do that, though. His large frame, tanned and muscular, was too much a man's to let her to remember him as a baby. It seemed so long ago. She quickly handed him the phone.

Like many mothers, she sensed things about her boy in a way that was prophetic. She knew that this phone call was the one that would take him from her for the last time, and that things would never be quite the same for the rest of her life. She felt she would surely cry, but she had learned through the years with her husband to bury the tears until she was alone. Besides, the excitement that lit up her boy's face made it hard for her to be sad. She remembered draft day, when the excitement had seemed to belong to her. Probably because then it was all a dream, but now she knew that Clay's agent had reached an agreement and he would be leaving. He would not come home again. He would have a home of his own, and when he did come, it would be for dinner, or coffee, and as a visitor.

Clay slammed down the receiver and let out a whoop of excitement and relief. He gave his mother a hug and a kiss on the cheek.

"Ma, I'm signed! Six point five million! Can you believe it? Six point five! Six point five!"

Clay held his mother's waist as he danced her around the kitchen. The water from his still damp body soaked quickly through her cotton blouse, and she found herself slightly dazed with the news—and thinking about the time he had pneumonia. He would wake during the night and call to her in a feverish panic, and when she went to him, she would hold him and calm him, and his fever-drenched body would soak her nightgown through and through with perspiration. He was too excited now to see the tears in her eyes, and she quickly wiped them away.

"Can you believe Bill Clancy!" Clay said. "Ma, he's a genius. Just last weekend I was bugging him to sign, but no, he said, wait, just wait. Wait? Can you believe it? We waited another five days and it's worth five hundred thousand dollars, half a million. This is unbelievable! I gotta call Katie, she's not gonna believe it. This is great!"

Now Clay's mother was laughing, caught up in the excitement of her son's happy moment.

"Katie," Clay said into the phone, "we got it! Bill Clancy just called. Six point five million over four years! Can you believe it? We gotta celebrate. Pack your stuff, I'm picking you up in an hour, we'll go up to the lake tonight and have a big steak and some champagne at The Wild Duck . . . What? No, who cares about workouts tomorrow, we gotta celebrate tonight! We'll start the weekend early, I gotta go to Birmingham first thing Monday. I'll see you in an hour."

"Clay," Mrs. Blackwell said when he had hung up the phone, "honey, you will stop by the plant on your way to tell your father, won't you?"

When she saw the frown on his face she added, "For me, honey."

"O.K., Ma, but I'm not gonna get him off the line. If he gets a hold of me he'll have me at Mickey's with a shot in my hand before I can get a word in edgewise. I'll leave a message at the break-room desk that I was there, and I'll write him a note and leave it."

"Clay, can't you just tell him yourself?"

"Ma, you know he'd leave work on the spot and make me stay out all night with him and his buddies. I want to spend this last weekend with Katie. You understand, Mom."

"All right, Clay." She smiled, knowing that he was right. She would not in all likelihood see her husband until the early morning. He would get Clay's note and declare a national holiday. She could count on making a sick call for him in the morning. Then he would spend the weekend between excitement for Clay's dream come true and resentment for the fact that he himself wasn't signing a million-dollar contract. Her husband could never understand why Clay spent so much time in the mountains with Katie, and would resent that as well.

The drive was pleasant. They passed by green pastures spotted with black-and-white Jersey milk cows, and farmers turning their equipment toward dull red or gray barns for the night. After an hour and a half of driving, the farm country began to be replaced with towering pines and the green Adirondack foothills, which soon made way for the oldest mountain range on the continent. It was a balmy summer evening, and they drove with the windows rolled down and the warm, rich mountain air whipping through the open windows as the old truck rattled down the highway. The sun had disappeared behind a bank of purple clouds in the western sky, and it left a red furnace glow that promised to fade to dusk. Clay felt for the headlights, then reached across the seat to find Katie's warm hand.

By the time they got to The Wild Duck it was dark, and the windshield was splattered with bugs. The Wild Duck was an old inn with the finest food in the entire Adirondack Park. It had been built at the turn of the century out of native stone and great pine beams. The atmosphere was extremely elegant, but the dress was casual because of the restaurant's resort location. Clay's and Katie's jeans and T-shirts weren't too unseemly, and since it was not the weekend, they were able to get a table overlooking the moonlit lake without reservations.

"Katie," Clay said after they had gotten their menus, "order anything you want, this is a celebration."

With that, he took a gold credit card out of his wallet. "All I have to do is put my John Hancock on that contract Monday, and I got myself a check for a two-million-dollar signing bonus. I had Bill get me this card a few weeks ago, and tonight we're going to break it in.

"Waiter," Clay said as he signaled the man, "a bottle of Dom Perignon, your best year. We're celebrating tonight and I want the best of everything for this beautiful lady."

Katie blushed.

"You know what else I'm going to do, Kate?" he said.

"What, sweetheart, what is my beautiful beau going to do?" she said, gazing across the candlelight.

"I'm being serious," he said.

"So am I, honey," she said, reaching for his hand. "What are you going to do?"

"Remember that old white Victorian house on Loon Lake that we looked at last week with the real estate lady?"

Kate nodded.

"I'm going to take you there tomorrow, and if we like it as much as we did, I'm going to buy it."

"Really, Clay? It's beautiful."

"You're beautiful," he said and kissed her hand.

"I love you," she said in a low, husky voice.

"I love you too, Katie."

They sat looking at each other for a few moments before Clay spoke again.

"That house is the kind of place we can have forever," he said. "When I'm done playing football, we could even live there and have a family. Can you picture it? On that lake, in that beautiful house?"

"It's like a dream," she said.

"It's my dream," he said.

"I hope it comes true . . ."

The ride to Raquette Lake was about a half hour, but it had begun to rain and the dark night made it seem twice as long. As they neared the lake, it seemed like the lightning was closing in on them. The rain came down harder. Clay could hear the threatening rumble of the dark skies as they pulled up in front of the boat slip at the marina. As the two of them worked together to untie the boat and rig the canvas covering that would keep them dry as they crossed the lake, the barnlike boat slip flashed alive with a blinding white light. A thundering crash exploded.

"Holy shit!" Clay said. "That sounded like it hit the roof!"

Another flash of lightning lit the night sky, this time farther down the lake.

"Clay," Katie said, her voice raised above the downpour, "we shouldn't go over in this."

"What are we going to do, spend the night in here?"

"Maybe we should go back to the inn and stay there."

A mountain lake at high elevation was like an enormous lightning rod, and Katie was not enamored with the idea of driving a boat through the middle of it. Clay, however, was feeling good from the meal and the champagne. The bed across the lake was only a five minute boat ride, and he knew the lake well, even in the dark. He felt confident that God had not brought him this far in his life only to knock him off with a bolt of lightning.

"Get in, Kate," he said decisively, "we'll be there in five minutes."

She didn't argue knowing there was no point. They would only fight and end up going over anyway. "This is crazy," she said, then got on board.

Clay fired up the engine, backing the boat out into the rain. He and Katie sat tucked up under the dry covering with their bags at their feet. The sky flashed alive and thunder split the night, echoing through the mountains. Clay saw the bolt clearly as it struck some trees less than a thousand feet away. The vibration shook his very bones. The flash lit up the lake as bright as day, but only for an instant. It became black again, and Clay spun the boat around quickly, heading away from the bare yellow bulbs that illuminated the marina. He peered through the windshield, straining for some sight of the flashing red and green buoys which marked a channel he would use to make his way out into the lake.

Another flash of lightning illuminated the lake and gave Clay his bearings. The water was rough, and fought the boat's progress. Then another bolt hit the water so close that Katie let out an involuntary scream. The hair on the back of Clay's neck jumped up, cold and prickly. He was quickly beginning to doubt his call, and found himself wishing they were back in his truck, heading for the inn. He shouldn't have tempted fate. He had gotten to where he was in life by making the right calls. To be out on the water in a storm like this was madness. But he found the flashing red light of the marker buoy, and in a panic he opened the boat's throttle as far as it would go. The windshield wiper thumped from side to side in a futile attempt to clear the glass of the spattering rain. More lightning flashed as they entered the channel, and Clay was forced to slow down to navigate more precisely. The sky flashed continuously now, like a waning fluorescent bulb as the lightning danced around them.

When he hit open water, he raced toward the opposite shore. Another bolt hit the water, this time not as close, but its exploding crack and reverberation sent another wave of fear down Clay's spine. He ducked his head instinctively and prepared for the next bolt, which he fully expected to hit him squarely on the head. The lake and mountains seemed possessed by unfriendly demons intent on his destruction. When he finally reached the Becker dock, he quickly lashed down the boat as Katie scurried for the front door. Clay didn't relax until he was under the porch roof, and even there the violence of the storm unsettled him. The great trees bowed and swayed to the awful gusts of wind and rain in a powerful display of nature's destructive capability.

After drying themselves off, Clay and Katie went right to bed, making the most of having the house to themselves. Her parents wouldn't be up until Friday night or early Saturday morning. They slept in Katie's bedroom, where Clay wasn't permitted when her mom was there. Her window looked out on the lake, and a smell of fresh, damp pine permeated the room. The old brass bed rose high off the plank floor. As Kate faded to sleep on his shoulder, Clay watched and listened as the storm raged against mountain and lake.

By the time Clay awoke, sunlight already filled the room. He kissed Katie until she too awoke.

"Clay," she said sleepily, "I was sleeping."

"I know, but it's time to get up."

Katie laughed quietly. "You're awake, so it's time for me to get up."

Clay grinned. "You know that's the way it is."

"But when I wake up for classes, it's never time for you to get up," she said, rolling in the soft cotton sheets.

"But when I wake up, I'm hungry," he replied.

"Just for this, I'm making you take me to Monte's for breakfast."

"Just what I had in mind," he said. "And after that we'll go look at that house."

"Don't you think we'll need an appointment?"

"When that broker hears that we're going to buy a six-hundred-thousand-dollar home, she'll make an appointment for us, real fast."

"Clay, how are you!" said the old man working the counter at Monte's, his face beaming as he reached over to shake hands. "Not like you to be here on a Friday morning."

"Well, Monte," said Clay, "Kate and I are celebrating my contract. It's all settled and I'm going down to Birmingham to sign it on Monday."

"Going down south, are you? Well, a good-looking boy like you oughta forget about football, marry that pretty girl you got there, and go to—"

"Hollywood. I know, Monte, but no one in Hollywood is offering me a big contract."

"Well, don't get yourself hurt," Monte said, turning his back and cracking some eggs onto his griddle. "The usual for you, Clay," Monte said, not as a question.

Clay nodded even though Monte couldn't see him.

"What about you, Katie?"

"I'll have a poached egg and some dry toast, Monte."

Clay watched Monte deftly prepare their food. When breakfast was well under way, he placed two steaming mugs of hot coffee in front of them. As he turned back toward his stove, Clay said to him, "Going to buy a house today, Monte."

Monte turned, his eyebrows raised appreciatively. "Well, that's the smartest move you could make. Up here, you mean?"

"Yes," Clay said. "There's a big old Victorian over on Loon Lake. Kate and I looked at it last week, and if we like it again today, I'm buying it."

"Just like that. I'll be damned," Monte said, more to himself than to Clay and Katie. "Well, you belong up here, so it's only right that you have a place to call your own."

As they finished their food, a long white BMW pulled up in front of Monte's. Elaine Gull got out, and her bleached hair shone like wheat. She was dressed smartly and wore large dark Porsche sun glasses. Two grubby middle-aged men at the end of the counter stared dully at her as she came through the door. She was in her mid-thirties, and even Katie had to admit to herself that despite a certain cheapness she was a striking woman. She eyed Clay suspiciously from the corner of her eye and caught him gaping at Elaine Gull's tight skirt. She kicked his shin. Monte, on the other hand, neither looked up nor said a word to the woman, but grunted an acknowledgment as he washed some dishes in the sink.

"Katie, dear," said Elaine, kissing Katie on the cheek as if she had seen her more than once before in her life. "And Clay," she said, kissing him too, leaving a conspicuous splotch of red lipstick on his cheek. "I'm so glad you called. Shall we?"

Even Elaine Gull's trashy white pumps couldn't detract from the dignity of West House, the name of the tall, gabled five-bedroom lake house that Clay now knew he had to have. He and Katie had always talked about having four kids, and they would all fit nicely into this house. He kept this thought to himself, though, not wanting to get Katie started on the subject of children. The thought scared him a little, and he wondered if maybe this house was something he should put off until Katie was done with school.

The two-acre property was bounded by towering old pines. Dark-green lawn chairs were placed in groups of two and three in various shady spots about the lawn. A plush grassy area lay cool in the shade between the house and the lake. Despite himself Clay envisioned the family, kids and all, playing touch football in the lawn and swimming together in the lake.

The house was old but obviously well maintained. Inside were two stone fireplaces on either end of the house, and the rooms, although not large, were cozy and trimmed with elaborate woodwork. The French doors in the master bedroom opened out onto a small terrace, and in the master bath was an oversized claw-foot tub.

"Think we can both fit?" Clay whispered to Katie.

Elaine pointed out the smallest bedroom and said slyly, "Really, this room is ideal for a nursery."

Katie looked at Clay with wistful eyes that made him vacillate back to uncertainty.

Almost all the homes on Loon Lake were elegant and expensive. It was the Adirondack summer retreat for the well-to-do. On either side of West House was a banker from New York City and a doctor from Albany. The banker, Elaine told Clay, flew in almost every weekend during the summer in a seaplane that landed on the lake and taxied right to his dock. The doctor drove his Mercedes. Clay had to admit to himself that he liked the idea of living among successful and accomplished people like that.

"The house has even been winterized," Elaine told them, "so if you ever decided to come up here in the winter to snowmobile or ski, you could. All the furniture comes with it."

"It must be kind of nice up here in the winter," Clay said. "I'm sure it's desolate, but it must be pretty. I can imagine the mountains covered with snow and the wind blowing through these pines."

"Well, it is nice in a way," Elaine said. "Of course, my husband, Thomas, and I winter in Palm Beach."

"Of course," Katie said.

Clay felt impulsive. His wish not to amplify Katie's expectations was outweighed by his desire to own a beautiful home in a place that he truly loved. He had Elaine bring them back to her office to draw up a purchase offer, which he signed with the understanding that Elaine wouldn't submit it to the sellers until he sent her a check for deposit on Monday. Elaine dropped them off at their boat and waved as they pushed off from Monte's dock.

"You really did it," Kate said to him as they cruised slowly across the lake back to her house. Her eyes were wide. She looked dumbstruck. "I mean, I knew that you would, that you could now, but it really seemed incredible to me to see you sign that paper for six hundred thousand dollars."

Clay was proud of her awe. "That's the way it'll be now, Kate," he said. "I've got some serious cash. But it is strange. A year ago Elaine Gull would have laughed at me if I said I wanted to look at house like that."

"But to buy a house that expensive so—so quickly, Clay."

"Why not? You heard what Monte said, I belong up here, and he's right. You know that these mountains are where I'm happiest, where I'm really at peace and where I can really relax. The rest of the time I'm always uptight about workouts, or football, or school. But up here I'm just me. I need a place like this, a quiet place away from everything."

She smiled at him, thinking about the two of them living in such a nice and peaceful home. Clay smiled back, thinking of the wonderful time they were having together, the wonderful times to come. Monday would begin a new life for him, and although he would miss the old one, he knew he would enjoy what was ahead. Besides, he could always come back.

After some difficult good-byes, Clay finally boarded a plane for Atlanta on Monday morning. The flight was not only taking him to another city, it was taking him to a whole other life. Bill Clancy met him in Atlanta, and together they flew to Birmingham and signed Clay's multimillion-dollar contract in front of the Alabama media.

Later that night, Max Dresden, propped up on pillows, sat naked on his bed watching TV. Only his lower body was covered with the sheet. He watched as Clay ceremoniously signed his contract and shook hands with the team owner and Vance White. It made Max's stomach turn.

He always tried to catch the eleven o'clock news before going to bed, and it was news he wanted to see, not some wet rookie getting more money for signing a contract than he would ever make in his whole career. No one had ever given Max anything to sign a contract. He had to work, and slave, and practically beg just to get looked at by the pros. The TV piece on Blackwell put Max in a dark mood, and he slapped the naked bottom of the blond girl that lay sleeping facedown on his bed. She gave a yelp, which made him smile as he whispered gently, "Move over, please, you're not the only one sleeping here tonight."

The girl was young, and she knew better than to backtalk to him. She just stuck out her lower lip in a pout and slid quietly to the other side of the bed.

CHAPTER NINE

ALTHOUGH MAX HAD STARTED his workout before Clay entered the room, he did so many more exercises than anyone else that it wasn't too long before Clay caught up to him. Max looked up to find Clay standing silently, waiting for him to finish a set of behind-the-neck shoulder presses.

"Want me to push you on these?" Max asked innocently as he got up off the seat.

"Not yet," Clay said, "I've got three sets. You can push me on the last one, though. I'd appreciate it."

Of course, Max said to himself, dodging the real tough work, just like I thought. To Clay he said nothing, but simply moved on to another part of the room to continue his own workout.

A few minutes later, Max felt a tap on his shoulder and he turned in confusion to see Clay.

"Give me that push?" Clay asked politely.

"Sure," said Max with his wolfish grin, thinking to himself that he would teach this rookie what it was like to work in the NFL.

"How many you going to do?" said Max as Clay positioned himself under the weight.

"Ten."

"Well, we'll just see if you can't get fifteen, rookie."

Clay merely nodded his head, sat down, lifted the weight off the rack, and began pressing the bar behind his head. On the ninth rep, Clay began to strain. Max touched the bar, lifting it just enough to allow Clay to get it back over his head.

"Six more to go, rook," Max shouted, getting excited now. He would show Clay the kind of mental toughness it took to play in the NFL. He was sure Blackwell would quit after the original ten. Then Max would scoff at him for being a quitter and a glamour boy who liked the cameras but not the weights.

Clay said nothing, just lowered the weight and began to push out another rep, then another, and another. Max had to give him more help with each rep, but he gave him only enough to get the weight up with an extreme struggle.

"Come on, Blackwell!" Max yelled. "Are you gonna quit on the field when it's fourth and inches? Are you really big-time?"

Clay was losing strength fast. On the fourteenth rep, he felt his arms go dead. He had nothing left. Max was screaming now, urging him on, insulting him, challenging him.

"Are you a little girl?" Max screamed. There was nothing the rookie could do. Max could see that Clay had no strength left in his arms and shoulders. They were limp.

Then Clay let out a primal roar: "Aghhhhhhh! Motherrrrrfuckerrrrrr!" His eyes bulged and his face turned purple. His limbs shook with the terrible strain of forcing muscles to perform, muscles with no oxygen that by rights should not work at all.

Then Max saw it, the rage seen only on the faces of the most intense players in the league. And he felt it too. Not much, but enough force to know that Blackwell hadn't quit. When Blackwell's body told him nothing was left, his mind blew a fuse and overrode the governors of the body. Somewhere deep inside him was an insane desire to win waiting to be released. It was something Max hadn't seen in any of his other Ruffians teammates, but he knew the feeling. It was an emotion that went beyond any drug. Max lifted the bar the rest of the way up and then toward the rack.

"Fifteen!" Clay screamed. "Fifteen!" and pulled the bar out of the rack, almost bringing it down on his head because of the lack of his own muscular control.

He let out another roar, enraged now and intent on finishing what he started. This time Max didn't let him struggle for long before he helped to bring the bar up and safely to the rack. Max looked up. The entire room was still, and every face was turned toward them.

"Rookie knows how to work," Max said calmly and pushed through them to get back to his own workout.

Clay sat panting, sweat streaming down his face. When he noticed everyone watching him, he stood. Spots danced across his vision, and he staggered, then caught himself and moved off to finish his work. His arms were numb and his head pounded. He was relieved to see everyone go back to work. No one would notice him using lighter weights and just going through the motions of his remaining workout. If he could have, he would have left that moment, but his pride made him stay and at least look like he was completing his remaining exercises even though his arms were now useless.

As he finished, he watched Max work. It was obvious to Clay that his teammate was not normal. He moved around the room like a wounded tiger, from exercise to exercise, attacking each piece of equipment. He groaned and shouted, cursed and screamed with a fanaticism that Clay had never seen before. Of course, the overall din of the weight room was more violent and aggressive than Clay had experienced in college. These men, his teammates now, were of a different breed and higher order of athlete than his teammates in school. They were working to keep their jobs. Each realized that every passing year brought on a newer and younger group of players from college who would try to usurp them, take their jobs, take food from their families. Yet even in this tough crowd of cursing men, Max stood out.

When Clay finished his lifting, he put on some grass cleats for a running workout on the practice field. The weight coach took the team out in different groups as they finished lifting. After he finished his running workout and just as he was stepping out of the shower, he saw Max stalk through the locker room, scuffing his cleated feet belligerently on the carpet on his way to join the last running group of the day. Clay would have liked to wait to see if Max was as focused on the practice field, but he had a meeting with White. The coach had told him yesterday after the press conference to report for workouts today and then see him as soon as he was finished. Clay instinctively knew White was a man who expected obedience, and he didn't waste any time heading to the coach's office.

"Clay," White said, "I'm glad you came right up like I asked. I watched your running from my terrace. Good to see you leading the pack."

Clay nodded and smiled despite himself. He felt uncomfortable showing any emotion in front of White. The man himself never seemed to smile. Clay thought that someone who didn't smile might look down on one who did, especially if it was over some simple compliment.

"You like to be the best, don't you, boy?" White said.

"Yes, sir."

"I know. That's why you're here," White said. "Clay . . . we have what I know is the best and most advanced training program in the NFL. It's something we don't want anyone to know we have. You may remember that you were given a personality test back in April?"

Clay nodded.

"That was a test that we give all our prospective players," White said. "We want all our players on the same page. We want them all training under the same program. In fact, I insist on it. That's why we like to make sure that you all have the type of character that would be receptive to advanced ideas. And that you're trustworthy."

White paused for several long moments, then continued. "We weren't one hundred percent certain with you, Clay. That's why I went and saw you myself. And then you said something to me, you said, 'I'd do anything to play the game,' and I knew you meant it.

"Clay, I know this isn't necessary with you, but I must insist that anything about our program stays within this team, and I need your word as a man that anything you learn will remain with you alone."

"Of course," Clay said.

White looked intently at him, "You will share it with no one." Then, in a more relaxed voice, "You see, to win in football, to be truly great, you have to have discipline before all else. You need to have players that act like soldiers, men who obey unquestioningly, men who have absolute faith in their leaders. That said, I don't expect you to question my instruction to see this doctor at the prescribed time and place." White handed Clay a handwritten note. "And I also don't expect you to ask why I'm telling you that I never gave you that piece of paper, and that I never had this conversation with you."

Before Clay could open the piece of paper, White held up his hand. "Your word."

Clay didn't know what to say, so he said what was expected of him, "Yes."

White stared silently.

"You have my word," Clay said.

"Your word that what?"

"You have my word that the program we have here will not be discussed by me with anyone else," Clay said.

"That includes even your teammates," White said with ice in his voice, and then stood suddenly, shaking Clay's hand. "Nice not talking to you." He laughed at his own humor, and Clay tried to join him.

Clay had gotten out the door when White's call brought him back. "Clay," he said with a twisted smile, "you're being paid a lot of money to be a part of this football team. I know you won't disappoint me."

On his way out of the coach's offices he ran into Gavin Collins.

"Clay," said Collins, eyeing the slip of paper, "what's up? Vance didn't take another bite out of you, did he? You haven't been goofing off . . ."

Clay stammered, "Uh, no, no I'm fine."

"You look kind of confused if you ask me." Gavin Collins looked around. "Why don't you come into my office for a minute?" he said.

Clay looked around too. "O.K.," he said, and followed Collins, who shut the door behind them.

"Sit down, sit down," said Collins, still eyeing the piece of paper. "Everything going all right?"

Clay looked at him. What did he want? "Sure."

"That must have something to do with our training program," Collins said casually, pointing at the paper.

"Yeah," Clay said, not knowing how much he was supposed to say or not say. "I guess it's a doctor I'm supposed to see. I guess I'm not supposed to ask about it—"

"Well," said Collins, clearing his throat and leaning forward to gently take the paper from Clay's hand, "I think it's probably best that some things are left unsaid."

Clay made no attempt to keep the slip of paper. He watched as Collins unfolded it and examined its contents. Clay didn't even know what was on it.

Collins folded it quickly and handed it back.

"Yeah," he said, "really, I probably shouldn't even be looking at this. You know how Vance is. Well, everything else O.K.?"

After a moment, he added, "Clay, you know you can call me anytime if you have any questions about anything."

He stood up, signaling the time to go.

"Sure," said Clay. "Thanks." He shook Collins's hand and left.

Gavin peered down the hall after him and shut his office door. He pulled out a pad and quickly wrote down everything that was on the paper. He sat staring at it on his desk. Why the hell were they involving Clay? If ever there was a natural player, it was Clay Blackwell. So why? Gavin tapped his pen on the pad and sat thinking with a disgusted look on his face. Finally he tore off the top page of the pad, folded it, and tucked it into the back of his file cabinet where it couldn't be found. It was always good to have a little something on file in case of a rainy day.

Clay's mind spun with all the possible outcomes of his strange meeting with White. His mind kept coming back to one conclusion.

As he descended the stairs, reading the slip of paper for the tenth time, his mind returned to steroids. Otherwise, why all the secrecy? Why all the rah-rah about doing whatever it took to win?

On the slip of paper was written the name of a Dr. Borne, his address, and an appointment time for Clay.

But Clay decided even White wouldn't do that. How could he? The NFL tested players for drugs, including steroids. No way could he risk losing his players to suspension. And what about the scandal that would result? White would be finished. No, it just wasn't possible.

Clay laughed at himself, he was getting as nutty as White. No matter how he thought about it, they couldn't get around the test. It had to be something else. He could only imagine what their great training method was, probably some hokey vitamin injection, or Borne was probably one of those sports psychiatrists—what a joke.

The locker room was empty when Clay entered, except for Max, who was drying off after his shower. Max's locker was directly across from his. Clay couldn't help notice Max's tanned skin, taut over his bulging muscles. Angry veins popped and strained up and down his arms and legs. Without thinking, Clay stuffed the piece of paper into his pocket. Max said nothing as Clay retrieved his keys. Max liked being the last one to leave, and he had taken an extra long shower to outlast Clay, who he had heard was meeting with White. Clay found the keys and started to leave. Then, on an impulse, he turned to Max, holding out his hand.

"I'm Clay, Clay Blackwell," he said.

"Max Dresden. You work good . . . I like that," Max replied, shaking Clay's hand.

"You pushed me hard," Clay said, "I like that."

"Yeah," Max said, and then smiled. "I saw you on TV. Figured you'd be kind of a prima donna, you know, with all the money—not that there's anything wrong with good cold cash."

"Yeah," Clay said, happy but not yet comfortable with his association with money, "well, I like the money, but I like the game too. No sense playing it if you don't try to be the best."

"You got that right. Hey," Max said, "you probably don't know your way around town at all. How about we get some food tonight and maybe a little tang afterward?"

He saw the look on Clay's face and asked, "You're not married, are you? I'd hate to get someone's wife pissed at me."

Clay wasn't certain what to say now. He didn't want to be a prude, but he didn't want to bullshit either. He didn't have to get laid. He could look.

"I have a girlfriend back home," he said, "but she's got two more years before she graduates."

"Good, where are you staying?"

"The Marriot."

"O.K., that's not far from me," Max said. "I'll pick you up at seven. We can go get some steaks and a few beers, then I'll show you around."

When Clay got back to his room, he called Katie. She was happy to hear from him, and he was glad to hear a familiar voice. She asked him what he was doing that evening.

"Not much," he said. "Just going out to dinner with a guy I met from the team. His name's Max Dresden."

"What are you guys going to do after dinner?" she asked, unable to hold back a pang of distrust and jealousy.

"Nothing, Kate. We're going to dinner, then for a couple of drinks. I don't even know where." He had a slight surge of guilt. Not that he was doing anything wrong. "Why'd you ask?" he couldn't help saying.

"No reason," she said defensively. "I was just making conversation."

Clay felt bad. Maybe he was being a little sensitive. Of course he was. She was just making conversation. He didn't know why he felt so defensive. Certainly Katie didn't want him to stay in every night.

But as much as he told himself this, during the rest of their conversation he couldn't help feeling that she wanted him to stay in. He said nothing more about it. Here he was in a new town with virtually no friends. He had worked hard for years to get here, and he was going to enjoy it. Part of that meant going out with his teammates and making new friends. If Katie stayed so uptight . . . well . . .

Max was waiting for Clay when he got down to the lobby. He looked much different dressed in jeans, an oversized yellow polo shirt, and tan loafers. In his workout clothes this afternoon, Max's over-exaggerated physique had made him look like a comic book character. Now he looked more like a model from *GQ.*

The car was parked right outside the main entrance and Clay gaped at the beauty of the machine. The black 928 had a deep shine. It looked like a car from a James Bond movie. Clay had never even ridden in a Porsche, and he had to admit that he felt a certain childlike thrill in going out on the town with a friend who drove one.

"This car is awesome," he said.

Max smiled uncertainly, and then remembered that Clay had just signed his contract the preceding day. He knew that Clay would soon become accustomed to nice things as even he had. Clay would certainly reach an even higher rung on the ladder of material possessions. After all, hadn't he just signed a $6.5 million contract? Max would never see money like that, but he did know how to live.

"If you like it," he said as they got into the car, "I'll take you to the dealer I got this from. The guy's a big sniffer and he'll give you a hell of a deal."

Clay nodded and discreetly buckled his seat belt as they surged past three cars on the ramp getting onto the expressway. "Do a lot of guys get deals?" Clay asked.

"Yeah, not bad, but no one gets 'em like Ferrone."

"Our QB?"

Max nodded. "That bastard gets free wheels, free vacations, free TVs, and all the free pussy he can eat. Ha, ha."

"You hang out with him?" Clay asked.

"Nah," Max replied. "He's a good guy. More balls than talent. But he hangs out with Pike and Sick. I don't go for those assholes."

"What's a pikensic?"

"No, Dan Pike and Pete Makozych, everyone calls them Pike and Sick. They're both offensive guards, and they are offensive. Slugs, if you ask me. You'll get to know them . . . real well. They're the dirtiest players I've ever met, except maybe me. They'll hold you, grab your mask, kick you in the balls, all that shit."

"They sound like trouble."

"They're O.K. I don't like them on the practice field. Neither will you. They're real rednecks. I don't go for that country shit, so I just don't hang out with them. They're O.K., though. Ferrone likes them."

They were silent until Clay said, "So . . . you get free stuff?"

"Well, I'm buying these shoes the other day at the mall and the manager asks me, do I play ball? I said, 'Yeah, I'm with the Ruffians.' I don't mind telling anyone I play for the Ruffians, win or lose. I worked my whole life to be in the NFL, and the NFL is the NFL, no matter what team you're on. So anyway, the guy gives me these shoes . . . free."

"Great," Clay said.

"I know, we make big money," Max said, looking from the road to Clay, "so what should it matter, a pair of shoes . . . but it's nice. Anyway, the Porsche guy would blow it if you walked through the door."

"I'd really appreciate it if you took me there," Clay said. He was beginning to see that Max knew the limits of the machine, and although he was going faster than he ever had gone before, he realized that the car was made for it. He relaxed a little. "I think I'd like a Porsche."

"Best car made," Max said.

"Hey, you must have been born lucky," he said after a pause. "I'm at home and I'm on my way out the door, thinking that this will be a pretty dull night, being Tuesday and all, when I get this phone call from this bitch I've been boning on and off, a nurse. Well, I'm not too happy to hear from her, 'cause I got plans with you, right? And I figure she's gonna start to whine. I'm about ready to cut this one loose . . ."

Max looked over to see if Clay understood, and Clay nodded.

"But the bitch tells me she's in some modeling contest put on by a suntan lotion company at the Acapulco Club, and she wants me to come see her. You know, to cheer her on? What a fucking joke! I don't think I've ever met a pretty bitch that didn't think she was some kind of model. But then I realize that if this bitch is there, there's bound to be plenty of others just as hot as she is, and she is hot. Your first night out on the town and we're gonna be knee-deep in pussy."

Clay smiled. This was where the fun started. Max was definitely a little over the edge, but he also seemed like a good guy.

"Max, what's the deal?" he asked. "Every girl's a bitch. Do you ever say girl or something?"

Max smiled and said, "Every once in a while I meet a girl that's more than a girl . . . then she's a lady in my book. Sounds like you have a special lady of your own."

"Yeah," Clay said sheepishly, "how'd you know?"

"Well, first of all you told me you got a girl back home, and second, why else would you care why I call every girl a bitch?" asked Max.

Clay shrugged.

"O.K., here it is. You got this great girl back home, right?"

Clay nodded.

"O.K. But you're gonna be here for at least two years on your own, right?"

"Yeah."

"O.K., here's the thing. Whether you know it, or admit it now, or not, you're going to end up with some strange tang, meaning not your girl-friend. Don't look at me that way. What the hell, you think you're really gonna go for two years with bitches throwing themselves at you left and right, and you keep on saying, 'No, sorry, I got a girlfriend back home?'

"I'll tell you right now, buddy," Max continued, "it'll never happen. I've been around pro sports long enough to know. Hell, even the married guys are lucky if they can hold out! It's nothing to get upset over. It's just the way it is."

Clay didn't know what to say.

"So the thing is," Max said, "since it's gonna happen, my advice to you is to just relax and enjoy it."

As the 928 raced down the expressway, the two players' minds traveled different paths. Max's was free from restraint, comfortable with the possibilities the night had to offer. Nights like this were at the core of his existence. There would be good food and plenty of drinking, and by the end of the night he was confident that he would assuage his drug-heightened lusts against the firm young body of some bitch.

He felt somebody had to set the kid straight. And what the hell good was all the shit he learned if he couldn't help some other guy out? Like a big brother.

Max smiled.

Clay had different thoughts in mind. He briefly wondered if he was soft in the head for mentioning Katie and asking Max about bitches. If the fun was about to really begin as he suspected, he hoped he wouldn't feel like so much of a heel that he couldn't enjoy it.

The steaks were thick and tender, and the beer was ice-cold, and when the meal was finished, Clay and Max sat for another hour, drinking steadily until their conversation flowed more easily. Clay talked about life after football, and of his house in the mountains. He gave Max an open invitation to visit him there. Max told his story and what he had gone through to be an NFL player.

When they pulled up to the Acapulco Club it was dark, and there was a line of people waiting to get in. A valet took the car and, spotting Max, the bouncers unhitched the felt railings and they walked right in.

Inside, the music was loud and the familiar thump thump thump of a bass set a steady rhythm for the dancers who moved amid the swirling lights that lit the dance floor. Clay felt a drunken rush of adrenaline as he took in the people and the noise and the lights. Many of the girls were clothed in revealing tight skirts or pants and high-heeled shoes. Their hair was teased wild and high on their heads. Shocking tones of lipstick outlined sensuous lips, and dark mascara highlighted enticing eyes. Many heads turned toward Clay and Max.

Max patted him on the back and said, "Relax. I can see the horns on your head, and so can every bitch in the place. Just be cool and they'll come to us. We don't want to go to them. Let me get you a drink. You want a vodka?"

"No," Clay said, conscious of the way he had gaped at the women he had seen, "I'll just have a beer. I don't drink drinks, just beer."

Max got a screwdriver for himself and a beer for Clay, and the two leaned against a section of the bar as they surveyed the club. Clay absently peeled the label from his bottle with his thumbnail.

"Knee-deep," Max said, "what'd I fuckin' tell you? Hey, tonight is a good night to get phone numbers. You know, just talk to a bitch and tell her you'd like to take her out sometime to dinner. There's enough good-looking pussy here to keep me busy for a month."

Clay said nothing. Max's nonchalance left him feeling like an adolescent at his first school dance. He guzzled some beer.

A tall and beautiful blonde suddenly appeared in front of them. She was the nurse model Max had talked about, and despite himself, as Max had predicted, Clay couldn't help staring at her. The low lights and smoke hid what minor flaws there might have been in her beauty. She was dressed in black. Her pants were shapely, but loose and light. She wore a halter top that displayed large tan breasts, hidden only by the lapels of an open silk blazer. Her long hair, thick and golden, fell straight to the middle of her back. Clay thought that if he had been Max and gotten a call earlier in the evening from this girl, he would certainly have canceled plans with his friend—in fact, done anything to please her. Max introduced her as Denise. Then, winking at Clay, Max blew her off by saying, "I gotta piss."

"Hi," Clay said, unable to think of anything else.

"Hi," she said sulkily, disappointed with Max's obvious lack of interest.

After a few moments of just standing and drinking and watching the people on the dance floor, Clay noticed Max across the bar mingling with two other girls. He was embarrassed, and wanted to prevent Denise from seeing what Max was up to. He started to talk.

"Max tells me you're a nurse, and a model too, of course," he said.

Denise perked up at the mention of modeling. "Yes," she said, "I met Max when he came into the office. I just do that to pay the bills. I try to do as much modeling as I can. The winner of this contest has a chance to go to the finals in L.A. I want to go to New York some day."

"I'm from New York," Clay said happily.

"Really? Where do you live? In Manhattan?" she asked.

"No, I'm not from New York City, I'm from upstate New York."

"Is that near the city?"

"No, I haven't even been there," Clay said, immediately regretting it, thinking that he must sound like a damn hick. "I just got here yesterday," he said, trying a different tact. "I play for the Ruffians, or I will."

"I figured that. I see a lot of you big guys here all the time. Most girls come here for that reason, but not me. I'm here for the contest. Max is the first football player I've really known. I don't really like jocks."

"Great," Clay said to himself, "this is only the hottest chick I've ever seen, and I can't get my ass off the floor. Now, if she was as drunk as me, and we were back at Northern, she might be impressed. But here I'm just a big dumb jock who hasn't even been to New York. Max will laugh his ass off if I don't even get her number. Well, desperate need calls for desperate action . . ."

"You know, Denise," he began, trying not to slur his words, "we live in the greatest country in the world. I can't believe it. Two days ago, I was just an average guy out of college. Yesterday I deposited two million dollars in the bank."

He watched Denise as he spoke, and he noted the reaction in her eyes.

"Unbelievable," he said. Her internal struggle with her snotty composure was obvious. It made Clay smile.

"How did you come across two million dollars?" she asked.

"I'm sorry," Clay said, the bullshit just rolling off his tongue. "I feel silly, really. I was the first-round draft pick by the Ruffians. I must sound really obnoxious. I'm sorry. I just signed my contract yesterday, and it's been such a big thing in my life, and with the whole thing being on the news and all, I stupidly assumed . . . well, I just thought you might have seen it on TV or something."

"I think I did hear something about you. I don't really watch the news," she said. "My God. It's amazing, it's like winning the lottery."

Clay grinned and congratulated himself. "The biggest problem I got," he said with a light chuckle, "is how to spend it. I mean, I'm gonna buy a Porsche. I'm gonna buy a house in the Caribbean. I already bought a summer lake house in New York . . . and I still got a ton of it. If you get any ideas, you'll have to let me know."

They laughed together. Clay had said it lightly, but he'd made his point.

"You know," he said, furthering his cause, "Max told me all about you."

"He did?" she said suspiciously.

"Yes, he said he had this girl who was a really great friend of his who he wanted me to meet."

"He told you that?" she asked, still suspicious.

"Yes," Clay said, the alcohol and the deceitful nightclub atmosphere allowing him to lie almost naturally now. "So naturally, I asked him if you were so great how come he hadn't snatched you up. He told me that you two were just friends though, although to look at you, I find it hard to believe."

"Why is that?"

"Because you're so beautiful," Clay said, giving his best imitation of Max's smile.

"Thank you," Denise said. "Yes, Max and I are just friends. That's really the only way to be with Max. He's very irresponsible, not someone you can count on."

Clay nodded with sincere understanding and said, "So, maybe we'll go out some night? You know, for dinner or something like that?"

"Sure, I'd like that."

Denise took a napkin from the bar and wrote her number down. Clay accepted it with a grin, knowing that it would be proof to his friend of his prowess. Clay would have abandoned the girl at this point, but, he had to admit to himself, the physical attraction prompted him to continue to speak.

"So, you work as a nurse when you don't model. Do you work at a hospital?"

"Oh, no, nothing like that," Denise said. "I couldn't stand anything like that. I work for a podiatrist. That's how I met Max. Dr. Borne does some work on the Ruffians players."

"Dr. Borne," Clay said, "I gotta see him this Friday. He's a what?"

"Podiatrist. You know, if you have problems with your feet, a foot doctor . . . Oh, my God! It's ten-thirty. Oh, my God! I'm supposed to be in the back for the line-up."

Without another word she hurried away, leaving Clay to the smoke and noise. He thoughtfully folded the napkin she had given him and placed it in his wallet as he would any other thing of value.

"A podiatrist?" he mused. "White's nuttier than I thought. What's he got going? A secret foot insert? The guy probably hides the toothpaste from his wife so she won't know his brand."

"What are you doing?" Max asked, appearing beside Clay suddenly. "Don't tell me you're goo-goo over that bitch. Hell, if I'd have known it was going to incapacitate you, I never would have left you alone with her. You better get to work. I got two numbers to your one already. You did get her number, didn't you?"

"Hi, Max," Clay said, coming out of his reverie. "Hey, what did you expect?"

He was certain that had been Max's intention, but it was polite to make absolutely sure before he boasted about her obvious attraction to him. Clay knew that no one liked a guy who worked on someone else's girl, even if she was a low-maintenance toy.

"Sure," Max said after Clay asked, "otherwise I never would have left you alone with her. Most people I wouldn't have to worry about. Most people are lucky if they have either looks or money, but you're danger- ous, you got both. If it's one thing a bitch likes more than a guy with good looks, it's a guy with money, and they like a guy with both more than rough sex," he said, and laughed. "And I know for a fact that bitch likes all three."

"Ahh, I probably won't call her. I just wanted to show you I could get her number . . . see?" Clay said, taking the number from his wallet.

"You're fucked up if you don't call her. She'll fuck you from here to New Orleans," Max said.

Clay laughed, as much at the serious expression on his face as what he'd said.

"Let me tell you," Max continued, coaching what he thought to be his young understudy, "she's the kind of bitch that thinks she's something special. Which means she's the same as the rest, only she likes to play make-believe. All that involves with her is taking her to an expensive place for dinner, then letting her pretend like she's never fucked on the first date before."

Clay nodded and said he'd remember that, and, so as not to disappoint his new friend, he tucked the number back in his wallet. By this time, both of them were drunk enough that their teeth and lips were numb. They drank to that fact and decided to use the men's room before the swimsuit contest began.

The rest room was remarkably quiet and the lighting subdued, a sharp contrast from the blaring noise and flashing lights outside. At the sink, a tall, lawyerly-looking guy in a double-breasted suit and crocodile shoes approached Max. Clay watched them speak as he washed his hands.

"You skiing tonight, Max?" the man asked in a slightly subdued voice.

"No, thanks, Martin, I'm good." It was all Max said. His words were not unfriendly, but they were firm, and Martin disappeared without another word.

"What the hell was that about?" Clay asked.

"Just a guy selling some blow," Max said. "He's scum, but if you need some snort, he's always here."

"You do that stuff?" Clay asked.

"You never snow skied? I guess not by the look on your face. Where did you grow up, on a farm?" Max said good-naturedly.

"Nah, beer's good for me," Clay said.

He continued to do just that, drink beer. Max matched him with screwdrivers. Not surprisingly, their friendship grew and blossomed with their intoxication. They watched the models prance about on the dance floor in swimsuits and chortled and leered with the other nightclub patrons. Denise was declared the winner, and that was last Clay saw of her that night.

CHAPTER TEN

THE AFTERNOON SUN WAS HOT. Clay searched for the air-conditioning control. The rental car he drove was a piece of shit, but it would have to do until he could get a chance to get together with Max's Porsche dealer. He was driving to his appointment with Dr. Borne, looking forward to seeing Denise, and wondering what was in store for him.

He pulled up to a tall Birmingham office building and took an elevator to the plush seventh-floor offices of the podiatrist.

Looking for Denise, Clay peered into the reaches of the doctor's office through the reception window. A middle-aged matron made a sour face at him and told him he'd be better able to fill out the information sheet if he sat down. Clay gave her an embarrassed smile and did as he was told.

Denise appeared and led him to an examination room. She wasn't nearly as friendly as she'd been when he left her the other night, and Clay told her so.

"Did you think I was going to fall all over you?" was her haughty reply.

Clay was miffed. He sat down on the sterile exam table. The stiff paper crumpled and complained. He wanted to say that he thought she might have been glad to see him, but instead imagined how Max might respond to such an unsettling welcome. With an expression that would have made his new friend proud, Clay stared at the girl impassively and said nothing. Denise didn't face his cold look for long. She gave him a coy smile and then leaned over, pressing her lips to his ear, briefly flicking her warm tongue inside it and sucking out cold air at the same time. Just as quickly Denise stepped away from him and was on her way out the door. With one last smile she said, "I can't be too friendly at work, but that was to let you know that you make me hot."

"Damn," Clay said to himself, "I gotta have that. I don't care what it takes, her I gotta have."

He failed to notice the entrance of Dr. Kyle Borne. The doctor had stood smiling dumbly at Clay and cleared his throat. He introduced himself with a handshake.

Clay thought he was a decent enough guy.

Borne was dressed in khaki pants and a pink oxford dress shirt with a bright green tie. The doctor told Clay to call him by his first name, Kyle.

"You know, Doc," Clay said with a congenial chuckle, "I don't even know why I'm here."

Dr. Borne gave him a puzzled look.

"Are you going to make me some inserts for my shoes or something?" Clay asked.

Borne's face beamed with an understanding and appreciation for Clay's humor, and for his discretion. "Oh yes," he said with a wink that confused Clay, "I've got just what you need. Let's get your vitals."

As Dr. Borne took his blood pressure and measured his height and weight, Clay became more and more confused. The doctor talked about football and the upcoming Ruffians season, not giving Clay the slightest indication as to the purpose of his visit.

Out of nowhere, Borne said to Clay, "Have you used injectables before?"

Clay looked around the room to see if there was someone else Borne was addressing. When Borne met his eyes, Clay, now utterly mystified, said, "What are you talking about?"

"Have you used injectable steroids or just taken a pill?"

"I–I've never used steroids at all," Clay stammered.

"Oh, no problem," Borne said, "I can show you how in two minutes." Then, seeing Clay's distress, he added, "It's no problem, really."

Clay reeled. Borne had actually taken out a syringe and begun to wrap a length of rubber tubing around his large biceps before Clay could even open his mouth. He was appalled.

"Are you fucking crazy?" Clay heard his own voice as if it was someone else who was speaking. His arm jerked away, freeing the tube to shoot across the room. With his other hand Clay slapped the doctor's hand down hard. The needle clicked off the floor. What Borne had tried to do to Clay scared him, and that fear made him angry.

Borne looked shocked and frightened. His dumb smile drooped slightly. Clay was standing over him menacingly, fists clenched. To Clay the presence of the needle and the tube was an assault, and his instincts told him to strike out violently. Borne winced as Clay's shoulders jerked in the fight to keep his fist from smashing into the man's face.

"What are you doing? What the fuck do you think you're doing!" Clay bellowed, venting the anger verbally.

"Please," Borne whined, "you can't use this drug without a syringe, it has to be injected."

"Who the fuck says I'm using some fucking drug? I thought you were a doctor, who the fuck are you?" Clay continued to rage.

"I am a doctor. I'm helping you. I'm helping your team."

"Get the fuck out of my way," Clay said with disgust, roughly shoving Borne aside and marching out the office amid the gaping staff and patients who had heard the yelling behind the door.

"I told you never to call me at my office," Vance White said coldly into the phone. "Remember, you and I don't know each other. We've never spoken or met."

"I'm sorry, Vance," the voice whined apologetically, "but there's a problem. A big problem."

"Go" was all White said in return.

"Vance, it's your player," Borne said, "Clay Blackwell. I don't think he wants to use this, you know . . ."

"What do you mean? How do you know?" White asked.

"He—he got upset. He stormed out of here. He pushed me. Vance, I don't know, I don't know, this isn't good. I don't want to get involved with something like this."

Vance White clucked his tongue in his cheek and stared vacantly into space. A dark cloud brewed in his eyes. "You listen to me," he said. "You'll do what I say if you have any desire whatsoever to continue practicing medicine. First, you never, ever call me again. I don't know you, and you don't know me."

White paused to let that sink in.

"Next, you will continue to do what it is you do. If you compromise this program, believe me, you will be the first one to go down, and you'll go down so hard, you'll wonder what hit you. Am I clear with you?"

White heard the doctor clear his throat on the other end and then say yes. He hung up the phone.

"What do you mean, relax! The guy tried to stick a fuckin' needle in me!" Clay exploded into the phone.

"Clay, Clay, Clay," said Clancy calmly, "just relax. We'll get this resolved."

"How the hell are we gonna resolve something with Vance White? Do you know Vance White? Have you seen the guy? He's not going to relax, I can promise you that. You gotta get me outa here."

Clancy was silent.

"O.K.?" said Clay.

"Clay . . . they didn't pick you with the third pick of the draft to trade you. They won't do it."

"I won't do their damned program," Clay said. "That'll make 'em trade me. White won't even want me here."

"Here's what you tell them," Clay continued. "Tell them that if they don't trade me, I'll blow the whole fuckin' thing in. I will . . . I can go to the papers and White'll be gone from coaching by tomorrow. You tell them that."

"Now, Clay, listen to me," Clancy said, "don't even talk like that. I have to look out for you, and anything like that wouldn't be a good idea. Really, it wouldn't. Let me set up a meeting and we'll get this all worked out . . . Come on, Clay, just trust me. Everything will be fine."

Clay was silent for a long while. "O.K.," he said finally.

"Shit!" Clancy said, after he'd hung up.

"Son of a bitch lied to me," Vance White reminded himself as he sat waiting for Humphry Lyles. "Said he'd do anything to play the game, anything to get better. Words. Well, he'll live up to those words or pay the price. No one deceives me. I've seen insubordination before, and I've crushed it."

The owner entered his office.

"Vance," Humphry said before he could get to his desk, "the first order of business is to contain this situation. We certainly don't need this thing getting out."

White looked stunned, as if he had not before considered the thought. Humphry could see from White's expression that he hadn't considered the far-reaching implications of what had happened. He guessed White's narrow viewpoint was what had gotten him into trouble at the college level.

"Vance," Humphry continued, "I know you don't like advice from anyone, even your friends. But I think that this situation is crossing over into the realm of business, which we have agreed is my domain. Right now we have something good going, something that we both know will help us win a championship. We have players getting stronger and better than the others around the league. Now, I have no doubt that Blackwell could go on CNN tomorrow with a story about our program and we could easily dismiss it as a ludicrous attempt to undermine a coach for whom he has ill feelings. I have no fear for you or me. I have a publicity firm in New York that could discredit Blackwell as a fool for the rest of his life. But you have told me that we need a winning edge, and I don't want to lose that. If Blackwell creates a disturbance, the program will have to be discontinued.

"Now, I know," Humphry said, holding up his hand, "I know that Blackwell is a player. And I know that on the field you need unquestioning obedience from your players. But right now Clay Blackwell is not on the field. Clay Blackwell is an investment, and one that I must protect from yielding a bad return.

"Vance, let me handle Blackwell. We'll bring him in here and calm him down, that's the most important thing in this matter right now. Then we'll spell the situation out for him, and let him think about it for a while. Once he sees the merit in his . . . discretion, and when he fully realizes that for two million bucks I have already purchased his skin and bones, then it will be the time for you to try again with him."

Humphry could actually see White bridle at the thought of such diplomacy. He knew White would prefer a fistfight or some other ugliness. He also knew that he was ultimately in control. This would be a good time for his friend to see that.

"I won't let you lose the ground we've gained these past months just trying to snap one player into line," Humphry said with all the severity he could muster.

"All right Mr. Lyles," said a constrained Vance White, "you do own this team. So if you want to keep this Blackwell around by pampering him even more, that's your prerogative. But one thing I can't do is be a party to it. I can accept Blackwell remaining here, even if that's not necessarily what I'd do with him, but I can't stop trying to mold him into a part of this team. That may not be pretty. He may not like my methods any more than our drug program. Then what will you do? Will you hold this program hostage to the whinings of one deceptive shit fresh out of college?"

"Vance, we're friends, don't yell at me," Humphry said calmly.

"Sorry." He wasn't.

"I know your concerns Vance, but this isn't college. We can't just take this kid's scholarship and send him home. We own Blackwell, and we have to work with him. Most importantly, we have to contain this situation."

White nodded his head. He had said all he had to say.

"Of course, you continue to run this team to your own standards," Humphry said. "Just let me take care of this Blackwell situation."

White nodded his head again. His face was sullen.

"What do you think, Max?" Clay said. "I mean, I know you use the stuff, right?"

Max looked at Clay long and hard, as if trying to decide just what to say. Then he laughed abruptly. "Ha!"

He held two fingers up to the bartender, signaling for two more beers.

"I'm their original boy," said Max, "their model player. Didn't know that, did you? Of course I'm on. I don't mind. I was going to use some shit to train for this season anyway. That's how I got in this league in the first place." Max looked keenly at Clay, cutting through the alcoholic fog. "They never would have even looked at me if I hadn't gotten on the juice and gotten bigger.

"This was my dream," said Max almost angrily, as if he were forced to do what he had done.

"Of course," Clay said.

"Really, I wasn't six four, two seventy-five, and I didn't come from a big football college."

"I know," Clay said apologetically. He had heard Max's story before. He knew that his own life had been blessed with the kind of talents and opportunity that young athletes dreamed of—size, strength, and natural speed. "But I worked too, Max."

"I'm not saying that. I guess I just . . . envy you, kind of. I mean, you know . . ." Max said in a subdued voice, looking down and turning the empty beer bottle in his hands.

Although they had spent much time together, it was the first time Clay had seen Max so pensive.

Then, abruptly Max said, "Aw shit, you do what you have to, you know. This shit is good for the team. You see what it's done for me. Hell, Clay, I'm stronger than you are and you outweigh me by thirty pounds."

Max saw the uncertain look on Clay's face and said, "Aw hell, I'm not sayin that what you're doin' is wrong, Clay. I'm just sayin' that this shit is good. With our guys on it we'll kick some ass and win. That's what this whole thing is about, winning. Believe me, you weren't here last year, but you don't want to go through a season like that, with everybody kickin' your ass and the fans booing you. Hell, if you can do without it and play great ball, then fuck it, you do it. And White can go fuck himself. You didn't do it in college, and you kicked ass there right?"

Clay nodded.

"Yeah, well, fuck, no problem," Max said, "you'll do it here too."

"I really think I can, Max," Clay said vigorously.

"Here's to kicking some ass this season," said Max, raising his new bottle. "You, me, and the whole fucking team.

"So," he added, "how about the Apex tonight?"

"What about Acapulco?" Clay said.

"Ah ha!" said Max. "Might see someone you know, huh? Why didn't you just call her for a date and bang her brains out instead of getting me out with you? Need me to hold your hand?"

"I wanted to talk to you," Clay said. "You asked, and I said Acapulco. It's not like I know many places . . . you think she'll be at The Acapulco?"

Max laughed. "Come on," he said. "Acapulco it is."

As it turned out, the Acapulco Club was just as satisfactory for Max as it was for Clay.

Denise's breath smelled strongly of bubble gum, and Clay found himself drunkenly thinking that surely a girl with bubble gum breath would not carry a venereal disease. She was probably very new at all this, an innocent nurse wanting only to help the sick and disabled, who had only recently fallen into the wrong company when she'd met Max.

The club was getting ready to close, and a thick-necked, grubby man was putting chairs up on top of tables. Clay could not remember exactly how long they had been there, only that it seemed a very long time. A friend of Denise's who was also a model, named Ginger, had seated herself on Max's lap and was stroking the nape of his neck. Besides Clay and Max, there were only a few businessmen in suits scattered about the club, finishing the last of their drinks, snatching greedy and indiscreet glances at the waitresses in their bikinis. Clay watched with dull eyes as one of the girls whose breasts he'd observed bulging from her costume all night made her way through the club and out the front door. She wore a trenchcoat and sneakers, which made Clay chuckle. Denise leaned her sinewy form against Clay's alcohol-soaked body, and pouted when he laughed.

"I don't know why that's funny," she said testily, even though she remained sitting on his lap with her firm breasts pressed up against his arm. She had been talking when Clay chuckled.

"What?" said Clay with a drunken slur.

"I said I didn't see what was funny about a broken hip."

Clay, who hadn't been listening to what she was saying, said, "Whose hip?"

"Oh, what do you care?" she said with disdain.

Clay didn't care, so he said nothing. Instead he turned to Max and hoisted what was left of a beer. "Thiz is to you . . . you an—an' me. Buddies for life!"

"For lives!" said Max. "An' now," he snickered, "it's time to take these young ladies, an' I use the term lightly, my frien', rather lightly indeed . . . an' now iz time to take these young ladies back to what I will call . . . my hummle abode. Exactly! My hummle abode."

"Layies," Clay said, "I believe my frien' has a tub which awaits us."

In the parking lot, Clay and Max argued about who would drive. It was finally settled that Ginger would drive Max's car and Clay would ride with Denise in her Honda Accord. During the ride, Denise continued to talk about what Clay deduced were family problems. Clay faded in and out of cognizance, but nevertheless learned enough about her family situation by the time they reached Max's apartment building to feel genuinely sorry for her.

Besides lust, any feelings, including sympathy for the unlucky girl, were quickly forgotten once the four of them had settled their naked bodies in the large, tiled hot tub on Max's roof. Max fondled Ginger indiscreetly under the bubbling water, and Clay likewise began to grope about Denise's superb body with intoxicated clumsiness. The tub, it seemed, was a mere formality. Before Clay had even begun to sweat from the steaming water, he found himself wrapped in a towel and stumbling behind the rest of the group down the stairs and through the hallway to Max's apartment. Clay declined as the three of them snorted cocaine from a mirror on Max's dresser top. Clay was too drunk to care what the others did, but nothing could sway him to snort the white powder himself. Instead he got another beer from the refrigerator.

By the time the cocaine was gone, only Clay remained with his towel intact. Then Denise led him silently by the hand out into the living room and gently undid his towel before she laid herself spread-legged on the plush gray carpet of Max's floor. She looked up glassy-eyed at Clay. The room was dark except for a thick, dull beam of light that seeped through the curtains from a streetlight outside. Clay was struck by how beautiful and vulnerable Denise looked. He felt no shame, only delight at the decadence of the entire night. There was some perverse pleasure, maybe it was pride, in taking the girl who only a few days ago at the bikini contest had been leered at and coveted by so many men. Clay smiled with drunken pleasure as he lowered his large frame onto the floor and pressed himself against her body.

Denise responded like a wild animal. She writhed and moaned as Clay entered her, grabbing his buttocks and squeezing them, forcing him into her still deeper. With surprising quickness she rolled them both over so that she was straddling him. Frantically she worked her hips, stroking his shoulders, then groping his chest as though he were a woman. Her long hair dragged across his face and his neck and chest. Then she arched back and with both hands caressed and toyed with him while she pumped herself ever harder and faster. He reached up and ran his hands from her long neck to her breasts, back and forth as if he couldn't feel enough of her body to satisfy him. Denise's hips stopped suddenly. Clay felt her shudder and she moaned in ecstasy. He flipped her on her back and violently rammed her, burning his knees on the rug until he winced and groaned, releasing himself inside her.

Max lay back on his bed and toyed with Ginger's hair. He wasn't normally given to such signs of affection, but it wasn't affection. Her hair was soft as silk and it felt good to Max's heightened senses to run it through his fingers. He was resting. Even though he'd had her once already, he wasn't tired, and he imagined he would be fucking her for the better part of the night. Her face rested on his muscular stomach and she purred lightly in response to his caresses.

"Oh God, I feel good," she said. "You feel good. Poor Denise."

"What the hell does that mean? 'Poor Denise,' " said Max.

"Nothing, just that Mr. Goody-Goody is probably out cold by now."

"What the hell is Mr. Goody-Goody?"

"I mean really, the guy couldn't even take a snort with us."

"Shut up," Max said coldly.

"What are you uptight about, honey?"

"I'm not your honey, and shut your fuckin' mouth about my buddy if you want to keep your teeth."

Max had a handful of her hair and was twisting it tightly now. He'd turned her head and he now looked into her eyes.

"Hey," she said in a frightened voice. "You're hurting me."

"Some people don't use drugs. You don't have a problem with that, do you? You think everybody's as fucked up as you and me?" Max said between tight lips and clenched teeth.

Fear flickered in her eyes now. Max rolled her onto her belly and got on top of her, still holding her hair.

"What are you doing?" she asked.

"Nothing you don't want me to do . . ."

CHAPTER ELEVEN

Humphry Lyles sat quietly drumming his fingers on the desktop. He was angry with the fact that Clay Blackwell was not cooperating, but unlike Vance White, Humphry at least had to admire the principles that the boy seemed to stand for. Of course, he would not let that admiration show; that would be a weakness in which he would not indulge. Instead he stared grimly at the young man who sat with obvious discomfort next to Vance White in front of his desk.

Clay explained, "Mr. Lyles, I plan on being a great player for you, everything you drafted me for, but there really is no need for me to use this drug."

He looked sidelong at White, who remained silent as a form of protest. White was angry with Lyles for not allowing him to handle the situation his own way, which would have been to threaten Clay until he submitted. White, in fact, had said nothing during the entire meeting.

"Clay, we hope you understand that our program is in the best interests of not only this team but you. This drug is perfectly safe. It has undergone extensive tests, and it has proven to be a certain aid in athletic performance."

"Mr. Lyles," Clay said, hesitating a moment and shifting in the leather chair, "I admit I don't know all there is to know about this drug, but I do know that it is a steroid, and I know that they aren't good for you."

"Well," said Lyles with a wan smile, "certainly the game of football itself isn't good for you, Clay."

"And how could I take this drug anyway, and not get caught and suspended when the league does its drug testing during training camp?" Clay asked.

"The drug has a built-in masking agent which hides its presence from the test that the league uses. There is no way for the NFL to detect it," said Lyles.

Then, seeing Clay frown at the mention of the drug, he added, "Of course, Clay, the reason we are meeting here today is to assure you that certainly if you do not wish to use the drug, we cannot make you. You know that, don't you?"

Clay nodded.

White, on the other hand, snorted his disapproval, still saying nothing.

"And I want you to know, Mr. Lyles," Clay said, "that I will be the football player you want me to be without using any drugs."

"Very well," said Lyles in a friendly way.

Then the owner's brow darkened, he screwed up his face and said, "But do know this, son . . . you are a member of this team, and Coach White runs this team for me. He has a job to do, just like the rest of us. You don't want to be involved in a program that all your teammates are required to participate in, and that rubs Coach White the wrong way, as it should. You see, son, his job is to take my team to the Super Bowl. We certainly can't expect him to do anything less than his best to get us there, and if he feels that part of that job is to get you involved in this program like everyone else, we can't fault him for that, can we?"

Here, Lyles glared at Clay. "I expect you to understand this and to act like a professional player, not threaten to run to your agent or the media every time Vance looks at you cross-eyed. You do understand me, don't you, son?" Lyles asked in a nasty tone.

"This asshole's going to ride me without mercy," Clay thought. "I disobeyed his very first instruction as a player. That's something he's got to get me for. And here Lyles is, telling him he can basically fuck me however he likes. He's telling me if I've got a problem to have it out now or don't come crying. Well, fuck both these guys. Whatever White's got, I can take. His shit can't last forever, especially when he sees me on the field. He'll forget about it quick when I crush a few quarterbacks. Meantime, go for it. That's what I should tell White, go for it."

"Yes," Clay said, "I understand."

"Vance White won't give you any special treatment," Lyles told Clay, "and I expect you to understand that it's his job to try to make you the best player you can be."

"I understand," Clay said, "I can live with that."

If nothing else, he thought White and Lyles would respect him for standing up for himself.

But to White, Clay had done nothing short of spit in his face. That was something Vance White would not forgive. Blackwell was done. He was no longer a soldier for the battlefield. His only value would be as an example to the rest as to just how seriously White treated insubordination. When the rest of the team watched him roast a first-round player, and a multimillion-dollar guy at that, they'd know no one was safe. They'd all drop to their knees. White would ride Blackwell until he either did as he was told, or he quit.

White remembered things of this sort he had done before. During his college tenure, when he was short on scholarships to give out to new recruits, he would occasionally run one of his unproductive players right off the team. As a coach, he was well versed in psychological manipulation. He had to be to motivate his players week after week. It was always easier to crush a player's morale than it was to raise it, and that was how he ran players off. He simply crushed their morale. That was what he would do with Clay Blackwell. He knew Blackwell's type. He had always been the coach's favorite and treated accordingly, praised incessantly and therefore looked up to by his teammates. That would end with White. Blackwell's psyche would become filled with doubt and insecurity.

Even though everyone had gone home, Gavin Collins looked around nervously. He pushed open the locker room door and peered into the darkness. "Anyone here?" he called. It was not necessary.

He felt around blindly and found the lights. He'd felt better when it was dark, but he had to see. If someone came, he planned to just say he was working late and came down here to take a crap. But he knew even that didn't make sense. He would have used the bathroom upstairs.

He removed the lid from the large waste basket, and with one more look around, he began to carefully remove the waste one piece at a time. He almost gagged when he removed a bit of toilet paper gooey from snot, but he kept on. More paper towels. More unraveled lengths of white tape. Pre-wrap. Soda can. Junk mail. Ahhh, wrapped neatly in a large wad of toilet paper was a needle. He held it up to the light. A few drops of amber fluid still remained in the syringe. Gavin was careful not to prick himself. He opened his gym bag and carefully placed the needle inside. He continued to pick through the garbage. His heart raced now, and he thought about leaving with the needle. But it had taken him enough time to get up the balls to do this, so he'd do it all the way. There would be more.

More paper towels. Another soda can. An empty cup. More mail. Snotty Kleenex. He was almost to the bottom. There! In the bottom of the basket was a small brown vial. He reached in up to his elbow, and lifted it into the light. Jackpot!

The label on the bottle read: Thyall-D.

Clay duffed his drive and it dribbled out about a hundred yards. Max chortled. The man with the poorest drive on each hole had to shotgun a beer. Max stepped up to the tee.

Whack! He connected cleanly with the ball, and it went straight off the tee.

"Yes!" cried Max, only to watch the ball slice wildly to the right and out of play.

Clay broke out, roaring with laughter.

"Fuck!" cried Max, swinging his club violently at the earth and tearing up a huge divot.

"Jesus, Max," Clay said, his laughter over.

"Fuck," Max said and did the same thing again.

Clay stepped back warily. They were only having fun, but today was a Thursday, and in the past eight weeks Clay had learned that Max, after injecting himself with Thyall on Wednesdays, was particularly violent and unpredictable for the twenty-four-hour period that followed.

"Max," Clay said in a low voice, "come on. This is a nice club. They're not going to let us come back if one of the members sees you. Chill out, man."

"Fuck that!" Max yelled and threw his club through the air halfway to Clay's ball. They both watched as the club bounced off the fairway twice before landing. Clay walked over to the larger of the two divots and put it on top of his head. The sod actually hung over his ears. "I'm serious Max," he said sternly. "This is a fancy club."

They both broke out laughing together.

"I dare you to let one of these stiffs see you with that on your head," said Max, inserting his car key into the bottom of a beer can. Pfft! Max immediately put the can to his mouth and popped the tab. Beer shot down his throat. Max crushed the empty can and let out an enormous belch. Clay said nothing. He simply got into the cart, adjusted his hat, and took off the brake. Max got in and they were off. Clay drove over Max's club with a thud-thud, then backed up over it again before Max could retrieve it. They laughed some more.

"Here come some," Max said.

"Aww, if they even notice, I bet they don't have the balls to say anything," said Clay.

He got out and approached his ball. A foursome with shiny leather golf shoes, knickers, and tweed caps came up the other fairway in two carts. They gaped as they passed. Clay tipped his divot before taking a hurried, wild swing at his ball which sent another patch of sod into the air. Max laughed wildly as each of the four men turned their heads in sync and drove on.

Max rolled out of the cart and lay face up on the fairway, now screaming with laughter. "You are so fucked up, ha, ha, ha," Max cried. "So fucked up, ha, ha, ha . . ."

Clay smiled. "I'm glad to see you can lighten up and enjoy yourself," he said.

"Aw, you know how I get," Max said, getting back into the cart and popping each of them a beer. "Especially golfing, it can really piss you off. That's just another good reason for you to keep yourself clean," Max said, tacitly referring to his violent outburst.

"Yeah," Clay said, "I have to wonder sometimes. White's been such an asshole—"

"Ah, he'll forget about all his hard-ass shit once camp starts. Camp'll be hard, don't get me wrong. In fact, he'll probably treat us all like shit in camp, but he won't keep singling you out, not once you start kicking people's asses on the field. White's crazy, but he's not stupid," Max said.

Clay nodded and said under his breath, "I hope you're right, buddy." Aloud, he asked, "How was training camp here last year?"

"Cake," Max said, "no running, not much hitting, it was easy . . . and we got our ass kicked. Not with White. Guy's a psycho. That's good, though, if it makes us win."

Clay thought about what Max said. Max was right, he should be confident. He was in good shape, he'd had enough time in Birmingham to acclimate to the hot, humid weather of the deep South. And he was a good player. He always had been. But if White's training camp was going to be brutal, he had a suspicion that it would be twice as bad for him. If White was going to break him, then his best opportunity was yet to come. In camp, the coaching staff had players for twenty-four hours a day, seven days a week, for six weeks. No one could leave. If he missed even one practice session, he'd be fined thousands of dollars and probably suspended without pay well into the season.

"Make sure you get your rest when you go up there in those mountains of yours," Max said, " 'cause you're gonna need it. By the way, the way you and I've been hitting the town? I'd cut back on all this shit if I were you. I'm going to. You can't be going into White's camp with all this shit in your system," Max added, raising his beer can to his lips.

Clay thought how good it was going to be to go home. Not only would he be glad to see Katie, but he couldn't wait to spend a week at the lake.

"Since tonight will be our last night on the town before camp," Max said, "I think it's only right we find two bitches and bring them back to my place for a rooftop Jacuzzi."

"I don't know, Max . . ." Clay said, "I'll be seeing Katie tomorrow. I don't think I'd feel right going home with some girl tonight."

"Oh, bullshit," Max said. "Stop talking like such a pussy. Two more beers and you'll be trying to fuck the girl at the snack bar.

"I know just the place to go too," Max continued, "the Acapulco Club."

"Uhh, can't you think of another place, Max?"

"Since when is it a problem going to the Acapulco Club?"

"Well," Clay pulled up to where Max's ball had gone out and took a swig of beer, "I kind of already said good-bye to Denise. I told her my flight left tonight . . . you know, she's apt to be there."

"Holy shit," Max exclaimed. "You're not only whipped by the girl back home, you got a bitch runnin' the show down here!"

"Come on, Max," Clay said remorsefully. "I just don't want to see her tonight, otherwise I'll never get rid of her."

Although Clay had made a point of not letting himself spend too much time with Denise, he had inevitably found himself out with her about twice a week. To her, this constituted some kind of relationship. Not wanting to alienate her, Clay had never come right out and told her otherwise.

Max laughed. "O.K., I guess you're right. If she latched on to you tonight it would mean no hot tub with two unknown bitches. I've had all I can take of Denise and that Ginger bitch. Hey, by the way, doesn't it make you laugh the way Denise talks around me, like we were friends or something? Do me a favor, when you cut that bitch loose, be sure to tell her that you know I boned her too, just so she doesn't think she got away with anything."

After a pause Max said, "When did you say good-bye anyway?"

"Today, I took her to lunch."

"Sure," Max said, "then you fucked her, and that's why you were late getting me. What an asshole. You're sitting here telling me you don't want to score tonight 'cause you'll feel bad, but you already got laid this afternoon. Now you want me to sacrifice my chances to get laid because you got yours already, and you're probably running that guilt trip again. Some friend."

"Oh, come on, Max. There's other places we can go. Tell you what, as a penalty, I'll talk to the ugly friend tonight."

"Ha," Max guffawed, "you always end up talking to the ugly friend. The hot ones always go for me. They can see you're scared right away. Unless you're good and tanked you're like a cold fish. You've got a habit of scaring them off . . . not to mention my superior looks."

"Yeah, right," said Clay sarcastically.

"Listen, Clay, the next time we see each other," Max said, referring to the six-week stint of isolation in training camp, "we're gonna go for a long time with no bitches. I just want to make sure that you've had enough action to hold you through camp, get you something wild to make sure you leave me alone."

"Very funny," Clay said, "but like I told you, I'll be spending a full week with my girl, alone."

"And like I told you," Max snickered, "I need to get you something wild. I don't want you hopping into my bed during training camp."

"Don't worry," Clay said, "you're not my type. I don't like guys with hairy asses."

"Faggot," Max said.

The bright sunlight streaming through the window finally woke Clay. He was lying naked in the middle of Max's living room. His head ached and his mouth was cotton dry. He knew immediately from the intensity of the light that it was late and that he was in danger of missing his plane. He hurried through Max's bedroom to the bathroom, careful not to make any noise that would awaken the two lumps under the covers. Clay found four aspirin in Max's medicine chest and washed them down with several big gulps of water straight from the spigot. He took a quick shower and as he dried off, he searched for a clean sweatsuit in the closet. He took one that he thought Max wouldn't miss. There was no time to go back to his own place, and his clothes from last night were damp from spilled beer and heavy with the smell of cigarette smoke.

Fortunately, he had packed his bags and left them in the trunk of his car, which was parked outside. He raced to the airport and dashed through the terminal, just making the last call for his flight back to New York. He had to change planes in Atlanta, and it wasn't until he got onto his connecting flight that he was able to get back to sleep.

Clay had closed on the house at Loon Lake right after signing with the Ruffians. Katie bought and supervised the delivery of some essential supplies. She also spent the entire week prior to Clay's arrival at the lake getting everything ready so that he could just relax.

Clay thought it would be fun to start off the week of vacation with Lever. Just like old times. So he asked his friend to come up to the lake for the weekend. He knew he'd made a mistake the moment Lever pulled up in his rusty green Impala. The car smoked and coughed all the way down the drive. Clay's neighbor, the banker, who had been planting flowers in his lawn, eyed Clay suspiciously when Lever's car door opened and an empty beer bottle rolled out. Lever heaved his sloppy bulk from behind the wheel and emerged from the car with an enormous fart.

"That one's been buildin' up," he exclaimed, beaming from ear to ear.

"Damn, this place is in the boonies," he cried. "How ya doin', buddy?

Long time . . ."

Lever grasped Clay's hand and pumped it enthusiastically. "Holy shit! What a place! It musta cost a fuckin' million. Check it out . . . "

Lever waddled up to the house and in the door with Clay close behind, glancing furtively at the banker.

"What do you mean, you won't have a chug with me?" Lever complained that evening.

"Really, Lev, I hit it hard last night. Besides, I gotta dry out for camp. I need to take it easy this weekend," Clay said. "It's not like college. Camp goes for six weeks and it's supposed to be a bitch."

Lever only frowned. "Well," he said, brightening with an idea, "I guess I'll have to drink enough for the both of us, ha, ha . . ."

Lever pestered Clay about drinking the whole weekend. When Clay did have a few, just to be sociable, Lever tried to induce him to drink more. But Clay wanted to follow Max's advice. He was an NFL player now, and he had serious work ahead of him.

Katie was glad to see Lever, and, as always, she enjoyed his buffoonery. When they headed out to the lake for a swim and Lever got stuck in an inner tube, Katie laughed. When Lever picked up the ice cream cone he'd dropped in town and ate it, she also laughed.

"Hey, Clay," Lever said, licking the sticky ice cream from his fingers, "what's up? You in a bad mood or something?"

"No, why?" Clay asked.

"I dunno. You just seem like you're not having as much fun as normal. You didn't even laugh at that. Did I do something?"

"No, Lev, I'm fine. Really, it's probably just camp coming up. I'm a little uptight, I guess."

Lever nodded happily.

That night Clay and Katie took Lever out for dinner to the Wild Duck. After dinner Clay ordered two cigars for himself and Lever.

"Sweet stogie," Lever said, chomping off the end and spitting it onto his coffee cup saucer.

Clay grimaced at his friend as he expertly clipped the end of the cigar with the silver clippers the waiter had left on the table.

"Hey, hoooo . . ." Lever exclaimed, "where'd you learn that trick?"

"Max showed me this in a place down in Birmingham called Nikkos. It's an unbelievable place . . . You should taste the clams casino," Clay said.

"You been talking about this Max guy all weekend," Lever said. "If I hadn't lived with you for the three best goddamned years of your life, I might think my best-friend status was in jeopardy."

Lever laughed at his own humor. Clay smiled wanly.

After Clay paid the check, the three friends said good-bye.

"Kate, I'll be seeing you around campus," Lever said as Katie hugged him and kissed his cheek.

"Clay," Lever said, holding out his hand. When Clay reached for it, Lever pulled him close and gave him a hug. "Kick some ass, buddy. I know you will."

"You too, Lev," Clay said. "Kick some ass."

Lever turned quickly and waved over his shoulder as he made his way across the parking lot to his beat-up car. He didn't look back.

"How come you're so quiet?" Clay finally asked. They were halfway back to Loon Lake, and Katie hadn't said more than three words.

"I just can't believe the way you acted to Lever," she said. "Did you see him when he left?"

"Well, shit, I didn't say anything to make the guy feel bad. I don't know what the hell you're talking about. If he was sad to say good-bye, it doesn't mean I did anything."

"Clay," she said in a firm voice, "I like Lever, but he's your friend. If you want to treat your friends like that, it's your business, but don't tell me you don't know what I'm talking about. All weekend, Max this and Max that—my God, Clay, even I noticed it."

"Yeah, well, did you notice the way every time I told some story about Max or Birmingham how Lever would come up with some damn story about back at school? Are you gonna tell me that wasn't annoying? What the hell, I'm not mad about it, though, so I can't see how Lever could be mad at me."

"He's not mad at you, Clay," Katie said. "You just weren't yourself."

"Well, shit." Clay said, then sat silently for a few moments before he said, "I'll give Lev a call tonight when he gets back. I'll just tell him that I'm uptight."

Max crammed an old pair of blue sneakers into the bag. The heels of the sneakers were crushed down so they could be slipped easily on and off. "Every bit of energy you can save counts," he said to himself.

He fished around his closet looking for an old brown box that he had somehow managed to hold on to since his college days. The box held things that he wanted to save, but that really had no place to keep. He found it. Inside were the two things he wanted. He never went to a training camp without them. The first was a picture of his family.

He had been fifteen when the picture was taken. His sister had been about to enter the state university. His father felt it would be the last vacation they might ever take as a family. He was right. Max stood between his mother and father, and his sister was tucked under his father's other arm. Behind them was the peeling yellow cottage on Lake Erie. Max could remember his father telling whoever'd taken the shot, "Make sure you get the lake." It was the only vacation Max could remember going on as a kid.

His mother and father had been killed that fall in an auto accident, and Max had suddenly found himself on his own. With his sister away at school and acting as his legal guardian, he was able to stay on in the house until he finished high school. The two of them then sold the house, and Max used what money was his to pay his way through Southeastern Ohio State, a Division 3 football school. He excelled in football, and although no one had ever gone on from SOS to the play pro ball, Max intended to be the first.

The picture was for good luck. Max kept it with him and he'd made it to the NFL. Now maybe it would make him a starter, his ultimate dream. The second thing Max needed was a laminated news clipping from Saskatchewan. It wasn't the headline that Max had saved the clipping for. It read: "ROUGH RIDERS LOSE FOURTH STRAIGHT." What he saved it for was about three inches into the article. He'd highlighted it in yellow before it had been laminated.

". . . If there could be a bright spot in such a dismal organization it would be Max Dresden. The unknown American from Southeastern Ohio State led the team with seventeen tackles, two quarterback sacks, and one interception.

" 'I can't feel great about today,' said Dresden, 'because the team lost. But this is the type of game I think I can play week in and week out. Hopefully it will help the team to win.'

"Even if Dresden can repeat his spectacular performance, the Rough Riders outlook at 0–4 is . . ."

The article gave Max inspiration. If he could have a game like that once, he could do it again. All he needed was the chance, and when he got it, he wanted to be ready. The clipping was something to read every night of training camp before turning in . . . to get his mind right.

Max tucked the two items carefully into his bag and zipped it shut.

CHAPTER TWELVE

THE RUFFIANS CAMP WAS HELD at a small state college about fifty miles south of Birmingham. In June, Max and Clay had driven out to see the facility where they would be spending the last six weeks of their summer. It was pretty grim. When they arrived after about an hour drive through parched cotton fields, the car was covered with hot dust and they were dying of thirst. They entered what looked like a club house near the playing field and found a drinking fountain. The water was warm and brackish, and did little to revive them.

They found a custodian in a blue work shirt and pants scraping blistered paint from the trim around the doorway of a nearby dormitory. The old man appeared to be hard of hearing. He didn't answer their calls as they approached him, and he jumped when he finally saw them.

"Who you?" he demanded. His dark skin was leathery and deep lines of age cut across his face. The nappy hair on his head was short and white.

"Hi," Clay said in a friendly tone, holding out his hand in an attempt to put the man at ease, "I'm Clay Blackwell and this is Max Dresden. We play for the Ruffians, and we just wanted to get a look around the place since we're gonna be here all next month."

The old man stared at Clay's hand. One of his eyes was a foggy blue color and the good one seemed to wander. He seemed to look up at Clay. "You with them football players? Not supposed to be here till July."

"I know," Clay said. "We just wanted to look around . . . at where we're gonna be staying."

The old man nodded and set his scraping tool down on the brick steps. Without a word he opened the door to the dormitory and stood holding it until they entered. They followed him down a worn hallway to one of the rooms.

"They all the same," he said, letting them in with a key.

Max flipped a switch on the wall and an old ceiling fan clanked noisily, circulating the thick, musty air. "Could you let us out on the field?" he asked.

Again the old man said nothing, but turned and led them out of the dorm through the large old trees down to the football field. There he fumbled with a padlock on the gate. He remained outside the fence watching them as they walked about. The practice field was a bumpy, uneven lot of crabgrass bounded by rusty goal posts and a rusty chain-link fence.

"My high school field was better than this," Clay said.

At one end of the field was a large, drab cinder-block building.

"Let's check it out," Max said. Inside was an empty training room, a large storage garage for equipment, and a large locker room filled with gray rusty lockers. The toilets and showers were laced with black mold. It was cramped and dirty, especially compared to the luxurious setting of the Ruffians complex.

Clay and Max said nothing as they emerged into the sunlight until they thanked the old man. He nodded, then locked the gate and shuffled away, stooping to pick up an old candy wrapper as he went.

"Why would we come to a rundown place like this in the middle of nowhere?" Clay finally asked. "It's a shit hole."

"That's just it," answered Max. "I'm sure White wants us to be here in the middle of nowhere. No distractions, just football. I think it's a damn good idea myself, otherwise we'd be sure to have some assholes sneaking out at night chasing bitches, getting drunk, you know, all that kind of stuff."

"That's exactly how you like to spend your free time, Max," Clay said.

"It is, but not during training camp. Camp is time to get your body and your mind in shape for football. This is the perfect place to do it. Last year we lived in the Days Inn off Exit 29, and camp was held at our own complex. Last year we got our ass kicked too. No, this place, as bad as it looks, is perfect. White sure knows what he's doing, huh?"

"Not if you ask me," Clay grumbled.

Clay had been back in Birmingham for one exhausting week of training camp when the alarm clock woke him from a deep and dark sleep. The room was pitch black. Clay winced when he sat up and reached for the clock. Every inch of him hurt. He felt a dull throbbing ache all over, and sharp jolts of pain when he moved. His forehead was swollen and chaffed from rubbing against his helmet. His neck was so sore that it hurt to turn his head in any direction.

Now that Clay was fully awake, the pounding in his head was fierce. His calves and thighs were knotted so tightly that he staggered as he rose from his bed. His arms ached too. Like his stomach and back, they were covered with cuts and bruises. His feet were covered with blisters, and his ankles were raw in places where ankle tape had come in direct contact with his skin, pulling it free in large patches. His fingers were covered with oozing, sticky sores.

Clay remembered practice the day before. It had been brutal and violent. Even Clay, who was unaccustomed to fighting with his own teammates, had gotten into it with Pike. He had thrown an upper cut under Clay's face mask during a scrimmage play. Clay surprised Pike by kicking his feet out from under him, then pinning him to the ground with his knees. He latched onto Pike's face mask with one hand and pounded the hulking offensive lineman with his free hand for all he was worth. But even though Clay appeared to get the best of Pike, the veteran player had sensed Clay's fingers in his mask and twisted his head sharply down and to the side, crushing the tips of Clay's fingers, which were caught in the bars of the mask.

Clay rubbed his aching hamstrings and remembered the running. After an already grueling practice White would line his team up across one end of the field and run them in the ninety-degree humid heat until the heavier and less prepared players began to drop from exhaustion. White would never stop the running until at least one player dropped to the steaming turf. In his mind Clay could still see the trainers as they raced to the fallen players, cut free their practice gear with large steel scissors, and packed them in mounds of ice right there on the field.

Max stirred from his bed but said nothing. He just slipped on a pair of shorts and some thongs, picked up his shaving kit, and headed toward the bathroom down the hall. Clay shuffled to the bureau, flipped on the light, and fumbled with an aspirin bottle. He took three and washed them down with some tepid water he kept by his bedside. There was nothing worse than this. There was no discomfort, or pain, or sleep deprivation as severe as at training camp. And this camp was ten times worse than anything he'd gone through in college. What was most depressing was that they had only just completed their first week, and the end seemed nowhere in sight. Right now the only pleasant thought was that at ten-thirty that night he could go to sleep again.

The first couple of days, Clay had felt ashamed at how mentally unprepared he was for the punishing routine of training camp. Max seemed to take even the worst conditions in stride, even though he had admitted to Clay that he too had never gone through anything as severe as this. Not that Max was cheerful. He had been in a dark and silent mood since day one. Clay hadn't even tried to talk to him in the last twenty-four hours. He knew Max must have given himself an injection yesterday. Although he was always aggressive, yesterday he had been brutal and plowed his way into three fights during practice. In one, he ripped the helmet off a rookie named Lee and smashed the offensive lineman's nose before his teammates and coaches could pull Max off.

Vance White thrived on the violence of this type, and although he would always say that he didn't want to see his players fighting each other, everyone knew he loved it. Clay had never seen so many fights during practice.

Each twenty-four hours of camp seemed like forty-eight. There was a practice in the morning and in the afternoon. The players would get up at 6:30 and eat breakfast. Then they would get taped and dressed for practice, which started at 8:00. Practice usually ended about 10:15, and then the team ran their sprints. Clay had never fallen out on the sprints, but still he was frequently dizzy after the harsh physical work and would have to stagger into the locker room and guzzle glass after glass of water before he felt steady enough to take a shower.

Lunch was at 11:00, and immediately afterward meetings began. The players would break up in groups by position. Clay and the rest of the defensive line met with their position coach, Gavin Collins, in an old classroom located in a building next to their dorm. The group would watch the film from the morning's practice, and Collins would correct any errors that the players had made. Everything they did was on film, each individual drill and every team scrimmage period. There was no escape from what the players called "the evil eye." Every mistake, every individual defeat, was captured for all to see on film.

Clay smiled in spite of his aches when he thought of Collins. The guy was so positive. He never rode his players. Even the free-agent rookies, who everyone knew probably wouldn't make the team, were treated with respect by Collins. Just two days ago during a film session, Doogie, one of Clay's fellow linemen, had berated a rookie that screwed up a pass-rush stunt. Collins stopped the film and turned on the light.

"O.K.," he said, standing up and fixing a glare on his players, "let's get something straight, Doogie, and the rest of you. No one in this unit calls anyone a piece of shit, or anything like it. I am the only one who says what's right and what's wrong. I'm the one that's gonna determine who among you are gonna make this team, and I'll tell you right now, I don't want anybody who's gonna be negative. We're all gonna make some mistakes. If we do, I'll point them out and we'll correct them, but not in that way. We've got to be a team, and no one benefits from that kind of talk. You understand that, Doogie? Anyone else got a problem with that? Good."

When the afternoon film meeting was over, the players were given an hour to sleep. There were very few who didn't. The hour nap rejuvenated Clay, but it gave his body time to stiffen. After the rest hour, the players would tape and dress again for another practice at 2:30 that went until 4:45. There was no running after the evening practice, but there was mandatory weight lifting. Dinner was at 6:00, and meetings after dinner went from 7:00 until 10:30.

The evening meetings began with a team gathering, then offense and defense would split up and go over the new plays that would be put in for the next day's work. When that was done, the team again broke down by position into meetings where the afternoon's practice film was critiqued. When the defensive line was let out of their meeting at 10:30,

Clay went straight to bed. If they were lucky enough to have Collins let them out a few minutes earlier than the rest of the team—say, at 10:20 like last night—Clay would hurry to one of the few pay phones in the dorm and call Katie.

By the morning, his talks with Katie always seemed long ago, and she seemed very far away. Clay found himself constantly reliving their time together at Loon Lake. He longed for the cool tranquillity of the lake, and he longed for Katie's comforting words and caresses. During the last week he had found himself more emotionally devoted to her than he had ever been. When he needed someone, that someone was Kate.

Max returned from the bathroom clean-shaven and looking fresh. Clay looked like he felt, sore and tired, and he stood staring blankly at the wall.

"What are you standing there for?" Max said.

"Oh," Clay started, "I was just thinking of Katie."

"Humph!" Max snorted. "That's a real smart thing to be thinking of."

"Hey, Max," Clay said with an angry stare, "seriously . . . what the fuck is your problem?"

Max glowered, his fists clenching.

"If I did something to offend you," Clay said in an apologetic tone, "tell me. I'm your friend, remember?"

Suddenly Max relaxed and looked at his hands, still balled. "No," he said. He sat down on his bunk. The springs squeaked. "No, there's nothing you did. I-I-I just . . ."

He looked up with a pained expression. He looked back down, burying his face in his hands with a tearless sob that was both angry and sad. Clay stood, frozen by what he was seeing.

"Clay, I-I don't know," Max shuddered. Staring at the floor, he did not look up. "I don't know what the fuck is happening to me. I feel like I'm crazy or something. I mean, it's good . . . the violence, it's good. It's just that I don't feel in control anymore."

Clay put his hand on Max's shoulder. Max sprang from the bed, knocking Clay's hand off him. He looked at Clay, his eyes wide. He laughed nervously. "I didn't mean it. I'm fine. I shouldn't talk about it. I don't want to talk about it, Clay," Max said. "I'm O.K., really."

He turned and left the small dorm room.

After a hot shower that helped relieve some of his stiffness, Clay left the room for breakfast at the school cafeteria. While he was plopping some eggs onto his plate at the buffet, Max passed him on his way out.

"Hey, buddy," Max said very matter-of-factly.

Clay did a double-take and was unable to get out a response before Max had disappeared.

Clay wondered what Max was up to all through breakfast. He was so distracted he almost forgot to eat any bananas. He always ate two bananas at each meal for potassium, which prevented cramping.

Later, after Clay was taped and putting on his shoulder pads, Max came up behind him and pulled down his jersey. "Ready for another big day?" he said with a cheerful smile and a pat on Clay's shoulder.

Clay could only search Max's face and smile uncomfortably.

"Gonna be a hot one," Max said in the same tone before heading out onto the field.

"It doesn't make sense," Clay said to himself over and over again as he made his last-minute preparations. Grease forehead. Put in mouthpiece. Rub some Flex-All on low back. Sun screen on nose. It was quiet in the locker room. Clay looked at the clock. "Damn."

He hurried out onto the field. He pulled his gloves on as he ran. He hated to wear the bulky leather gloves in the heat. But it was either that or have hamburger hands.

He fell into line. He saw White look at his watch, and Clay figured he must have just made it, otherwise he would have heard.

Clay wondered again about Max. What was the deal? He reached for his toes. He moaned. The stretch wasn't doing anything to relieve the ache.

Clay reminded himself as he ran mindlessly through agilities that Max had always been tense. But the intense mood swings were bizarre. It had to be the drug.

Even when the team scrimmage was a full hour into practice, Clay was still pondering his friend's odd behavior during a break between plays.

Vance White's shrieking brought him back to where he was. "Blackwell, you damned rookie, you damned worthless rookie," he was yelling from the middle of the practice field, "get your ass out here!"

Clay began to run from the sideline, his muscles aching with the effort. The entire team was staring at him, some with disgust, others with pity. Doogie hawked a loogie and spat it at Clay's feet. Spike Norris, the other inside tackle, frowned. The others stared at him wide-eyed in disbelief. He had let down the D-line. He was the rookie of the bunch and he'd made them all look bad. The first team had been called to scrimmage, and they were all there except Blackwell. They knew White would take it out on the whole first-team defense with some extra running.

"He must be thinkin' about all that big money, Coach," yelled out Todd Ferrone from the offensive huddle. "Ain't got time to play with us."

Pike and Sick snickered loudly.

Clay's ears were burning. When he finally got into the huddle, no one moved. Max, the defensive signal caller, was silent. The offense didn't move either.

Everyone's eyes were on White. His face was contorted with anger and told them all that they were not continuing until he vented it. His mirrored sunglasses, baseball cap, and whistle gave him the look of a malicious trooper. He marched over to the defensive huddle. As he approached, Clay felt Keith Neil, the cornerback who stood behind him in the huddle, tap him on the butt and say under his breath, "Stay cool, babe."

The caring words made Clay feel sick.

White reached the huddle, wound up, and cracked Clay on the head with his metal clipboard as hard as he possibly could. Clay reeled despite his helmet.

"You son of a bitch. You worthless piece of shit!" screamed White. "This is a scrimmage! Is this what you'll be doing when we're in a battle? When your teammates are fighting for their lives, you'll be on the sideline daydreaming?"

Clay staggered and then stood facing White's angry face. He was still dazed and unsure.

A voice inside Clay was screaming, "Kill this fuck! Rip his fucking throat out! Mash his face into a bloody pulp! No one does that to you! No one!"

"No!" said another voice. It was one he was more familiar with. "You don't do that. You don't hit a coach any more than you'd hit your own father. You don't do it. It's wrong. It's unacceptable. This is a coach. You do what he says. You take what he gives you. That's the way."

"Well?" shouted White, who showed no sign of any doubt or fear. He knew exactly what Clay would do.

Clay thought hard. What was the question . . . ?

"No," Clay said definitely.

"No. Damn you, Gavin," White said, turning to Collins, "I want Blackwell off the first team until I say he's back on. You got that? I don't give a shit who he is. I don't give a shit how much money we wasted on him."

"Yes, Coach," Collins said, and called to the reserves on the sideline, "McGuire! Get your ass out here!"

McGuire set a speed record getting to the huddle.

"I don't know why you put him there in the first place," White said in a voice that everyone, even the players on the sideline, could hear. "He doesn't merit any special treatment. He's given absolutely no indication that he's willing to make any sacrifices for this team. He's the most selfish son of a bitch I've seen in all my years of coaching. It wouldn't surprise me if his own damn teammates run his ass out of here.

"You," White continued, turning back to Clay and pointing with his clipboard, "you get the hell off my field. You watch for the rest of practice. And you got ten extra sprints after practice, Mr. First Rounder. That's ten more on top of the extra ten you got the whole first defense doing. You think I don't remember that you're the only guy on this team who has shown me that he's got a serious attitude problem? I sure as hell haven't forgotten. And I'll tell you something else, boy. You keep this shit up and even the owner himself won't be able to keep me from shipping your sorry ass home in a box. Now get the hell off my field!"

Clay jogged off the field and stood alone on the sideline. The shame of being hit and insulted and demoted made him forget about the ringing in his head. He had lined up as the starting end on the defense since the beginning of camp. Normally rookies were relegated to second or third team, depending on their draft status. But a first- and sometimes a second-round pick was usually given the starting job based on the fact that an owner would not think well of paying out big money to watch a player sitting on the bench.

Clay was still sweating despite his inactivity. The air was hot and humid, and the dry field stirred a dusty haze that stung the players' eyes and filled their nostrils with crud. The rest of the team eyed Clay enviously from the practice field. In the middle of all their running and hitting, their sweat and punishment, Clay's spot seemed like an oasis.

In reality, though, no one would trade places with Clay. No one wanted to piss off a coach. If it was done too many times, it was a sure ticket out of town, and everyone knew that if a player got on White's bad side, he might as well pack it in. Most of them had worked all their lives to play in the NFL, whether it was for the glory or the money, or both. There were eighty of them there in camp, and each one knew that in six weeks almost half of them, no matter how hard they worked, would be gone. Those who were more secure in their positions weren't carefree either, because White decided who played and who sat. The pressure to please him consumed each player.

Clay felt it too, and so he couldn't enjoy the break. In the end, he was worse off. The sprints the team had to run after practice were one hundred yards in length. The players had to sprint the hundred yards in under eighteen seconds, then jog back and do it again. Clay's extra sprints totaled over an extra mile of running. His already sore feet and legs burned with pain, his mind whirled, and his chest felt as if it would collapse. When the rest of the team had completed their running, White made them all stay in the hot morning sun, doubled over and panting, to watch Clay. Only his anger at Vance White, who ridiculed him every step of the way, kept Clay focused enough in the oppressive heat to finish the sprints. He staggered off the field. It wasn't fear of White, or even shame that got him through it. It was pure rage, hatred. He refused to be beaten by White.

The next day, Clay learned that White's abuse wouldn't be limited to after-practice running. When the team broke up by position to work on fundamental skills, White appeared at the D-line's area. Clay and his teammates were working on a tackling drill, where they would take turns as the ball carrier and the tackler.

"Gavin," said White, "let Blackwell run for these boys."

Gavin shrugged and tossed Clay the ball. Clay got out of the tackling line and went over to the running side.

"And I want to see if you pussys can hit," White added in a nasty tone. "I won't have any D-linemen on this team that can't put a ball carrier to the ground."

Sky was next to tackle. Clay, ten yards away, ran at him full speed with the ball. Sky popped him hard, wrapping Clay up in his long arms. He held Clay in the air, driving him backward, and then dropping him to his feet as was custom in the drill.

"Sky, you mother-fucking piece of shit!" White screamed. "You dumb son of a bitch! I said drive him into the fucking ground! Get your ass off my field! You can join Blackwell after practice, you dumb-ass!"

Sky looked wide-eyed at Gavin, "I-I th-th-thought—"

"Off!" shouted White, pointing at the water buckets.

Norris was next in line. He pounded Clay to the ground, not wanting any of what White was giving out.

"Umpphhh!" went Clay.

"Sorry," whispered Norris, then started to help Clay to his feet.

"Don't help him up, Norris!" bellowed White. "If I wanted you to help a ball carrier up, I wouldn't have you tackle him! This isn't a fucking tea party!"

Doogie was next. He hit Clay under the chin and drove him into the ground. Doogie got up quickly, leaving Clay in a heap.

"You'll be here in September, Doogie," White said. "I like the way you hit."

The drill went on like that every day, with White motivating Clay's teammates to punish him in order to preserve their own jobs.

White also ran Clay extra every day. The tackling drill and running alone were unbearable, but after the first three days White added a "double team" drill after the running.

Clay had almost reached the cool locker room when he heard White shout, "Blackwell! Get your ass back out here, you're not through. You need some work on the double team."

Clay turned to see Pike and Sick waiting beside White. They looked rested, and fresh as daisies compared to Clay. They were leering.

"You just line your ass up right here," White said, pointing at the ground directly across from the two huge offensive linemen. Clay looked up to see two sets of mean eyes. Sweat dripped off their bulging arms and legs. One of them reeked horribly of body odor. Clay thought he would gag.

Clay got down in his stance and almost fell on his face. He was still exhausted from the extra running. Before he was even ready, White called, "Hut," and the two loads fired out at him, knocking him back five yards before he landed on his back. Pike and Sick landed with their full six hundred pounds on top of him.

"That's bullshit!" White screamed at Clay. "This is the NFL, boy! You can't let two offensive guards blow your ass off the ball like you aren't even there! Now get your ass up and do it again . . ."

Next time Clay jumped the count, grabbed hold of Pike, and pulled him to the ground. Sick got there a split second late, and the three of them lay in a pile-up on the line of scrimmage. Clay had trouble getting up.

White spat. "Not bad," he said blandly. "You two gonna let this rookie pile you up on the line like that? I thought you two were tough."

"Fuck," said Pike.

"Cunt," said Sick.

The two ogres whispered between themselves and lined up.

"Hut! Hut!"

Clay went for Pike's chest again. He was too slow, but that didn't matter. Pike had launched his full bulk at Clay's knees. The impact twisted Clay's joints and left him in an awkward position. Sick hit him high before he could recover. The back of Clay's head hit the ground first with a thud, bouncing off the turf. He winced from the shock to his head and from the anticipated snap of a knee.

Exhausted as he was, a rush of adrenaline allowed Clay to jump to his feet and kick Pike in the head. Sick was up and on him, and Clay could only land one punch to Sick's belly before he was taken to the ground.

What happened next was a blur in Clay's mind. He was outnumbered. Pike and Sick punched and kicked him repeatedly, cursing as they did it. Through it all Clay could hear the maniacal laughter of Vance White. He had nothing left. He lay there and took what they gave him. Sooner or later he knew they would tire of beating him.

White finally turned and walked away. Pike and Sick followed when they realized White had gone.

". . . ever kick me . . . teach that fuckin' rookie . . ." Clay heard them mumbling.

Clay lay still until he caught his breath. He smelled the hot turf. It reminded him of cutting the summer lawn when he was a kid. He rolled over, got up, and marched into the locker room.

"Fuck them," he said. No one could hear him.

One night during the defensive line meeting, Clay sat watching the practice film.

"Clay," Gavin Collins said, "you gotta get wider on this play, you've got contain. You're the last player that can make this play. If the back gets outside you on this, like he does here, it's a touchdown. We can't have you doing this. I know it's not a physical thing, I can see you've got the tackle beat, but you have to concentrate. You have to know that when we run a Bronco, you're the contain."

Collins corrected Clay in the same patient tone he used with all his players. He wasn't being an asshole; he was just explaining the job and how to do it. Clay felt that Gavin respected him despite White's campaign. It was nothing spoken, Clay just had a sense that Collins wanted no part of White's program of intimidation and humiliation.

And now, as he watched the film, Clay had to face the fact that he had fucked up for the one guy who was on his side. He started to get anxious.

Collins backed the film up so they could all see the mistake again. Clay tensed his muscles, urging his image on the film to stay outside and make the tackle. He urged and urged, and then he shot up out of his seat.

"Auggggggh! Ooooow!" he almost screamed.

Every muscle in his body tightened at one time. He tried to stand but couldn't. He fell over onto the floor, writhing in pain, the agony of the cramps making him light-headed.

"He's cramping up," he heard someone say.

The rest of the defensive line tried to hold him down, to subdue him and massage his cramping limbs.

"Sky!" Clay heard Collins yell. "Get a trainer! Go get a trainer!"

It was only ten minutes before Sparks the trainer came rushing into the meeting room with an IV. To Clay, those few minutes seemed like forever. He lay on the floor and moaned with pain more intense than any he had ever experienced. His teammates and coach stood about helplessly. Once Sparks had the needle in Clay's arm and the IV started flowing, he instructed the players on how to rub Clay's limbs to help ease the cramps. Sparks sent one of the players to the training room for some more IVs. After four quart bags of IV fluid Sparks removed the needle and helped Clay slowly off the floor. The rest of the defensive linemen had gone to the dorm. Only Collins remained.

"What the hell happened, Sparky?" Collins asked, relieved to see Clay up and on his feet, even if he was unsteady.

"Dehydrated," Sparks said. "Been working out in that sun, not gettin' enough fluid in his system between practices. Get dehydrated like that and the whole body goes. Cramps up tighter than a drum. Painful sumbitch, huh?"

Clay nodded.

"Well," Sparks said, patting him on the back and then packing up his black bag, "you best get some rest. I'll bring by a couple of six-packs of Gatorade to your room, and you make sure you're drinking it all night."

When Sparks had gone, Clay turned wearily to Gavin Collins. "Sorry about this, Coach."

"Hey, there's nothing for you to be sorry for, Clay," Collins said with a smile. "You can't help what happened. But next time you guys want to get out of a meeting early, just ask me instead of scaring me half to death."

Clay chuckled softly, shaking his head. The joke broke the ice.

"Clay," Collins said seriously, "I've been meaning to talk to you anyway. I know that Coach White is being unusually hard on you, and I know why."

Clay's eyes quickly focused on his coach's face.

"The thing is," Collins continued, "I really can't do anything about it except to tell you that you're a fine football player, and I know that you can come through all this. I can't say anything against Coach White—he's my boss, and that would be unprofessional. But I can tell you between you and me that I respect what you're doing. I really can't say any more to you. I'm going to treat you like the rest of my players. I'll ride you extra hard on the field because that's the orders from above, but I want you to know that I am behind you. I'd like to see you do well, and I think that once you get through this camp, you will."

Clay waited to see if Collins would say more. "Thanks, Gavin," Clay said after a few silent moments.

Clay left the meeting room and made his way slowly through the dark, towering trees between the old college buildings and back to the dorm. He smiled at the thought of Collins's vote of confidence. Then it was gone. Gavin, after all, was one coach. The rest were going right along with White. Even his teammates were disdainful. After all, he was a first-round draft pick who wasn't even in the starting line-up.

"Face it," Doogie had said to him one day after practice, "You're gettin' big money, so if you don't perform, it makes 'em all look like shit."

Ralph Scott, a three-hundred-pound former All-Pro who was in the waning days of his illustrious career, heard Doogie's comment, and he leaned toward Clay.

"Listen," he said, "don't listen to that shit. I made a million dollars in Houston one year, and I had a hell of a year . . . but it didn't matter. No way could I have done enough to make people think I deserved that money. There's nothing you can do either, so don't mind that asshole a bit."

But the worse things got on the field, the more Clay heard cracks about how much money he was making.

Clay wondered how White could be doing this to him. His head was pounding as he staggered across the grass to his dorm. He couldn't stop asking himself why. So he wouldn't take White's drug, big fuckin' deal! He could play. He would be the best D-lineman they had if White would cut his shit. Gavin knew it. Clay knew it. Even White must know it.

Clay shook his head.

He climbed the stairs to the second floor, where his room was. It was only 10:15, and there was no one using the phone. Clay dialed Katie. She picked up on the first ring.

"Clay?" she said, her voice echoing on the long-distance line.

"How'd you know it was me, honey?" he asked.

"Just guessed. I had a feeling you might call. What's wrong, Clay? You don't sound good."

He told her what had happened.

"Oh, my God, Clay," she said, clearly upset. "I hope you're going to take it easy for a few days."

"Ha!" Clay laughed. "That's a good one. I'll be out there tomorrow morning sweating my ass off with everyone else. I'll be lucky if White doesn't make me run extra just because I cramped up tonight."

"You're not really serious, Clay. It's barbaric. They never would have had you practice the day after something like that at school."

"Well, this isn't college anymore, Katie. There's no such thing as taking it easy here."

"Maybe you should talk to them, Clay, tell them. You're a first-round pick. I thought that meant that they wanted to make sure you were ready to help the team right from the start of the season."

Clay rested his forehead against the cold, shiny metal of the pay phone. Tears welled up in his eyes. He wanted to tell here she was absolutely right, but that logic meant nothing to the Birmingham Ruffians.

"It's so fucked up down here," he thought, "no one would even believe it. If the son of a bitch would just give me a fucking chance!"

He didn't want Katie to know how upset he was, so he took a deep breath and steered the conversation away. "I just want this to be over," he said, "and be back together with you. The season isn't even started, and all I can think of is getting home."

"I'm sure you'll feel better when you get out of training camp."

"Holy shit," he thought, "you don't get it, Kate, you just don't get it."

"Yeah," he said, "I'm sure things will get better."

They talked for a few more minutes, then Clay hung up the phone and rested his head against his arm on the wall. "The bad thing is," he said to himself, "I can not only see things not getting better, I can see them getting worse."

He limped awkwardly to his room. The rest of the players, now done with their meetings, were beginning to filter into the dorm. Clay flopped down on his bunk, not bothering to turn on the light. As he lay in the darkness, he felt completely exhausted. His limbs were heavy and his various cuts and bruises throbbed incessantly. Even before Max got back from his meeting or Sparky stopped by with his Gatorade, the shuffle of feet and the muffled voices from beyond his door lulled Clay into a deep sleep. Sleep was his only reprieve from the panic that was beginning to grip him and the feeling that for the first time his world was collapsing around him and he was powerless to stop it.

"Jesus, there's some hittin' goin' on out there, Gavin," Stepinowski murmured to Collins.

"What do you expect, Step?" Collins replied. "This is a full scrimmage and these guys are—what should we say—highly motivated?"

Step glanced over at White, then snorted, "Gavin, I like you, and you know it, but you gotta watch your sarcasm."

Collins just smiled and signaled the play in to Max.

Max called the play with authority; even Clay could hear him from the sideline, "Okee Double Slant Cover Three . . . Ready . . ."

"Break!" The shout went up from the entire defense in unison. They knew by now that if it wasn't loud and crisp Max would make them re-huddle and do it again, and no one questioned Max. He was their leader.

Clay watched McGuire line up next to Doogie, checking to see if McGuire would align outside the tackle and then shift inside at the last second, the way Clay knew it was supposed to be done.

McGuire did it right.

"Shit," Clay said to himself.

The ball was snapped and the offense surged as one to the open side of the field. Only the off-side guard, Pike, pulled from his stance and went the other way. The back too, after a jab step to the strong side, turned and countered back. It was a counter O play. Doogie saw it, McGuire saw it, even Sky saw it. But they all saw it too late, they had committed to the strong side.

Max wasn't fooled. With amazing speed he charged straight toward the line of scrimmage. Just before Pike turned the corner to lead-block up the field, Max threw his entire body, head first, directly at the ear hole of Pike's helmet.

"Crack!"

The sound exploded. Pike went backward, slamming into Davis Green and popping the ball from his hands. Norris jumped on the ball, a defensive turnover.

"Owwwwwwwwww!" went Max's war cry at the top of his lungs. He was standing over the immense motionless body of Pike with both fists raised.

"Owwwwwwwwww!" shrieked the rest of the defense, mimicking Max like wild animals and swarming him with high fives, shoulder slaps, and head butts. They loved when Max made a big hit. It made them want to make big hits. A turnover got the entire defense out of two sprints after practice.

"Anybody can cause a fumble," Clay said to himself in disgust. Immediately he felt ashamed, and glanced around to make sure no one had read his thoughts. He chided himself privately. Max was his friend, even though everyone else was down on him. In fact, the worse things got for Clay, the nicer Max was.

When the howling and slapping subsided, Max walked away without so much as a glance. The trainers ran out onto the field to attend to Pike, and the scrimmage had to be moved to the other end.

"Two's will go against two's next, and I want to see more hits like that!" White yelled to his team. "Max, everyone's tired of hearing it, but great job! Hell of a play! Everybody take five and get some water."

They all pushed toward the water table, where full cups were laid out by Sparky. Max pulled off his head gear and found Clay.

"How 'bout it, buddy?" Max said, putting his arm around Clay's shoulder, his eyes a-gleam.

"Great hit," Clay said, a little blandly.

"Yeah, but how 'bout the revenge factor?" Max asked, hugging him. "I did that fucker for you. I told you that fat fuck would pay . . . and I'll get the other fucker, Sick, too before the end of camp. Not that you can't do it yourself, but hey, what are friends for?"

Clay had to smile. "Thanks, buddy."

Clay put his arm around Max's waist and gave him a light squeeze before grabbing them both a cup of water.

White blew his whistle and Clay took the field along with the rest of the second-string offensive and defensive squads. Max stood apart from the rest of the first-teamers and kept a close eye on Clay as the scrimmage began. Doogie appeared at Max's side.

"Hey, Max," Doogie said, "since we got no meetings tonight after dinner, me and Sky and Spike are gonna get a couple beers at that roadside dive out on 23, how 'bout it?"

"I don't know," Max said coolly. "I'll talk to Clay."

"Well," Doogie said jovially, "We were thinking just getting a few of the starters together, you know?"

"No, I don't know."

"Come on, Max," Doogie said in a light-hearted way, "what's the hang-up with you and Blackwell? You don't say shit to the rest of us, and we're the guys gonna be in the trenches with you. Why don't you hang with us a little?"

"Hey, man," Max said, "I don't see the big deal. I don't mind going with you guys, but what the hell's the problem with Clay coming too?"

"Listen, Max, most of us guys don't see much reason to hang with Blackwell unless maybe you need a loan or something, ha, ha," Doogie chuckled at his own wit. "The guy's a bust."

Max's hand whipped out like a flash. He grabbed Doogie's mask and yanked it until it clanked against his own.

"You and 'most of us guys' can fucking kiss my ass," Max said, and shoved Doogie away.

"Crazy fuck," Doogie mumbled, straightening his helmet as he stalked off.

CHAPTER THIRTEEN

THE CHICAGO BEARS WERE STILL referred to as the "Monsters of the Midway." They had recaptured the physical style of play that earned them the name in the Butkus era. Any team that took the field against the Bears knew they were in for a hard-hitting game of smash ball, and considered themselves lucky to get out of the game in one piece.

For the Ruffians, who were accustomed to the brutal heat of Alabama, it was a cool July evening in Chicago when they took the field against an opponent for the first time under Vance White. The first cut was still two weeks away, and there were still eighty members on the team. The players had to double up in the visitors' locker room, and there was a cramped, uncomfortable feeling that was exacerbated by the testiness of many of the key players, who had discreetly given themselves an injection.

White's eyes burned with intensity. "You men have kicked each other's ass for the past three weeks," he said to them right before they took the field for the kickoff. "Now it's time to kick someone else's ass.

You've lived through hell, now it's time to make someone pay for it. Men, this is a fucking war . . . and I don't expect any goddamned prisoners."

With a roar, the team burst from their locker room and took the field. The Ruffians took control of the game on the opening kickoff. The entire kickoff team swarmed the return man, with nine out of the eleven defenders pummeling him to the ground on the Bears thirteen yard line.

Even the quarterback, Ferrone, seemed inspired by his teammates' intensity and at one point in the second quarter did something totally uncharacteristic. He pitched the ball to Davis Green, then turned and threw a vicious block at the head of a pursuing back-side linebacker. The oversized meatgrinders Pike and Sick always gave Green the two or three yards he needed for a first down on a short yardage play up the middle.

Near the end of the game with the team up 27–6, Spike Norris leaned over to Doogie and McGuire on the bench and said, "More like the Midwives of the Midway."

The D-line laughed together. They were having their way with the Chicago offensive line, who in comparison to their own Ruffians offensive line seemed pretty lame. They had sacked the Bears' quarterback three times by the third quarter and tackled the runner for a loss of yards on four other occasions. During the "battle" six Chicago Bears had to be assisted from the field.

Two of these injuries were caused by Max. The first was on a pass play. Max dropped back into the hook zone. The tight end dragged across on an underneath route and tried to catch a pass. Max hammered him and broke his hand. The other play was when Max intercepted the ball and ran it back to the Bears ten yard line. He looked like he had a clear shot at the end zone until one of the Bears receivers caught up to him on an angle. Instead of trying to outrun the faster player, Max dipped his head and careened full-bore into him, knocking both himself and the other player through the air. Max got up with the ball in his raised hands. The receiver lay still, unconscious from the hit.

Standing on the sideline, where his jersey remained bright and clean, Clay heard Tim Tyrone say to his buddy, Spencer Clayton, "I told you, man, that motherfucker is bad."

White's post-game speech was severe, and he seemed unimpressed with the way his team had performed. But Humphry Lyles, who had traveled with the Ruffians, could not contain his excitement and held the charter plane on the ground an extra half hour in Chicago so the flight crew could stock up plenty of cold beer for his players' ride home.

Before takeoff White made an announcement over the plane's inter-com that although of course he would not countermand the owner's pro-vision of beer, he would expect his players to use discretion, since they had a full practice tomorrow afternoon.

"You men have won an important battle," White's voice squawked impersonally over the intercom, "but it's just one battle. We have a war to win, and only a hell of a lot more hard work will get us there. We'll go to the Super Bowl, but we'll have to suffer before we get there. But think about this, for every minute we suffer on the practice field, we'll make the rest of this league suffer twice as much when we meet them on the battlefield. Don't forget, you've got tonight and tomorrow morning off, but I expect you to be ready to go tomorrow afternoon like it was the first day of camp."

The players, pent up for the past three weeks with no reprieve, wal-lowed in drunkenness, scarfing cold beer after cold beer despite knowing that they would have to pay dearly for it in the heat of the upcoming day. White being a hard ass might normally have pissed everyone off, but the Ruffians had been expected to be fodder for the Bears and were so ecstatic at the apparent revival of their sorry team that they looked at White's strictness with respect and admiration.

"Here's to White being a hard ass," slurred a drunken Pete Makozych for the fourth toast.

"To Whitey boy, and his ass," chorused Dan Pike, and the rest of the offensive line as they slammed down their beers.

Clay was slumped in the corner of his row, staring vacantly out the window. He had played a total of seven plays at the end of the game, less than in any contest he could ever remember. Max, who normally sat in the aisle seat, was back drinking and shooting dice with Ralph Scott and Davis Green.

Gavin Collins sat in the first-class compartment with the other coaches and Humphry Lyles. He was even indulging in a cold beer. Gavin looked at Step, who sat next to him poring over the stat sheet. Gavin had to smile. For whatever the reasons, his defense had just crushed the Chicago Bears. It was too soon to be sure, but if they could keep this up, he'd be a hot commodity in the NFL.

Denise was laying naked on the bed, facedown when Clay walked out of the bathroom. He hadn't had sex in three weeks, and the last thing he wanted tonight was to be alone. He'd called her the minute they touched down in Birmingham. He only had about eighteen hours before he had to be back in camp, so it was good that Denise wasn't wasting any time. Clay wanted to do her and fall asleep. He stripped himself in seconds but stopped before lowering himself on top of her. On the dresser he saw a bottle of baby oil. He took the bottle and splashed oil over Denise's back.

"That's cold!" she protested.

"I'll warm it for you," he said in a husky voice.

He worked his hands around her ass, then slithered across her back, covering himself with oil before he flipped her over. He splashed more of the oil across her breasts and belly and began to rub it in. She reached up to him and grabbed hold of his wrists.

"Stop," she said. "Fuck me."

For an hour they writhed and moaned, and Clay forgot.

The Ruffians next faced Tampa Bay. It was one of two teams that had finished behind the Ruffians in the league standings the year before.

"Don't you motherfuckers lose this game tonight," White said through clenched teeth in his pre-game speech. "This team is horse shit. We're no longer in their class. We're champions, and when champions face a horse-shit team, they don't make a game out of it, they squash the fuckers out of existence! I don't want you to just win this game, I want you to punish these fuckers like there's no tomorrow! I want them to hurt! I want them to bleed!"

Despite the muggy Florida heat, White's team played with a fury, and Tampa bled. Eight Tampa players were carried from the field during the game. Tim Tyrone caught two touchdown passes. Sky had three sacks. Davis Green ran for two hundred and eleven yards and three touchdowns. Max had fifteen tackles and two forced fumbles. The Ruffians won 35–3. Clay's jersey remained clean.

Gavin Collins stretched his legs onto the ottoman and eased back into his leather recliner. After the trouncing they had given Tampa, White gave the coaching staff their first night off in over a month. Gavin slept in until seven o'clock, then snuck downstairs to make his wife, Leena, breakfast. While she cleaned up the kitchen, Gavin decided to read the morning paper with his coffee.

"I'll find out what the hell's going on in the world," he told himself, but then immediately turned to the sports page.

"Holy shit," he said with a chuckle.

"What's that, honey?" Leena called from the kitchen.

"Nothin', baby."

The headline on the top of the sports page read: RUFFIANS "DEATH SQUAD" LED BY "MAD" MAX.

The article went on to explain that the Ruffians players had come up with the nickname based on their "body count" and that Max Dresden was their unofficial leader. Most of the article was devoted to Max, his hard-luck background, the tough road he had to the NFL, and his apparent blossoming into an NFL superstar.

"Hmmm, I could live with this kind of press." Gavin murmured to himself when he read his own name in the article. "Sensational it might be, but . . . 'a defensive genius' . . . that could move things along faster than I'd hoped."

Gavin read everything about the Ruffians through to page five. Leena came in and sat on his lap. "What's the frown for?" she asked. "Did you get some bad ink?"

"Hmmm? Oh, no . . . in fact," he said with a smile, "if things keep going this way, baby, you and I could make the big time."

"I thought we were in the big time," Leena said, waving her hand around their extravagantly furnished living room.

"This is big, but there's bigger if we keep doing this," he said, tapping the paper with the back of his fingers. "I'm talking about maybe my own team in a few years," he said.

Leena nodded, "So why the frown a minute ago?"

"Ahhh," he said, "it's Clay Blackwell, he's a damn good kid. I feel bad for him. Look at this . . ."

Gavin showed her a small blurb in the lower corner of page five. The caption read: IS BLACKWELL A BUST?

"Wow," said Leena, "harsh stuff. Your guy too, huh?"

"Yeah," Gavin, said shaking his head.

"Well, if everything else is going so good, they won't hang you for it. It was White and Humphry Lyles who had the final say on him anyway," she said.

"No, I wasn't thinking about myself," Gavin said. "I was just thinking that Blackwell's a good kid, and a hell of a player."

"So what's all this about White calling him a major disappointment?" Leena said, squinting at the page.

Gavin looked up at her for a few silent moments. His eyes told her something wasn't right, but she knew when not to ask questions.

"Just a personality conflict." was all he finally said.

CHAPTER FOURTEEN

THE THIRD PRE-SEASON GAME was at home in Birmingham against the Pittsburgh Steelers. Clay was in the locker room early with Max. He sat at his locker putting the thigh and knee pads in his game pants when he felt Max directly behind him.

"Clay," Max said, rummaging in his travel bag, "I'm not trying to get you to do anything you don't want"—Max pulled a syringe from his bag and held it up—"but this shit will get you into a serious frenzy tonight. I could even tell White that you took some of it, and the fucking guy'd be so happy he'd probably start you. I don't know, I just wanna help you. You can tell me to go to hell. I won't mind."

Clay looked at the needle. Under the bright locker room lights he could see it glinting through its translucent plastic cap. All the self-doubt and emotional pain of the past month resurfaced. Never had he hurt so much or felt so miserable. It was as though White had pushed him into his own little hell. Ending all that pain was as simple as giving himself a shot. One little shot. He'd get beaned up for about six hours and prob-

ably play the game like he'd never played it before. He could see himself, crushing opponents like Max, slapping high fives with his teammates.
White would not single him out. He'd be part of his team. The headlines
would read: BLACKWELL FINDS NICHE, EXPLODES AS RUFFIANS
WIN.

Then his stomach turned. He was disgusted with himself. "Fuck that,"
he said flatly to Max, turning back to his locker.

"Clay," Max said, calm considering he'd just been cursed at, "really, I
don't care. I just wanted to try to help. I hate to see you this way, that's
all."

Max turned and walked away through the still empty locker room.

Without turning toward him, Clay, who now had his head resting in
his hands said quietly, "Max, I just think I can do it without it. Maybe
tonight I'll get a chance. It's not that I think I'm better than anybody, or
above anybody. I just think I can do it without it."

Max stopped and said, "I think you can too, buddy. I just hope you
get the chance."

He made his way into the bathroom, bag in hand. He entered a stall
and locked the door. He pulled down his pants and underwear to his
knees. When the right amount of Thyall was in the syringe, he dropped
the bottle into his bag. He twisted around and grimaced as he punched
the needle into his buttock. The now familiar hotness of the drug under
his skin was almost comforting. He knew it was working. He knew what
it would do for him. He rubbed the spot gingerly, easing the sting and at
the same time working the Thyall quicker into his system. He knew
some players injected it right into a vein in their arm, but that was something he couldn't stomach. He assumed that would give him an instant
rush, but he liked the slow, methodical increase in the feeling the drug
gave him.

He probably could have injected himself out in the open. No one else
was there yet, but he never knew when someone might come. Even if
someone had seen him, he doubted whether it would make any impression on them. Many of his teammates would be doing the same thing
today. Most, he assumed, injected themselves in their rooms before leaving for the game. But Max liked to get the feel of the stadium before he
got himself wired up on Thyall. He also knew that the amphetamine
effect would only last about six hours, and he would hate to chance losing that effect any time before the game ended. Max was secretive

because he knew that was the way he was supposed to be. That was what White had demanded.

Max's behavior since March had been a series of actions that had all pleased Vance White. His career was approaching proportions that he had dreamed of but never really thought possible. There was no doubt in Max's mind as to why he was having the sudden success he was. He had always believed he had the talent to play in the NFL, and now he was being given that opportunity. Still, it was more than just opportunity that accounted for his prosperity. It was Thyall.

Max also knew that the drug was responsible for the team's success. There was no doubt that this team, more than any other Max had seen, was more violent and more intent on winning. There was never a let-down with the Ruffians. Even the skill players who were not using the drug were carried by the emotion of the majority of their teammates who were. Even though it was only pre-season, already those who had seen them play knew that the Ruffians were a new team with a new attitude. No one suspected the real reason why. They were crediting White's rigorous off-season training program that included the entire team. The Ruffians were about to ride a big a wave and Mad Max would be at the wave's crest.

The Steelers, like the Bears, were known throughout the NFL as a team that played football the old-fashioned way—mean, tough, and physical. When they played the Ruffians, the game went back and forth, each team having their share of big plays on defense, and each team scoring ten points. It was the first time the Ruffians were playing at home this season. The stadium was packed with fans, many of whom screamed for the Death Squad Defense by name. Death Squad . . . Death Squad . . . Death Squad . . . went the chant every time the Ruffians defense took the field. It was late in the third quarter when their offense completed a long bomb to take the lead for the first time that night. The crowd went wild.

Clay's black-and-gray uniform wasn't drenched with sweat or soiled with dirt and grass stains. He hadn't played in the game, and the crowd noise, irrelevant to him, made him feel as though he were in a dream. In all his football experiences up to now, the crowd had been a source of inspiration for him. But now he was detached from the energy of the game and had little interest in how it turned out. It was all about whether or not he would play, and if he did, if he'd perform well enough to get himself out of White's doghouse.

Suddenly McGuire, the player who had replaced Clay in the starting line-up, tapped Clay on the shoulder. "Collins wants you," he said.

Clay made his way through a throng of teammates and found Gavin near where the action was.

"Yeah, Coach," Clay said.

"Clay," Collins said, turning to him, "this is a critical time right now. We've got to keep our momentum going, and we can't let them return our score. You take McGuire's place at right end. I already told him, so you just get out there for this series and stay in until I tell you otherwise."

"O.K.," Clay said, his heart now pounding from nerves.

"Clay, I know what you can do," Collins said, looking Clay in the eye. "Just relax and think of your responsibilities and kick some ass."

Collins, busy with many other things, turned away without another word.

Clay buckled his chin strap and adjusted his pads, which had settled from all his standing around. He found Max on the sideline watching the Ruffians kickoff team take the field.

"Max," Clay said to his friend through the din, taken by a fervor that suddenly made him feel a part of it all, "Collins is putting me in with the first team."

When Max turned, Clay saw that his eyes were wide open and on fire with excitement. It looked almost as if Max did not recognize him. The wild look on his face gave Clay an adrenaline rush. He was pumped up to take the field with the Death Squad and Mad Max. As silly as it all had seemed when he was not part of it, now the names seemed to fit Clay's own emotion.

"Time for fucking blood, baby!" Max screamed to him almost incoherently through his mouthpiece. "It's your time, my friend. It's your time to show these motherfuckers what you can do."

Max grabbed Clay by the shoulders and smashed heads with him three or four times, giving them both further rushes of adrenaline. The Ruffians kicked off and three defenders sandwiched the ball carrier on the fifteen yard line. Again the crowd went berserk. Clay and Max and the rest of the Ruffian defense took the field.

Death . . . Death . . . Death . . . went the cheer of the crowd. It was more like a college crowd to chant and cheer. Most NFL stadium crowds were more reserved in their enthusiasm, but until only recently Alabama had known only college football and the fans kept that frenzied atmosphere alive at the Ruffians' home games.

Max called a blitz and the defense broke the huddle. Clay lined up. The ball was snapped and he rushed up field toward the quarterback. He clubbed his blocker and sidestepped him, coming free, but not before Max had shot up through the line unblocked and leveled the quarterback with a crunch that seemed to reverberate across the field. Max was on his feet, both hands in the air, shrieking his war whoop.

"Owwwwwwwww!"

Clay and the rest of the Ruffians defense surrounded him, pounding each other's shoulders and heads in celebration. Clay felt the thrill of being part of it all, and it made him yearn to make a big play like Max had.

Pittsburgh ran a draw on the next play, and the Ruffians defense, expecting another pass, was caught in a blitz. The runner broke through the line and nearly gained a first down before one of the defensive backs could bring him down. It was third and one, a short-yardage play, almost certainly a run.

"Now, let's kick their fucking asses back on this play and make 'em punt," Max implored his teammates in the huddle, and then gave the call. "Okee Bronco Cover One. Ready . . ."

"Break!" shouted the entire defense.

Clay lined up just outside the left end of the Steelers line. Bronco . . . he had to stay outside no matter what. If the ball came his way, it was his job to turn the runner back into the pursuing defense. If Clay let him get outside, he'd have plenty of room to run for the first down.

The ball was snapped and the tight end fired out at Clay. He saw the running back headed his way with a lead blocker in front of him. It was a sweep play right at him. He had to contain. He struck the end with all his might, knocking him backward and off balance. Clay immediately knew that he was in control of his blocker. He had good position to make the outside play. The back dipped to the inside, freezing Clay for an instant. The end, unable to handle Clay, grabbed for his jersey and pulled with all his strength, jarring Clay off balance. The runner saw the weakness created by Clay's awkward position and darted for the sideline, gaining distance on Clay.

In his mind, in that brief instant, Clay could see Gavin Collins in the film meeting. He could see White on the sideline. He could see Max's face in the locker room, the face that had wanted him to succeed so badly. And in that instant Clay knew that he could not fail. He simply could not let it happen, not after all that had happened to him. It was critical that he make the play. The back was already outside him when he dived to his right, throwing his body with all his might and at the same time swinging his right arm like a club, using the full force of his body's momentum as well as all the strength he could muster. His forearm struck the runner directly on the knee cap, leveling him in his tracks.

There was a pop, and Clay saw a flash of white light in his mind like a bolt of lightning. The sound and the flash registered in his brain before the pain. But the pain was soon to follow and it was excruciating. Clay knew that he had hurt himself.

The rest of the defense, in a frenzy of excitement and enthusiasm for the play that would send out the Pittsburgh punt team, rushed toward Clay. They lifted him from the ground and began slapping him and each other in celebration before they realized that Clay was limp. He staggered among them and made his way to the sideline, not wanting to be assisted from the field, as most injured players were. As he stumbled amid his celebrating teammates, he saw Vance White's face. He was actually making his way onto the field to greet Clay. Clay smiled to himself despite the dizzying pain in his elbow. If he had gotten hurt seriously, he had done it while proving to White that he was a player worthy of respect. He could be the player he was expected to be without any help. As he got closer to White, he felt more and more like a hero, sacrificing his body to make a great play that proved his worth as a player. He would be humble to White, and would not try to remind him of his former doubts or animosity. It would be a good way to start over with the head coach.

"You fucking son of a bitch!" White screamed when his face was six inches from Clay's. "Who in the fuck put you out there? I'm the only one that makes changes in my line-up! You almost lost contain on that play, you worthless piece of shit! Who the hell told you you could go out there!"

Clay was too shocked to say a word to White. He just stood there staring dumbly. White adjusted his headphones as if he weren't certain what he was hearing on the other end. Collins, who had heard the tirade through White's microphone on his own headset, informed him that he had put Clay in the game.

"Coach, this is Gavin," he said, "I told him to go in."

White said simply, "I'll settle this with you later, Gavin," and turned to walk away. Then he stopped, turned back to Clay, and said, "You're out of the game, Blackwell, and you don't go back in until I tell you."

Sky and Spike Norris stared uneasily at Clay as White stomped away. From the yelling they heard, they assumed Clay had put himself in the game. It was something everyone knew better than to do. Clay found Sparky and held his limp arm out weakly to the trainer.

"Great play, Clay! That was great!" said Sparky, unaware of what had happened.

"I think I hurt my elbow," Clay said, then plopped himself down on the bench, tears of pain and humiliation clouding his sight.

"Christ, Clay," said his father on the phone, "I've been calling you all damn day. Why didn't you call when camp broke? What the hell's going on with you down there?"

"Hi, Dad" was Clay's only response.

"Hi, Dad? Well, what the hell's going on?" came his father's reply.

"What do you mean?"

"First of all, I haven't heard from you since camp started. That's bullshit. Second, I don't get the games up here on TV, so I check *USA Today* every Monday to see how you're doing and I don't see a goddamned thing. Nothing. No sacks, no tackles, no assists . . . Then today I read that you broke camp and I see you got one tackle this weekend. One. What the hell's gotten into you? I hope all this money hasn't gone to your head, boy. They'll take that money away real fast if you don't start doing something down there—"

"Is that why you called, Dad?" Clay interrupted. "You worried about the money? Let me tell you something, Dad. I'd give all the money I've got to have things going well down here, but they're not."

"So why the hell not?" asked his father irately. "You got a bad attitude all of a sudden?"

"Dad, listen, I hyperextended my elbow, so you don't have to worry about it for at least five weeks."

"What? You got hurt? When?"

"Against the Steelers."

"Well, that explains this weekend, but what the hell happened the first two games?"

"Jesus Christ, Dad, I got my arm in a sling and you want to know why I'm not the superstar down here? I've played eight damn plays the whole pre-season. Did you ever stop to think how I feel?"

"I knew it. I knew you had some kind of attitude now," his father said. "Can't you think how I feel?" he whined sarcastically.

"Christ," he continued, "It doesn't take a genius to see what's going on. No one sits the third pick of the draft unless something major is wrong. But I can hear it in your voice. You got too fucking big for your britches all of a sudden, and they said no way to that. Well, I don't blame them. You got a bad attitude. I can see that—"

"I don't need this. Good-bye, Dad," Clay said and hung up the phone.

"Fuck you!" he said out loud, punching a pillow on his couch. "Fuck off!"

The phone rang again almost immediately, but Clay would not pick it up.

When Clay spoke with Clancy the next day, the news was not what he wanted to hear.

"Why won't they just trade me?" he asked into the phone.

"Clay, listen to me," Bill Clancy implored. "They're not going to do anything with you. They say they have made a financial commitment to you and will see it out for at least four years."

"But why?" Clay demanded. "How can they even want me around here when the damn head coach is calling me a bust?"

"Clay, first of all, White did not call you a bust. Some cracker reporter implied that you might be a bust, which we both know is absurd. White simply expressed displeasure with you, and we both know that has nothing to do with your talents as a football player."

"But I thought when I agreed to drop the whole thing with the drug that White was going forget it too! What happened to that deal? This guy's acting like a total asshole."

"Clay," said Clancy, talking calmly, "White is an asshole to everyone. You're just overreacting to some bad press."

"Bill, I'm not. I'm telling you, you can ask anyone down here, the guy hates my guts. He's tough to everyone, but me he hates, there's no doubt about that."

"Clay, listen to me," Clancy said sternly. "This is professional football. The object is to make as much money as you possibly can, remember? You will have made almost three million dollars by January. Now, don't you think you can put up with a little grief for that kind of money?"

Clay was silent as he digested what Clancy was saying. He wanted to tell him that it was more than that. He wanted to remind him about his last college game, about the crowd that had screamed for him. He wanted to tell him about countless autumn days in backyards with grass-stained knees, days when he'd dreamed of playing in the NFL. The money wasn't even part of it back then. It was playing, that was the dream. But Clay said nothing.

"Clay, I know that right now it's particularly hard because your whole life is football. You just got out of camp, and now to top it off you'll be on injured reserve for a few weeks. But once you get well, you'll realize that what I'm saying is true. Just trust me, Clay. I haven't let you down this far, have I?"

Clay was silent another moment and then said, "No, you're right. I guess if they want to pay me that much money to criticize me and have me sit the bench, then I can take it. I just wish I could get out of here."

"Well, you can't," Clancy said. "So the best thing to do is ignore the bad and think of the good. Think of that house up there on the lake. You'll be back there before you know it. Besides, I think maybe this whole thing with White will blow over. He's probably just giving you a hard time because you're a rookie. He'll get over it. Now, you get some rest and I'll talk to you in a couple of weeks, O.K.?"

Katie checked the clock for the eighth time. It was still 7:59 A.M. She'd sworn to herself she wouldn't call Clay until eight o'clock.

She told herself she wasn't being silly to wait and straightened a picture of the two of them set on her dresser. She knew he needed rest and suspected he'd be happier to hear from her when he was already awake.

Katie knew Clay set his alarm for eight and that these days he always slept until the last minute. He hated to go to the Ruffians complex, he'd told her that. He was like a non-person since he'd been hurt. He'd go in and get treatment from Sparky, then attend meetings that meant nothing to him. His name was never called. He was never on the film. The opponents they watched together were meaningless to him. He wouldn't be facing them. Then he'd have to go outside and stand for three hours watching his teammates practice for the upcoming game. Besides an occasional word from Max, who was always busy during practice, no one talked to him. No one had anything to say. Katie knew Clay even preferred being yelled at to having people act as if he wasn't even there.

"But the doctor said it's only for five weeks," she'd reminded him. "It could have been worse, you could have broken it. Then you might have missed the whole season."

"Everything considered, that probably wouldn't have been so bad," Clay had said dejectedly.

Katie sat on the edge of her bed and placed the phone down beside her. She thought about how training camp had ended the day after the Steelers game. Clay told her White was so pleased with his team that he decided to make his final cuts and get them into the regular routine of the season back in Birmingham. Clay had almost made it to the end, but now he was hurt. She frowned. She was sure things would have gotten better if he had stayed healthy.

Katie knew Clay had gone out with Max last night, and he'd sounded low. She usually didn't call him in the morning because she knew he got up and ran out the door, but she couldn't stop thinking all night about how down he'd been on the phone.

Ahhh! 8:00!

" 'ello," Clay's voice sounded rough. Katie checked her clock again. She was right.

"Hi, honey," she said.

Clay cleared his voice abruptly, "Uh-um, oh, hi! How are you?"

"Hi, how are you?" she replied. "Are we always so formal in the morning?" she teased.

"No, no, sorry, I'm glad you called."

"Well," she said, "I know you've got to run, but I worried about you all last night. You know . . . you sounded so down."

In the background Katie thought she heard a cough. "What was that?"

"What? Nothing. Nothing" came Clay's voice. Then he coughed himself.

"Owwww! Clayyyy, why'd you pinch me?" rang a girl's voice clearly from the other end of the line.

"You son of a bitch!" Katie yelled into the phone. "Who have you got in that room with you! You son of a bitch!"

"Kate, I—"

"How could you, Clay? How could you?" Katie screamed, then slammed down the phone.

"How could he do this to me! To me?" she shrieked to her empty room, pulling her own hair. Her face was crimson, and hot tears began to spill down her cheeks.

She picked up her address book from her night table and flung it across the room. Its pages flapped and fluttered wildly, and it crashed against her closet door. She tasted bile in her mouth and she choked on it, almost vomiting. She threw herself facedown on the bed with her hands over her face.

"No . . . no . . . noooooooo . . ."

Her body shook and heaved in convulsions of anger and shame.

Clay, disgusted with himself and humiliated by the unexpected turn of events, ran into the kitchen, where he picked up the phone and frantically dialed Katie's number, but the phone rang and rang without being answered. He felt like shit.

The Ruffians' final pre-season game was at home against Houston. Clay stood in street clothes on the sideline with the handful of other players who had been placed on injured reserve. Some of them were happy just to be on the team and get paid. Others, like Clay, had aspirations of glory and felt miserable because they weren't in on the action. The sell-out crowd was wild with enthusiasm, and the Ruffians did not let them down.

The locker room after the game was crazy. Reporters were everywhere. Players yelled and shrieked and hugged each other in congratulations. There had been a body count of five. White led the team in a prayer. Clay knelt in the corner near the door with the other injured players.

"Dear God," came White's strong voice, "thank you for the gift of victory. Thank you for letting each of these men know what it takes to be a champion. We know that these past games haven't counted for the record, and we pray that in the coming months, you'll give us strength to rise to the challenge ahead of us, and to rise to the standard we have established in this pre-season . . . in Jesus's name . . . Amen."

"Un-fuckin'-believable," Clay mumbled as he rose and pushed his way out the door.

He was thirty feet down the tunnel when he heard Gavin Collins say,

"Clay! Wait up a minute."

Collins was still in his coaching gear and he still clutched his game-plan clipboard in his left hand. "How you doin', buddy?" he said when he caught up.

Clay looked at him to see if he was serious. "O.K., I guess," he said finally.

"Well, I just wanted to tell you to hang in there. I mean, I know things are tough right now, real tough . . . but stick with it. Injury is part of the game . . ." Collins said, glancing to see that no one else was around, "and stay clean too, huh? I mean, things can only get better. I'm still behind you, O.K.?"

Collins held out his hand and Clay shook it.

"O.K.," Clay said blandly, "thanks."

"O.K.," said Gavin, "well, see you."

He turned and, after glancing around once more, walked away.

Clay watched him go back into the locker room. He stood alone for a moment, frowning. "Don't worry. Don't worry?" Clay said to himself with a bitter chuckle.

"Bullshit," he said out loud, then turned and walked away.

Clay retched in his toilet, spraying vomit on the white porcelain rim. He heaved until there was nothing left, then lay back on the tile floor to catch his breath. He looked up at the lights. They spun slowly around. He blinked. They still spun, so he rolled over and crawled to his knees, finally rising to his feet. He staggered into his bedroom. Out on the coffee table he could see the almost empty bottle of schnapps standing next to an overturned glass. The sight made him start to heave.

He flopped onto his bed and propped himself up against the headboard. He pulled his clothes off clumsily, struggling with his boots. When he was naked, he pulled up the covers and picked up the phone. He carefully punched the number of Katie's apartment.

"Hello . . ." came her voice.

"Katie, Katie, I'm sorry, honey, please lis—"

" . . . this is Katie. I'm not home right now, but if you leave a message, I'll get back to you when I return."

Beeeeeep.

Clay cleared his throat. He tried to clear his mind. "Katie, honey . . . this is Clay. Are you there? Listen, honey," he said, "I'm sorry . . . Katie,

I'm so sorry. I'm sorry, honey. It was a mistake. I was an asshole. I'm a fool. I promise, honey. Just talk to me . . . I need to just talk to you. I promise it will never happen again . . . never . . . honey? Are you there? I start practicing again on Wednesday. I need to talk to you about something. You're the only one I can talk to. Please pick up, honey . . . I'm sorry."

The machine beeped off, and Clay listened until there was a dial tone. He left the phone off the hook and lay back in his bed. He was sick, not only from drinking, but from what he'd just done. It must have been the twentieth time he'd spoken to that machine, and he knew he was beginning to sound pathetic. He was sick of everything. He was sick of his life. He lay there. The room turned slowly and there was a constant buzzing in his ears.

"I could leave," he said out loud. "I could just leave here."

He knew that wasn't possible. It was possible, but he wouldn't. This was what his whole life had been about, playing in the NFL. It was what he'd dreamed of. It was who he was. Everyone from his hometown knew Clay Blackwell. Everyone knew him as a football player. But beyond what everyone else thought, it was how he thought of himself. It was even how Katie thought of him.

"She thinks you're shit," he said out loud to remind himself. "Better face up to it. She's gone, man, so stop makin' an ass out of yourself and stop callin'."

Clay was silent while he digested that idea.

"Hey, did ya hear about Clay Blackwell?" he said aloud suddenly, in a voice that was not his own.

"Yeah," he answered himself, "he's a bust. A fuckin' bust!"

"Yeah, and all that guy had goin' for him too. What a fuckin' loser."

He was silent for a while, thinking and spinning.

"What's a fucking drug?" Clay said. "What's that to me? What do I really care?"

He thought about what it would be like, to have his life back again. To be Clay Blackwell again. He struggled with the idea that Clay Blackwell wouldn't use a drug.

"Face it, pal," he finally said out loud. "Without the drug there is no Clay Blackwell. You don't exist anymore, so it's kind of irrelevant, huh?"

He reached over and fumbled open the night table drawer. He pulled out the phone book and opened it to the yellow pages. B, C, D, P . . .

Paint . . . Photographers . . . Physicians . . . Crowley . . . Adler . . . Baxter . . . Bolton . . . Borne!

Clay tore out the page and threw the book across the room. He laid the page neatly over his wallet on top of his night table. He turned out the light and rolled over to sleep.

On Tuesday afternoon, Vance White was in his dark office watching film of the Raiders, his team's upcoming opponent. His players had the day off, but there were no days off for a coach, not during the season anyway. He saw a big hole in Art Shell's nickel defense and smiled to himself.

"I'll bury that big coon," he murmured to himself, exhaling a big drag from his cigarette.

His intercom buzzed and a timid female voice said, "Coach White, I know you said not to be disturbed, but there's a Dr. Borne on the line and he insists you'll want to talk to him. I didn't know what to do."

"Fine!" White barked, disconnecting his secretary and punching the blinking line. "I don't like telling anyone any goddamned thing twice!" he bellowed.

"Vance, before you say anything, listen," Borne said in a quavering voice, "I know you'll want to hear this . . ."

"Go, damnit!"

"It's Clay Blackwell," Borne said. "He just left my office . . . with the drug! He made me promise I'd tell you."

"You told me. Now don't ever call here again," White said and hung up the phone.

Vance White began running the film again. The orange ember flared every minute or so as he smoked his butt down to a tiny roach. On his last drag he held the smoke as if he were holding his breath, then blew it out through his nose and his mouth, filling the air with his smoke and the maniacal laughter of a prison guard who has clubbed a smart-ass inmate into submission.

On Wednesday afternoon Clay was moved from the injured-reserve list directly into the starting line-up. White gave Gavin the news right before they went out to practice. Gavin had all afternoon during practice to speculate what had happened. It was possible that Humphry Lyles had had enough of White's military bullshit and put an end to Clay's condemnation. But he noticed as practice wore on that Clay wouldn't make eye contact with him, even when he spoke directly to him. Gavin began to fear the worst.

After practice the defensive line had a half hour film session. When it was over, Gavin said, "O.K., you guys, good work today. Tomorrow we're going to work hard on our nickel stunts, so a couple of you guys may want to go over your game plans tonight at home. You know who I mean . . . Sky . . ."

His players busted out laughing and kidded Sky, who took it all in stride.

"Clay," Gavin said as they filed out of the meeting room, "stick around a minute. I want to talk to you."

Clay sat down and watched as his teammates left the room. Doogie and McGuire threw him sidelong glances. It was curious and irritating enough to them that he was back in the starting line-up, and now he was being held after for God only knew what.

When they were gone Gavin crossed the small room and shut the door. Pulling up a chair, he sat down in front of Clay. He had never seen the blank stare from Clay that met him now. Gavin started to speak, then hesitated. Clay sat motionless, waiting. Even his eyes were dull.

"I think it's great that you're back in the line-up," Gavin finally said.

Clay nodded.

"Clay, I want to ask you what happened. You know all along I've been pulling for you, and I've told you what I think of the moral position you took. I admire it. And now with Vance suddenly putting you back on the first team, well, I'm sure it's because Mr. Lyles has had enough of it. I guess I just wanted to hear it from you, I mean what happened . . . I hope you don't mind."

Clay snorted through his nose and shook his head. His smile was grim and contemptuous.

"What's funny?" Gavin asked, annoyed.

Clay sat staring at his hands, turning them over and over as if to find an answer. He snorted again, then looked up. Finally he spoke. "You've got to be kidding me, Gavin, you really do. I've been shat on since I got here. Yeah, you said you were behind me and all that. You even put me in the game that time, but the fact is that when it came right down to it, you went along with this shit just like everyone else. So now I decide to join the fuckin' club and you get off on this morality shit like you and I were in some kind of fraternity together, and we got some secret pledge to be the good guys. Well, before you go telling me the way you think things oughta be, you just remember that you were going along with this shit long before I was."

Gavin's face flushed with anger. "Listen, Clay," he said quietly, "I might be able to do something about this situation for both of us, but not right now. I'm lucky just to be here at all. There's a big difference between having to keep quiet to keep your job and using some drug to make you play better."

Clay chuckled softly to himself, shaking his head. "O.K., Gavin, if that's how you're going to look at it, then you and I really don't have anything else to talk about, do we?"

Gavin sat silently, searching for something more to say. Clay got up and left the room.

CHAPTER FIFTEEN

THE RUFFIANS HAD BEGUN what people were calling a miracle season. At 3–1 the team was creating a national stir, and their game with the 4–0 L.A. Raiders was nationally televised. If the Ruffians could win, they would be legitimate. If they lost, maybe they were just a flash in the pan. If anyone could match up to the Ruffians' physical challenge, experts said it was the Raiders.

There was only 2:47 left in the game. The Ruffians were down by four points and they needed the ball back. Max's eyes were wide. They were crazed eyes and they held the attention of every player in the huddle. The crowd roared for the Death Squad.

"Listen," Max barked, "someone's gotta make a play. We gotta stop 'em here. Third and fifteen, they're gonna pass. We need a big play."

He looked from face to face, stopping at Clay. "You been kicking that guy's ass all game," Max said, leaning his head gear toward his friend. "Can you get us one? Can you get the quarterback?"

"I'll get the fucker," Clay said, spit flying from around the edges of his mouthpiece. "Call a Mac Trailer, and use up the guard for me. I've been pounding this guy's outside all day, and if you can use up the guard, I'll up and under the motherfucker and nail that fuck."

Max grinned. "Keith, if we go Mac Trailer, we'll have to cover man-on-man. Can you guys give us four seconds?"

"Three fuckin' seconds," Clay said, "give me three."

"We got you," Keith replied. The other defensive backs nodded.

"O.K., Mac Trailer Cover Six Man, ready . . ."

"Break!"

Clay walked to the line and eyed the Raiders' offense. Louis Lewis jogged to the line with his teammates. Clay looked up his six-feet-seven, three-hundred-twenty-pound frame and sneered. "Buckle up, mother-fucker," he said under his breath.

Lewis eyed him warily. Clay had been racing around his outside all game and had already gotten to the quarterback several times, even sacking him once. Lewis shifted his weight back on his heels. Clay saw it and grinned. He jabbed his cleats into the earth in a sprinter's stance. His legs quivered in anticipation. His head shuddered. He could feel his heart deep in his constricted chest pounding wildly like some berserk clock. The entire stadium swam in noise. Clay felt like he would explode.

"Make the play. Make the play. Make the play," he mumbled to himself. "Hurt that fuckin' quarterback."

He glanced back. Max was lined up inside of him, grinning wildly.

"Three forty-seven blue . . ." called the Raiders' quarterback, "three forty-seven blue . . . Hut, Hut!"

Lewis flinched on the second hut and Clay sprang from his stance. Lewis lurched, backpedaling to keep Clay boxed out of the pocket. Clay was fast, he was beating him to the corner. Lewis stabbed hard with his long arms at Clay's torso. The shot was strong enough to knock Clay off his feet, but Lewis's hands whiffed through the air. Clay clubbed the giant's inside shoulder with his fist, knocking him off balance and stepping deftly to the inside. The guard was still on the line of scrimmage with Max's helmet buried under his chin. The lane to the quarterback was clear.

Without missing a step, Clay headed straight for him. Like a giant bird, he spread open his arms just as the quarterback saw him. He tried to step away, but Clay's arms wrapped him up. The step saved the quarterback from taking the full blow of Clay's helmet in his ribs, but as

Clay's body rocketed through the air, his arms brought the opponent with him. Clay whipped his body around in midair, almost gracefully lifting the quarterback up and then slamming him viciously to the ground.

Cheers and foot-stamping erupted as though the stadium was falling in. Clay was on his feet, hands raised over his victim.

"Owwwwwww!" he bellowed.

Max came at him first, butting heads viciously, then bursting out in his own war cry. Then came Doogie and Sky and Norris, butting heads and slapping high fives.

"Owwwwwww!" they cried.

Clay jogged to the sideline to the tumult of a crowd that was cheering just for him. The rest of the defense jostled and slapped him as he made his way. Clay looked up at the large screen on the scoreboard. He saw the replay and himself sacking the quarterback once again.

Clay's heavy helmet hung from his hand. He stood at the edge of the field with the rest of his team. He was on edge. The Raiders punted the ball, and Tim Tyrone returned it ten yards to the Ruffians forty-seven yard line. The field position was good, but the Ruffians had used up all their time-outs.

Ferrone dropped back to pass and completed an underneath route to Clayton. They got five yards, but the clock ran down to the two-minute warning.

Clay watched Gavin Collins make his way through the defensive players, congratulating them and saying, "We're gonna win this. We're gonna win this."

The two-minute warning ended.

Ferrone handed off to Davis Green on an off-tackle play, and Green was stuffed at the line of scrimmage.

When Gavin got to Clay, he turned abruptly and made his way back down the sideline to where White and the entire staff had clustered to urge their offense into the end zone for the winning points.

"Did you see that?" Clay said, poking Max in the arm.

"I know," Max said, "I can't fuckin' believe we ran the ball with only two minutes left."

"Not that," Clay said. "Collins, did you see Collins? The guy was hand pumping everyone on the D, then he gets to me, the fuckin' guy who made the play, and he just walks away."

"Collins? Shit, man, we need a touch!"

The offense lined up quickly since the clock was running, and Ferrone threw a wild pass that deflected off the hands of Tim Tyrone. The clock was stopped, but it was fourth and five, and the Ruffians had more than forty yards to the end zone. Ferrone took three drop steps as if to pass, then sprinted up the middle of the line. He got seven yards and the first down. The crowd went wild.

"Holy shit! Holy shit!" Max yelled, pounding Clay's shoulder with his fist. "What balls, a fuckin' quarterback draw! What balls!"

Ferrone lined the offense up instantly. The clock was at 1:18 and running down. The ball was snapped and Ferrone dropped back again. Again he threw a wild ball. The clock stopped at 1:09. The offense huddled. They came to the line. Ferrone dropped back again. No one was open. A Raider burst through the line. Ferrone scrambled. Another defender broke loose in the backfield. Ferrone ran from the pocket, gesturing wildly for his receivers to adjust and get open somehow. Just as the defenders were going to bring him down, Ferrone ducked and doubled back. Pike was waiting for the closest pursuer and laid him out with a vicious forearm to the head. The crowd "ooohed." Ferrone ran all the way across the field and just before he was brought down he launched the ball. Tyrone caught it on the five and was smashed to the ground.

The crowd was on its feet.

"Hurry! Hurry!" cried the players from the sideline. The clock read :54 and was running down. By the time the offense was lined up the clock read :36. Ferrone hiked the ball and threw it into the ground, stopping it at :33.

"They can't run it now," Clay said.

"They can't," said Max, "and I bet they will. White's got brass balls."

The offense broke the huddle and jogged up to the line. Ferrone dropped back, this time five full steps, then sprinted up the middle of line. Raiders flew at him from every direction. He was stopped at the one. The Raiders sat on the pile to keep Ferrone down. Referees frantically tried to clear them out so the Ruffians could get lined up. Ferrone finally popped up. :09 seconds were on the clock,

:08, :07 . . .

Ferrone hiked the ball and threw it into the turf. Three seconds remained on the clock. The Ruffians had one play to win the game. Ferrone ran halfway to the sideline to get the call, then nodding, ran back to his huddle. The Ruffians came to the line. The crowd roared and Ferrone waved his hands down to quiet the crowd so his linemen could hear the count. The ball was snapped. The line surged forward. Ferrone handed the ball to Davis Green, who launched himself through the air.

"Touchdown!" Clay screamed, hugging Max and Norris and Sky all at once.

"Touchdown! Owwwwwww!" they screamed together and jumped up and down like schoolboys.

Players and coaches alike all ran onto the field and swarmed Ferrone and the entire offense. The noise was deafening.

After the reporters had asked the reborn Clay Blackwell their last question, he shuffled wearily to the showers. By the time he got back, most of the team had dressed and gone. Only a few TV cameras remained at Ferrone's locker. Max sat in his locker, wet hair slicked back, waiting for his friend. Clay slumped to his stool.

"Auuuugh," Clay moaned.

Max chuckled. "Coming down?" he said.

"What do you mean?" Clay asked with another moan.

"Stomach cramps, nauseous, itchy skin, general shittiness," Max said.

"Yeah, how'd you know?"

"It happens."

"Yeah?"

"Yeah," Max said, "but you kind of get used to it. I feel it, but it doesn't bother me as much as at first."

"God, man," Clay said, "I feel like I'm gonna die. It hit me all of a sudden."

"You'll be O.K. Coupla beers and you'll forget all about it."

Clay dressed in silence except for an occasional moan.

"You had a hell of game," Max said finally.

Clay pulled his shirt on and ran a brush through his wet hair. He looked around, then smiled. "I did, huh?" he said.

"Damn straight," Max replied. "You like bein' in the land of the living, huh?"

"Damn straight," Clay said.

Monday was a light day for the team. They didn't have to be at the complex until noon, and got to sleep off their hangovers. At twelve was a team meeting where they watched the game film from the day before. When they won, it was a lighthearted, happy event. Their one loss against the Vikings had been like a funeral. After films there was running. Players would go outside with their positional group and run. Collins had the D-line run an easy mile and he ran along with them. After the run was lifting. That was mandatory. White insisted on having the best-conditioned team in the league. Part of that was continual weight work-outs.

Since Tuesday was their one day off during the week, most of the players would meet at some bar to watch the Monday night game. They were usually able to find a place that would give free drinks to the team just for advertising, but the most times they got asked back was twice. Bar owners could get a lot of advertising for the dollars they used up on the Ruffians' bar tab.

Clay and Max arrived together at Sportex. It was the first time either of them had been to the bar.

"Damn," Max said, "I never seen so many hot bitches on a Monday night."

Clay gave a low whistle as a busty redhead strutted by them.

"Let's get a beer," Max said, "I'm buying."

"Why is it you always buy on Monday nights?" Clay said, slapping Max on the shoulder. "You're a hell of a guy."

Before they could get to the bar, Davis Green handed them two cold ones.

"Sweet touch yesterday, Davey," Max said, slapping Green with a high five. "Thanks for the brew."

"Yeah, great play, Davey. Thanks," Clay said.

"No prob, boys. You the ones that did it. We didn't get that ball back, it was all over," Davis said with a sniffle.

"Hey, bud," Max said, "your eyes are a little shot."

Davis grinned at Max and winked. "I'm just feeling good, babe," he said. "How 'bout you?"

"Nah," said Max, "I'll be up all night if I do, and I didn't go to bed until six last night."

"Oh, babe," Davis said, taking a swig of his beer, "you were workin' it last night, I know."

"Nah," Max said, "you ain't gonna believe this. I was readin' a damn book."

"Don't shit me, boy," Davis said.

"No shit, man, *Catcher in the Rye*," Max said.

Davis looked at him warily and said, "Don't bullshit me when I'm high, man."

"I'm not bullshittin'," Max said. "Clay, did you give me the book or not?"

Clay nodded.

Davis broke out laughing.

"Hey, Ralph," he called, "com'ere, my brother. Clayboy give Max a damn book and the crazy fucker tellin' me he was up till six this mornin' readin the motherfucker. Do you buy that?"

Ralph looked down at them all and smiled big. "People do read books," he said to Davis in his low baritone voice. Ralph had his degree from Cornell.

"Yeah, not Mad Max, though," Davis replied, poking the big man lightly in the chest. "You read books. Blackwell read books. Mad Max blow snow, lift weights, play football, and freak till his dick blue, but he don' read no books."

"I win the game for you," Davis said, turning to Max good-naturedly, "git you a beer, an' you fuck with me. Ain't that a bitch," he said and walked away into the crowd, shaking his head.

They all laughed.

There was a crowd around the main bar. Max was trying to tell Ralph what he'd learned from his reading, so Clay slipped away to see what was up. Ferrone was on the bar laying face up while Sick poured a pitcher into his mouth. When the pitcher was gone, the crowd cheered, and Ferrone hopped off the bar, grabbing the nearest pretty girl for a kiss. The crowd cheered even louder.

"Fuckin' QBs get it all," murmured a drunken voice next to Clay. He turned to see Doogie looking sourly at Ferrone, who was still locked up with the girl.

Clay put his hand on Doogie's shoulder and said, "Damn it, Doogie, you're right, and it's bullshit. A guy like you busts his ass all day yesterday in the trenches, makes a bunch of big hits, and what thanks does he get?"

"You ain't fuckin' kiddin'," said Doogie, draining his bottle of beer.

"Hey," Clay said, "You could do that shit man! You could down a pitcher like that. Get up there and down one of those pitchers, Doog!

Don't let Ferrone look like he's something special to all these people here!"

"Yeah, I could drink two of those fuckers!" Doogie replied.

"Go on, man!" Clay said, gently shoving him from behind.

Doogie pushed his way through the crowd and got up on the bar. The crowd parted and Clay called for a pitcher while Doogie laid back, pulling his shirt down over his gut, then putting his hands dramatically behind his head.

The crowd was watching. Even Ferrone came up for air.

"You ain't the only big shot," Doogie announced, lifting himself up and pointing rudely at Ferrone. He lay back and Clay began to slowly pour the beer into his mouth.

The crowd began to chant, "Go Go Go Go . . ."

Doogie gulped down the beer. Clay poured a little faster. Doogie gulped and gulped.

"Go Go Go Go . . ."

Clay poured faster. Doogie worked his mouth frantically. Beer began to spray off his teeth as he gulped.

"Go Go Go Go . . ."

The beer now spilled over Doogie's face.

"Hey, you motherfucker!" he yelled, trying to get out from under the beer. But Clay quickly emptied the rest of the pitcher onto his head.

The crowded thundered with laughter. Girls screamed with delight, and the other players doubled over, slapping their thighs and each other. Clay dropped the pitcher and scrambled away through the crowd. Doogie got to his feet, swinging wildly at the laughter. Pike and McGuire put him in a headlock, and with the help of three bouncers carried him outside before he could hurt anyone.

"Mind if I park here and we walk up the hill?" Andrew Becker asked his daughter.

She shook her head. She didn't mind. He pulled up against the curb, shutting off the engine of his Lincoln Town Car. The cold bit into them as they got out of the warm comfort of the car, but despite the cold it was a pleasantly clear fall evening. They followed the winding road as it climbed up the hill to the dormitories.

"Thanks for having dinner with me. I hate to ruin your Saturday night," Andrew said.

"Oh, Daddy, don't be silly," Katie said quietly.

After a long silence Andrew said, "Wanna talk?"

"I thought that's what we've been doing for the past three hours," replied Katie, without any disrespect.

"I mean really talk," Andrew said. "That's why I'm here."

"I thought you had some business in the city," said Katie.

"Well, I did, but I usually let Mary Anne drive in for work like this. All I had to do was drop off a federal court deposition at a local attorney's home. He needs it for first thing Monday morning, and I didn't finish it until late last night."

"So why did you come?" Katie asked. "I know it wasn't just to take me to dinner."

"No, it wasn't just to take you to dinner. I promised I wouldn't run down here on a whim only because I missed you, although the thought has crossed my mind. It's just that I hate to be away from my girl for too long."

Andrew squeezed his daughter's hand in his own. She stopped suddenly and flung her arms around him, sobbing violently. He stood there simply holding her until her sobs became sniffles. He took a handkerchief from his pocket, and she blew her nose on it. She laughed nervously at the sound of her honking in the silence. A car crept slowly up the hill, and they stepped off to the side until it passed, then began walking again.

"How did you know?" Katie asked her father.

"Well, my first hint was the phone," Andrew said. "You've called less than usual. That means you've wanted to call more, but you wouldn't let yourself. The second hint was what you said—actually what you didn't say—when you did call. Oh, you sounded happy enough, almost too happy, but you stopped talking about Clay. Usually it's Clay did this and Clay said that, and you know that I like to talk about Clay too. So I figured I'd put you to the jury and come down for myself. I saw it in your eyes right away, but I knew if I brought it up at dinner there was no way you'd cry right there in the restaurant. I could tell you needed to cry."

At that she stopped again and, hugging him with her face buried in his chest, began to cry again. "It's horrible," she said, her voice muffled by his coat. "Daddy, it's horrible. He was with someone else. I called and heard her. I never thought that Clay would ever do that. Ever." Her crying renewed.

Stroking her hair, he said softly, "I'm sorry, honey, I'm sorry. We don't have to talk about it. I just want you to feel better, that's all."

"Daddy, I still love him," she said, with an angry sob, her eyes shining with the tears as she looked up at him in the dim light.

Andrew Becker bit his lip. The night hid the redness in his face. "I imagine you do, honey," he said finally.

Silence followed, finally she said, "I thought you'd be mad at him. That was part of why I didn't want to tell you."

"Mad?" Andrew said as if it were the first time he had considered the word. "Yes, I guess I'm mad. Anything that hurts you makes me mad."

He was silent for a moment. He peered into the autumn night sky. "I think . . . I think maybe you should use this to do some thinking, Katie. Maybe you should think about how you really feel about you and Clay, whether he's what you really want."

Katie threw her hands up in the air. Fresh tears flowed in her eyes. "I don't even know what I want," she said, looking to the sky in desperation.

They were both silent. Katie stared through the trees at the lights of the city. "He calls a lot," she said quietly. "But I don't talk to him. I just listen . . . to his messages. I think he's sad. I know he is. He's really sad."

Andrew shut his eyes and said nothing. He knew what she wanted him to say, and part of him wanted to say it, but the other part of him hurt for her, and wanted to prevent it from happening again.

"I don't know what to do, Dad," she said, looking at him for an answer.

"I can't tell you what to do with Clay, honey," he said. "You're the one who has to decide what to do about Clay."

He was trying to hold firm, then he looked into her eyes. She was begging him and he couldn't refuse. "I do think," he said, giving in, "it's always good to give someone a second chance. But I also think you might want to wait till the end of the semester, let Clay miss you, and you do some thinking on your own about what you really want. But take some time, Katie, don't just rush into it again."

"Wouldn't that be like asking him to go on seeing whoever it is he's with?"

"No, not really, Kate. Clay is going to do what he wants anyway, and if this is something that he just needs to get out of his system, then he'll do it whether you talk with him or not. The fact is, if he is going to change back into the person you and I both thought he was, then the fastest way for that to happen is for you to let him think about things a little bit. Don't make it easy for him."

"I can promise you I haven't done that," she said, then took her father's hand and turned to walk again.

They were almost to her dorm when she said, "I think you're right, Dad. I think I'll let Clay think about it for a while, and I'll do some thinking myself, but I probably will give him another chance."

Andrew smiled. "Good, honey, I think that's smart."

When they reached the door, Katie said, "If I ever got back with Clay, do you think people would call me a fool?"

"Some people might," Andrew finally replied. "But I think if you can live with what happened, then anyone who matters to you can also live with it."

"You won't tell Mom about this, will you?"

He shook his head no.

Katie was quiet, and Andrew knew she was very happy with what he had said.

CHAPTER SIXTEEN

MAX LEANED OVER and brushed some lint off Clay's lapel. They were both dressed in tuxedos and seated in the back of a limousine that Max had insisted they rent.

"I don't know why we need a damn limo to go to some fashion show," Clay had said. "I heard this thing was a real bore last year."

"That was last year," Max said. "Trust me. Will you trust me on this? This town is on fire; you know that. Everyone who's anyone in this town will be there, and you and me are gonna pull up in a limo with two hot bitches on our arms. Besides, it's for charity, so we can write it off.

"Clay," Max said in a tone that Clay knew was meant to change the subject, "I heard you on the phone before we left."

Clay looked out the window.

"It's not my business, but I gotta tell you that this bit with calling Katie is getting old, man," Max said in his friendliest manner.

Clay sighed.

"Hey," Max said, "you got the world by the balls, man! You got everything! You're playing great football, you got more money than a bank, you got bitches throwing themselves at you like you're fuckin' Elvis or something. Look, I know how you feel about Katie, she's your college girlfriend, you'll always care about her, but you gotta start livin' in the here and now. Don't let this business with her bring you down. I hate to say it, but it's time to move on, Clayboy."

Clay nodded. "I know, and I'm trying to do it. But I guess I just want to keep trying . . . until I can at least talk to her. I just want to talk to her. I don't know, I can't go on like this forever either, this whoring-around bit. It's fun, but someday I'd like to get back with her."

"Well, my man," Max said cheerfully, "you got time for all that, but right now I'd just keep doin' what you're doin'. You know, grabbing these dumb bimbos and bangin' their fuckin' brains in. You need to stop thinkin' about her. At least until the season's over. When you get back up there, then you can talk."

The car stopped and they picked up Denise and a girl named Linda. The two of them climbed in and began twittering between themselves in the seats across from Clay and Max.

Max leaned over to Clay and whispered in his ear, "This is just what I'm talking about, fuckin' gorgeous, and dumb as two birds."

Twenty minutes later the long black car rolled up to Sammy's, the biggest, swankiest nightclub in Birmingham. A doorman opened the car door. There were hundreds of people waiting in line. They were a festive crowd and cheered as Clay and Max stepped from the limosine.

Cameras appeared from nowhere, their lights blinding them. The girls, excited about the cameras, clung tightly to their dates. After answering a few questions about the evening and the upcoming game, Clay and Max led the girls into Sammy's through the VIP entrance. The people inside were all elegantly dressed. The men all wore tuxedos. Many of the women were in sequined dresses. Sammy's was packed.

Clay whistled. "Two hundred bucks a pop's a lot of money. Can you believe all these people?"

"I told ya," Max said. "They're here 'cause of us. Are you kiddin'? This town would follow this team to the gates of hell. You win football games in Alabama, you're there, buddy.

"Hey, I'll get us some drinks," he said and disappeared.

Clay looked around while the two girls talked. He noticed Ferrone and his two sidekicks had set up in a corner booth and were entertaining some girls and some of the general crowd with a game of quarters. He saw Ralph Scott with his wife and waved at them. Doogie and Sky walked in with their wives. Neither of them were particularly attractive. Doogie looked smart despite his gut, but Sky's pants were too short. Clay turned his head, pretending not to see them. Max reappeared, drinks in hand.

"Hey, Clay, you're not gonna believe this!" he said. "I'm at the bar ordering, and this guy comes up to me an' asks if I'm Mad Max. I say sure and the guy says he wants to give me this vacation to St. Thomas. No shit! The guy owns a travel agency and he says he loves the way I play and he wants me to have this free trip he's got. It's for a week and everything's first-class. I figure the guy wants something, but he says no. He just hands me his card and this envelope here. Can you believe it, man? We're gonna go to St. fuckin' Thomas for free! I told you we were big time!"

"Let me see that," Clay said, taking the envelope. "Hmmm, yeah, it looks like the guy was for real. I'll be damned."

"Of course," Max said with a sarcastic wink, "we'll have to buy two more tickets for you lovely girls. We certainly couldn't go away to some exotic place without our best girls, could we, Clayboy?"

Denise's and Linda's eyes brightened at the thought. Clay rolled his eyes in his head.

"Ladies and gentlemen," came the voice of the M.C. from the main stage, "the Birmingham Children's Hospital would like to thank you all for coming here this evening to help what we all know is a very special cause."

The crowd clapped politely.

"And most especially, let's all give a big welcome to the man who made it all happen, the owner of the first-place Birmingham Ruffians . . . Mr. Humphry Lyles!"

The crowd cheered as Lyles strode importantly out onto the stage. His smile was enormous and he held his arms open to receive the applause.

"Give me a break," Clay said, leaning close to Max's ear as he clapped along with the rest of the place.

Lyles soaked up every last clap before he began to speak. "Thank you, thank you," he said. "This is a wonderful cause we have here, and I want to thank you all for coming tonight. I'm sure you'll all have a very enjoyable time mingling with my players and seeing some very exciting new fashions for you ladies. I had a dream a short time ago, and that dream was to bring an NFL franchise to this great city."

Applause.

"But my dream didn't stop there," Humphry said, raising his voice. "No, my dream went beyond that. I wanted to give this town a winner, and that is what we've got."

Cheers and applause.

"Ladies and gentlemen, I'd like you to look around. You see among you the makings of the finest football team in the country. Let's give our team a hand, ladies and gentlemen, and thank you all for coming."

The people went wild.

That same week, the night before their game against the Eagles, Clay drove downtown in the warm fall evening to the Hyatt, where Philadelphia was staying. He'd gotten a call during the week from his former Northern teammate Cooper O'Brien, the Eagles fullback. Clay had always thought Cooper wasn't too bright, and he'd had little contact with him in college. Clay thought it was almost strange that Cooper wanted to meet him for a beer the night before the game. But Clay knew from listening to his teammates that it was kind of an NFL tradition to meet your college buddies for a drink whenever they came into town. So even though he had never been particularly close with Cooper O'Brien, the novelty appealed to him.

Clay pulled up to the main entrance in his shiny new Porsche. He'd gotten a wax job that same day to make sure Cooper would fully appreciate the ride. Cooper was standing in the front waiting when Clay pulled up. He beeped the horn and waved. The players greeted each other with big smiles. Any bystander would have thought that they were close buddies.

"Hey, Coop!" Clay said. "Hop in."

"Hey, Clay! Nice ride, man, I like this," Cooper replied running his hand over the car as he got in.

They shook hands and Clay roared off.

"I thought I'd take you to one of my favorite places," he said. "It doesn't really move until about eleven, but it's a good place and it's close."

"No problem, buddy," said Cooper. "I just figured we could get together and grab a quick beer. I got bed-check at eleven, so I always make sure I'm back by ten-thirty."

Clay took Cooper to the Acapulco Club, where he knew the parking valets and bouncers would recognize him and be deferential. They went in and sat down at the bar.

"So you guys are havin' a hell of a season," Cooper said, raising a beer to his lips.

"Yeah, thanks, Coop," Clay replied, "you too, you guys are in the hunt."

Cooper nodded. "Yeah, it feels good."

The two of them sat in silence for a while, each of them looking around at the relatively quiet nightclub.

"I told you this place doesn't really get going till eleven," Clay said.

"Oh, I don't care about that," Cooper replied, "I like to take it easy on game night anyway."

Clay nodded. "Yeah, me too."

"So what's up with you guys, anyway?" Cooper said from out of nowhere.

Clay laughed lightly. "Whadaya mean?"

Cooper looked around and leaned closer, "Well, I was talking with Tommy when we played in New England last week . . ." He looked around again and leaned even closer. "And he says that the word is White might be up to his old tricks again . . ."

Clay looked down and took a swig of his beer. "What kind of crazy shit is that?" he said.

"Aw, don't get pissed or nothin', man," said Cooper. "We were just talking. I mean, you know, the way White takes over and your team is all of a sudden kickin' ass. I guess a bunch of guys on the Patriots and Tommy were thinkin' White could be doin' somethin' illegal. I guess one of those guys played for White in college and said he liked his guys on the shit. Plus they said you guys were geeked for their game. That Dresden guy's like a psycho."

"Seldon would think that," Clay said, " 'cause he's that dumb. You think this team could be usin' drugs, man? What about the testing? Even if just a couple of guys were on somethin', don't you think one of them would get caught?"

Cooper looked blankly at Clay. "Man, I feel kinda stupid," he said. "I didn't even think of that. What a dumb thing. Gee, Clay, you know, I wasn't thinkin'. I didn't mean nothin' by it, you know that."

"No, I know that," Clay said. "It just pisses me off that our team kicks the shit out of the Patriots, and Seldon has to start some shit instead of just admittin' that we got a good team."

"Awww, you know how Tommy is," Cooper said, "He don't mean nothin'."

The two of them sat without saying anything for a while. Clay looked at his watch. "Well," he said, rocking back in his stool, "unless you want another one, I guess I should get going back myself. We've got an eleven o'clock curfew too, and we stay at this dump that's twenty minutes outside the city."

"O.K., man," Cooper replied glumly. "Hey," he said brightening as if with a new idea, "thanks for the beer, buddy."

Clay looked at him warily. "No problem . . . no problem at all."

Clay sat at his locker before the game, looking through his game plan. He was dressed in his uniform except for his shoulder pads and jersey and helmet. He began to feel hot. His leg started to twitch, causing his cleated shoe to click click click against the metal of his locker. His skin itched. Without thinking, he reached back and rubbed the sore spot on his ass.

"Fuckin' piss me off," he mumbled to himself. He mumbled a lot to himself before and during the games. He was beginning to feel an anger in him that was just right for playing football. He wasn't nervous; he certainly wasn't scared. He was just pissed off, and he felt like kicking someone's ass.

"Let's kick some fucking ass!" Max cried suddenly.

Everyone looked up. Max was in the middle of the locker room. His fists were clenched and he had no shirt on. Muscles bulged with angry veins in his arms and shoulders and back.

"Are you motherfuckers ready?" Max screamed, spit flying from his mouth.

The faces that met him were angry ones, not at him but angry with him. They mumbled things like "Fuck, yes" "Hell, yes" "Fuckin', A." It was almost time to go out on the field. Every game at this time Max would start cursing and goading them all like the mad leader that he was. He began to circulate around the room. He slapped high fives with Davis Green and Pike and Sick and Ferrone. He shook hands roughly with Ralph and Sky and Doogie and Keith Neil. Max went around the entire room exhorting everyone on the team to fire up. Then he came to Clay. Clay sat still, continuing to stare into his locker. Max reached down and grabbed a firm hold of his shoulder.

"Are you ready too, my brother?" he said in a whisper that made everyone stop what they were doing and stare. It was a bizarre sound, soft and peaceful. It was like the calm before a storm.

Clay looked over his shoulder. He looked up at Max's bulging red eyes and his almost purple face. There were beads of sweat on his brow. His lips trembled slightly.

Clay's mouth pulled back into a sneer. "I'm gonna rip one of their fuckin' heads off and shit right down their fuckin' throat!"

"That's why we're gonna fuckin' win! 'Cause we're fuckin' violent and we want fuckin' blooooooooood!"

Max screamed the words and then began slamming his head into Clay's locker with a terrific force.

Crash! Crash! Crash! Crash!

Clay blinked. Flecks of blood spattered his face. He looked down at his white T-shirt. It too was splattered with blood.

Crash! Crash! Crash!

"Jesus Christ!" Clay said, jumping to his feet. "Max . . . hey, Max, what the fuck?"

Clay grabbed his friend by the shoulders, pulling him away from the locker. Max struggled and Clay looked around wildly for help. Ralph Scott grabbed Max from the front and put him in a bear hug.

"Ahhhhhhh!" Max screamed, his head now pounding harmlessly against Scott's enormous chest.

"Hey, hey, hey, buddy," Ralph said in his booming voice, "ho, buddy, slow down, easy, buddy . . ."

"Holy shit, Max, you're all blood," Clay said.

Max's forehead was cut in several places, and blood literally poured down his face. He laughed maniacally. "Ha, ha, ha, ha. I fuckin' love blood! Owwwwwwww!"

"O.K., you motherfuckers, O.K. I'm O.K.," Max said, shaking himself free from Clay and Ralph. "O.K., let's go. It's time. Let's go."

He rushed over to his own locker and began to speedily throw on his shoulder pads and jersey. His movements were quick and jerky, and he mumbled and chortled to himself as he dressed. Finally he had his helmet on and buckled.

"Let's go, you fuckers! Let's go!" Max cried and charged out the locker room doors. The Ruffians followed.

The Ruffians lost the coin toss. Clay smiled. It was better to start on defense first. It was better to start hitting right away. Standing on the sideline watching the offense always made him sick to his stomach. Clay grabbed a cup of water, drank a little, then swished the rest around in his mouth and spat. The defense was gathered together on the thirty-five yard line closest to where the ball would be kicked. Clay hustled over to the group. They were in a circle with Max in the middle.

"Hey, Gavin!" Max shouted. "Coach Collins!"

Gavin looked over. He was standing between Step and Cody Wheat with his headphones already on. The kickoff team lined up and prepared to begin the game. Max waved his arm frantically. "Gavin!" he said, "come break us!"

Collins broke the defensive huddle before they hit the field for the first time in every game. It wasn't something he had instigated. He always waited to be asked. But one of the defensive starters would invariably grab him or motion to him to come do the honors. Gavin handed his headset to Step and walked over. The kickoff team tackled the Eagles runner on the twelve yard line. Gavin walked into the center of the circle and raised his hand. They all reached in to put their hands on his.

"O.K.," Gavin said, "you guys ready for this one?"

"Yes!" came the cry.

"O.K., kick ass on three, ready . . . one, two, three . . ."

"Kick ass!" screamed the entire defense, throwing their hands down and running as one onto the field.

Vance White was standing on the fifty yard line next to Jim Nelan. White looked out of the corner of his eye to see whether or not Nelan had seen what he had. White stared malevolently at Gavin Collins. He tugged on the brim of his hat and murmured something inaudible. Then he spat out an enormous glob of tobacco juice in the direction of Collins.

Clay was one with the game that day. He felt like he couldn't make a mistake. He thrashed and pounded and assaulted anyone who faced him. He spat and cursed and stomped around the field, hitting with a crazed violence he had never known.

At one point, the Ruffians were winning 17–3 and it was third and eight. Clay lined up and hammered into the offensive tackle, trying to knock him back into the quarterback with a power rush. Just before Clay's man banged into the QB, he threw the ball. Clay turned on a dime and raced down field. It was something every D-lineman was supposed to do, pursue the ball after the pass was thrown, but it was also something that was never easy.

Rushing the passer takes a lot of energy, and it is not unusual for a D-lineman to simply turn and watch the play. But since he'd returned from his injury, Clay felt like his energy was unlimited during the game. He never felt himself get tired, and he never let up on a play until the whistle was blown.

Keith Neil picked off the pass, and Clay turned once again, this time to throw a block. He would always look to throw a block on an interception, that was the rule for all defenders. But on this play he felt like a hunter looking for meat. He didn't want to just throw a block, he wanted to hurt someone. Clay sprinted toward the Eagles' line of scrimmage. There was the center, but Clay passed him up. There was the quarterback, he even passed him up. There was something in his mind driving him on. It wasn't something conscious. Then he saw him. The setup was perfect.

It all happened in less than a second. Clay veered toward the Eagles fullback, who was in hot pursuit and who had the angle to bring Neil down from behind. Cooper didn't see Clay until the last instant, and then it was too late. Clay had accelerated his two hundred and seventy-five pounds to its ultimate speed. With precision timing he launched himself headfirst at his former teammate.

Crack!

Clay heard a terrible snap and saw stars. He rolled over on the ground. He was groggy. Cooper lay beside him in a heap, rolling and moaning loudly on the grass, clutching his arm. Clay's helmet had struck him square in the upper arm and snapped the bone like a stick. Clay hit him so hard that he almost knocked himself out. Clay staggered to his feet and made his wobbly way to the end zone with the rest of the defense, who were celebrating Keith Neil's touchdown.

"Sorry, buddy," Clay mumbled as he jogged, "just part of the game."

The game was now out of reach for the Eagles. They were down 24–3 and there wasn't much time left till the end of the game. But Philadelphia would not lie down. They came out after the kickoff and began to throw the ball, moving down field on the Ruffians' prevent defense.

"Fuck this!" Max said in the huddle after another Eagles completion that put them into scoring position. "We're gonna take this fucker out, and I mean out."

His eyes were popping. "I need a fuckin' body," he said, looking wildly at his teammates. "Clay, you owe me, man. I'm callin' Mac Trailer and I want you to pull the tackle and come inside and pick the guard. I want that QB to bleed!"

Clay nodded.

"O.K., Mac Trailer, with a switch, Cover Nine, ready . . ."

"Break!"

As Clay put his hand down in the dirt, he reminded himself that the game was really over. But if Max wanted a big hit, who could blame him? Clay had his big play already today. He couldn't fault Max for wanting to get one too.

Clay eyed the guard who was lined up inside him. Then he looked at the tackle who faced him. The ball was snapped. Clay shot forward into the tackle, latching onto his jersey with both hands. Clay pushed to get him off balance, then yanked and pulled the behemoth with him to the inside. Max ran straight at the guard to get him to set hard, then just before he hit him, Max darted outside at the same instant Clay came crashing down with the combined weight and inertia of his own body plus the offensive tackle's.

Bam!

The three of them went down in a heap. Clay stuck his head up to see Max swinging around free as a bird and accelerate to lay a hit on the quarterback. The QB saw Max coming and dumped off the ball out of bounds. Max was four good steps away from the QB, but he didn't stop even though the ball was thrown. Clay watched in slow motion. Max reared back his elbow like a plank and fired it directly at the quarterback's head as he crashed into him with the full force of his body. The quarterback went down in a motionless heap.

Max stood and raised his hands.

"Owwwwwwww!"

Yellow flags came at Max from all different directions. Then three Eagles offensive linemen were on him. Max swung crazily. Clay struggled to get to his feet. He grabbed the guard who he had just picked off and swung him to the ground again before he could throw a punch at Max. Clay glanced back. Max was kicking a Philadelphia lineman who had fallen to the ground. Then a swarm of bodies engulfed them both. There was a lot of pushing and shoving. The referees finally got to the middle of it. Three of them along with Spike Norris and Sky pulled Max away from the crowd, and the ruckus ceased. The quarterback was taken from the field by two trainers and a doctor. Max was ejected from what was left of the game.

Clay took two beers from his refrigerator.

"Good party, huh?" he said as he fumbled through the drawer for an opener.

There was no response from the other room. Clay kept talking. "It's always good when ya win, I guess . . ." he said, popping the caps off.

He stumbled into his living room. The girl—he thought her name was Wendy—was nowhere to be seen. "Shit," he said to himself.

Then he heard giggling from his bedroom. Clay laughed and staggered through the doorway. It was dark except for the light from the bathroom. Clay stumbled on one of her shoes, but caught himself and only spilled a little of the beer.

"Wanna drink?" he asked.

"I want more than that," she said in a quiet, husky voice.

Clay's eyes adjusted to the gloom, and he saw that she was on her knees on top of his bed staring at him. Her pink blouse was still on, but that was all. She had let her dark hair down. It fell past her shoulders and spilled into her opened blouse, drawing his eyes down to her breasts. Clay felt a rush in his loins.

He dropped the bottles to the carpet and stripped himself quickly. Her hands were on him before he reached the bed. She guided him into her mouth. He stood at the edge of the bed with his head tilted back. He ran his hands through her long, silky hair. He reached down and touched her breasts. She moaned and he pushed her gently back on the bed. He climbed on top of her and kissed her neck. His lips moved up to her ear, and he smelled something that made him freeze.

"What's wrong?" she asked after a moment.

Clay was silent. In the dark the smell brought a million images to his mind, and they swirled around in his spinning head. It was a good smell. He liked it, no, he loved it.

"What's wrong?" she asked again.

"Nothing," he said. Then he rolled her roughly over onto her stomach.

"Hey!" she said in a feeble protest.

"Quiet," he murmured in disgust as he thrust himself inside her.

Her perfume was the kind that Katie always wore.

Humphry examined the cork and then tasted the champagne. "You can pour," he told the waiter.

Vance White lit a cigar. The waiter looked up at him but said nothing. Even if he didn't know who White was, he did not look like the kind of person you asked to put out his cigar.

"A toast," Lyles said.

The three of them raised their glasses.

"To a new order in the NFL," said Lyles.

Percy Stone took a quick gulp of wine and picked up his pad to jot down what Lyles had said.

"Do you mind if I turn this on during dinner?" he said, revealing a hand-held tape recorder and setting it on the table. "It'll be a lot easier than having to pull out my pad every time one of you gives me a quote."

"No problem at all," Lyles said. "You don't mind, do you, Vance?"

"No," White said, blowing a plume of smoke into the air, "I don't."

Percy Stone looked and dressed like an Ivy Leaguer, right down to his tortoiseshell glasses. White figured he had never put the pads on in his life, and he would just as soon slit Stone's throat as have dinner with him. But judging from the smile that appeared to be almost hurting Lyles's face, he knew it was best to be pleasant. White had been featured in *Sports Illustrated* many times before. It had lost its thrill for him. Still, he had no intentions of raining on Humphry's parade.

"So," said Stone, "how did this all happen? I mean, how did the Ruffians go from the shithouse to the penthouse in just two years of existence? It's unheard of."

Lyles's eyes were brilliant with excitement. He inhaled as if to speak, but then threw up his hands and looked at White for help.

"It's simple," White said, looking impassively at Stone. "It's as simple as where you always find greatness."

Stone couldn't help his mystified look. Despite perennial dealings with football coaches he could never get used to their sometimes strange phrases.

"Greatness is where success is," White continued, "and Mr. Lyles has been a success in everything he does. He knows what winning is about. He knows what it takes. That's as simple an answer as I can give you."

He knew from past experience that one of the surest ways to get all the credit was to give it to someone else. Writers loved to think they were heralding some unsung hero.

"I'm not saying that Mr. Lyles isn't a tremendous success. Of course, we all know he is," Stone said with a smile. "But almost every man who can afford a professional franchise at this level is a success. Still, no one has ever taken an expansion team in this short a time and made it a contender."

"If you're trying to say that it's me, you're wrong," White said, giving them both what his wife would recognize as a false smile. "This is Mr. Lyles's organization. He's the reason."

"Oh, come on now, Vance," interjected Lyles. "I admit that picking you was the best and most important decision I made for my team, but you've got to take credit for what you've done with these boys."

White shrugged and smiled as meekly as he could. The waiter took their orders and poured them each more wine.

"What is it that you've done, Vance?" Stone asked after taking a sip.

"I just believe in old-fashioned hard work and discipline," White said from behind cold and impassive eyes. "I run my training camps like boot camp. I run my game plan like it's a battle, and I look at each season like it's a war to be won."

Percy smiled. This was good stuff.

"But like I said before," White continued, "everything comes from Mr. Lyles. It's his team. He's given me the best facilities and the ability to pick the best staff that money can buy. He went out and got every free agent my staff wanted to sign, and he got every rookie into training camp. That's why we're in the penthouse."

White sucked on his cigar. Deep in the tip of ashes a dull orange ember came to life.

"What we really have," Lyles said, "is something like the Al Davis/John Madden team of the seventies. Remember I talked about a new order?"

Stone nodded. Of course he remembered.

"Well, that's part of what I meant. Humphry Lyles and Vance White are the owner/coach success team of the nineties."

Humphry almost felt embarrassed for the way he was talking. But he knew that he'd have no regrets once he saw it in print. The three of them ate and drank into the evening. With the passing of time, each story the other told about his counterpart became even more flattering and embellished. Finally, despite being nearly drunk, Percy Stone couldn't stand it anymore and he had a cab called.

CHAPTER SEVENTEEN

CLAY WOKE UP ONLY FIFTEEN MINUTES before they started closing down the pre-game buffet. He liked to get as much sleep as possible. The hotel room was empty. Max had awoken over an hour ago and was probably sitting in the dining room reading the paper and having some coffee. Clay drew back the curtain and looked out the window. The weather was damp, the sky gray. He could just make out the Washington Monument through the mist.

"Shit," he said, letting the curtain fall back.

He took a quick hot shower, then wiped the mirror with a towel. He hurriedly brushed his teeth, checking his watch all the while. His hair needed a quick brushing too. Clay fumbled in his bag, pulled out his brush, and ran it through his hair. He set the brush down on the white countertop.

"Son of a bitch," he said, picking the brush back up and holding it to the light. "Son of a bitch," he said again, this time pulling a wad of dark hair from the brush. He cleaned it out good, then ran it through his wet hair again. "Son of a bitch!"

The brush was filled with hair. Clay looked in the mirror and pulled his hair up off his forehead. His hairline looked O.K. He tried to see the top of his head. He couldn't.

"My damn hair is falling out," he said pulling the new hair out of the brush with a stunned look on his face. He looked at himself in the mirror again. He looked O.K. Except . . .

"Jesus."

He noticed for the first time how many pimples there really were on his back and shoulders. He turned as far around as he could, still looking in the mirror. He tried to remember when he'd gotten them all. He knew he had a few zits, most of the guys did. But he was suddenly realizing his whole back was covered with festering acne. He hurriedly pulled on a T-shirt to cover himself. He couldn't remember the last time he felt self-conscious about the way he looked. He started to fuss with his hair again, then he checked his watch.

"Shit, I better get going if I want to eat," he told himself.

Max was right where Clay thought he'd be. Clay filled a plate with toast and eggs and fruit and two baked potatoes just before the waiters took away the trays. He sat down next to Max and poured himself some orange juice. Max looked up from his paper.

"You ready?" he asked. "It says here that their O-line is concerned with your outside pass rush, but they think the Hogs can handle you as far as the run game goes. What a crock of shit! I bet they don't get a hundred yards on the ground today, even though they prob—"

"Max," Clay interrupted, "I gotta ask you something."

Max looked at his friend. Clay looked around then leaned closer.

"Is your hair coming out or anything?" Clay said.

Max set the paper down. He too looked around. One of the waiters asked Clay if he would like coffee. When he'd gone, Max said, "Yeah, of course. You're gonna lose a little hair with this shit, but it's no big deal. I'm thinned out a little, but it's not like I'm bald or anything."

"Could you go bald? Could I go bald, I mean?" Clay said.

"Well . . ." Max said, "I guess you could . . . not that you will. I wouldn't worry about it. Most guys I've known lose a little hair, it's no big deal."

"Most guys . . . but did anyone ever lose all their hair, or go bald up top?"

"Come on, man, we got a big game today," Max said. "What the hell are you worried about this all of a sudden for?"

" 'Cause I just noticed it, that's why," Clay said. "I'm standing there in the mirror, and I notice all this hair in my brush. Then I look in the mirror and I realize that my whole back is zitted out. On the way down here in the elevator I started feeling my balls to make sure they didn't start shrinking on me."

Max laughed with delight, "Ha, ha, ha . . . you're worried about your damn balls . . . relax, will ya? Whatever happens won't last. A couple months after the season you'll be back to normal, so I wouldn't worry about it."

"Yeah," Clay said, "but what about next year? They'll want us training with this stuff in the off-season too, you know."

"Sure, but not right away," Max replied. "They'll have us take a couple of months off to give it a rest before they kick back into high gear. We won't start hitting the weights hard until about April. Come on, man! We got a game today. This is a big one!"

Clay ate his meal in silence.

The team bus took them past the Capitol and the Supreme Court. The drizzle had turned to rain. Clay rested his head against the window. Every minute or so he'd wipe a clear spot on the steamy glass to get a better view of the city. Max was right. Today was a big game. The Redskins were 7–1, one game in front of Birmingham. A win for the Ruffians would put them in a good playoff position; a loss would put them behind the Redskins, Giants, and Falcons. But as big as this game was, Clay was distracted by his experience with the hairbrush. He was sick over it. He didn't want to lose his hair. He was only twenty-two years old! He ran his hand over his head. Without thinking, he put his hand inside his shirt and picked at a scab on his shoulder.

When the bus arrived at the stadium, Clay hurried through the rain and into the stadium tunnel. He shivered from the cold and stamped the water off his shoes when he reached dry concrete. The locker room was damp. It made him think of a basement that had been cheaply remade as a living space. The carpet was worn and the cinder-block walls were painted with a thick blue paint that had begun to chip. The sour smell of the place made him wish he were anywhere else.

Clay sat down and began to stuff his pants with the appropriate pads.

Davis Green had a boom box a few lockers down, and Clay's leg jiggled involuntarily to the rap. When his pants were ready, Clay checked the air in his helmet and tugged the straps on his shoulder pads to make sure they were snug. Next he pulled off his socks and went in to have Sparky tape his ankles. When they were bound tightly with white medical tape, Clay returned to his locker and discreetly shoved a vial of Thyall and a fresh needle from his bag into his pocket before heading to the bathroom. When he got halfway there, he stopped.

"Damn," he said to himself, "I don't want to use this shit. I don't feel like it, I really don't."

He continued to himself, "I feel like shit. But maybe that's exactly why I should take it. If I feel like shit, I'll probably play like shit. It'd be tough to run wild out there all afternoon without a little juice."

Someone put their hand on Clay's shoulder, and he turned around to see White standing there. "You don't look too ready to play," White said. He was smiling like a shark.

With a solemn face Clay said, "I'll be ready."

"Good, we need you," White said, patting Clay roughly on the shoulder before walking away.

The steamy mist that seemed to be rising from the field was actually a low cloud cover. It obscured Clay's vision. He wiped a clod of mud from his cheek with a cold, wet finger. His heart hammered in his chest. It was almost frightening how fast it was beating, but Clay didn't have time for fear. He was in a dog fight. Washington had one of the biggest and most physical offensive lines in the league, and his bad elbow was acting up. He'd caught it between the guard and the running back one play and hyperextended it against the joint. The cold and wet probably did nothing to help. Clay was a wounded animal driven to fury by his pain.

"Fucks! Fucks and shits!" he cursed.

"What's that?" Keith Neil asked him as they both joined the huddle.

"These motherfuckers, that's all," Clay said with a wave of his hand.

The Ruffians were down by six points and it was late in the third quarter, but the Redskins were backed up deep in their own territory on the four yard line.

"O.K., O.K., O.K.," Max said, "huddle your asses up! That was a hell of a play, Sky . . . Now listen to me, we can't let these fuckers out of the hole. We got 'em where we want 'em, third and long. We make this play and we get a rest while our offense shoves it up their ass for the lead."

He looked over the bowed heads of his teammates at the sideline. Gavin Collins made a series of hand motions, and Max said, "O.K., Blue Hornet Blitz Cover Six Man, ready . . ."

"Break!"

Clay thought quickly of what his assignment was. Blue Hornet put him in a stunt with Spike Norris. On the snap, Clay would crash down inside at the guard. Spike would take a jab step at the center, then loop around to Clay's outside. The outside 'backer would use up the tackle with his blitz, and if the running back blocked weak to cover the other outside 'backer's blitz, Spike would come free. That is as long as Clay wiped out the guard.

"I can take this fucker out," Clay said to Spike as the Redskins broke their huddle and approached the line. "So if you want, you can bag the jab step and come right away."

Spike looked at Clay. His face was muddy and blood streamed freely down both sides of his nose from a split in his skin directly between his eyes. Spike smiled. Even in the gloomy mist his gold front tooth gleamed.

"My man, you get me a sack and I'll buy you a cold case," Spike said.

The Redskins were at the line. Clay put his fingers on the ground, and they sank into the mud up to his second digit. He wiggled his feet down into the slop to try to get some kind of traction. He snorted and blew a wad of snot from his nose that stuck to his mask. The center wagged his head from side to side, assessing the front, then barking out the protection scheme. The quarterback checked the secondary alignment and started his cadence.

"Red sixty-seven . . . red sixty-seven . . . down, hut hut hut!"

Clay exploded from his stance, spewing mud in all directions. He hit the guard like a freight train, grabbing tightly onto his jersey at the armpits. There wasn't much cloth to grab, but Clay got hold of some skin, which made the guard all the easier to pull with him. Clay was aware that Spike's form was looping outside of him. The center, not slowed down at all without Spike's jab step, was waiting for Clay and he dived with all his might into Clay's knees. He felt his legs go out from under him. His right hand slipped off the guard, who was trying desperately to pull free so he could get a hit on Spike, but his left hand held true and the guard tumbled over with him. Clay was sandwiched between two players and lying face up in the cold mud. From the corner of his eye he saw Spike crash into the QB, but not before he had dumped off the pass.

Most players would have still been on the ground, but Clay was already in motion, twisting to free himself from the pile and scrambling to his feet despite the slop. The pass was complete to the tight end, and as Clay accelerated down field, he saw Max hurl himself at the Redskin receiver from behind. A deft cut left Max nothing but air. The tight end straight-armed Keith Neil, who'd lost his footing. Neil fell uselessly to the ground, leaving only a cornerback between the tight end and eighty-five yards of open turf. The cornerback dived at the tight end's feet, trying to bring him down by taking out his legs. It wasn't enough to bring him down, but it was enough to slow him up. Clay churned toward him and slammed into him from behind with such a violent hit that the tight end's head whiplashed back and the ball popped free. Doogie, who was also in hot pursuit, dived on the ball and slid ten feet with the ball in his hands, all the way to the Ruffians' sideline and out of bounds.

Clay got up and raised one fist. "Owwwwwwww!" he cried.

His teammates hit him like a wave. They had seen the hit. The tight end was still lying at his feet.

"Owwwwwwww!" they cried, slapping Clay's hands and shoulders.

Max raced up and slammed his helmet into Clay's, butting heads again and again. The Ruffians made their way to the sidelines amid the cheering offensive players who were taking the field. Everyone wanted a piece of Clay. The crowd was almost silent. Clay could clearly hear his name being announced as the one who'd made the tackle. Doogie strutted up and down the sideline with his recovered fumble raised in one hand over his head.

On the sideline everyone took the opportunity to shake Clay's hand and tell him, "Great play." The offense ran the ball on the first play and gained four yards. The clock ran out, ending the third quarter. There was a time-out on the field and everyone on the sideline relaxed. Clay went to the bench and pulled a rain poncho over his helmet and shoulders. He got a cup of water from the drink table and swished the mud out of his mouth. When he turned around Gavin Collins was standing in front of him. Gavin was bundled in rain gear. His hood covered the large headphones he wore, and the only thing on him that seemed to be wet was the brim of his hat. Gavin looked at Clay coolly, reaching past him for a cup of Gatorade.

"Nice play," Gavin said.

"Thanks."

"Ya know," Gavin said, "you could've made it even if you didn't stick that needle in your ass."

Clay wasn't going to say anything, but Gavin lingered.

"What do you care?" Clay said finally.

Gavin put his hand on Clay's forearm and gave it a firm but gentle squeeze. "I care," he said, then turned away and headed toward Step and Wheat, who were conferring with each other on the edge of the field.

There was only a minute to go in the game. Clay's play had enabled the Ruffians to take a one-point lead, and they'd held it through the entire fourth quarter. The Redskins had the ball on their own thirty yard line. The clock was stopped. It was third and ten. Gavin looked down at his clipboard. He needed something good, but something they hadn't used all day. He signaled a Lightning Safety Blitz out to Max. The Ruffians defense broke their huddle at the same time as the Redskins. The crowd roared for their team to get into field goal range. Gavin changed his mind. He gestured frantically to Max. He yelled at the top of his lungs. Cody and Step saw what he was trying to do and they joined in. No one could hear them.

The quarterback started his cadence and the ball was snapped. Gavin leaned toward the field, willing his line to get to the quarterback. The Redskins picked up the blitz.

"Shit," Gavin said as the unmolested QB launched the ball through the air. He heard White curse at the same time over his headphones. The tight end was wide open across the middle, and the ball was headed straight for his numbers.

Max flashed like a bullet from nowhere and struck the tight end just as he reached out and grabbed the ball.

Whack!

Gavin heard the sweet sound clearly from the sideline and watched the ball bounce harmlessly to the ground.

Yaaaaaa!

Gavin had to lift the headphones away from his ear. His fellow coaches had erupted with joy. The phones slipped down over his ears and around his neck. Gavin looked down at his clipboard. Fourth and ten, late in the game . . . Gavin had plotted every possible game situation during the week and gave himself a group of the best alternatives from which he could quickly choose from. He looked wildly around him.

"Prevent!" he yelled to the players around him.

"Prevent!" the players yelled to each other as three extra defensive backs ran out onto the field to replace two linebackers and one defensive lineman.

Gavin signaled in Zone Pinch Man Under to Max. The Redskins were already approaching the line in an attempt to take advantage of the Ruffians' confusion from the late substitution. Max quickly broke the huddle and the Ruffians scrambled for their positions. The Redskins were already at the line.

A hand grabbed Gavin by the shoulder and spun him around.

"God damn it to hell!" White, red in the face, screamed at Gavin above the cheering crowd. "I told you to run that blitz again and you fuckin' send out the prevent!!! Who the hell do you think you are, Collins?"

Gavin was baffled, but nothing could keep him from turning his head away from White to see the play. The quarterback was back in the pocket with what seemed like hours of time. Finally he chose his target and launched the ball. Keith Neil, who was the man under in the zone, leapt up and picked the ball from the air before it could reach the receiver. He tucked the ball and ran it down to the five before one of the Redskins offensive linemen brought him down. The crowd went dead. The Ruffians sideline exploded with cheers. They had won the game. Gavin turned back to White. He had also watched the play.

White turned his attention back to Gavin. As much as he tried, Gavin couldn't keep the grin from his face. White's brow furrowed and his face grew dark.

"Don't you ever . . . and I mean ever, countermand an order of mine. You—you—I'll have your ass on a fuckin' stick!" White said and quickly turned and stalked off.

"Good Lord, Gavin," Step said in his ear, "didn't you hear the man calling for the blitz? That took some balls . . . but I gotta admit, you made the right call."

The next day the phone rang just as Clay was heading out the door. He thought it might be Max calling to tell him to come on, so he picked it up.

"Whaaaat?" he said into the phone.

"Clay?" came the gruff voice at the other end of the line.

"Oh, hi, Dad," Clay said. "I thought you were Max. I'm late picking him up."

"Goin' out for a little celebration, huh?" his father said. "Big win requires a big party . . . but I know you got a few minutes to talk to your dad. You had a hell of a game yesterday, son. I was damn proud of you. I tell you, you're playing the best ball of your life. I knew that money wouldn't go to your head. And what a team! I swear, you guys go at it the way we did back when I played: tough, mean, physical, some real ass-kickers . . . I love the way you guys hit. You got some coach in that Vance White, the guy's a genius. I think everybody and their mother saw the game up here. I couldn't pay attention to shit on the line today. I fucked up at least two water seals on some suckers' windshields, I can tell you that. But hell, every other minute somebody's comin' up to me on the line and tellin' me how good my kid did. Even the damn boss said somethin' to me!"

"That's great, Dad," Clay said out of respect.

"Yeah, I told 'em all that's why you're gettin' the big money, 'cause you win games. That's what you always did, I told 'em. I told 'em I taught you how to strip the ball carrier when you was just a little guy. Remember that? When I used to tell you to strip 'em when you tackled 'em. It paid off yesterday, by God."

His father chuckled good naturedly to himself. "Uh, Clay . . . there's somethin' we gotta discuss sometime."

"Yeah, Dad?"

"We gotta talk about that business deal I was tellin' you about, you know? When would be a good time to talk about that? Pete and Joe and me are real hot to get started. I tell ya it's a hell of an idea. It's not really any risk for you either. We'll pay you back first thing, and the way I got if figured we can get your money back in less than six months, no kiddin'."

"Dad . . . Dad. Listen," Clay said as patiently as he could, "you and I are gonna sit down and talk about this, but you gotta wait until I get home from the season. I wanna have time to really talk about what you got in mind and see what you got down on paper, O.K.? You told me yourself I gotta be focused in on football, right? You taught me that, otherwise I probably wouldn't even be here right now, you know? So just let me say a quick hi to Ma and go get Max. He gets crazy when I'm late. O.K.?"

There was silence for a moment, and then Mr. Blackwell said, "Yeah, you're right, son . . . and I told those guys that I didn't want to bother you about it right now. I don't know why I let them push me into it. I'm just thinking it would be good to make some extra cash so I could do some nice things for your mother, but we'll talk about all this like you said, when you get home, huh?"

"Thanks, Dad," Clay said, "and thanks for calling."

"O.K., son, here's your mom."

"Clay?"

"Hi, Mom! It's good to hear you."

"It's good to hear you too, honey. Did you get my package?"

"Oh, Ma, I'm sorry I didn't call you! The books are great. I love them!"

His mother cleared her throat, "Well, I'm glad . . . Have you heard from Katie?"

Clay rapped his keys on the countertop. "No, I haven't spoken to her in a while, Ma," he said.

"I'm sorry to hear that, Clay, I know how much she means to you. I don't know what happened, but I'm sure things will work out between you, and when you do speak to her, tell her to give me a call. I miss seeing her."

"O.K., Ma."

"Well, your father's telling me you have someplace to go that you're late for, so I'll get off now and don't worry about calling us, you just have a good time with your friends. I love you, Clay."

"I love you too, Ma."

CHAPTER EIGHTEEN

CLAY TOOK A BIG BITE out of the ham-and-cheese sandwich he'd
made for himself and washed it down with a gulp of Heineken. A blonde
with a perfect shape walked up to the buffet table and smiled at him. She
was wearing a white halter under a short leather jacket and a short, tight
leather mini-skirt. Her face was tan and beautiful. Clay stopped in the
middle of his second bite to smile. Mayonnaise oozed from his grin and
the girl giggled. Clay laughed too.

"Kinuff a slov, huh?" he said, lettuce spilling out of his mouth.

"Are you a bodyguard?" she asked him.

"Me?" he said after swallowing. "No, I'm a football player. But my best
friend on the team is good buddies with Johnny Zero's bodyguard, and
he got us backstage passes."

"A football player? Who do you play for?" she asked.

"I play for the Ruffians."

That drew a blank stare.

"I don't know much about football," she said. "I know the Ruffians, but

I don't know who you are."

"That's O.K., I like girls who don't like football," he said. Then to himself he said, "You'll say anything."

Max appeared suddenly with a brunette on his arm. "Gina, these guys are football players," Max's girl said.

"I know."

"You two know each other?" Max asked.

"Susan and I are VIP hostesses," Gina said haughtily. "We usually work here for all the big concerts."

"You know Simon?" Max said.

"Yeah, I know who you mean," said Gina, "the big black guy . . . he seems cool."

Max gave the girl a wolfish smile and said, "You two should come over to my place tonight. Johnny and Simon, and I think most of the band, are coming."

"Johnny Zero? Really? The whole band?" Gina said, caught off guard.

Clay looked at Max and said, "Really?"

Max nodded and pulled Susan closer.

"Gina, this is Mad Max," Susan said, putting her hand on his chest, obviously impressed.

"And this is Clay Blackwell," Max said, introducing Clay to both of the girls.

"Come on, Gina, you've heard of the Death Squad Defense," Susan said.

"No, I haven't," Gina said.

Susan waved her hand. "Aw, she just doesn't like to be impressed."

Gina's face turned red.

"There's nothing to be impressed about," Max said humbly. "We're just a couple of football players out having fun with some friends. So you two will join us?"

There was a rush of screaming and cheering outside the room, and the long-haired Johnny Zero made his way through the door with Simon close behind him, pushing people who weren't part of the band back outside. When the last member of the band had gotten inside, Simon and a couple of other lugs shut the door. Johnny Zero sandwiched himself between two girls on one of the enormous overstuffed couches. Simon grabbed a beer from a tub of ice and walked over to the buffet table.

"Damn!" Simon said to Max. "Reminds me of Saskatchewan."

"I don't remember you pushing anybody around like that on the football field," Max said.

Max and Simon laughed together.

"Simon," Max said, putting his hand on the huge man's shoulder, "you met my buddy Clay. This is Susan and this is a not-so-impressed Gina."

"I seen these girls," Simon said. "Very fine."

"Well," Max said, "we're still on for my place, right?"

"Yeah," Simon said, "Johnny said he couldn't wait to meet you guys. You saw him wearing your Ruffians T-shirt with the skull 'n' dagger, didn't you? The crowd loved it . . . went ape shit. Johnny likes that. Come on over, you gotta meet the guys. They'll want to have a few beers here, then we'll hop on the bus and head on over."

"The whole band?" Clay couldn't help saying.

"Why not?" Simon said with a shrug and led them over to the band.

"Holy shit, Max," Clay said. "I can't believe this! I really can't believe this! Zone Seven! I really can't believe this!"

"O.K., so you can't believe this. What else?" Max said, steering his car onto the freeway. "What did you think I had you help me move all my furniture around for and get all that beer? Did you think I was doing that for my health?"

"No, I just can't really believe they're really coming over to your place," Clay said. "I love this band! I listened to these guys all through college, and I never thought I'd be hanging out with them. It's just unbelievable."

"Yeah, well, speaking of unbelievable," Max said, "how about those two bitches? Did you see the tits on that Susan? I'm all over that, man, I can tell you right now."

Clay seemed not to have heard him.

"Johnny Zero," he said quietly to himself, "I can't believe it."

When Clay was good and drunk, he got up the nerve to talk to Johnny Zero. Johnny was now on Max's couch with the same two girls he'd seen him with at the concert.

"Hi, Clay," Johnny said in his Australian accent, shaking Clay's hand but not getting up. "Ya met my wife, Julie, an' my sheila, Nan, right?"

"Yeah, hi," Clay said, nodding to the two women. He couldn't believe Johnny had remembered his name. "I just wanted to see how you were doing. I don't know if I told you at the concert, but me and my buddies in school listened to you guys all the time."

"Well, I thank ya for that, my man," Johnny said. "I gotta admit, I'm kinda a fan o' yours too. When I got 'ere from Australia two years ago, I wanted me a football team ta root for, an since the Ruffians an' my band got the same logo, well, I figured it was meant ta be, eh?"

"Yeah," Clay said, "definitely. It's perfect, huh? That T-shirt looked great. Well, hey, it was really nice meeting you, Johnny, and both of you too."

"Right, Clay, nice meetin you, mate."

Clay smiled and shook hands with the rock star, then faded back into the crowd. When he got safely across the room he looked back to see what Johnny was doing. He was kissing his wife, or his girlfriend, Clay wasn't sure. Clay finished what was left of his beer and looked around for Gina. He was pretty sure he had her, but he had to make sure one of the band members didn't get a clean shot at her or he might be out of luck.

Clay was pushing his way through the crowd toward the kitchen when Susan burst out of Max's bedroom. "Make some toast! Make some toast!" she screamed frantically. Her hair was disheveled and she was dressed in just her bra and panties. She was raving and pushing her way toward the kitchen. "He's bugging out!" she screamed. "Somebody burn some god-damned toast!"

Clay stood staring dumbly with almost everyone else. One of the band members, Clay thought the bass player, pulled some bread from the refrigerator. He ripped right through the wrapper and jammed the bread into the toaster. Clay found his legs and pushed past the dumb crowd into Max's bedroom.

"Oh, my God," Clay said.

Max was lying face up on the bed in his underwear. He looked like he was having some kind of seizure. His body was rigid and his hands were twisted up like a praying mantis. Max was moaning something incoherently. His eyes were bugging out of his head. Clay had no idea what to do. He ran to the bed and put his hand on Max's shoulder.

"Are you O.K., buddy? What's wrong?"

"My friend's dying," was all Clay could think, "and I'm standing here like an idiot."

The bass player rushed in with Susan close behind him. He had two pieces of black toast in his hand and he began jamming them into Max's mouth. Susan was at Max's feet, sobbing hysterically. Max chewed and coughed. The bass player continued to feed him the disgusting toast. Clay stood watching with his mouth open. It seemed like forever, but in a few minutes Max began to relax and come around. Susan stopped sobbing and only cried quietly.

"What happened?" Clay said to her.

"Jesus, he almost O.D.'ed," she said to Clay, pointing to a half-empty glass of orange juice on Max's bed table.

"What?" Clay said.

"We were drinking it," Susan said still crying, "drinking the coke . . ."

"That's why the toast, mate," the bass player said, looking up from his patient. "The cha'coal from tha burnt toast absorbs tha cocaine an keeps ya alive if ya get it quick enough."

The bass player smiled at Clay. Max looked up at Clay too, black crumbs stuck about his face. Clay reached down and brushed the worst of them away with a discarded T-shirt. Max smiled weakly.

"What's up, buddy?" Max said sounding sick.

"You gonna make it?" Clay asked.

Max nodded. "Yeah, I'm O.K.," he said weakly.

Then to the bass player Clay said, "Is he O.K.? Should we take him to the hospital or something?"

"Naw," said the musician, getting up from the bed, "I seen a lot worse than 'im. 'E'll be fine if 'e sleeps it off."

Clay looked down on his friend.

"I almost bought the fuckin' farm there, buddy," Max said in a strained voice. "That's it for this guy. That's the last snort. I'm through with coke, man. I'm through . . ."

"You gonna stay with him?" Clay asked Susan.

Susan nodded and began covering Max with the blanket.

"He's gonna be O.K.?" Clay said again.

"He'll be O.K. now," Susan said, "I'll take care of him."

"Go ahead, Clay," Max said, "I'm all right. I just gotta get some sleep. I'll be O.K., I'm fine."

Clay shrugged. "All right," he said. "Call me in the morning when you get up?"

Max nodded.

"Susan," Clay said, handing her a scrap of paper, "here's my number in case anything happens tonight."

When Clay got back to his apartment, he handed Gina a wine cooler from the fridge and told her to sit down and make herself comfortable. He flicked on MTV and glanced over his shoulder at her before he went into his bedroom.

"I'll be right out," he told her, then shut the door and turned the lock quietly.

Clay dialed the phone. It rang four times. The machine picked up. Clay waited for the beep.

"Katie . . . are you there? Katie, come on . . . it's me, you've got to talk to me sometime . . . Katie? Well, maybe you're out . . . anyway, I was with Zone Seven tonight and I thought of you. I can think of so many good times we had with these guys on the radio. I was just hanging out with Johnny Zero, and he's just a regular guy . . . Well, anyway, Max and I went to their concert and they all came over to Max's after and the whole time I kept thinking of you . . . well . . . I just want you to know that I'm thinking of you. I miss you, Katie. I want to talk to you sometime. I'm still sorry about what happened. If I got the chance it wouldn't happen again, really. This must be getting kind of old, hearing me on your machine all the time. Well . . . I still love you, Kate . . . bye."

Clay hung up the phone. He sat thinking for a while. He yawned and remembered Gina was outside. He considered calling for her to come in, but decided it wasn't nice, so he got up and walked out of the bedroom to get her.

Humphry Lyles sat alone in his office. It was late and there was no one else to be found in the entire building. Beside his desk sat a box full of magazines. He'd sent his secretary out, and she'd gotten about fifty of them. On his desk were five of the fifty. They were all laid out, each one to a different page. The first one was just the contents, which had a small version of the picture that particularly pleased Humphry. The other four made a sequence of pages that constituted an article entitled THE NEW AGE OF THE NFL.

Humphry got up and poured himself a scotch. He stood over the desk, examining the words and pictures from this new perspective. He laughed out loud and gazed up at the painting above the fireplace.

"Who would have guessed it?" he asked the empty room, raising his glass to the painting of the dilapidated storefronts from his childhood.

"I love it," he said out loud, holding up the pages of the article at arm's length. "I really love it."

It was the first picture that kept luring his gaze back again and again. In fact, it was the picture that had kept him in his office until such a late hour. It showed him and Vance White standing together, with their backs against a goal post. White was in coaching gear. Humphry was dressed in a suit and tie, looking like the quintessential owner. White looked hard. His jaw was set and he wore a slight frown. Humphry fancied that he looked hard himself.

"I guess I do," he said to himself.

The shot was taken from a lower angle. Humphry looked every bit as tall as White, he liked that. Both their arms were crossed, and the goal post was lit a bright yellow from the flash. Behind them was the blood-red Alabama sunset.

Humphry checked his watch. It was one-thirty. He yawned and stretched. His glass was empty. "One more," he told himself. "Last one, then I'll call it a night."

It would be the third "last one."

CHAPTER NINETEEN

MAX WAS ALREADY IN A BAD MOOD. They had lost yesterday to the Cowboys in overtime. He had dropped an interception that was in his hands. So when he saw the blue slip on the stool in front of his locker, he cursed out loud.

"Shit!"

Max had gone the entire season without having to take a piss test. Yes, he knew there was supposed to be no way the drug could be detected. But the test still made him nervous. He seemed to be running low on luck the past couple of weeks. He could just see it. He'd somehow be the one to go down. There'd be something in his body chemistry that would fuck up the masking agent. Maybe the coke he'd done last week? Who could say? All Max knew was that he was going to have to piss in a cup and wait to hear from the league whether or not it came up dirty.

Max picked up the blue slip and headed to the bathroom, where he knew the NFL testing agent would be waiting for him and five other players who had been picked at random.

"Come on," he told himself, "no one has tested positive yet. Someone would have gotten busted before now if the shit didn't work."

During training camp he'd passed the pre-season piss test that everyone had to take. But Max was a survivor, and knowing about the pre-season test he had decided not to take a chance. He had snuck out of camp the night before, gone back to his apartment, and gotten the skinny kid with glasses who washed his car to piss in a bottle for him. After he was assured the kid hadn't used any drugs, Max flipped him a fifty not to ask any questions. Max filled an empty bottle of saline solution with the piss and hid it in his shorts the next morning before the test. He'd even taken the trouble to buy a thermometer and warm the kid's piss to ninety-eight degrees in a basin of hot water right before the test. Then, while the lab coats watched from behind, Max squirted the kid's clean piss into the cup.

That was what made Max worry. Even though he knew others must have passed the test, he had yet to be tested.

At seven o'clock on Friday morning Max sat in the parking lot outside the Ruffians complex. He sat slumped down in his car seat until 7:05, when the equipment manager arrived and opened up the locker room. Max waited a minute, then went in to sit at his locker. From there he could see the door to the training room. It seemed like hours, but it was only ten more minutes before Sparky appeared at the door and fumbled with his keys to open up his room. He turned around suddenly.

"Jesus, Max!" Sparky gasped. "You scared the hell out of me! What are you doing here so early for? You look like hell. You sick?"

"No."

Max pushed his fingers through his unkempt, wavy hair. There were blue circles under his eyes and a few days' growth on his face. "I gotta talk to you, Sparky," he said, looking around.

"Come on in," Sparky said, flicking on the lights.

"This may seem like a funny question," Max said once they were inside Sparky's inner office, "but I gotta know. When do you get the results from the league on those piss tests they gave on Monday morning?"

Sparky sat down and grinned smugly. He examined his fingernails. "Not worried about anything, are you, Max?" he said.

"No, no . . . I just wondered about it . . ."

"That's why you're here two hours before the rest of the guys, huh?" Sparky said, still looking over his nails. "You were just curious."

He looked up into Max's eyes. They were bloodshot, but lit with a fire that wiped the grin from Sparky's face. Sparky cleared his throat and sat up straight.

"Don't worry, Max," he said. "I would have heard by now if anything turned up."

Max's fists were clenched, his knuckles white. "You're sure?" he said, gritting his teeth.

"I'm positive, Max," said Sparky. "I'm sure. The league gets the results from the lab on Thursday morning, so I'd hear by now if something was up . . . really."

"O.K.," Max said, smiling a little. "O.K.," he said again in a lighter tone, then turned and walked out.

It was one of those games where the better team was playing down to the level of their inferior opponent. The Ruffians, who were 8–2 and in the playoff hunt, were punishing the 2–8 Browns. The Ruffians had over 400 total yards of offense compared to Cleveland's 120, and three unnecessary roughness penalties against the Ruffians defense accounted for 45 of those yards. Still, there were only a few minutes left in the game, and the Browns, who were only down 10–9, had the ball. All afternoon the Death Squad had denied the Browns a serious drive, but turnovers, stupid mistakes, and two outrageously long field goals by the Browns kicker had kept the game close.

A Ruffians punt had gone awry, and the Browns were taking over at midfield. Their first pass was knocked down by Doogie at the line of scrimmage. The Birmingham crowd went berserk. Doogie strutted around the field with his arms raised. The next play was a draw. Max hammered the ball carrier and drove him back to the line of scrimmage. The ball popped free and the Ruffians scrambled to get it and win the game. Spike Norris came up with the ball. The line judge signaled a first down for the Ruffians. The stadium roared. Ruffians leaped and jumped about, head-butting and high-fiving. There were only forty-two seconds left on the clock.

But the referees were gathering together. They were arguing. The head official appeared from their midst and flicked on the microphone in his lapel.

"The play is being reviewed," squawked the voice over the P.A. The crowd instantly booed. The ref hurried back into the huddle of zebras.

Some of the officials nodded, others shook their heads. After a full minute, the head official emerged from the bunch.

"After further review . . ." came the voice, "the ball was ruled dead. No fumble. Cleveland's ball, third down."

The crowd went animal. They booed and hissed and stamped their feet until it seemed the stadium would collapse.

Max was in a frenzy. "We gotta kill these motherfuckers!" he screamed at his teammates. "We gotta stamp their fucking guts out! They're trying to rob us!"

"Max! Max!" shouted Keith Neil. "The play, get the play."

The Browns were about ready to break their huddle, and Max had still not gotten the play from Gavin on the sideline. Collins was waving his hands wildly, as were the coaches around him to get Max's attention.

"O.K.," said Max after getting the signal, "Double Loop the Gap Cover Two, ready . . . Break!"

The Ruffians lined up hurriedly. The Browns were already on the ball. The clock was running. :36, :35, :34 . . .

The Browns quarterback examined the defense.

"Pass! Pass! Pass!" Max shouted from behind the defensive line, where he stood crouched and ready to go.

The defensive line heard him and wiggled their cleats into the earth, leaning forward with their weight. Max was usually right when he read a pass. Besides, even the dimmest lineman knew the situation. It was third and eight with the clock running down. The Browns had no time-outs and twenty yards to get into good field goal range. Everyone in the stadium knew it would be a pass.

The ball was snapped and the quarterback dropped back. Mike Patterson, the Browns right offensive tackle, gave Sky a pitiful bump and he burst free through the line. He knew he had the screen. He knew it was too easy. Patterson had pounded him all day. Now, on the biggest play of the afternoon, Sky had an open lane to the quarterback. Somewhere in Sky's mind came a voice. The voice said, "Screen, cover the screen. Double Loop, you got screen, it's yours." But that voice was drowned out by another, less familiar voice in Sky's brain:

"Kill that fucking quarterback!"

Sky raced forward at the retreating QB. Back, back went the quarterback. Then, as Sky and Clay and Doogie were all ripping into him at the same time, the QB lofted the ball gently over their heads.

Crunch!

The QB went down, but the running back pulled in the ball and followed his wall of offensive linemen down field for twenty-five yards before Keith Neil could finally bring him down.

Vance White threw down his headphones and his hat at the same time. Then he stomped on them both. Then he found Gavin Collins and got in his face.

"You never should have been cover two!" he screamed. "What in hell were you in cover two for? Why weren't you in man? You just cost us the fuckin' game, God damn it!"

Gavin was sick when he saw the play, but not because he'd called cover two. That was the right call. Gavin ripped his own headset off and pushed his face forward until his nose almost touched White's.

"That's not what cost the game, God damn it!" Gavin screamed back at him. "I told Sky all week he's got the screen on Double Loop! You know that, I know that, and every goddamned guy on this team knows that! The problem is that the fuckin' guy is so beaned up he can't think straight! The problem wasn't the play, Vance, and you know it! The problem is whatever these guys are on!"

White looked around involuntarily and stepped back with a dumb look on his face. It lasted only a split second. Then he was at Gavin's throat. Nelan grabbed White, and Wheat got hold of Gavin. Step got his bulk in between the two of them.

"God damn it!" cried Step, catching a blow in his shoulder that was meant for Gavin's face. "God damn it! You two take it easy! Vance! . . . Vance!"

Cleveland's field goal team trotted out onto the field. The Birmingham crowd watched with anticipation. No one noticed the squabble between coaches. The ball was snapped, the hold was good, and the Browns kicker popped the ball straight through the uprights to win the game by two. The crowd, like a whipped schoolboy, was quiet and sullen.

CHAPTER TWENTY

ANDREW BECKER SAT IN THE LIVING ROOM with his two sons, Eric and Seth. A fire crackled in the hearth, and the room was cozy and warm. Andrew and his boys were not tremendous football fans, but they all liked tradition, and Thanksgiving Day meant football and a large family meal. Today they even had something to watch. They couldn't wait to see Clay. Even though the family knew there were problems between Clay and Katie, they still couldn't resist the excitement of watching someone they knew play in a game that they had watched together for the last twenty odd years.

"How about a beer, Dad?" Eric said.

Andrew nodded. "Sure."

"Get me one too, will ya?" Seth said above the voice of Dan Fouts, who was hyping the importance of today's game on the TV. Both Birmingham and Detroit had 8–3 records and were in contention for the playoffs.

Andrew watched Eric disappear into the kitchen just as Katie appeared with a tray of vegetables for the dining room table. Andrew admired her grace as she put down the tray and arranged the red candles in the center piece. Her hair fell into her face and she brushed it behind her ear. She was certainly a pretty girl.

On the TV, Dan Fouts was saying, ". . . for the Ruffians. But certainly one of the bright spots this season has been the way rookie defensive lineman Clay Blackwell has come on to perform. Blackwell was—"

"Hey, Eric!" Seth shouted. "Get in here! They're talking about Clay!"

Andrew saw Katie freeze. Her back was to him now and she stood motionless at the table while the TV commentator talked on and on about how well Clay was doing for a player fresh out of college. Andrew glanced at the screen to see a highlight of Clay sacking the Redskins quarterback. He looked back at his daughter. She was still standing there, listening, he knew. He went into the dining room and put his arms around her. She jumped.

"I didn't know you were there," she said without looking back at her father. "The turkey should be ready by halftime."

"You O.K.?" he asked.

Katie nodded. She was biting her lip. "I just miss him . . . that's all," she said.

Eric's wife came in from the kitchen with a basket of dinner rolls, and Katie wiped her face quickly on her sleeve and returned to the kitchen to help her mother. Andrew forced a smile at Eric's wife and shrugged before returning to the living room.

"Geneane! Get in here!" Ward Blackwell bellowed at first mention of his son's name. He looked over at his father-in-law and brother-in-law, who were sitting on the couch, and smiled apologetically at them. At least he wanted her to see it.

Geneane hurried in from the kitchen with her hair up and her apron on. Her mother and her sister-in-law peeked out from behind her. They were busy trying to get everything ready before the game started, so when it was over they could just sit down and eat. In Geneane's left hand was a spoon that was dripping brown turkey juice on her white apron. No one noticed.

They watched clips of Clay's best plays and listened to him being praised by the TV commentators. Then Clay himself appeared. He was being interviewed and modestly spreading praise for his team's achievements among his teammates. Clay's family was silent until a Miller beer commercial filled the screen.

"Can you believe it?" Mr. Blackwell said to everyone and no one. "Do you know how much money that little piece was worth? You can't buy that kind of exposure!"

Geneane beamed. Everyone beamed. They were all so proud to see their Clay on TV, and on Thanksgiving Day, no less. The entire country had seen him.

"I wish he could be here with us," Geneane said quietly before turning back into the kitchen to finish her preparations.

Clay felt queasy. It was that pre-game feeling he'd had ever since he was a kid. It never seemed to go away, no matter how many games he played. In fact, it was worse now. For the past seven weeks he hadn't felt that knot in his stomach. He had only felt hot and angry and nasty and hyper. He began to jiggle his left leg from nerves. He was completely dressed for the game except for his shoulder pads. Everyone around him was hyped. Max was beginning his rage by pounding a locker with his fist. Clay thought he might vomit. A sweat broke out on his upper lip.

"Ten minutes!" Cody Wheat called through the locker room, letting the players know that they should finish whatever pre-game preparations they had to make.

"I must be crazy," Clay said to himself. "Things have been going great, and all of a sudden I'm gonna stop doing it? I must be nuts!"

He frantically began pulling the tape and glove off his right hand. He looked up at the clock. "Damn!"

He rummaged quickly through his bag and palmed an unopened needle and a bottle of Thyall in his thickly gloved left hand. The sounds of the locker room were intensifying.

He closed the stall door and pulled his game pants down. He tore open the plastic, popped off the cap, and stuck the needle into the top of the vial, lifting them both to the light so he could measure accurately. Amber fluid bubbled into the syringe. Clay pulled the needle free and pushed some of the drug back out. It shot a fine spray into the air. Just right. He put his left hand on his right hip to steady himself as he twisted around. He chose his spot and stabbed the needle at his buttock . . .

"Three minutes!"

"Shit!" Clay cried, biting his lip in pain.

He'd rushed the shot when he heard the call from Wheat and stabbed the bright needle into a knot that remained under his skin from a previous injection. It hurt like hell! He pulled the needle out, and although he was going to have to run out late for pre-game, he measured his spot more carefully this time and found some virgin skin. Once the needle was in deep, he quickly emptied the syringe into his ass. He felt a hot, stinging rush under his skin. By the time he got back to his locker, his teammates were already milling at the door.

"I don't know what the hell I was thinking," he muttered, chastising himself as he began to frantically retape his hand.

"Time!" called Cody Wheat, opening the doors, releasing a mad rush of drooling snarling Ruffians out into the Pontiac Silverdome.

The buzzing of the lights overhead could be heard above the drone of the crowd. The Lions were already out on the field. Clay jogged out onto the artificial turf. He skirted the Lions and took his place among the Ruffians on the far end of the field. The team was already halfway through their stretch. Clay was glad to see Vance White distracted on the sideline with a TV crew. Only Gavin Collins gave Clay a cold look for his late arrival. It didn't really bother Clay that much. By kickoff he was beginning to feel the effects of his shot.

The Ruffians came out strong, keeping the Lions pinned down in their own territory for the entire first quarter while they scored a quick ten points of their own. The touchdown came on a long bomb to Tim Tyrone, and the field goal went up after a ten-play drive in which Davis Green chalked up over fifty yards on the ground. Max was having a tremendous game. He was in on almost every tackle and seemed to be shutting down the Lions running game almost single-handedly. Midway through the second quarter, deep in their own territory, Ralph Scott got beat by a blitzing outside linebacker, and Todd Ferrone took a brutal hit that made him cough up the ball. Detroit recovered on the five yard line. Sky got too far up field to contain a QB bootleg, and Detroit scored on the first play.

After another Ruffians offensive drive that sputtered at midfield, Detroit got the ball back on its own eighteen. Clay jogged out onto the field with the rest of the defense and waited for a TV time-out to end. There were only a few minutes left in the half.

Max exhorted his teammates in the huddle. "Let's stuff their fuckin' ass right here," he said. "Let's get a fuckin' turnover and bring the fucker in for a score ourselves."

Everyone nodded. "Yeah . . . O.K. . . . Let's do it . . ." they said.

"I gotta make a play," Clay told himself. He hadn't even assisted on a tackle so far and he was pissed. He knew everyone was watching the game. Damn! He couldn't believe he'd waited so long to give himself a boost. He had to make a play.

Twice Detroit ran the ball, but the most they could get was five yards. Third and five meant pass. Clay pinned back his ears and jumped on the second "hut," taking a chance by anticipating the count. The gamble paid off. Clay raced by the offensive tackle. There was only the running back between him and the quarterback. Clay barreled down on the runner, lowering his shoulder in order to blast him right back into the QB. The back crouched down at the last instant to cut out Clay's knees. Clay saw the quarterback's arm rear back to throw the ball and he sprang. The back just clipped his feet, but it only flipped Clay's legs up, propelling his head down into the quarterback's shoulder that much quicker. With a crunch they both went down in a heap before the quarterback could release the ball. Clay was up in an instant. The crowd got strangely quiet, but the Ruffians on the field were making noise enough.

Clay raised his hands high. It was a big play, and he knew the TV would be replaying it again for everyone at home to see several times from several different angles. He shook his fists at the crowd and slapped and butted with his teammates. The crowd came to life. They booed and hissed. They booed even more when the Lions punter came out and shanked one, giving the Ruffians a shot at the end zone with only seconds to go in the first half. Todd Ferrone used the opportunity well by connecting on three straight pass plays that ended with Spencer Clayton shaking his rear end in the end zone after scoring six.

During halftime, White threw a can of Coke against the locker room wall. It exploded, spraying half his team with droplets of the syrupy drink.

"No one knows how much this game means!" he raved. And for the umpteenth time that week he told them, "It's more than just a win . . . it's a loss for a divisional opponent. This game could be the entire season! This game could be the difference between the playoffs and sitting home on your asses like a bunch of losers!"

He continued, pacing, "Every damned person in America is watching you guys, and they want to see some ass-kicking! How many of their players have been taken off? How many?!"

"Max, how many?" White said, looking wildly at Max, who was looking just as wildly back.

"Not a fuckin' one, Coach," Max said through gritted teeth.

"Damn right," White said. "Now I want you guys to go out there this second half and not just win this game, but knock some of those bastards out of it. I want to see some asses kicked! And if the guys that are out there can't do it, then I promise you I'll get some guys that can!"

The Ruffians burst out for the second half on fire. There were two fifteen-yard penalties against them in the first two minutes of the second half, and it wasn't more than four minutes before Doogie jumped on a pile of Detroit players near the end of a play and a Lion had to be carried from the field. The Ruffians kicked a quick field goal, then hung on to their thirteen-point lead for the entire third quarter. Scoring was no longer their main objective; the infliction of punishment and pain was. Early in the fourth quarter, Tim Tyrone fumbled a Detroit punt, and the Lions scooped it up and ran it in for a score. It made for a more exciting game for the viewers, but everyone on the field knew that the outcome had already been decided. The fumbled punt was just a lucky break. The Ruffians continued to physically pound their opponent in a way that caused White and Nelan to chortle and slap each other high fives on the sideline.

Clay piled up a few tackles, and although it wasn't his best game, he was satisfied at having gotten at least one critical sack on national TV. By the time the game was over, three Lions had been carried from the field. The Ruffians offense had put together a twelve-play drive that made the score 27–14, and the Ruffians defense added icing to the cake when Max forced a fumble that Sky was able to scoop up and carry into the end zone to make the final 34–14.

Clay drained what was left of his beer and signaled the bartender for another. He sat with his back to his friends, who were drunk and rowdy and didn't notice him. Half the team were there at Sportex, almost all the single guys. Max came up with a girl under each arm and tapped Clay on the shoulder.

"This is 'im," Max said to the girl on his right. "This is my buddy, Clay. Now, you can't ass for better 'an him, 'cause Stacy's already got me, and he's the next bes' thing, honey."

Clay had a good buzz on, but Max was stinking drunk. Clay thought he sounded foolish, but neither of the girls seemed to mind.

"Fools themselves," Clay thought, looking at their bleached hair, red lipstick, and tight clothing with a frown.

"Hey, come on, good buddy," Max said drunkenly. "Give theez girls that smile tha' you're so famous for. This is Stacy . . . an' this is your date for tonight . . . Clara . . ."

Clay turned back to the bar.

"He's jus' shy," Max whispered loudly to Clara with a wink. He put his hand firmly on the back of Clay's stool and spun him around. "Don' be shy, good buddy," Max said, "theez girls won' hurt you. . . . They might bite a little, but they won' hurt you. Ha, ha, ha . . ."

Max broke out laughing at his own drunken humor. Clay got out of his seat and brushed past Max.

"Be right back," Max said to the girls with another wink.

"Hey, hey, hey," he said, putting his arm around Clay, who was still headed for the door, "wha's the rush? Where ya goin'?"

Clay stopped and said, "I'm just not in the mood for this shit tonight, Max. It's fuckin' Thanksgiving and I'm goin' home."

Max held his head close to his friend and whispered, "Look, I don' care if you turned fag on me . . . it happens, ha, ha, ha . . . but you can't tie my nuts in a knot 'cause you don' wan' any pussy. You're my buddy! You gotta take tha' Clara bitch home so I can hang her fuckin' frien' from my ceiling."

Clay could smell the screwdrivers on Max's breath. "Max," he said, "don't you ever get sick of this?"

"Sick of wha'?" Max said, raising his eyebrows.

"Just all this!" Clay said, waving his hands up in the air. "We play football. We get drunk. We fuck. We play football. We get drunk. . . . It's all we do!"

"You're drunk," Max said flatly.

After rolling his eyes, Clay said, "Look, tell that girl . . . what's her name?"

"Clara."

"Tell Clara I'll pull up the car and give her a ride home so you can hang her friend from your ceiling and fuck her twenty different ways."

"Can't ya jus' come over and get her?" Max pleaded. "Come on. I'd do it for you an' ya know I would."

"O.K.," Clay said, shaking his head, "but I'm not screwing around. I'm leaving, so if she won't go right away, you're on your own."

"Deal!" Max said, patting him on the back.

"Hi, I'm Clay. Could I give you a ride home?" Clay said to the girl named Clara.

"O.K.," Clara said.

"What an idiot," Clay murmured under his breath.

"Come on," he said, and left Max, who was smiling and winking at him uncontrollably, with his girl for the night.

A valet brought up Clay's Porsche and they got in.

"Nice car," Clara said.

Clay guessed she was about nineteen. "Where do you live?" he asked.

"You know where Dumont Street is? Out past the Starlight Mall? I live in the apartments on the corner of Dumont and Boland."

"O.K.," Clay said nodding.

They drove for a while in silence.

"Nice game today," the girl said finally. "Nice sack."

"Thanks."

When they pulled up in front of Clara's building, she asked if he was coming up. Clay shut off the car and followed the girl up the outside stairs to her apartment, which was on the second floor. Clay didn't want to be there, but he didn't want to leave either. There was nothing waiting for him at home. They sat on Clara's couch and she got them each a beer. The room was dimly lit by a single lamp on an end table. She sat close and rested her arm on the back of the couch. Her fingers barely touched Clay's shoulder. He swigged his beer.

"Stacy's my roommate," Clara said. "I think she's staying with your friend Max tonight."

"Yes. I think so," Clay said.

They sat for a while in silence. Clara was looking at him dreamily.

"So, where'd you eat dinner today?" Clay asked.

"Dinner?" she said.

"Yeah, Thanksgiving, you know?"

"Oh, nowhere really, I guess," she said. "Stacy and me were at Sportex watching the game and we just had some nachos. Actually, they were turkey nachos." She giggled.

"Jesus," Clay said, almost to himself, "that's pathetic."

Clara frowned.

"The thing is," Clay said, "is that it's a holiday, and everybody's supposed to be at home, you know . . . the whole family thing. It's been that way my whole life. Then all of a sudden this year everybody in the world is eating turkey and pumpkin pie and I'm playing a game, then getting drunk afterward with the guys. I don't know . . . it's just depressing."

They sat quietly for a while just drinking their beer. Clara began to stroke the hair on the back of Clay's head. He reached over and gently cupped her breast. They began to kiss and she reached for his crotch, caressing him through his jeans. He pushed her back on the couch. She stretched her arm and reached up behind her. She fumbled with the light, and the room went dark.

CHAPTER TWENTY ONE

Two and a half weeks later, Vance White finished the team prayer, then held his hands up for silence. The entire team was gathered around him in the locker room. Most of the players were stripped to the waist, their bare chests beaded with perspiration. Sweat-drenched shoulder pads and filthy jerseys were flung about on the floor. Many of the players were bleeding, and each wore a smile.

"I'm damn proud of you guys today," said White. "You played piss poor last week and it cost us. But the sign of a true champion is when you can come back and play the way you did today. The offense hung in there and kept moving the ball; the defense got it back for us when we needed it.

"I can think of a bunch of you guys who played your ass off today," White continued, "but we had one guy who really stood out, and I want to give him the game ball."

Everyone looked around. Clay stood at the edge of the group. His eyes met Ralph Scott's from across the room. Ralph winked at him.

". . . This guy had a ton of tackles today and three quarterback sacks," White said. "One of them caused a fumble that ended up giving us the lead."

He held the game ball high over his head.

"Clay," he said, "come on up here, son, you earned this damn ball."

All the Ruffians hooted and cheered. Those who were near enough clapped Clay on the shoulder or shook his hand. White gave out only one game ball and that was only when the team won. He had never given one immediately following the game.

"Now," White continued when the team had quieted again, "before the press gets in here, I want to say one more thing to you guys. I'm not a guy to look at what other teams do, but we're all thinking it, and I'm gonna say it. If the Vikings lose on Monday night, then we can clinch a playoff spot with a win in Buffalo next week.

"Now, I don't want anyone talking about it. This is just between us, but if they lose, then next week we can make history."

Again the team cheered and slapped high fives among themselves. White turned and left the locker room. The press came streaming in. Most of them headed right for Clay's locker.

When the last question had been asked, Clay looked around to see that besides him and Todd Ferrone, the rest of the team had showered. Only a few even remained in the locker room. Max, always a favorite of the media, was just returning from the showers.

Drying his hair, he said to Clay after the last reporter had departed, "You coming down off that shit yet?"

"What do you mean?" Clay asked.

"You know," Max replied, "the Thyall. Are you feeling it wear off?"

"I'm feelin' a little shitty," said Clay, "nothin' unusual. I'm still pumped up over the game."

"I don't know," Max said, "I must have fuckin' heartburn or something. I feel like shit."

"Couple beers an' you'll be good as new," Clay said, pulling off the last of his uniform. "Or so you always tell me."

Max smiled weakly.

Clay gimped to the showers, taking his time and letting the hot water pound his aching muscles. When he was finished, he combed his hair in the mirror and then came still dripping back out into the locker room. There was no one left now. Even Ferrone had gone.

Max was sitting on a stool in front of Clay's locker, hunched over and breathing heavily. He was clutching his left arm and he looked pale.

"Max," Clay said, ambling up to him with the towel stuck in his ear, "are you O.K.?"

"Yeah, I'm O.K.," Max said, although it was obvious he was in discomfort. "I'm just coming down real hard, that's all. Fuck, it hit me all of a sudden too. I felt a little bad, but now I really feel like shit."

"You look like shit. Maybe I should see if Sparky is still around, or one of the doctors."

"No," Max said. "I'm fine."

Clay shrugged. "Suit yourself," he said, and finished toweling himself dry.

When Clay had dressed, the two of them walked slowly through the tunnel that led to the players' parking lot. They passed a gray-haired custodian in a battered blue uniform who was sweeping dust and cigarette butts along the damp concrete tunnel. As they went by, the shabby old man turned to stare at the two younger men, especially the one who looked sick as all hell.

"You know what?" Max said as they sped down the street in Clay's Porsche. "I think I might just head home and lie down for a little while. I feel like if I could rest for an hour of so, I'll be O.K. You wouldn't mind dropping me off, would you?"

Clay looked at his friend warily. "Max, this is really weird. I mean, you not going out to party after a big win? Something must really be wrong."

"Look," Max said in a strained voice, "would you cut me some slack? I told you, I'm just coming down real hard. I feel like shit."

"I feel like shit too," Clay said. "You're the one that told me that's the way it is when the amphetamine wears off."

"Yeah, well, maybe I'm coming down with something, I don't know. Just take me back to my place and cut me some slack, O.K.?"

"Max, it's not that I won't cut you some slack, it's just that if you feel that bad, maybe you should see someone about it. I've got Doc Simon's home phone number. Maybe we should just give him a call," Clay said, referring to the team's physician.

"Oh, sure," Max said. "I'll just call him right up. 'Hello, Doc? Yeah, this is Mad Max, and I'm coming down off that shit we're all on, you know, the Thyall-D, the stuff no one's supposed to talk about, and I just wanted to know if you could give me something for my crash.' Are you fucking crazy? Just ease up and take me home. I'll be O.K."

Max was slumped in the leather seat of the Porsche, looking very pale.

"Well, I'll take you back," Clay said, "but I better see you at The Club by eight, or else I'll know something is wrong."

Max nodded vacantly, and Clay swung his car around to head toward Max's apartment. Actually, when Max slumped out of the car, giving Clay an absent wave and some assurances that he'd see him later on, Clay was kind of relieved. He felt a little down himself, but he was still anxious to get to The Club and celebrate with his teammates. He could tell Max wouldn't be much fun in the state he was in, and he certainly couldn't have fun himself with his best friend swooning at his elbow the entire night.

Tonight would not only be a celebration of a win. For him it would be a celebration of his best game as a pro. He wanted to enjoy it. It was selfish, he admitted. But Max would understand. Hell, Max would be the first one to call him a pussy for worrying.

When Clay walked in the door, he saw the D-line waiting for him at the main bar. Doogie was motioning to him, and he wore a shit-eating smile.

"I don't see Mad Max around," said Doogie. "That's a shame," he continued. "Well, I'm sure he knew that since the rook was the big star today, he was going to finally have to drink with the big boys. He probably didn't want to see the rook embarrass himself."

He didn't attempt to hide the winks between he and Sky and Spike. Clay smiled, aware of the game and happy to be jibbed by his fellow linemen.

"I just hope you three don't plan on standing around all night winking at each other like a couple of fags," Clay said. "All those tackles and sacks I had today made me damn thirsty."

"Oh, ho! So that's the way it is, huh?" said Spike, and he waved to the bartender for a round of drinks.

Within an hour and a half Clay was having a hard time just getting to the bathroom. He bumped into tables and chairs and people. One of them was Gavin Collins.

"Sorry," Clay said sullenly and moved on.

Gavin caught him by the arm. "Can I talk with you?" he said.

Clay was too drunk to hide his surprise. "I gotta piss," he said above the music. "I'll be right back."

When Clay returned, Gavin appeared engrossed in the Sunday night game that was on the enormous screen. Clay hesitated and was about to walk away when Gavin noticed him. He motioned with his head for Clay to follow. He led Clay to the VIP lounge, which was decorated in plush leather and thick green carpet and where a person could be heard without shouting. They sat down in a booth.

"Want a drink?" Gavin asked.

"Sure."

Gavin signaled to a waitress in an aerobics uniform, who took their order and disappeared. Clay sat looking dully at Gavin. He had drunk enough so that he did not feel like he had to talk without first being talked to. After their drinks arrived, Gavin held out his hand across the table.

"Look," Gavin said, looking intently at Clay, "I want to say I'm sorry about the way I've been acting."

Clay was not used to coaches apologizing. When he recovered, he shook Gavin's hand firmly. "It's O.K.," he said.

"Thanks, but it's not O.K.," said Gavin. "You're not the guy I should have been down on. If anything, you're the only guy I really respect. At least you tried. I guess that's what got me down. I figured after I told you that you could do it on your own, you'd stay away from the drug."

"I would have liked it that way," Clay said, "but I wasn't happy about the idea of riding the bench for my entire career."

"I know, Clay, I know. That's why I regret being so hard on you."

"If anything," Clay said, "I'd think you'd be the guy to do something. You could walk out of here tomorrow if you wanted. They can't hold you like they can me."

Gavin chuckled. "No, huh?" he said. "You think I can just leave? You can leave a hell of a lot easier than me. I've worked my whole life to get a shot in the pros. If I walked away from this job, it'd be the last time I had to worry about working in the NFL. I'd be a black that was given every opportunity but squandered it. No, a guy in my shoes has to just bide his time and hope for the best."

"Like when we get into the playoffs?" Clay said.

"Exactly."

"Awww, I bet you could get a job with almost anyone," Clay said.

"You're the biggest defensive thing since Buddy Ryan."

"Clay, trust me," Collins said, "no one can walk out on their team during the season and expect to ever work in this league again. Even Buddy Ryan couldn't do it when you think about it, and I bet he hated working for Ditka as much as I hate working for White. Besides, we really do have a great bunch of guys. I'd hate to let them down at this point."

Clay looked out through the soundproof glass at the milling crowd of players, bimbos, and just plain average Joes. He could just make out his own reflection in the glass. "Well," he said, raising his beer, "here's to you getting out of here. Who knows what's next for you? I bet three years from now you'll be running your own team."

Gavin laughed.

"You've had a little too much to drink," he said. "But if I do go . . . maybe I'll take you with me."

Clay spotted his reflection as his face broke out in a twisted grin that was somewhere between pain and pleasure. He raised his beer bottle in a toast and said, "Now who's been drinking too much?"

Clay awoke the next morning in a familiar alcoholic fog. Over the past few months he had grown quite accustomed to the cotton mouth, the sick feeling in his gut, and the throbbing headache. He tried hard to recollect what had transpired the previous night. Even despite his aching head, he smiled remembering yesterday's game and the ensuing celebration. He remembered the game ball, and the good time he'd had with his buddies. He remembered talking to Collins. It was a good memory. They had drunk together like soldiers who were fighting for the same cause, which was what in fact they were.

His phone was thrown down on the floor beside his bed. The receiver had been knocked from its cradle. He remembered vaguely having tossed it when its shrill ring had disturbed his sleep. He wasn't sure if that was last night or just this morning. His alarm clock too lay askew and face-down on the carpet. He picked it up.

"Holy shit!" he said.

He had forgotten to set his alarm and overslept. Or more likely, he had disabled the clock, as well as the phone, in his sleep. It was eleven-forty. The team meeting was at twelve. He was about twenty minutes from the complex. He threw himself out of bed and scurried around his bedroom, throwing on a hat and a sweatsuit and some sneakers without bothering to look for socks.

He hurried out the door and sped to the complex. White was intolerant of lateness, and Clay hated the thought of tarnishing yesterday's performance. The nervous adrenaline worked against his stomach, which was already suffering from last night. He felt nauseous and his heart raced. There was no way he would be on time.

It was 12:06 when he dashed into the locker room out of breath. He looked around, confused. Clay found his teammates milling about and whispering to each other in subdued tones when they should have been in the meeting room. Clay tried to listen to bits and pieces of conversations as he made his way quickly to his locker, relieved that the meeting had not yet started.

". . . don't know, I guess meetings are canceled . . ."

". . . heard he's going to talk to us . . ."

"Did you hear who it was?"

". . . really true?"

Just as Clay hung up his sweat jacket, Coach Stepinowski announced in an audible but subdued voice that Vance White wanted to speak to the team before anyone left.

Clay shuffled into the meeting room with the rest of his teammates. They were all silent, and Clay searched their faces, looking for the answer to what he had obviously missed by arriving late. The tension in the air prevented him from asking. He chose a seat in the back of the room and sat down. He noticed the coaches, all except White, standing in a gloomy group in one corner of the room. Vance White entered, and all eyes were riveted on his stiff figure. The look on his face shot an electric charge through Clay's body. Without having any idea what it was, he knew that he was about to hear something awful.

White cleared his throat. "I hate to be standing here right now," he said, his voice choked with uncharacteristic emotion. "As many of you have already heard, Max Dresden died early this morning at Memorial Hospital."

CHAPTER TWENTY TWO

CLAY'S MIND SWAM. He was alert, but his thoughts were spinning out of control. He felt the muscles in his face twitching, and his stomach turned over and over again. He did not, could not believe he had heard White correctly. He had seen Max. Max was not dead. Max could not be dead.

". . . We're not sure of the exact cause of death, but to tell you guys the truth—and this stays in this room, within this team—it appears that Max had a heart attack."

White was silent a moment, and so was the rest of the room. Clay continued to listen in disbelief.

"It also seems . . . that the police found some cocaine in Max's bedroom . . . where he apparently phoned the ambulance for help. When the ambulance got there, Max was already unconscious and his heart had apparently stopped beating. I'm told that they did everything they could to revive him, but, well, he didn't make it. I don't have to say what a shock and devastating loss this is for all of us. Max was a teammate and friend, and one of the most dedicated players I've ever coached.

"You guys just go home today. We won't be doing anything here. Max has a sister, and the authorities have contacted her. She's having his body brought back to Ohio for the burial, but she's agreed to allow us to have a viewing here in Birmingham tomorrow. We'll be having a memorial service for the team at the McNally Funeral Home at one o'clock tomorrow afternoon.

"I know you guys all respected Max. We all did. So you guys just go home and be with your families. I know this is hard to take, but we've got to pull together and get through this as a team. That's the only thing we can do, and it's the only thing Max would have wanted us to do. . . . You guys can go."

White said no more. He walked from the room with the rest of the coaching staff following in his wake.

Clay sat. He didn't know what to do or what to think. He found his mind floating from one trivial thought to another, all of them totally unrelated. Where would he go for dinner tonight? What was Katie doing right now? The idea of Max being dead left him feeling vacant. He vaguely wondered if he should be crying. After all, Max was his best friend. He also wondered whether the ringing phone he had knocked over that morning was a call from someone to let him know what had happened.

The rest of the Ruffians players also continued to sit noiselessly. It was ten full minutes before the first guy got up and quietly left the room. After the first few left, there was a steady stream. One by one they rose and left. It was as if they were ashamed of leaving, as if it were disrespectful to continue on with their lives when one of them was dead. Soon Clay was the only one remaining. He didn't know how long he sat there. He wouldn't remember a single thought. His mind seemed stuck in a daze, and only an occasional thought penetrated its fog, and then not long enough to be remembered.

Clay had never been through the formalities of death before. He knew he should wear a dark suit to the memorial service and that was all. No one he had been close to had ever died. Once when a high school teammate's mother had died, Clay had instinctively avoided him until a few weeks passed and then he had acted as if nothing happened. He assumed that people wanted it that way. And that was how he wanted it now. He didn't want any of his teammates to try to console him. He wanted to go through what had to be done without having to talk about it with anyone.

As he drove to the funeral home it began to rain. After the team meeting the day before, Clay had returned home and shut himself in for the rest of the day. His phone had rung several times. He didn't answer. He was incapable of doing anything but sitting and staring. He couldn't eat. Only when it was well after midnight did he fall asleep on the couch where he'd been sitting all day.

Clay's hands trembled despite the tight grip he had on the steering wheel. He had arrived at the funeral home and pulled into the lot, parking his car away from the others, who had gotten as close to the building as they could to avoid the rain. He turned off the car and sat, his whole body shaking now. Agony and shame rushed from deep within him, racking his body with sob after sob. Tears flowed freely down his cheeks, and he cried uncontrollably for the first time in his life. Max was dead.

The windows of his car were all steamed up. No one would have been able to see him even if he cared. He cried for Max and he cried for himself.

By the time the tears stopped, he couldn't even breathe through his nose. Clay composed himself as well as he could and went into the funeral home. The service was already well under way when he entered the large viewing room. The entire team sat in folding chairs arranged in rows in front of Max's coffin. A priest stood at a podium off to one side of the coffin and conducted a service that seemed to Clay only a formality. The priest didn't know Max, and that, in Clay's mind, seemed to invalidate the substance of what he had to say. Clay knew Max better than anyone in the room, and even he knew nothing of Max's religious sentiments. He probably had none.

The priest spoke in generalities, many of which had no application at all to the type of person Max was, or to the type of life he led. Nevertheless, when the priest began to speak of Max's love of life and his zest for football, it struck a nerve in the entire team. Many of Clay's teammates began to cry silently.

It wasn't until the service was over and the last few Ruffians were shuffling silently from the room that Clay had an opportunity to really see Max for the last time. He made his way to the front of the room, and was horrified to see Max's lifeless form slightly propped up in his coffin. His eyes were shut tight, and his arms lay crossed stiffly across his chest in a way that let Clay know Max was gone forever. What Clay saw now was a shell, stiff and pale, and so unlike Max Dresden that it was disturbing. Gone was that lust for life, and that hot-blooded arrogance that made everyone know that Max Dresden was not only alive, but that he was living life in a way that few others dared or knew how to. Hot tears welled in Clay's eyes. He moaned pitifully for his friend and wanted to touch Max's face, but he was too horrified. He turned and stumbled out.

Denise was waiting for him outside. "Clay," she said, hugging him, "I'm sorry about Max. I can't believe it happened."

After a minute Clay gently detached himself from her. It seemed so out of place, Denise being there. "I gotta go," he said.

"Sure. You want me to come over later?" she asked.

"No, thanks," Clay said turning to walk away. He stopped and turned back. "Denise," he said, reaching out for her hand to shake it, "I want to say good-bye."

"What do you mean?" she said, pulling her hand free.

"I just mean good-bye. Take care," he said, then turned away without looking back.

Although Clay was exhausted and depressed, the crying had actually made him feel better. He felt as though part of the heavy weight that compressed his chest had been lifted. He drove absently and was suddenly struck with the idea that if he had stayed with Max instead of dashing off to celebrate, Max would probably still be alive. If he had stayed with his friend, he most certainly would not have been snorting cocaine.

Then it hit Clay like a fist in the mouth. He could see Max lying there that night of the Zone Seven party. He couldn't forget Max's frightened, ashen face. No way would Max have been snorting cocaine after what had happened. No way.

His mouth dropped open. Could he be wrong? No. It all made sense. There was nothing he could have done to save Max. Max hadn't used cocaine. Even White himself said that they only found cocaine in Max's room, and that they weren't sure what had killed him. White said that to imply that Max had died from cocaine. Maybe they had found the powder in Max's bedroom, but Clay knew that was not what killed Max. It was the drug.

Clay slammed the steering wheel with his palm. Hadn't Max complained of a tightness in his chest, and a pain? A pain in his left arm! It was a heart attack, all right, but it had nothing to do with cocaine. Max had shown the symptoms before he had even gotten home! In his debilitated state he had probably lain down on his bed, and only when it was too late had he realized that he needed help. The thought of Max lying in pain, alone and helpless on his bed, crowded all other thoughts out of Clay's mind.

He slammed the car into third gear and jumped into the passing lane, leaving a path of shrieking car horns in his wake. He sped past the exit for his apartment and didn't stop until he pulled up in front of the offices of the Birmingham Ruffians. He jumped from his car and stormed into the building. He pushed past a gaping secretary outside the office of Humphry Lyles. When he burst open the doors, he found the owner and Vance White together. They looked up with surprise at the unannounced intrusion.

Clay stood trembling from head to toe. His voice wavered, but the sheer force of his anger propelled the words from his mouth. "You sons of bitches!" he shrieked, pointing at the two men. "You killed him! You killed him!"

At first, even Vance White was too shocked to respond, but the sight of one of his players standing there pointing—actually pointing at him—was too much. White had neither the experience nor the self-control of Humphry Lyles. It never occurred to him to deny what he knew to be true. He was being called out, and he knew of only one way to answer that call. Before Lyles could speak, White was on his feet.

"You're way out of line, boy," he yelled angrily. "Do you realize who you're talking to?"

"You son of a bitch," Clay repeated. "I know your drug killed him, and soon everyone will know. The party is over for you, you son of a bitch. Your next stop will be the fucking jail."

"Why, you worthless shit!" White stood as if he were about to come after Clay with his fists.

"Vance!" Lyles shouted, seeing the severity of the situation. "Get hold of yourself!"

White blinked, then looked angrily from Clay to the owner, waiting for the reason why this shouldn't be settled his way.

"Sit down," Lyles said after seeing that his words had had their desired effect on both coach and player, "You too, Blackwell."

After a few moments of staring, Clay sat.

"Good. Now," Lyles said, drawing himself up to his full height in the elevated chair, "Clay, what you've just said is not only very serious, it's absurd."

Clay gave the owner a vacant look. Right now he didn't care whose toes he stepped on. Max was dead and he shouldn't be. These two men were responsible. That was all Clay knew, yet despite his outrage he found himself seated and listening to the owner's demand. His rage had vented itself and then suddenly lost its force. He no longer felt the surety that had caused him to burst in here uninvited and hurl accusations. Yet despite the cooling of his temper, he was still convinced that he was right about Max's death, and he set his jaw with determination to meet any contradictory information the owner might throw at him.

"First of all," Lyles said, "you, like the rest of us within this organization, have agreed not to mention any kind of drug. This drug, in fact, does not exist.

"Do you know why it does not exist, Clay?" he asked, raising his eyebrows.

"It does exist," Clay said flatly.

"No, it does not!" shrieked the owner, slamming his fist against the solid desk with a thud. "It does not exist because I say it does not exist!"

Then, very calmly, he said, "Throughout history there are great men, Blackwell. And great men are the ones who write history, this is the nature of things. What is true is what the men of power say is true. I am one of those men."

The room filled with silence. Clay met Humphry Lyles's stare as he felt Vance White's malevolent gaze bearing down on him from the side.

"Max Dresden is dead" was the only thing Clay could think of to counter what had just been said.

"Clay," said Lyles, "Max had a heart attack. This is unusual for a boy his age, yes, but Max was a cocaine user, and things like this happen from time to time."

"Max didn't die from cocaine," Clay said, speaking fast, wanting to explain, wanting them to understand that he knew. "There was no cocaine in Max's body, was there? It was in his bedroom, but Max didn't use it that night. And he was sick before I even dropped him off at his apartment. He was sick right after the game. He said his chest was tight and his arm hurt."

"Clay, I know you're very upset," said Lyles. "You probably feel somewhat responsible. Max was your friend. But facts are facts. There has already been an autopsy which says Max died of a heart attack, that's it. The coroner's report has no mention of cocaine, true, but the police report and every newspaper in the country have stated that Max was found dead of a heart attack with a modest stash of cocaine right next to the bed where he died. People will remember Max as a guy who died from cocaine. That is what history will say. That is what is."

Clay saw exactly what was happening. Both the owner and the coach understood all too well what had really happened, and Lyles had far more control of the situation than Clay had guessed. Without saying it, Lyles was saying that Max had in fact died from Thyall-D, but no one would ever know that. The cocaine in his bedroom was incriminating evidence. There would be no proof that Max had taken Thyall—it was undetectable unless someone knew they were looking for it. There was probably not even any solid proof that the Ruffians had any direct control over the drug even if someone could find it in Max's system. And if he wanted to make a fuss about it, it would be his word against the team's. No other player would come forward to back him up. They probably all believed that Max had died from cocaine. They all believed Max was crazy enough to take such a risk; he was Max.

Clay's mind was fogged. How could people ever know what had really happened? Who would listen to him? Who would believe him even if they did listen? But just because Lyles and the whole world said otherwise, Clay knew in his heart that Max had died because Humphry Lyles and Vance White wanted to win football games, and they did not care about the cost, even if it included the life of a young man who was Clay's friend. The thought sickened him. No one would care about Max. To the world, he was just another foolish and spoiled professional athlete who couldn't be satisfied with what so many others dreamed of, so he turned to the rich man's high, cocaine. No one would want to hear about the real Max Dresden. No one would overcome the prejudices already instilled by the implications of a cocaine death to care.

After a long interval Clay realized that White and Lyles were waiting to see what his response would be. He looked from the coach to the owner. They both were staring intently. Clay felt constricted. He wished himself away from them, away from the whole situation. Why did he have to be drafted by Birmingham? He could so easily have been chosen by another team. If he had only been honest from the start, and let White know that he wasn't some moronic football-soldier looking for a maniac to lead him into battle. He never should have put on that front. But that was a foolish train of thought. He was here, and he had to do something about it.

But what could he do? Ask for a trade? One thing he did know, he wouldn't play in Birmingham, not for these men. How could he, knowing what he knew? He certainly wouldn't keep using their drug. It had killed Max. Even if it was a freak thing, the point was that it could kill. Clay was not so sure in his mind that it even was a freak incident. What did any of them really know about this drug? It only made sense that something which was apparently so good had serious side effects. Wasn't that the way things were supposed to work? Wasn't that why a person was supposed to do things right in the first place?

And if he stopped using their drug, then he would be right back where he had been in training camp. He had no intentions of going back to that. Life was too short.

"I want to be traded," Clay suddenly blurted out.

Lyles smiled widely and said, "Now, what do you think people would say about me if I were to trade a rookie I had just spent over two million dollars on and who had been the defensive MVP in his eighth game back from a serious injury? I'd be laughed out of the league, and probably tarred and railed out of the state of Alabama." Lyles chuckled as if they were just a couple of good old boys having a laugh. "No," he said, "you're just too valuable to trade, Clay. You're just going to have to get through this personal crisis and pull yourself together like the rest of us."

Clay sat and thought. White continued to stare malevolently. Lyles smiled.

"You have to trade me," Clay said. "I won't play here for you."

Lyles's face grew dark. "Then, son," he said, "you won't play football in the NFL." Then he added, "This team will hold your rights indefinitely, boy, until you recover from your injury."

"I'm not hurt," Clay said.

"Well," Lyles replied with a smile, "history will say that you tried to come back too soon from that elbow, and despite a tremendous showing Sunday, it was reinjured to the point where we don't know if you'll ever make it back. You'll go on our injury list and stay there until you're ninety-nine if need be, boy. No other team can touch you. They can't even give you a physical because you're the property of the Birmingham Ruffians."

White too was smiling now. "Mr. Lyles," he said, delighted to strike a blow at Clay, "I'm happy to inform you that from a coaching standpoint, we don't need this piece of shit no matter how good he played on Sunday."

Clay stood up, looked White directly in the eye, and said, "Fuck you."

He turned before White could respond and walked from the room. Behind him he heard the owner shrieking, "Blackwell! Blackwell! You get your ass back here, boy! Where the hell do you think you're going, son?"

Clay slammed the door with a bang that sounded like a shot.

CHAPTER TWENTY THREE

IT WASN'T LONG AFTER CLAY had stormed out that Gavin Collins appeared in Humphry Lyles's office as well. Vance White looked up malevolently at him.

"What can I do for you, Gavin?" Lyles asked without offering him a seat.

Gavin looked at White, who was now staring blankly ahead, before saying, "We've got to stop using this drug. I think that it may have had something to do with Max Dresden's death. I think we're into something that's more dangerous than any of us knows."

White laughed mechanically, "Ha. Ha. Ha. Ha."

Gavin looked at him to see if he was laughing or pretending to laugh. White continued to stare strangely in front of him.

"I'm really not aware of this whole drug situation in any great detail, Gavin," Lyles said. "So any feelings you've got about it, you'll have to bring up with Vance, and quite frankly, I'd prefer the two of you did that between yourselves."

Gavin looked at him incredulously. "Don't you realize what I'm saying, Mr. Lyles?" he said. "One of our players may have died because he was using this drug! Doesn't that mean anything to you?"

"First of all," White said abruptly, "Max Dresden died from a cocaine overdose—"

"That's not proven—"

"Second," White said, now glaring at Gavin, "you're way the hell out of bounds by bringing up something like this. If anyone has benefited from this drug, it's you, Collins. You're the defensive coordinator. You're the mastermind of the Death Squad. Mastermind! Ha! Without this drug you're just another token black on an NFL coaching squad."

White smiled as he watched Gavin go tense and clench his fists. "Go ahead," he said menacingly, "make a move. Not only will you never coach again, I'll rip your fucking heart out."

Gavin went cold. He felt a rush to his head. It was all he could do to control himself. "You may have it right about me coaching," he said, "for now. But one thing you got wrong, and you got it wrong bad. If you and I ever go at it, I'll leave you lying in a pool of your own blood."

Gavin turned and walked out.

Clay wanted to make sure that the drug had the capability to kill Max. He called the only man he could think of who he could trust and would have the knowledge to confirm or deny his fears. Dr. Norton had been Clay's family doctor since he could remember. He'd always shown a keen interest in Clay and his success in sports.

When Clay had finished telling Dr. Norton the entire story, there was a moment of silence before the doctor asked, "What was the name of that drug, Clay?"

"Thyall-D."

Clay heard the rustling of paper as the doctor paged through what sounded like a phone book.

"Clay," the doctor said after a minute, "I've spelled that drug in every way I can think of, and I've looked at the most recent supplement to the FDA's list of new drugs. There is no such drug."

"But I know that's it. I took it, I know that's the name," Clay said, frustrated.

"Well, from what you've told me," said Norton, "I would assume this is a black market drug. Many times performance drugs are. This certainly supports what you think happened to your friend. The drug he took, this Thyall-D, certainly hasn't been tested as thoroughly as it should be if it isn't FDA-approved. And if you're right about the drug being a combination of a metabolic steroid and an amphetamine, well, only a fool would use the two of them combined. The steroid itself used over time is enough to cause coronary seizures in even young men. Combining the adverse effects a steroid has on the blood pressure with the obvious stress created by an amphetamine . . . well, it's insane."

There was silence as Clay again considered that his friend was gone forever.

"I don't know what more to tell you," said Dr. Norton. "If your friend displayed signs of a coronary—I'm referring to the soreness in his arm and the constricted feeling in his chest—then it seems almost certain that he was suffering the effects of the performance drug and not the cocaine found in his apartment."

Clay nodded to himself and thanked the doctor. Before he hung up, the doctor said, "Clay, I don't want you to use that drug again. I've known you for a long time, son, and I'd hate to lose you for something as foolish as that."

Clay started to pack his bag. He already had a seat on the first flight out of Birmingham. The phone rang.

"Hello."

"Clay, thank God I've got you," said Bill Clancy on the other end of the line. "What the hell is going on? Clay, come on, talk to me." Clancy sounded more excited than Clay had ever heard. "I just got off the phone with Humphry Lyles. Clay, are you crazy? I'm sorry about your pal, but Clay, have you thought about what you're doing? I told them that I was sure that what happened was just a reaction to your pal's death, but Clay, come on . . ."

When Bill finally stopped talking, Clay allowed a moment of silence before he spoke. "Do you know what happened, Bill?" he asked calmly.

Clancy repeated the version of Max's death that, as Humphry Lyles had said, would be how history remembered it.

"Bill," Clay said, "Max died from that drug. I've been taking the damn thing myself . . . every Sunday, Bill. Every damn Sunday. White wasn't going to let me on the field if I didn't."

"Clay," Clancy said, "I know what you think, Lyles told me what you said to him."

Lyles had told Bill Clancy everything that was said, and called on Clancy to contain Clay Blackwell, threatening to expose Clancy's previous improprieties. Clancy knew containing Clay would be much more difficult than before, but he also knew that he was now in deeper than ever. Payoffs, drugs, and now a death—he wanted no such associations to be made with his name. Any scandal could cost him his business.

"Clay, what happened to Max is horrible, and you should be upset, but they found cocaine in Max's room," Clancy whined. "Everyone knows that cocaine can kill you, even if you're only an occasional user. How can you say that Max's heart attack was caused by the team's drug? It's tested. It's safe."

"How the hell do you know it's tested?" demanded Clay.

"They wouldn't let their players use something that wasn't safe. Come on, Clay, this is the NFL," said Clancy.

"What the hell does that mean? That drug is from the black market. There's no drug like that anyone can buy or prescribe. I spoke with my own doctor. He told me there was no such drug approved by the FDA. He told me that the kind of drug we're using is dangerous, for Christ's sake."

"You spoke to your doctor? Clay," Clancy said, "I thought you gave your word to them that you wouldn't mention this drug to anyone."

"Are you fucking kidding me?" Clay asked. "Max is dead. They don't give a shit, and you're worried about my word to them. Anything I promised to them no longer means a damn thing. That's the way it is, Bill. They killed Max, and I have to figure out what to do about it."

"What do you mean, Clay? What is there to do?"

"I'm not sure. I'm out of here, though. I won't play for the Ruffians."

"Clay," Clancy said, "we've already been through this once. They won't trade you. You know that, now more than ever, especially after the way you've been playing."

"Bill, I've been thinking about it. If they won't trade me, I don't think I'll play football."

"Clay, I know you're upset, but you're really not thinking rationally," said Clancy. "Clay, you and I are friends, I can't let you talk like this. If it's just a reaction to the shock of Max's death, that's one thing, but you have to get over it. You've got a job. You've got a contract! What about all the rest of your teammates? You guys are about to go to the playoffs! You can't let everyone else down. What about your Coach Collins there?

What about Max himself? He'd have wanted you to stay in there and win it all . . . for him. You've got to stay, Clay."

There was a long silence before Clay finally said, "I'll have to think about it. O.K.?"

"Sure, Clay," said Clancy. "I know this is a hard time, but that's why I'm here for you . . . to think for you when times get tough. "

"I'm still going to New York. I'm going up to the lake. I've got to get away from here right now," Clay said with finality.

Not wanting to lose the ground he knew he'd just gained, Clancy said, "I'll talk to Lyles about it. I'm sure under the circumstances they'll be willing to give you a few days to get over this tragedy. But I'm going to tell them that in all likelihood you'll be in Buffalo on Sunday to play, O.K.?"

"O.K., Bill, whatever you want to say," Clay said, "and Bill . . . thanks."

"No problem. That's what friends are for. I'll call you tomorrow in New York."

When Bill Clancy hung up his phone, he pumped the air with his fists. He was smiling.

Clay was on a plane to Syracuse two hours later. He wanted to put as much distance between himself and the Ruffians as fast as he possibly could. The first thing he planned on doing when he got home was to find Katie and talk to her face to face. He would get on his knees if he had to, but he was determined to win her forgiveness. No matter what happened between him and the Ruffians, he was done with life in the fast lane. Max's death made that certain.

When the plane lifted off, Clay felt relieved and suddenly free of the Ruffians, of Vance White and Humphry Lyles and all their lies. He almost ordered a beer, but he wanted to keep his thoughts clear. The first thing he would do when he got off the plane would be to take a cab to his house. He'd say a quick hello to his parents, get the old Bronco from the driveway, and head straight to Katie's dorm. He didn't want to show up with even a hint of alcohol on his breath. He wanted her to know that what he was going to say came from him, and that it was not some drunken self-pity that prompted him to seek her forgiveness.

When Clay arrived home, he was met by a suspicious glare from his father.

"What are you doing home, son?" he asked. "Don't you have practice tomorrow?"

"They gave me a few days off, Dad," Clay said. "You know, 'cause about what happened to Max."

"Yeah, yeah, I know. I heard about it," his father said glumly. "That's too bad." He brightened. "Your mom's in the shower, which is good. It'll give you and me a chance to talk. No sense wastin' time moanin'. Come on . . .

"Damn, it's good to see you, son," he said as he led his son into the kitchen and pulled a bottle of Jim Beam from the cupboard. "I told all the boys that the first chance you got, you'd kick some ass, and sure as shit, me and the boys all saw you do it down at Mickey's on the satellite dish," he said in an excited tone, referring to Sunday's game.

"That's great, Dad. Look," he said as his father carefully poured two shots of whiskey, "I really can't hang around. I just wanted to say a quick hello to you and Mom and get going. I've got to get up to school and see Katie before she goes to bed. She doesn't know I'm coming."

"Well, just one quick one can't hurt," the father said, ignoring his son.

"Dad, no, I'm sorry, I just can't drink. I—" he stuttered, then said quickly, "It's too close to the playoffs. I gotta cut back—"

He didn't tell his father the real reason, because he wouldn't have wanted to hear it.

"Son of a bitch, that's right!" his father said, slapping his knee. "My boy is gonna be in the playoffs! Well, by damn, I'll drink to that, and I'll have your shot for you."

With that, he downed two quick shots.

Clay's mother appeared suddenly in the kitchen, wrapped in a thick terry-cloth robe. Her hair was dark and glossy and wet and made her look young enough to be his sister. When she saw Clay sitting there unexpectedly, no words had to be spoken between them; she knew he was troubled. Her eyes flickered with a mixture of joy and sorrow. The joy was for seeing him, and the sorrow for the pain she knew he must be feeling. The conflicting emotions brought tears to her eyes. Clay stood abruptly, cutting off his father in mid-sentence. His mother rushed to him, hugging him tightly.

"Oh, my poor baby," she said in a soft voice, rubbing his back to soothe the shudders of sorrow that now shook Clay's large frame. "I'm so sorry . . . I'm so sorry."

The sudden acknowledgment of Max's death made Clay cry again as if for the first time. That he had been sitting there with his father, who had not even mentioned the death, made the telepathy between him and his mother all the more poignant.

"He didn't have to die," Clay sobbed, "he didn't have to."

"I know, honey," his mother said softly, "I know."

Clay's father, overwhelmed with embarrassment and confusion, two emotions that for him quickly converted into anger, mumbled, "Bullshit crying, the damned cokehead asked for it."

Clay wheeled instantly and violently. "Who the hell are you?" he screamed, the tears still clouding his eyes. "Who the hell are you? Who gave you the right to judge?"

Clay's father was stunned at the reproach. "You don't talk to me like that, boy!" the older man bellowed, slamming down an empty shot glass and rising from the table. "I can still whip your ass from here to fucking Toledo."

The two men moved toward each other. Clay's mother got between them and looked at Clay with pleading eyes.

"No, honey," she said to him, "please."

At that moment Clay felt as though he could pound the very life from his father. That his mother, so good, yet abused and unappreciated, should jump to his father's defense galled him beyond description. His father didn't deserve her loyalty. Yet here she was, protecting him, knowing that later that same night, after his alcoholic haze had thickened, he would berate her, maybe even strike her, for interfering. It was for her only that he swallowed his anger. He turned quickly, grabbed his keys from a drawer, and left through the front door without another word.

It was a good while before Clay began to cool off. He was beginning to feel exhausted. The emotions of the day and the traveling left him spent. He simply wanted to pull off the road and sleep. But he wouldn't. He had to see Katie. That was one thing he had to try to resolve. It was the one thing that he felt would give him something to hang on to. He wanted her back.

As he drove, he began thinking how bizarre it all was. This very morning he had been looking at Max's corpse. Now he was halfway across the country chasing down the girl he loved, who might very well reject him. Max would have cringed at such a venture. But Max was dead, and the way he had done things was no longer something Clay set his sights by. Nevertheless, the whole day seemed like a dream. And as the Bronco rumbled through the dark streets, it would not have surprised Clay to be shaken by the arm and awakened by Max to find himself back in Birmingham, subject to a fine for having overslept the team's Monday morning meeting.

Instead Clay soon found himself winding his way to Katie's dormitory. He parked the truck in the visitors' lot and made his way into the building. A few girls who lived on her floor regarded him silently, and Clay wondered if everyone knew of the rift between them. If so, then he must certainly seem a strange sight. If these girls recognized him, as he suspected they did, they were probably wondering why he wasn't in Birmingham.

Clay pretended to read the inspection certificate on the elevator wall to avoid eye contact with the girls. He didn't want to talk with anyone but Katie, not even small talk. When the elevator reached the fourth floor, Clay got off quickly and made his way to Katie's room at the end of the hall. On the door was a message board, and Clay couldn't help but look for any messages left by another guy who might have tried to move in while he was apparently out of the picture. He was relieved to see nothing but foolish and insignificant memos about study groups and laundry. Gathering himself again for the purpose that had brought him there, Clay knocked.

"Yes," came Katie's muffled voice from behind the door, "who is it?"

Clay froze for an instant, saying nothing. What if she told him to go away? What would he do? Wait? Keep banging until she answered or until security dragged him away? The thought of the alternatives made him blush. He cringed, praying she would let him in. He didn't want a scene, standing here as he was like some abandoned soul in the hall of the dormitory.

"Katie?" Clay said hesitantly, "it's me."

There was a moment of silence that turned his stomach. He felt as if he would run away rather than face the possible rejection, and if he wasn't so exhausted, that is exactly what he would have done. But the door opened suddenly, revealing Katie dressed in baggy sweat pants and a worn football T-shirt that had been his. Her face was filled with surprise. He was the last person on earth she had expected to see at her door. To him, she was a beautiful sight, and he instantly felt a sharp pang of guilt and regret for what he had done to her.

"Clay," she said quietly and gave him a hug. He looked pathetic. His eyes were sunken and puffy. He was obviously exhausted and distressed. "I'm so sorry. I know what happened. I know Max was special to you."

Clay's eyes filled again with tears. How could she say what she had just said? After what he had done to her, after how he had hurt her, all that, and she felt bad for him!

He began to sob. "Katie, I'm sorry, I'm sorry . . . Max is dead. I could have helped him. I hurt you. I hurt everyone . . . I don't deserve you. But please . . . I'm so sorry . . ."

Katie sat him down on her bed and closed the door. Then she sat next to him and held his head against her chest while he cried himself out. When he began to sniffle, she handed him a box of tissues and he blew his nose several times.

"I must look pretty foolish," he said, "sitting here crying like a baby."

"No," she said, "it's not foolish. If you didn't cry, it would mean that what happened to Max didn't matter to you."

"I'm sorry about you too," he said.

"I know you are, Clay," she said, "and I had a whole bunch of games I was going to play to make you prove it, but this is no time for things like that. Just your being here lets me know that you're sorry."

"Katie, I love you," he said.

"I know," she said, "I love you too."

Clay hugged her and they fell back on the bed, holding each other tightly. They lay like that until Clay's grip loosened and the room began to fill with the sound of his heavy breathing. He was so deeply asleep that he was completely unaware of Katie pulling off his boots before covering them both for the night.

Chapter Twenty Four

THE NEXT MORNING, THEY SAT DRINKING coffee after having had breakfast in the same diner they had eaten in hundreds of times.

Clay reached across the table to hold Katie's hand and said in a low voice, "I love you."

"Clay, there is one thing I have to tell you," she said, after hesitating.

"What, honey?"

"You can't do what you did to me ever again," she said, looking directly into his eyes. "If you do, I promise that no matter how much I love you, and no matter what you do, I'll never be with you again."

He nodded, shame filling him again. "I'll never do anything," he said.

They sat for a few moments in silence.

"I tried to call you," she said, "after I heard what happened to Max on the news Monday. I kept calling, but I guess you weren't home."

"No," he said, "I was home. After I found out about Max, I just went home and sat there. I don't think I moved until this morning."

Clay then told her about the service for Max and what he thought actually happened.

She interrupted him, saying, "Then Max didn't really die from cocaine?"

"No," he replied, "he couldn't have. Besides the fact that I know he wouldn't use it, he was already showing signs of a heart attack before he even got home. I should have known. I should have stayed with him."

"Clay," said Katie, "how could anyone have guessed that a person as young as Max and in the shape he was would have a heart attack? It's not your fault at all."

He nodded. They sat there silently for a while, then he told her how he had confronted the owner and the coach.

"And you used the drug too, Clay?" she asked. Even though he had told her why he had used it, she found it hard to believe, knowing how opposed to such things he had been.

He nodded and said, "Yeah, like I said, I figured it was use it or keep living in limbo. Nothing was worse than that."

"But not now," she said, "you don't still think that after what happened to Max—"

"No," he said, "not now. I wouldn't do it again for all the money in the world. Even if I never play another down of football, I won't use it."

"What will you do now?" Katie asked.

"Well," he said, "I was hoping you could miss some classes and go up to Loon Lake with me. I don't know what I'm going to do. I've got four days before the Buffalo game . . . but . . . I don't know, I don't want to go back to that. It's sick what they're doing."

"Do you think you could really not go back?" she asked.

"I don't know," he said. "When I think of the guys and getting to the playoffs, I'd hate to not be there. I'd hate to let them down. I imagine White will give me shit if I stop using the drug. I could end up right back where I started."

"But they won't let anyone take it after what happened," she said.

He looked at her blankly. "You wouldn't think so, would you?" he said. "But they don't care about Max, or me, or any of the players. We're meat to them. We're less than meat. They don't even care if I won't play for them. They won't trade me or give me up, that's what they said. They said they'd hold my rights until I was an old man. They own me."

"But if they held your rights, they'd have to pay you, wouldn't they?" she asked.

"Yeah, but then I'd have to do whatever they wanted me to do, and if I didn't, they'd suspend me without pay. They'd make my life so miserable that it wouldn't be worth even that kind of money. Believe me, they can make your life miserable."

Kate nodded, and they sat in silence once more.

After a while she asked, "So, what will you do?"

He seemed to consider, then said, "I was thinking on the plane . . . with the money I've got, I don't have to worry all that much. I can do pretty much whatever I want."

"But what about football?" Katie asked.

"I thought about that too," Clay said. "It's not really football anymore, Kate. I mean, it's football, but it's not the game I signed on to play. I mean, you're not a person to them. It's bullshit. It's sick. It's a dirty business. I'm through in Birmingham. I'm not their 'boy.' There's other things I can do with my life besides football. They think because they've got millions more waiting for me that I'll kiss their ass and kill myself just to make them happy, but I don't need millions more. I've got enough now to live good—at least better than anything I've come from. Maybe I'll just surprise them all and walk away. No one owns me."

"Clay, it's not that I don't believe you, but are you absolutely sure that you're right about this drug killing Max?" Katie said. "I mean, I know how much you cared about him, but isn't it possible that the cocaine killed him? I'm not saying it did, but maybe you should talk with someone else about this, someone who knows about what these kinds of drugs can do."

Clay scowled. "I thought the same thing," he said, then recounted his conversation with Dr. Norton.

Before they left town, Clay called a local handyman at Loon Lake to plow out his driveway and turn up the heat in his house before he and Katie got there. It had snowed overnight, and as they got farther and farther north into the mountains, the roadside drifts deepened and began to block their way. Clay had to rely more and more on his four-wheel drive. In a way, the snow was soothing. The clean white powder covered everything, and gave the world the brand-new look that only freshly fallen snow can. It was as though they were entering another world. The disparity between the calm of the countryside and the chaos of yesterday gave him the feeling that the events of the past twenty-four hours might all have been a dream.

They stopped in the town to get enough groceries to hold them over should they get snowed in. There was a stack of newspapers on the checkout counter, and Clay bought one to see if anything more had been written about Max's death. It was possible that if he had figured out what had happened, someone else had too. Maybe a coroner or a policeman or someone had investigated the situation more thoroughly than White and Lyles imagined. But if there was any news about Max's death, it wasn't in the paper.

By the time they got to the house, it was almost noon. The sun was bright now, but some western clouds promised more snow before the day was through. The house itself was laden with a thick cap of snow, as were the surrounding pines. The towering trees partially protected the house from the wind that blew across the great white field that now covered the lake. The snow had drifted high against the trees and along one side of the house. Gusts of wind blew white powder that had collected high up in the trees. The snow dust sparkled in the sunshine as it swirled to the ground. It was almost magical, and Clay felt a surge of pleasure knowing that this place belonged to him.

The snow crunched under their feet as they unloaded the truck and lugged their packages into the house. Inside, it was warm, and Katie went to the kitchen to make sandwiches while Clay brought in some wood. Setting up a fire in the hearth, Clay felt a pang of guilt, thinking of his teammates back in Birmingham. They would be working hard to get ready to play the Bills.

The phone rang.

"Clay? It's Bill. Are you feeling any better yet?"

"Hi, Bill."

"You sound kind of glum," Clancy said.

"I've just been thinking about it. I'd be crazy to use a drug like that anymore. I just don't see how it could work."

"Don't forget your teammates, Clay," Clancy reminded. "It really wouldn't be fair for you to bow out now . . . when they need you. Especially since Max isn't there. Look, there's only three regular-season games left. I'm sure you could get by for the next few weeks without using the drug, and no one would even know."

Clay doubted that. "I just don't know how I could do it, Bill. I'm sitting here in another world that seems a whole hell of a lot saner than the one I've just come from."

"But think of how long you've worked, Clay," Clancy said desperately. "You can't throw it all away now. Think of the money involved."

"I've got enough money, Bill," Clay said.

Bill Clancy hadn't made it to the top of his field without being able to quickly assess any situation and immediately influence its outcome to meet his needs. If Clay didn't play on Sunday, trouble was likely to ensue. And even if it didn't, Clancy would lose five percent of the remaining $4.5 million which Clay stood to make over the next four seasons. The problem now was that Clay's comfortable financial situation was inhibiting Clancy's power to get his client back where he wanted him. Although Clay was correct in the appraisal of his financial situation, he was only correct if he could keep the entire two million he had now in the bank. It was that premise which Clancy knew he could assault with a mixture of truth, fiction, and lawyer talk that would quickly destabilize Clay's comfortable state of mind.

"Clay," said Clancy in a fatherly tone of voice, "if you don't go back to play for the Ruffians, you may have very little of that money left over to enjoy."

"What the hell is that supposed to mean?" said Clay.

"You have a contract with the Ruffians to play for four years. If you breach that contract, you are very liable to lose your entire signing bonus. First, you will undoubtedly be sued in a federal civil court, which will be costly for you. You will have to hire a lawyer. I couldn't handle it. I would have to insist that you get someone who is the best in the field of litigating contract disputes such as these. Second, the Ruffians will not only seek your signing bonus for failure to perform, they would undoubtedly seek expectation damages for the draft pick they used in order to sign you. Even if they don't succeed in getting all your money, by the time it was all through, after what a good civil attorney gets, you would have very little left."

Clancy let the words sink in before he added, "As for your house on the lake . . . you could certainly never afford to carry the expenses of that place, even in the best-case scenario."

Clay looked around him. This was something he hadn't figured on. Lose the house? No way. Clay stared out the window at the frosty snow. Clancy cleared his throat on the other end of the line, bringing him back. Clay gulped involuntarily.

"They could take everything?" he said quietly.

"Damn near," replied Clancy, adding drama to his case with a sad and equally subdued tone.

Finally Clay said in a flat voice, "See if you can get me a ticket back to Birmingham tomorrow. If I'm going to do this, I might as well do it right."

"You got it, Clay! You're really doing the right thing. I knew I could count on you."

Clancy slapped his leg and congratulated himself soundly after he'd hung up.

Clay sat staring out the frosty window at the falling snow until Katie entered with a tray of sandwiches and two cups of coffee.

"Hey," she said, "that fire looks like it's ready to go. What are you waiting for . . . Clay? Clay, what's wrong?"

She set down the tray on the coffee table and sat next to him on the couch. She took his hands and began rubbing them gently. Clay continued to stare blankly out the window.

"Clay . . ." Katie said again, "what's wrong, honey? Are you all right?"

Clay shook his head and said, "I want to do things right . . . with everything, you, football, I want to do what's right, but I don't know how."

"What do you mean?" she asked.

"I don't mean with you," he said, detecting the alarm in her voice. "I mean with football. It's not right to go back. It's not right not to tell someone about what happened to Max. It's not right."

"So you don't have to go back, you already said you didn't," replied Katie. "And if you think someone will listen, you can tell someone about Max, maybe even get them to do something about it."

"I can't."

Clay listened to the words and thought how weak they sounded. "That was Bill Clancy on the phone. If I don't go back and keep my mouth shut, I'll lose everything," he said with the wave of his hand. "This house, my car, my money, I could lose it all. I guess they really do own me."

"Clay, why did Bill tell you you'll lose everything? How could that be?" Katie asked.

"He said something about my contract," Clay replied, "a breach or something. If I don't play for them four years like I agreed to, they can get their money back—most of it anyway. I can't win. Quitting won't do any good."

He put his face in his hands and rubbed his eyes wearily for a moment.

"Max is gone," he said, looking clearly into Katie's eyes as if to make sure she understood. "No one would believe me about this whole thing anyway. And Bill's right about the team. They'll need me, this weekend especially. They will."

They sat for a long while in silence before he said, "I'm going back tomorrow."

CHAPTER TWENTY FIVE

CLAY EMERGED FROM THE TUNNEL and pulled the turtleneck up over his chin to take away some of the bite of the cold Buffalo afternoon. He gazed up at the stands, which were only half filled with heavily bundled people. He saw a middle-aged couple sitting near the railing in a dark-blue double sleeping bag. They were drinking something hot from a thermos, but they still looked cold. Clay stuck out his tongue and felt a pellet of ice melt as soon as it hit. The sleet, or ice, or snow, or whatever it was that was falling, was clicking loudly off his helmet.

Clay looked around nervously. He wasn't used to being distracted during pre-game. Usually his mind was churning and his body was tense for action. Usually he could still feel a slight sting in his ass where the needle had been.

But that was over. If he was going to keep playing the game, it was going to be on his own terms.

He heard a ruckus in the stands behind him. He turned and looked up into the end-zone seats to see his parents amid a throng of his father's friends from Ford. They were screaming his name. Buffalo was the closest place an NFL team ever got to Syracuse. Clay's father had bought the tickets back in August. Clay thought about snubbing them all, just to get his father. But it was something he could never do. Instead he waved and the small band cheered. Clay could see his father's large, proud figure in their midst, both fists raised high.

He turned away and searched the stands for Katie and Lever. He knew they'd be there, and he found himself thinking that a loyal friend like Lever was something of value. They would be sitting apart from the Syracuse contingent in seats he'd bought for them. He finally spotted them on the ten yard line about thirty rows up. Katie had already seen him and was waving frantically at him, smiling. Lever stood up and hoisted a beer high in the air as a salute. Clay waved to Katie and gave his old friend a thumbs-up. He was glad to see them both.

Clay jogged out onto the field and began stretching with the rest of his team. The crowd was starting to pour in from whatever shelter the tunnels of the outdoor stadium offered. The Bills started to filter out of their locker room and assemble for a stretch of their own. As Clay was reaching down for his toes, he heard Gavin Collins's voice.

"How do you feel?" The voice was subdued, sad.

Clay stood up so he could look Gavin in the eye. "I feel like shit," he said.

"Me too," returned Collins. He seemed to examine the turf for a while before saying, "But you know something? We still got a job to do, so let's take about a three-hour break from feeling sorry and kick somebody's ass. Know what I mean?"

Clay shrugged and looked at him blandly.

"I'm not bullshitting," Gavin said seriously. "We're here, both of us, so we might as well do our jobs. We got a whole lot of guys around us who are damn good people depending on us both."

Clay looked from Collins up past the confines of the stadium to the gloomy sky. The sleet made him blink. He looked back to Gavin. "I guess so," he said.

"Have a good one, Clay," Gavin said, then patted him on the shoulder and walked away.

Clay watched him go. Gavin passed by White, who was also strolling through the ranks. It was as though neither existed for the other.

When the team emerged for the kickoff, the capacity crowd filled the stadium with boos.

"Welcome to Buffalo," Keith Neil shouted to Clay above the din.

The entire defense was gathered under one of the goal posts. They were pelted with sleet and insults while they waited to be introduced. When his name was called, Clay ran out onto the field and into the sea of his waiting teammates. Most of them were geeked, their eyes bulging.

"Let's kill! . . . Fuck them! . . . Kick ass!" came the angry spit and cries from all around him.

The kickoff set the tone for the entire game. The Bills return man fumbled and bumbled the ball, then finally advanced ten yards before a swarm of Ruffians drove him into the turf. The ball popped out, but the Bills recovered fifteen yards farther up the field. The weather made it a game of slipping and sliding and mistakes. After two stalled scoreless drives by both teams, Spencer Clayton fumbled a punt and gave Buffalo the ball on the Ruffians ten. Wheat and Nelan had to restrain White from running out onto the field and bashing the already shaken Clayton.

"We gotta hold them to a field goal! No touchdown!" cried Doogie in the huddle. The rest of the defense agreed.

Clay looked over to the sideline at Gavin Collins. He was cool and calm, apparently in no rush, as he signaled the play in to Don Wallace, Max's replacement as inside linebacker.

"Double Okee Cover Six Split," said Wallace, "ready . . .

"Break!"

Clay lined up on the outside shoulder of Ike Newwal, the Bills All-Pro offensive tackle. Above, the announcers in the TV booth were heralding the match-up as the ultimate battle in the trenches. Newwal was an enormous man and a grizzled veteran of thirteen NFL campaigns. Clay was quick, fast, strong, and aggressive. So far everyone watching the match-up had been disappointed. Newwal had pushed Clay around pretty well for the first two series.

Clay felt listless and weak. He looked up from his stance at the face of Ike Newwal. His nose was twisted and covered with ugly freckles. His eyes were large and heavy-lidded. He had a twisted smile. Clay didn't want to be there. The ball was snapped anyway. Newwal drove Clay well clear of the runner and the Bills gained six yards. Doogie had to make the tackle from the back side.

"What the fuck is up with you?" Doogie demanded in the huddle.

"This is the fuckin' playoffs if we win this one. Does that mean anything to you? Don't let that fucker run right over you!"

Clay took the rebuff in silence, looking straight ahead and waiting to hear the next play.

The Bills QB rolled out to pass. Newwal stuffed Clay at the line. All he was able to do was watch as the ball floated between Keith Neil and Wallace into the hands of the Buffalo tight end for a touchdown. The crowd's cheer was deafening as the Bills celebrated in the end zone.

White was waiting on the sideline. He started to shriek at Clay before he got there. Again, Nelan and Wheat each had an arm tightly grasped.

"Fuckin' dammit!" White cried. "You gotta contain that roll-out, you fuckin' shithead Blackwell!"

"Bring your ass right here!" White screamed, grabbing Clay's arm as he tried to edge past him toward the bench.

Clay looked down into the coach's face. It was almost purple with rage, and Clay thought that White might have a heart attack of his own. He smiled at the thought.

"What the fuck are you smilin' at, son? Do you realize what this game means? Get your head out of your ass, boy!" White said, "or I'll put in McGuire!

"Are you on the program, Blackwell?" White yelled two inches from Clay's face. "Are you with it? 'Cause you don't look with it, and if I have to, I'll give you a fucking booster at halftime, personally."

"I'm on," Clay said blandly, not because he was afraid of White anymore or because he believed White meant what he said, but simply because he wanted to end this bullshit and go sit down on the bench.

White had an unsure, dazed look in his eye, so Clay simply walked away. By now everyone knew that even at his worst, Clay would hold up better against Newwal than McGuire even if they gave McGuire ten shots of Thyall. And anyway, if they pulled him, well, Clay didn't give two shits. White quickly turned his frenzy on the special-teams coach for only getting the kickoff back to the twenty-three yard line.

"Do you think our fucking offense can score from there all fucking day!" White screamed in the man's face before pacing back down the sideline to where Nelan was signaling in the offensive play.

Ferrone dropped back on the very first play and heaved a long ball to Tim Tyrone, who caught it and ran to the Bills thirty before being cut off by the pursuit. The Ruffians cheered among themselves on the sideline. Clay watched from the bench as Spike Norris and Sky slapped each other high fives. The offense was shut down for the next three plays, and the field goal unit ran out. Clay didn't even bother to get up to see if the kick was good. Part of him wanted to put on a show for his family and friends, but it wasn't happening. When he saw three light up the visitors' side of the big board, Clay sighed, buckled his helmet, and got to his feet.

The defense was able to keep the Bills out of the end zone, but their consistent running game behind Newwal was enough to get them into field goal range and kick a long one to go ahead 10–3.

When the Ruffians got the ball back, Davis Green went on a seven-play rampage that put the Ruffians again deep into Buffalo territory. With only seconds to go in the half, Todd Ferrone hit Davis on a delay pattern in the end zone and tied the score at ten all. The Ruffians went into the locker room at halftime with all the momentum on their side.

White stood on a chair so that even the players in the back could see and hear him clearly. His voice was almost completely shot from screaming. It rattled and squeaked and sounded as if it hurt so much to talk that Clay would have felt sorry for another man.

"I don't give a fuck about anything!" White rasped. "This game is the most important thing I've ever experienced in my fuckin' life! And if you don't feel that way right now, then get the fuck out of this room!"

He looked around at his silent players, glaring.

"I want each of you to look into yourselves right now. Look!" he said, pounding his palm with his fist and then pointing. "What do you see? Do you see a man? A man that can accomplish greatness? Or do you see a fucking coward that doesn't even deserve to fuckin' be alive and that should be crawling around in some hole of shit somewhere?

"I want men to go back out there with me!" White yelled. "I want men that have pride! And guts! I want men that love to hit! And men that love fucking pain! That's what this is all about, you know! Pain! Now, let's get our asses out there and make those scummy motherfuckers hurt like they never hurt before!"

White's descent from his chair as he spoke his last words signaled that it was the end of his halftime speech. The team bellowed in agreement. They were all talking at once and moving for the door.

"This is it, this is it . . . Kill those fuckers . . . Pain, it's all about pain . . .

Win, baby, we gotta win this . . . Come on, you fuckers, let's do it . . .
Playoffs, baby, we're takin' it all the way . . ."

Clay was the last one to leave the locker room, and he ambled out
slowly. The dampness had set in and made his entire body stiff. He honestly didn't give a shit. That was how he felt and no matter what he said
to himself, he couldn't get pumped up. He wouldn't use the drug again
even if it meant he would get the shit pounded out of him for the rest of
his career. He was wet and cold, and he was tired. He wanted to go
home, and he wanted everything that had happened with Max to be just
a shitty dream. He felt certain now that it had been a mistake to come
back.

The Ruffians took control right from the start of the second half.
They received the ball and Clayton brought it back to the fifty. Ferrone
and the offense pounded down the rest of the field and got to the Bills
one. But on a pass play to a wide-open Tim Tyrone, Ferrone's hand
slipped on the ball and it flipped up through the air. A Bills lineman
grabbed the wayward pass and rumbled to the fifteen before he was
caught by Pike, who proceeded to try to pull the ball free from the lucky
lineman's hands. A fight ensued and it was five full minutes before the
officials gained control. Yellow flags were everywhere, but they offset
each other. Apparently in the spirit of modern football the refs chalked it
up to good violence and ejected none of the perpetrators from the game.

For the entire third quarter, both teams moved the ball well, but critical turnovers prevented any points from being scored. In the early minutes of the fourth quarter the Bills put together a running drive behind
Newwal that got them into field goal range. This time there were no
Buffalo turnovers, and the Bills went up 13–10.

Clay jogged over to the sideline and was happy to see White spending
his wrath on Sky, who had just missed blocking the kick. Clay slipped
back to the bench and slumped down for a breather. The shock of having
no lift from the drug was having an exhausting effect on him.

He sat breathing heavily with his head down when Gavin Collins
appeared. "Clay," he said firmly, "Clay, you gotta give me more than
you're giving right now . . . Clay?"

Clay looked up. His eyes were bloodshot from a week of little sleep.
His face was haggard and unshaven, and his fatigue made him look even
worse.

"Listen, you gotta give me more, man," Collins said, kneeling down in front of Clay. "I've been doing everything I can all game long to help cover for you. I know Newwal is a tough son of a bitch, but you gotta help stop that weak-side run. I know you can do it, Clay."

Clay looked Gavin in the eye and said, "I can't help it. Winning this game is everything they want. I can't help not giving a shit. They don't deserve to win this and have everyone talk about how wonderful they are. They're scum. They killed Max, they're fucking everybody—"

"Hey, Clay," Collins said firmly, "you gotta snap outa this, man. Look around you. Look at these guys . . ."

Clay looked around the sideline. Sky and Doogie and Spike were gathered anxiously in a group, rooting and watching for the offense to put them back ahead or at least tie the game. Sky had his hand on Spike's shoulder pad, and the tension of his nervous grip made his knuckles white. Keith Neil was sitting on the bench having the trainers tightly wrap a bad hamstring so he could finish the game. He winced with pain as every loop was pulled tightly against his damaged muscle. Then Clay saw Davis Green limp off the field, bleeding from his nose and staggering from exhaustion, but refusing the attention of the team doctor, who wanted to look at him. All he would do was rest a play and go back in for more punishment.

"O.K.," Clay said to Gavin. "I'll try, I really will . . . for you, and these guys. I'll try . . ."

Both of them looked up as the Ruffians sideline erupted with cheers. The Ruffians had scored on a reverse pass with Tyrone running the reverse to the left while Ferrone jogged nonchalantly and unnoticed into the end zone, where Tyrone hit him with the touchdown pass. After the extra point, the Ruffians held the lead by four.

Clay played better through the entire fourth quarter, but he still didn't feel like he was all there. It was enough, though, to dissuade the Bills from running his way on almost every play as they had earlier. The Ruffians were holding their lead. With only a few minutes left in which to score a winning touchdown, the Bills began to move the ball with a series of runs and passes that seemed to outguess everything Gavin Collins could think of. When the Ruffians blitzed, the Bills ran a screen. When the Ruffians went to short-yardage defense on third and inches, the Bills threw a twenty-yard pass. With a little less than a minute to play, the Bills were sitting first and goal on the Ruffians ten yard line.

The first play was a pass. The Ruffians were in a blitz, and the Bills quarterback had to dump it off to a running back. The Ruffians swarmed him and punished him. The next play would be a run. That was where the Bills had gotten the majority of their yardage all afternoon, and they would surely go back to it when it counted.

"Come on," Clay told himself as the Bills came to the line and their quarterback started his cadence, "snap out of it! This is it! This is the whole game! This is the playoffs! Do it, Clay! Do it!"

The ball was snapped, and Newwal surged off the line straight at Clay. He was a split second slow off the ball and braced up against him, but Newwal pushed him back four yards, enough to get the runner to the one yard line before Clay could bring him down by the ankles.

"Shit!" Clay said out loud from under the pile of bodies.

As Newwal got up, he used Clay's back to push himself off the turf. Clay swung his arm around, knocking Newwal off balance. Newwal stepped toward Clay with his hands in fists. Three Ruffians were on him instantly, and the pushing and shoving and swinging began. The crowd booed and cheered. As the refs broke up the commotion, Newwal, who was now restrained by two officials and two Bills players, pointed a gnarled finger at Clay and shouted, "You pay for that, rookie! I'm kicking your fuckin' ass now! We're comin' at you! We're comin' right over your sorry ass!"

"Fuck yourself!" Clay shouted back.

Newwal tried to break free, but they had him good.

"That's it!" cried another ref, waving his hands in Clay's face. "That's enough now. Get back to your huddle and let's play ball!"

Clay was pumped. He almost forgot all about Max and White and the whole thing. He was pissed and he had an adrenaline rush of his own. It came from him, and it reminded him of what the game was about. The game he loved.

He could play the game anyway the asshole Newwal liked.

The Bills came to the line. It was third and one at the one. The Ruffians were in goal-line defense, and Clay hunkered down as low as he could to meet Newwal's challenge. They would come right at him. Newwal was their game winner, their bread and butter. Newwal had handled him all game. But Clay was pissed off, and that made a differ-ence. The ball was hiked and Newwal surged at him. This time Clay was lower and got off the ball quicker, so it was almost a stalemate and the runner was only able to push an extra half yard to make it fourth and goal from the one foot line. Clay and Newwal continued to push at each other after the play was blown dead. Whistles blared as Newwal took a shot at Clay with an upper cut. Clay grabbed Newwal's mask and twisted it, trying to rip his head off at the neck. Again players from both teams and the officials had to separate the two of them.

"You're not going to throw him out?" Clay cried at the official. "You had to see him take that shot! Are you fucking blind?"

"That's enough of that, son," said the official pompously, "just play the game—"

"What's the matter, rookie?" yelled Newwal before the refs could quiet him. "Want me out of the game so we don't ram this ball right up your ass this next play?"

Clay flipped him the bird. A ref saw it and scowled. The Bills had called time-out to stop the clock at twenty-seven seconds and give them time to consider the play that would either win or lose the game for them.

Clay knew that it would come right at him. He also knew that with only a foot, it would be almost impossible to stop Newwal from advancing enough to prevent the score. It wasn't that Clay wasn't confident, but he knew that the other player outweighed him by almost fifty pounds. Clay had one thing better than anyone, though: quickness. If he could focus and get the jump on Newwal, he could get into the backfield and make the play before the runner ever hit the line.

Then Clay felt like he was hit with a one-two punch. The first thought that hit him was of Lyles and White. He could see them sitting there in the owner's office, smugly explaining to him the cruel and corrupt ways of their world. The image made him determined to simply lie down and let the Bills run right over him for the score. He could actually envision himself doing it. The Ruffians dream would be ruined.

The second thought that hit him was just as powerful. It was on him like a flash. It was as though Clay's mind had skipped a beat from all the previous games, and Max, filled with energy and violence and life, his face red and his brow dripping with sweat, was giving him the same exhorting he would always give.

"Kill 'em, Clayboy! Kick their fuckin' ass! We gotta win!"

Then it was gone, and Wallace was calling the play.

Clay lined up, dazed from confusion and exhaustion and stress. The quarterback started his cadence, and if it was a short one, the Bills would have won the game. Clay was still thinking. Then he did it. He slid down into the gap between Newwal and his guard and looked intently at the ball instead of the men in front of him. When it moved, he would move. It was in the quarterback's rhythm, and it was just a slight tightening by the center of his grip on the ball. Clay took off!

The ball was snapped and both teams rushed at each other from across a very narrow space. The players came low and hard. They swung arms and fists and helmets and shoulders at one another. The crack of pads filled the cold, wet air. Clay got his jump and he twisted his shoulders ever so slightly to just avoid a full collision with both Newwal and the guard.

Clay dipped and accelerated. He was in! Before he could think, he collided with the ball carrier with a crack. The runner spun and churned like an animal with no head and no sense for stopping. Clay clutched his jersey and got a hold. His fingernails tore, but he held on for the split second it took for several other Ruffians to get there. The ball carrier went down under a pile of black helmets. He was two feet short of the goal line.

CHAPTER TWENTY SIX

GAVIN COLLINS MADE HIS WAY THROUGH the bustle of the locker room. The players were all cleaning out their lockers. Most of them were either headed back to their homes or at least on some vacation for a month or so. Gavin, like many of the players, had a large grin on his face. Clay was sitting glumly in his locker, sorting through different pairs of football shoes and worn socks. Gavin sat down on an empty stool next to him. Clay looked up.

"How's it going?" Gavin said.

"Fine."

"Hey, I got the Giants job."

"Yeah, I heard, congratulations, Gavin. You get to get out of here after all, huh?"

"Can we talk?" Gavin said quietly.

"Sure."

"How about in my office?" Gavin said after looking around.

"Sure," Clay said and followed him upstairs.

"Clay," Gavin said when they were both sitting down, "last week you came to me with an idea, and I said I wanted to think about it."

Clay straightened up and looked Gavin in the eye. "Did you?"

"Not only did I think about it . . . well, believe it or not, I've had the same idea myself," Gavin said. "But before I talked with you, I wanted to see if the Giants thing panned out."

"And . . ." Clay said.

"You don't happen to have that stuff with you, do you?" Gavin asked.

"It's in the trunk of my car."

"Get it," Collins said.

A half hour later, the two of them walked right past Wendy, Humphry Lyles's secretary, who blurted something about a private meeting. They burst in on White and Lyles. In Clay's hand was a clear plastic bag.

The two men that Gavin and Clay interrupted were happy ones. The Ruffians had failed to go all the way to the Super Bowl. They'd lost to the 49ers in the NFC championship only two days ago. Still, they had made history. Humphry Lyles and Vance White had done the impossible. They'd taken a lowly expansion club and a bunch of unknown players and turned them into a team of bad guys that were now the darling of American sports fans. In fact, the meeting they were interrupting was a cheerful strategy session for the upcoming year.

". . . I know we're going to win it all," were the exact words coming from Humphry Lyles's mouth as Clay and Gavin entered. White and Lyles both looked up in surprise.

"Sorry to interrupt you," Gavin said blandly, "but I thought you'd be as happy about my news as I am." Looking directly at White, he continued, "I'm taking the coordinator job in New York with the Giants. I know you'll be more than happy to let me out of my contract and let me go."

White chuckled condescendingly. "So they've got quotas to make in New York too?"

Gavin let the slur go. He had more important things to talk about.

"He's taking me with him," Clay said authoritatively. "We figure you two can trade me for the Giants first-round pick this year."

Both the other men laughed out loud before Lyles could gain enough control to scowl and say, "Get the hell out of here, Collins. You're no longer part of this organization, and that's a damn good thing in my eyes.

Blackwell, you're a fucking problem, but you might as well buy a big house here, boy, 'cause this is your home."

"No, Mr. Lyles," Clay said, "this isn't my home, and I'm not your boy."

He tossed a clear plastic bag onto Lyles's desk.

"What the hell is this!" Lyles shrieked.

White, sitting in a chair opposite the desk, craned his neck to see what was in the bag.

"You know damn well what it is, Mr. Lyles," said Clay, "or you ought to. It's an almost empty vial of the shit you've been pumping into this team for the past eight months. There are also a few used syringes for effect."

"I've never seen this before, Blackwell. I don't know what the hell you're talking about. What the hell is this all about, Collins?" Lyles glared. "I'll have your ass."

"No," Gavin said, "we've already got your ass. Humphry."

Clay wondered which had shocked the owner more—being called by his first name, or what Gavin had actually said.

"You will trade Clay like he said," Gavin continued. "You'll get a decent pick for him, and no one will ask why. You may look a little foolish after the way he's played, but you can cite personality differences as the reason."

"You're forgetting one thing!" said White, grabbing the bag from the desk and clutching it to him. "This stuff never existed! And even if it did, you're both into this as much as anyone! You'll be blackballed from coaching, Collins! You're a traitorous motherfucker!"

It was Clay's and Gavin's turn to laugh. White looked silly, standing there clutching the plastic bag.

"Do you really think that's all we've got?" Gavin sneered. "That's just Clay's stuff. There's an envelope full of things that I've collected that a friend of mine is holding for me. It's got the same stuff that's in there. I thought someone might want to put that shit through some tests or something. Anyway, the best part of the whole thing is a little note in your handwriting, Vance. It's the name and address of a Dr. Kyle Borne. Along with all that is a nice little story I put together about the two of you that I'm sure all your fans would like to see. It's all in an envelope—addressed to the *New York Times*."

He looked from the coach to the owner to see the effect of his words.

"Don't tell me you'll take me down too," Gavin said, "because it's bull-shit, and even if you did, I don't really care. I'm not letting you two have your cake and eat it too. If you want to keep the Ruffians, then I get Clay."

Clay could tell by the look on the two men's faces, and their lack of response, that the deal was done, but he wanted to hear them say it. "Do we have a deal, Mr. Lyles?" he said.

Lyles was looking down at his desk, his hands bunched in rage. "Go," he said. "Get the hell out of here, both of you."

Clay looked at the astonished White and grinned. White twisted his mouth in rage and glared at Clay.

"Make a move," Clay said, his face suddenly dark and threatening. "You're not my coach anymore, and you know what I got."

White sprung from his seat, but stopped, standing.

Clay's fists were tight. His muscles quivered and his eyes were lit with that same fire that separated him from the rest.

White studied his eyes for a moment, then sat down.

Gavin nodded to Clay that it was time to leave. On his way out Clay paused and looked up at the painting of the small-town street of Humphry Lyles's humble beginnings and said, "What a shitty little town."

He shut the door firmly behind them.

"It worked," Gavin said, breaking into a grin as soon as they were out the door.

"It worked," Clay said, beaming. He shook Gavin's hand firmly, and the coach pulled him into a hug.

"Let's get the hell out of here," Clay said.

A special thanks to my mentor in all things written, Professor Judith Weissman, Ph.D., for her belief in *Ruffians*.